BY HIS MAJESTY'S
GRACE

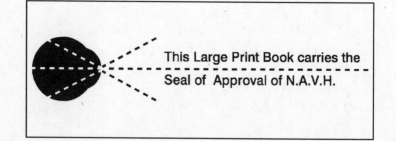

This Large Print Book carries the
Seal of Approval of N.A.V.H.

By His Majesty's Grace

Jennifer Blake

THORNDIKE PRESS
A part of Gale, Cengage Learning

GALE
CENGAGE Learning™

Detroit • New York • San Francisco • New Haven, Conn • Waterville, Maine • London

GALE
CENGAGE Learning™

Copyright © 2011 by Patricia Maxwell.
The Three Graces of Graydon Series.
Thorndike Press, a part of Gale, Cengage Learning.

Thorndike Press® Large Print Romance.
The text of this Large Print edition is unabridged.
Other aspects of the book may vary from the original edition.
Set in 16 pt. Plantin.

LIBRARY OF CONGRESS CATALOGING-IN-PUBLICATION DATA

Blake, Jennifer, 1942–
    By his Majesty's grace / by Jennifer Blake. — Large print ed.
      p. cm. — (The three graces of Graydon series) (Thorndike
Press large print romance)
    ISBN-13: 978-1-4104-4089-1 (hardcover)
    ISBN-10: 1-4104-4089-3 (hardcover)
    1. Large type books. 2. Large type books. I. Title.
PS3563.A923B9 2011
813'.54—dc22   2011024151

Published in 2011 by arrangement with Harlequin Books S.A.

Printed in the United States of America
1 2 3 4 5 6 7 15 14 13 12 11

To Bertrice Small and Roberta Gellis.

Many thanks, ladies,
for prodding me to write this story,
for fun and friendship at the 2008
Romantic Times convention in
Pittsburgh and, especially, for the warm
welcome into your medieval world.

1

Braesford was finally sighted in late afternoon. It stood before them on its hill, a walled keep centered by a pele tower of massive proportions that loomed against the gray north sky. Rooks wheeled and called above the turret, soaring about its corbelled and battlemented walkway. A pennon topped it to show the master was in residence. That sturdy fabric of blue and white fluttered and snapped in the brisk wind as if trying to take flight.

Isabel Milton would have taken flight herself were it not so cowardly.

A trumpet sounded, indicating their permission to enter. Isabel shivered despite the late-summer warmth. Drawing a deep breath, she kicked her palfrey to a slow walk behind her stepbrother, the Earl of Graydon, and his friend Viscount Henley. Their mounted party approached Braesford's thick stone walls with their ragged skirt of huts and small shops, clip-clopping over the dry moat, beneath the portcullis and through the gateway that gave onto a barmkin where the people of the country-side could be protected in time of trouble. Chickens flapped out of their way and a sow and her five piglets ran squealing in high dudgeon. Hounds flowed in a black-and-tan river down the stone steps of the open turret stairway just ahead. They surrounded the arriving party, barking, growling and sniffing around the horses' fetlocks. Lining the way to the turret entrance was an honor guard of men-at-arms, though no host stood ready to receive them.

Isabel, waiting for aid to dismount, stared up at the great central manse attached to the pele tower. This portion was newly built of brick, three stories in height with corner medallions and inset niches holding terra-cotta figures of militant archangels. The ground floor was apparently a service area from which servants emerged to receive the baggage of the arriving party. The great hall, the heart of the structure, was undoubtedly on the second floor with the ladies' solar directly above it, there where mullioned windows reflected the turbulent sky.

What manner of man commanded this fortress, which rose in such rugged yet prosperous splendor? What combination of arrogance and audacity led him to think she, daughter of a nobleman and an heiress in her own right, should wed a mere farmer, no matter how wide his lands or impregnable his home? What rare influence had he with the king that Henry Tudor had commanded it?

A shadow loomed inside the Roman arch of the turret doorway. The broad shape of a man appeared. He stepped out onto the cobblestones. Every eye in the bailey turned to fasten upon him.

Isabel came erect in her saddle as alarm banished her weariness from the long journey. She had been misled, she saw with tight dread in her chest, perhaps through ignorance but more likely from malice. Graydon was fond of such jests.

The master of Braesford was no mere farmer.

He was, instead, a warrior.

Randall Braesford was imposing in his height, with broad shoulders made wider by the cut of his doublet. The strong musculature of his flanks and legs was closely defined by dark gray hose and high boots of the same color. His hair was black, glinting in the pale sunlight with the iridescence of a raven's feathered helmet, and worn evenly cropped just above his shoulders. His eyes were the dark silver-gray of tempered steel; his features, though well cast, were made somber by the firm set of his mouth under a straight Roman nose. Garbed in the refined colors of black, white and gray, he had not the faintest hint of court dandy about him, no trace of damask or embroidery, no wide-brimmed headgear set with plumes. His hat was simple, of gray wool with an upturned brim cut in crenellations like a castle wall. From the belt at his lean waist hung his knife for use at table, a fine damascene blade marked by a hilt and scabbard with tracings of silver over its black enamel.

It was no wonder he was a close companion to the king, she thought in fuming ire. They were two of a kind, Henry VII and Sir Rand Braesford. Though one was fair and the other dark, both were grave of feature and mien, forbidding in their strength and obvious determination to bend fortune to their will and their pleasure.

At her side, Viscount Henley, a veritable giant of a man on the downside of forty, with sandy hair and the battered countenance of those who made a pastime of war and jousting, swung down from his courser. He turned toward Isabel as if to assist her dismount.

"Stay," Rand Braesford called in the firm command of those accustomed to being obeyed. He advanced upon her, his stride unhurried, his gaze keen. "The privilege is mine, I believe."

An odd paralysis gripped Isabel while a hollow sensation invaded her midsection. She could not look away from Braesford's dark eyes, not even when he paused beside her. They were so very black, with shimmering depths that beckoned yet defended against penetration. Anything could be hidden there, anything at all.

"My lady?"

The low rumble of his voice had a vibrant undertone that seemed to echo inside her. It was as intimate and as possessive as his mode of address. *My lady.* Not *milady,* but *my lady.*

His lady. And why not? Soon she would be his indeed.

Aware, abruptly, that she was staring, she veiled her gaze with her lashes, unhooked her knee from her pommel and turned more fully toward him. He reached for her waist with hard hands, lifting her from the saddle as she leaned to rest her gloved hands on his broad shoulders. He braced with his feet set, drawing her against him so she slid slowly down his long length until the skirt of her riding gown was drawn up and crushed between them and her booted toes barely touched the ground.

Her breath caught in her chest. Her future husband had no softness about him anywhere. His body was so unyielding from his chest to his knees that it was more like steel armor than living flesh. The sensation was particularly evident in the area below his waist. She jerked a little in his grasp, her eyes wide and fingers clenched on his shoulders, as she recognized that heated firmness against the softness of her lower belly.

He cared not at all that she knew, or so it seemed. His appraisal was intent behind the thick screen of his lashes, which seemed to permit her the same right of inspection. His eyes, she saw, carried a gleam in their depths like honed and polished silver, and thick brows made dark slashes above them. Lines radiated from the corners, perhaps from laughter but more likely from staring out over far distances. His jaw was square and his chin centered by a shallow cleft. The firm yet well-molded contours of his mouth hinted at a sensual nature held steadfastly in check.

"Well, Braesford," her stepbrother said with the rasp of annoyance in his voice.

"Graydon," the master of the manse said over his shoulder in acknowledgment. "I bid you welcome to Braesford Hall. And would do so with more ceremony if not so impatient to greet my bride."

The words were pleasant enough, but carried an unmistakable note of irony. Did Braesford refer, most daringly, to his appreciation for her as a woman? Did he mean he was otherwise barely pleased to make her acquaintance, or was it something more between the two men?

This knight and her stepbrother had known each other during the Lancastrian invasion of the previous summer that had ended at Bosworth Field. Braesford had earned his spurs there, becoming Sir Randall Braesford. It was he who had found the golden circlet lost by the usurper, Richard III, and handed it to Lord Stanley so Henry Tudor might be crowned on the battlefield. Graydon, by contrast, had come away from Bosworth with nothing except the new king's displeasure ringing in his ears for his delay in bringing up his men. Braesford no doubt knew that her stepbrother had waited until he was sure where victory would fall before lending support to Henry's cause.

Graydon, in keeping with his dead father before him, preferred always to be on the winning side. Right was of little importance.

"A brave man, you are, to lay hands on my sister. I'd think you'd want her shriven first."

Isabel stiffened at the suggestion. Her future husband did not spare her step-brother so much as a glance. "Why would I do that?" he asked.

"The curse, Braesford. The curse of the Three Graces of Graydon."

"I have no fear of curses." Rand Braesford's eyes lighted with silvery amusement as he smiled into hers. "It will be done with, betimes, when we are duly wed and bedded."

"So that's the way of it, is it?" Graydon gave a coarse laugh. "Tonight, I make no doubt, as soon as you have the contract in hand."

"The sooner, the better," Braesford agreed with deliberation. Setting Isabel on her feet, he placed her hand upon his arm and turned to lead her into the manse.

It was a moment before she could force her limbs to move. She walked with her head high and features impassive, leaving behind the winks and quiet guffaws of the

Graydon and Braesford men-at-arms with the disdain they merited. Inside, her mind was in shivering chaos. She had thought to have more time, had expected a few days of rest before she need submit to a husband. In a week, or possibly two, reprieve could easily appear. It was years since any man had dared brave the curse of the Three Graces, so long that she had come to depend on its protection. Why should Braesford be the one to defeat it?

He meant to prove it false by a swift home strike. It was possible he would succeed.

Turning to look back, Isabel instinctively sought the familiar face of her serving woman, Gwynne. One of her stepbrother's men-at-arms had helped her from her mule and she was now directing the unloading of their baggage. That Gwynne had heard the exchange along with everyone else seemed clear from the concern in her wise old eyes that followed her and her future husband. An instant of communication passed between them, not an unusual thing as the woman had been her mother's body servant and had helped bring her and her sisters into the world. Bolstered by Gwynne's silent support, Isabel faced forward again.

The curse was a fabrication if Braesford but knew it, a thin defense created from

15

superstition, coincidence and daring. It had been Isabel's inspiration, begun in hope of some small protection for her two younger sisters that she had helped rear after their mother died. To guard them in all ways had been her most fierce purpose since the three of them had been left with a brutish, uncaring stepfather. She had feared Cate and Marguerite, so lovely and tenderly nubile, would be bedded immediately at fourteen, the age of legal marriage following betrothals made in their cradles. By fate and God's mercy, the three of them had, between them, escaped from ten or twelve such marital arrangements without being joined in formal wedlock or losing their maidenheads. Disease, accident and the fortunes of internecine warfare had taken the lives of their prospective grooms one by one. A malignant fate surely had them in its keeping — or so Isabel had suggested to all who would listen.

Mere whispers of it had served well enough for three or four years.

Then Leon, King Henry's handsome Master of Revels, who had traveled with him from France the year before, had taken up the tale out of mischief not unmixed with kindness. Well, and for the challenge of seeing how many credulous English nobles he

16

could persuade to believe it. Dear Gwynne had helped it along among the serving wenches and menservants at Westminster Palace. The supposed curse had become akin to holy writ, a universally believed truth that death or disaster must overcome any man who attempted a loveless union with any one of the Three Graces of Graydon — as Leon had styled them in token of the classical Roman fervor sweeping the court just now.

It had been a most convenient tale, regardless of the notoriety attached to it. As the eldest of the Graces, Isabel had been grateful for its protection. She had enjoyed the freedom it allowed, the endless days of peace with no one to order her except a stepbrother who was seldom at home. To be stripped of it through such an obvious misalliance as the one before her would be near unbearable. Yet how was she to prevent it?

The arm beneath the slashed sleeve of her future husband was as hard as the stone of his keep walls. Her fingers trembled a little on the dark wool that covered it, and she gripped tighter in the effort to still them. Did this man have none of the superstitious fear that ran rampant through those who prayed most mightily before every altar in the kingdom? Or was it only that he, like Henry VII, had known the Master of Revels in France?

Braesford glanced down at her with the lift of an inquiring brow. "You are cold, Lady Isabel?"

"Merely weary," she said through stiff lips, "though the wind was somewhat chill for summer, especially during the last few leagues."

"I apologize, but you will grow used to our rough weather in time," he replied with grave courtesy.

"Possibly."

"You think, mayhap, to escape it." He led her into the tower, keeping his back to the curving wall as they mounted the narrow, winding treads so she might retain the support of his arm.

"I would not say that, but neither do I look forward to a long life spent at Braesford."

"I trust you may change your mind before the night is done."

She gave him a swift upward glance, searching the dark implacability of his eyes. He really meant to bed her before the evening was over. It was his right under canon law that recognized an official betrothal to be as binding as vows before a priest. Her heart stumbled in her chest before continuing with a more frantic beat. There must be some escape, though she could not think what it might be.

The staircase emerged in the great hall, a cavernous room with dark stone walls hung with banners and studded by stag horns. A dais lay at one end with musicians' gallery above it, and trestle tables were spaced in a double row down its length. The mellow fragrance of fresh rushes mixed with lavender and cedar hung in the air from the newly laid carpet of them that softened the stone floor. Overlaying these was the wafting scent of wood smoke from the fire that burned low on the hearth of the huge fireplace against one wall, taking the dampness from the air. As they entered, menservants were already laying linen cloths for the company.

"You will wish to retire to your chamber before the feasting begins," Braesford said as he surveyed the progress in the hall through narrowed eyes, then glanced back at the male company crowding in behind them. "I'll see you to it."

Dismay moved over Isabel. Surely he did not intend to join her there now? "You have far more important duties, I'm sure," she said in some haste. "My serving woman and

I can find our way."

"No duty could ever be more important."

Humor gleamed in the depths of his eyes, like light sliding along a burnished sword blade, though it was hidden as he inclined his head. Did he dare laugh at her and her fears?

In that moment, she was reminded of an evening at court some months ago, just after the announcement that Henry had agreed to marry Elizabeth of York. Isabel, like most unwed heiresses over the country, had been ordered to attend, though against Graydon's wishes. There had been a great feast with dancing and disguising afterward. She had been dancing, moving through the figures of a ronde with a light heart and lighter feet, when a prickling awareness slid along her nerves. Glancing about, she noticed a gentleman leaning in the entrance to an antechamber. He had seemed set apart from the general merriment, grim of feature and dress, oddly vigilant. Yet a flash of silver appreciation had shone in his eyes for the space of a heartbeat. Then he had turned and vanished into the tunnellike gloom behind him.

That man, she realized now, had been Braesford. She had heard whispers of him about Henry's court, a mysterious figure without family connections who came and went with no let or hindrance. He had endured Henry's uncertain exile in Brittany and his later detainment in France, so they said, and was honored for that reason. Others whispered that he was a favorite of the new king's lady mother, Margaret Beaufort, and had sometimes traveled between her and her son on missions that culminated in Henry's invasion. No one could speak with accuracy of him, however, for the newly made knight remained aloof from the court and its gossip, occupying some obscure room in the bowels of whatever palace or castle Henry dwelled in at the moment. The only thing certain was that he had the king's ear and his absolute trust. That was until he disappeared into the north of England, to the manse known as Braesford, which had been gifted to him for his services to the crown.

Was it possible, Isabel wondered in some perplexity, that her presence at Braesford, her betrothal to such a nonentity, sprang from that brief exchange of glances? It seemed unlikely, yet she had been given scant reason for it otherwise.

Not that there need be anything personal in the arrangement. Since coming to the throne, Henry had claimed her as his ward, given that her father and mother were dead, that she was unwed and heir to a considerable fortune. Graydon had raved and cursed, for he considered the right to manage her estate and its income to be his, though they shared not a drop of blood in common. Still, her stepbrother had been forced to bow to the will of the king. If Henry wanted to reward one of his followers with her hand and her property, including its munificent yearly income, that was his right. Certainly, she had no say in the matter.

Rand led Isabel Milton of Graydon from the great hall into a side vestibule and up the wide staircase mounted against its back wall. At the top, he turned to the left and opened a door leading into the solar that fronted the manor house. Glancing around, he felt the shift of pride in his chest. Everything was ready for his bride, though it had been a near thing. He had harried the workman with threats and not a few oaths to get the chamber finished in time. Yet he could not think Henry's queen had a finer retreat.

The windows, with their thick, stacked circles of glass, gave ample light for the sewing, embroidery or reading of Isabel and her ladies. The cushioned benches beneath them were an invitation to contemplation or to observe what was taking place in the court below. The scenes of classical gods and goddesses painted on the plastered walls were enlivened with mischievous cherubim, while carpets overlaid the rushes here and there in a manner he had heard of from the Far East. Instead of a brazier, there was a fireplace in this room just as in the hall below. Settles of finely carved oak were drawn up on either side, their backs tall enough to catch the radiating heat with bench seats softened by embroidered cushions. A small fire burned against the advancing coolness of the evening, flickering beneath the massive mantelpiece carved with his chosen symbol of a raven and underlined by his motto in Latin: *Interritusaum,* Undaunted. Beyond it was the bed, resting on a dais fitted into the corner. As he was not a small man, this was of goodly size, and hung with sumptuous embroidered bed curtains, piled with feather-stuffed mattresses and pillows.

"Your solar, Lady Isabel," he said simply.

"So I see."

Rand had not expected transports of joy, but felt some word of appreciation might have been extended after all his preparations for her comfort. His disappointment was glancing, however, as he noted how she avoided looking at the bed. A faint tremor shook the hand that lay upon his arm, and she released him at once, drawing away a short distance.

She was wary of him, Rand thought. It could not be helped. He was not a superstitious man, put little credence in curses, prophecies and other such foretelling, yet neither did he leave things to chance. It was important that he take and hold Lady Isabel. He would do what was necessary to be sure of her and make his amends later.

And if holding her promised to be far more a pleasure than a duty, that was his secret.

"You will need to quench your thirst, I expect," he said gravely. "I will send wine and bread to sustain you until the feasting."

"That's very kind. Thank you," she said, speaking over her shoulder as she turned her back on him, moving farther away. "You may leave me now."

Her tone was that of a princess dismissing a lackey. It grated, but he refused to take offense. No doubt she feared his attack at any moment, not that she lacked cause. It happened often enough with these alliances of great fortune, wherein to bed the lady was to take her virginity and her wealth in the same act. He thought briefly of living up to her expectations, of sweeping her into his arms and tossing her on the bed before joining her there. The surge of heat in the lower part of his body was a fine indication of what his more base self thought of the idea.

He could not do it. For one thing, being closeted with her for any length of time would expose her to more of the ribald, lip-smacking comment she had endured already. For another, forcing her was not a precedent he wanted to set for their life together.

Let her have her pride, then. She was in his power whether she accepted it or not. There would be time enough and more to see that she understood that fact.

"I regret that you were embarrassed just now," he said abruptly.

"Embarrassed?" She turned to give him a quick glance from under her lashes. "Why should I be?"

"What may take place between us is not a matter for rough talk. I would not have you think I view it that way."

Color as tender and fresh as a wild rose invaded her features. "Certainly not."

"It's only that there is bound to be speculation, considering the misfortune met with by your previous suitors."

Between them lay the knowledge that he made the fifth in a line that had begun when she was in her cradle. The first was to a baron her father's age who had expired of the colic. Afterward, the honor had descended to his son, a youth of less than six years who did not survive the childhood scourge of measles. A match had been arranged then with James, Marquess Trowbridge, a battle-scarred veteran of almost fifty. Trowbridge had been killed in a fall while hunting when Isabel was nine, after which she was pledged, at age eleven, to Lord Kneesall, merely seventeen years her senior and afflicted with a harelip. When he was executed after choosing the wrong side in the quarrel between Plantagenet factions, the betrothals halted.

This was in part, Rand knew, because the lady carried a reputation for being one of the accursed Three Graces of Graydon, sisters who could only be joined in wedlock to men who loved them. A more pertinent reason was the constant warfare of the past years which made selecting a groom problematical, given that the man chosen could be hale and hearty one day and headless the next.

The lady began to remove her gloves with

meticulous attention to the loosening of each finger. Rand watched the unveiling of her pale hands with a drawing sensation in his lower body, his thoughts running rampant concerning other portions of her body that would soon be revealed to him. It was an effort to attend as she finally made reply.

"You can hardly be blamed for the vulgarity of others. My stepbrother, like his father before him, takes pleasure in his lack of refinement. Being accustomed to Graydon's ways, I am unlikely to blush for yours."

"Yet you flushed just now."

She kept her gaze on what she was doing, carefully inching the leather off her little finger. "Not for the subject of the jest, but rather at having it raised between us."

"So I am at fault," he said evenly.

"There is no fault that I see."

Her fairness touched him with an inexplicable tenderness, as did her courage and even her unconscious pride. She was a jewel there in that perfect chamber he had created for her, the final bright and shining addition. Her eyes were the soft green of new spring leaves, alive with watchful intelligence. Her lips were the rich, dark pink of the crusader's rose that climbed the courtyard wall. Her mantle was a mere dust protector of russet linen, and her riding gown beneath it of moss-green summer wool. She had thrown back the cloak's hood to reveal a small, flat cap of crimson wool embroidered with fern fronds, attached to which was a light veil that covered her hair so completely not the finest tendril of it could be seen. Rand's hands itched, suddenly, to strip away that concealment, to strip her bare in truth, so he might see in full the prize he had been given.

"You relieve my mind," he said, his voice harsh in his throat. "If the bedding others mentioned is in advance of the wedding, I trust you will understand the cause. The best way I know to dispel a curse is to disprove it."

Her chin lifted another notch, though her lashes shielded her expression. "You will at least allow me to remove my cloak first?"

The vision his mind produced, of taking her in a welter of skirts and with her stocking-clad legs clamped around him, did such things to him that he was glad for the unfashionable length of his doublet. It would be so easy to manage since it was doubtful she wore braies of any description under her clothing, unless to prevent saddle soreness during her long ride. Moreover, her challenge sounded as if she might resent the necessity he claimed but would not fight him. That was promising, and fully as much as he had any right to expect.

She stripped away the glove she had loosened, but stopped with a gasp as her hand slid free of the soft leather. The color receded from her face and a white line appeared around her mouth.

Rand stepped forward with a frown, reaching to take her wrist in his hard fingers. "My lady, you are injured."

A small sound somewhere between a gasp and a laugh rasped in her throat as both of them stared down at her little finger, which was bent at an odd angle between the first and second knuckle. "No . . . only a little."

"It's broken, obviously. Why was it not set?"

"There was no need," she said, tugging on her arm in the attempt to free it from his grasp. "It's nothing."

Her skin was so fine, so soft under his calloused fingertips, that he was distracted for an instant, intrigued also by the too-fast flutter of her pulse under his thumb. "I can't agree," he answered. "It will heal in the shape it has taken."

"That isn't your concern." She twisted her wrist back and forth, though she breathed quickly through parted lips and her eyes darkened with pain.

"Anything that touches upon my future wife is my concern."

"Why, pray? Because you expect perfection?"

She meant to anger him so he would abandon her. It was clear she knew him not at all. "Because I hold myself responsible for your well-being from this day forward. Because I protect those close to me. Also, because I would know how best to serve you."

"You will serve me to a nicety by leaving me in peace."

She meant that literally, Rand thought. As granting that particular wish was impossible, he ignored the plea. "How did it happen? A fall? Were you thrown from your palfrey?"

"I was stupid, nothing more."

"Were you indeed? I would not have thought it your habit."

She refused to be drawn, pressing her lips together as if to withhold any explanation. The conviction came upon him that the injury might have been inflicted as a punishment. Or it might have been in the nature of persuasion, perhaps to cement her agreement to a match she considered beneath her.

He released her with an abrupt, open-handed movement. An instant later, he felt a constriction around his heart as she cradled her fingers with her other hand, pressing them to her midriff.

"I will send the local herb woman to you," he said in gruff tones. "She is good with injuries."

"So is the serving woman I brought with me. We will manage, I thank you."

"You are quite certain?"

"Indeed." The lady lifted her chin as she met his gaze. She let go of her mistreated hand and, with her good one, tucked the glove she had removed into the girdle of leather netting she wore across her hip bones.

He swung toward the door, setting his hand on the iron latch. "I will send your woman to you, then — along with your baggage and water for bathing. We dine in the hall at sundown."

"As it pleases you," she answered.

It didn't please him, not at all. He would have liked to stay, lounging on the settle or bed while he watched her maid tend her. It would not do, not yet. He sketched a stiff bow. "Until later."

Rand made his escape then, and didn't stop until he was halfway down the stairway to the hall. His footsteps slowed, came to a halt there in that rare solitude. He turned and put his back to the wall, leaning his head against the cool stone. He would not go back. He would not. Yet how long the hours would be before the feasting was done and it was time for him and his betrothed to seek their bed.

How was he to bear sitting beside her, sharing a cup and plate, feeding her tidbits from the serving platters or their joint trencher, drinking where her lips had touched. Yes, and breathing her delicate female scent, feeling through linen and fine summer wool the slightest brush of her arm against his, the gentle entrapment of her skirts spreading across his booted ankles?

Ale, he needed a beaker of it. He required a veritable butt of ale immediately. Oh, but not, pray God, so much as to dull his senses. Not so much that he would disgust his bride with his stench. Certainly not enough to unman him.

Maybe ale was not what he needed, after all.

He could go for a long ride, except that he had no wish to be too tired for a proper wedding night. He could walk the battlements, letting the wind blow the heat from his blood while staring out over the valley, though he had done that far too often this day while waiting for his lady. He could descend to the kitchen to order some new delicacy to tempt her, though he had commanded enough and more of those already.

He could entertain his male guests, and hope it wasn't necessary to stop their crude comments with a well-placed fist. And, just possibly, he could learn something from Isabel's stepbrother that might tell him how strenuously she had objected to this marriage, and what had been done to her to assure her agreement.

What he would do with any knowledge gained was something he would decide when he had it.

2

Isabel emerged from the solar at the tolling of the Angelus bell. Her spirits were considerably improved after a warm bath to remove the dirt of travel, also the donning of a clean shift beneath a fine new gown of scarlet wool, the color of courage, with embroidery stiffening its hem and edging the slashed sleeves tied up at intervals with knots of ribbon. Sitting before the coals in the fireplace while Gwynne brushed her hair dry and put it up again under cap and veil had also given her time to reflect.

She had avoided being bedded at once by Braesford, though she could hardly believe it. Had he changed his mind, perhaps, or had the possibility never been anything more than Graydon's low humor? She hardly knew, yet it was all she could do to contain her giddy relief. Pray God, her good fortune would continue.

It was not that she feared the intimacy of

the marriage bed. She expected little joy from it, true, but that was a different matter. No, it was marriage in its entirety she desired to avoid. Too many of her friends had been married in their cradles, given to much older husbands at thirteen or fourteen, brought to childbed at fifteen or sixteen and mothers to three or four children by her own age of twenty-three. That was if they were not dead from the rigors of childbirth. Her own mother's first marriage had been similar, though happy enough, possibly because Isabel's father, Lord Craigsmoor, had spent much time away at court.

The second marriage of her mother's had not fared so well. The sixth earl of Graydon had been brutal and domineering, a man who treated everyone around him with the same contempt he showed those attached to his lands. His word was law and he would brook no discussion, no disobedience in any form from his wife, his stepdaughters or his son and heir from a previous marriage. Many nights, Isabel and her two younger sisters had huddled together in their bed, listening while he beat their mother for daring to question his household rulings, spending too much coin on charity or denying him access to her bed. They had watched her turn from a smiling, animated woman into a pale and cowed shadow of herself, watched her miscarry from her beatings or deliver stillborn infants. It had been no great surprise when she failed to rally from one such birth. The saving wonder had been that the monster who was her husband had been killed in a hunting accident not long afterward.

No, Isabel wanted no husband.

Yet to defy Braesford would avail her nothing and might anger him to the point of violence, as it did her stepbrother, who had been formed in his father's image. Her only weapons, if she was to escape what the night had in store, were patience and her God-given wits. What manner of good they might do her, she could not guess. The pain of her broken finger was a flimsy excuse at best. More, Braesford seemed all too likely to press for how she had come by it. To admit her stubborn refusal to agree to the marriage was the cause could not endear her to him. She might claim the onset of her monthly courses but had no certainty that would deter him. A vow of celibacy would give him pause, though only long enough to reason that she would not have been sent to him had it been binding.

No, there had to be something else, some-

36

thing so immediate and vital it could not be ignored. Now, she thought with conscious irony, would be a fine time for the curse of the Three Graces of Graydon to make its power felt.

In truth, she feared nothing would stop Braesford from possessing her. So many women must have prayed for escape from these entrapments, most to no avail. It was fated that those of her station should become the pawns of kings, moved at the royal will from one man to another, and all their tears and pleas changed that not a whit. The most Isabel could do was to make herself agreeable during the feasting while watching and waiting for a miracle. And if it did not occur, she must endure whatever happened in the bed of the master of Braesford with all the dignity she could command.

To retrace the way to the great hall was not difficult. She had only to follow the low rumble of male voices and smell of tallow candles, smoke from kitchen fires and the aroma of warm food. She had sent Gwynne ahead to see to the table arrangement made for her in what appeared to be primarily a male household. Female servants abounded, of course, but there seemed to be no woman serving as chatelaine — no mother, sister or wife of a trusted friend. Nor, if Gwynne was correct, was there a jade accustomed to warming the master's bed and giving herself airs of authority, though Isabel was not entirely sure that was the blessing her serving woman claimed. A man used to bedding a mistress might not have such rampant need of a wife.

As she neared the head of the stairwell, a shadow moved in the far end of the dark corridor. The shape grew as it neared the flaring torch that marked the stairwell, taking on the form of her stepbrother. He had just emerged from the garderobe, or stone-lined latrine, that was let into the thickness of the end wall. Square built and heavy with a lumbering gait, he had a large head covered to the eyebrows with a thatch of rust-brown hair, a beard tinted orange-red and watery blue eyes. As he walked, he adjusted his codpiece between the parti-colored green-and-red legs of his hose, prolonging the operation beyond what was necessary when he caught sight of her. The odor of ale that preceded him was ample proof of how he had spent the time since their arrival. His lips were wet, and curled at one corner as he caught sight of her.

Tightness gripped her chest, but she refused to be distressed or deterred. "Well met, Graydon," she said softly as he came closer. "I hoped to speak to you in private. You were quite right, the master of Braesford doesn't intend to wait for our vows, but to try me like a common cowherd making certain his chosen bride is fertile."

"What of it?"

"I would be more comfortable having the blessing of the priest first."

"When will you learn, dear sister, that your comfort doesn't matter? The cowherd is to be your husband. Best get used to it, and to the bedding."

"Isn't it insulting enough that I must be thrown away on a nobody? You could speak to him, insist he wait as a gesture of respect."

"Oh, aye, if it was worth running afoul of one who has the king's ear. You'll do as you're bid, and there's an end to it. Unless you'd like another finger with a crook in it?"

He grabbed for her hand as he spoke, bending her little finger backward. Burning pain surged through her like the thrust of a sword. Her knees gave way. She went to the stone floor in front of him in a pool of scarlet wool, a cry stifled in her throat.

"You hear me?" he demanded, bending over her.

"Yes." She stopped to draw a hissing

breath. "I only . . ."

"You will spread your legs and do your duty. You will be honey-mead sweet, no matter what he asks of you. You will obey me, or by God's blood I'll take a stick to your —"

"I believe not!"

That objection, delivered in tones of slicing contempt, came from a stairwell nearby. A dark shadow rose over the walls as a tall figure mounted the last two stair steps from the hall below. An instant later, Graydon let go of her hand with a growled curse. He fell to his knees beside her. Behind him stood Rand Braesford, holding her stepbrother's wrist twisted behind his back, pressed up between his shoulder blades.

"Are you all right, my lady?" her groom inquired in tight concern.

"Yes, yes, I think so," she whispered without looking up at him, her gaze on his dark shadow that was cast across her, surrounding her on the floor where she knelt.

Braesford turned his attention to the man he held so effortlessly in his hard grasp. "You will extend your apology to my lady."

"Be damned to you and to her —" Graydon halted with a grunt of pain as his arm was thrust higher.

"At once, if you value your sword arm."

"By all that's holy, Braesford! I was only doing your work for you."

"Not mine, not ever. The apology?"

Graydon's features contorted in a grimace that was half sneer, half groveling terror as his shoulder creaked under the pressure Braesford exerted. He breathed heavily through set and yellowed teeth. "I regret the injury," he ground out finally. "Aye, that I do."

Rand Braesford gave him a shove that sent him sprawling. Her stepbrother scuttled backward on his haunches until he struck the wall. He pushed to his feet, panting, his face purple with rage and chagrin.

Isabel's future husband ignored him. He leaned to offer his aid in helping her to her feet. She lifted her eyes to his, searching their dark gray depths. The concern she saw there was like balm upon an old wound. Affected by it against her will, she reached out slowly to him with her good hand. He enclosed her wrist in the hard, warm strength of his grasp and drew her up until she stood beside him. He steadied her with a hand at her waist until she gained her balance. Then he let her go and stepped back.

For a stunned instant, she felt bereft without that support. She looked away, glancing toward where Graydon stood.

He was no longer there. Fuming and cursing under his breath, he retreated down the stairs, his footsteps stamping out his enraged withdrawal.

"Come," Braesford said, guiding her back toward her solar with a brief touch at her back, "let me have a look at that finger."

She went with him. What else was she to do? Her will seemed oddly in abeyance. Her finger hurt with a fierce ache that radiated up her arm to her shoulder, making her feel a little ill and none too steady on her feet. More than that, she had no wish to face Graydon just now. He would blame her for the humiliation at Braesford's hand, and who knew what he might do to assuage his injured conceit.

Braesford's features were grim as he closed the two of them into the solar again. Turning from the door, he gestured toward a stool set near the dying fire. She moved to drop down upon it and he followed behind her, dragging an iron candle stand closer before going to one knee in front of her. His gaze met hers for a long instant. Then he reached to take her injured hand in his and place it carefully, palm up, on his bent knee.

An odd sensation, like a small explosion of sparks from a fallen fire log, ran along her nerves to her shoulder and down her back. She shivered and her hand trembled in his hold, but she declined to acknowledge it. She concentrated, instead, on his features so close to her. Twin lines grooved the space between his thick brows as he frowned, while the black fringe of his lashes concealed his expression. A small scar lay across one cheekbone, and the roots of his beard showed as a blue-black shadow beneath his close-shaved skin. An odd breathlessness afflicted her, and she inhaled deep and slow to banish it.

He did not look up, but studied her little finger, following the angle of the break with a careful, questing touch, finding the place where the bone had snapped. He added his thumb, spanning the injured member between it and his forefinger. Gripping her wrist in his free hand, he caught the slender, misshapen digit in a grip of ruthless power and gave it a smooth, hard pull.

She cried out, keeling forward in such abrupt weakness that her forehead came to rest on his wide shoulder. Sickness crowded her throat and she swallowed hard upon it, breathing in rapid pants. Against her hair, she heard him whisper something she could not understand, heard him murmur her name.

"Forgive me, I beg," he said a little louder, though his tone was quiet and a little gruff. "I would not have hurt you for a king's ransom. It was necessary, or else your poor finger would always have been crooked."

She shifted, moved back a space to stare down at their joined hands. Slowly, he unfurled his grasp. Her little finger no longer had a bend in it. It was straight again.

"You . . ." she began, then stopped, unable to think what she meant to say.

"I am the worst kind of devil, I know, but it seemed a shame that such slender, aristocratic fingers should appear imperfect."

She would not deny it, was even grateful in a way. What she could not forgive was the lack of warning. Yes, and lack of choice. She had been offered so little of late.

He did not wait for her comment but turned to survey the rushes that covered the floor behind him. Selecting one, he broke its stem into two equal lengths with a few quick snaps. He fitted these on either side of her finger, and then reached without ceremony to slip free the knotted silk ribbon which held her slashed sleeve together above her left elbow. Shaking out the shining length, he wrapped it quickly around his makeshift splint.

Isabel stared at his bent head as he

worked, her gaze moving from the wide expanse of his shoulders to the bronze skin at the nape of his neck where the waving darkness of his hair fell forward away from it, from his well-formed fingers that worked so competently at his task to the concentration on his features. His face was gilded by candlelight, his sun-darkened skin tinted with copper and bronze, the bones sculpted with tints of gold while the shadows cast upon his cheekbones by his lashes were deep black in contrast.

A strange, heated awareness rose inside her, the piercing recognition of her response to his touch, his inherent strength, his sheer masculine presence. They were so very alone here in the solar with the gathering darkness pressing against the thick window glass and only a single branch of guttering candles for light. She had few defenses against whatever he might decide to do to her in the next several minutes, and no expectation of consideration at his hands.

Husband, he was her husband already under canon law, with all the privileges that entailed. Would he be tender in his possession? Or would he be brutish, taking her with all the ceremony of a stag mounting a hind? Her stomach muscles clenched as molten reaction moved lower in her body. A shudder, uncontrollable in its force, spiraled through her.

Braesford glanced up as that tremor extended to the fingers he held. "Did I hurt you?"

"No, no," she said, her voice compressed in her tight throat. "I just . . . I should thank you for coming to my aid. It was fortunate you arrived when you did."

"Fortune had no part in it," he answered, returning his gaze to the small, flat knot he was tying in the ribbon. "I was coming to escort you to the hall."

"Were you?" Her wonder faded quickly. "I suppose you felt we should make our entrance together."

"I thought you might prefer not to face the company alone. As there will be no other lady present, no chatelaine to make you comfortable, then . . ." He lifted a square shoulder.

"It was a kind thought." She paused, went on after a moment, "Though it does seem odd to be the only female of rank."

"I have no family," he said, a harsh note entering his voice. "I am the bastard son of a serving maid who died when I was born. My father was master of Braesford, but acknowledged me only to the extent of having me educated for the position of his steward. That was before his several estates, including Braesford, were confiscated when he was attainted as a traitor."

Isabel tipped her head to one side in curiosity. "Traitor to which king, if I may ask?"

"To Edward IV. My father was loyal to old King Henry VI, and died with two of my half brothers, two out of his three legal heirs, while trying to restore him to the throne."

"You followed in his footsteps, being for Lancaster?" She should know these things, but had barely listened to anything said about her groom after the distress of being told she must wed.

"Edward cut off my father's head and set it on Tower Bridge. Was I to love him for it? Besides, he was a usurper, a regent who grew too fond of power after serving in his uncle's place when he became a saintly madman."

Her own dead father had sworn fealty to the white rose of York, but Isabel held the symbol in no great affection. Edward IV had stolen the crown from his pious and doddering uncle, Henry VI, and murdered him to prevent him from regaining it. He'd also executed his own brother, Clarence, for treason in order to keep it. When Edward died, his younger brother, the Duke of Gloucester, had declared Edward's young sons and daughters illegitimate and taken the crown for himself as Richard III. Rumor said he had ordered the two boys murdered to prevent any effort to restore them to the succession. Mayhap it was true; certainly they had disappeared. Now Henry Tudor had defeated and killed Richard III at Bosworth Field, becoming King Henry VII by might as much as right. He had also married Elizabeth of York, eldest daughter of Edward IV, thus uniting the red rose of Lancaster with the white rose of York, ending decades of fighting.

So much blood and death, and for what? For the right to receive the homage of other men? For the power to take what they wanted and kill whom they pleased?

"And the present Henry is wholly deserving of the crown he has gained?" she inquired.

"Careful, my lady," Braesford said softly. "Newly made kings are more sensitive to treasonous comments than those accustomed to the weight of the crown."

"You won't denounce me, I think, for that would mean the end of a marriage greatly to your advantage. Besides, I would not speak so before any other."

He met her gaze for long seconds, his own darkly appraising before he inclined his head. "I value the confidence."

"Of course you do," she said in short rejoinder. Few men bothered to listen to women in her experience, much less attend to what they said.

"I assure you it is so. Only bear in mind that in some places the very stones have ears." He went on with barely a pause. "In any case, Henry VII is the last of his blood, the last heir to the rightful king, being descended on his mother's side from John of Gaunt, grandfather to Henry VI. With all other contenders executed, dead in battle or presumed murdered, he has as much right to the crown as any, and far more than most."

"Descended from an illegitimate child of John of Gaunt," she pointed out.

His smile turned crooked, lighting the gray of his eyes. "Spoken like a true Yorkist. Yet the baseborn can be made legitimate by royal decree, as were the children of John of Gaunt by Katherine Swynford, not to mention Henry's new consort, Edward IV's daughter, Elizabeth. And as with the meek, they sometimes inherit the earth."

"Do you speak of Henry," she said after an instant of frowning consideration, "or mean to say that you inherited your father's estates, as he was once master at Braesford?"

"I was awarded them, rather, for services rendered to Henry VII. Though I promise you I earned every hectare and hamlet."

"Awarded a bride, as well," she said with some asperity.

Rand tipped his head. "That, too, by God's favor, as well as Henry's."

The former owner of Braesford, if she remembered aright, was named McConnell. Being baseborn, Rand had taken the name of the estate as his surname, identifying himself with the land rather than with his father. It was a significant act, perhaps an indication of the man. "I was told the reward was, most likely, for finding the golden circlet lost by Richard in a thornbush at Bosworth. Well, and for having the presence of mind to hand it to Lord Stanley with the recommendation that he crown Henry on the field."

"Don't, please, allow the king's mother to hear you say so." A wry smile came and went across his face. "She believes it was her husband's idea."

Henry's mother, Lady Margaret, was married to Lord Stanley, Earl of Derby, as everyone knew. Though she had set up her household at Westminster Palace with her son, living apart from her husband by mutual consent, she was yet protective of Stanley's good name.

"It was the reason, nonetheless?" Isabel persisted.

"Such things come, now and then, from the gratitude of kings."

His voice was satirical, his features grim, almost forbidding. He was not stupid by any means, so well knew the fickle nature of royals who could take away as easily as they gave.

Yet receiving the ripe plum of a fine estate that had once belonged to a traitor was not unusual. The late bloodletting, named by some troubadour as the War of the Roses, had gone on so long, its factions had shifted and changed so often with the rise and fall of those calling themselves king, that titles and estates had changed hands many times over. A man sitting at the king's table today, lauded as a lord and dressed in ermine-lined velvet, could have an appointment with headsman or hangman tomorrow. Few so favored died in their beds.

She noted, of a sudden, that Braesford seemed to be avoiding her gaze, almost ill at ease as he smoothed a thumb over the rush stems of her splint as if checking for roughness. Disquiet rose inside her as she wondered if he had overheard what she'd said of him moments ago. Clearing her throat, she spoke with some discomfiture. "If it chances you were near enough to overhear what passed between me and my stepbrother just now —"

He stopped her with a slicing gesture. "It doesn't matter. You were quite right. I am nobody."

"You were knighted by Henry on the battlefield," she replied with self-conscious fairness as heat rose to her hairline. "That stands for something."

"So it does. Regardless, I will always be a nobody to men like your brother who were born to their honors."

"My stepbrother," she murmured in correction.

"Your true father, your mother's first husband, was an earl, as well. You, therefore, share this birthright of nobility." He glanced up suddenly, his eyes as hard as polished armor. "You will always be Lady Isabel, no matter what manner of man you marry."

"For what good it may do me. But the lands you have been given will provide sufficient income to maintain a place at court, one from which you may gain more honors."

He shook his head so firmly that the candlelight slid across the polished ebony strands of his hair in blue and yellow gleams. "I will always be the mere steward of this estate in some sense, a farmer at heart with little use for Henry's court and its intrigues. I want only to live in this manse above its green valley. Abide with me here, and I swear that you and your aristocratic fingers will be forever safe from injury, including that from your husband."

It was a promise well calculated to ease the fear in her heart. And so it might have if Isabel had dared trust in it. She did not, as she knew full well that oaths given to women were never so well honored as those sworn between men.

Removing her fingers from his grasp, she got to her feet. "I will be glad of your escort below, for now."

If he was disappointed, he did not show it. He rose to his feet with lithe strength and offered his arm. Together, they descended to the wedding feast.

The hall blazed with light from wicks set afloat in large, flat bowls perched upon tripods. The double line of trestle tables led toward the low wooden dais that held the high table with its huge saltcellar. The alcove behind it was wainscoted with whitewashed wood and painted with allegorical scenes in the tall reaches above the paneling. A pair of chests set with silver plate flanked the great stone fireplace that soared upward. Above them hung bright-colored banners, swaying gently in the rising heat.

The men-at-arms that lounged on the benches drawn up to the tables numbered thirty at most. It was not a large force; that brought by Isabel's stepbrother for protection on the journey northward was half again as large. Between the two complements, however, the room seemed overfull of men in linen, wool and velvet.

Their voices made a bass rumble that ceased abruptly as Braesford appeared with her on his arm. With a mighty scraping and rustling, they came to their feet, standing at attention. Silence stretched, broken only by a cough or low growl from one of the dogs that lay among the rushes beneath the trestles, as the two of them made their way to the high table.

Isabel flushed a little under such concentrated regard. Glancing along the ranked men, she caught open speculation on the features of one or two. They believed dalliance in the privacy of her solar had delayed her arrival, particularly after Graydon's comments in the courtyard. It made no difference what they might think, of course, yet she despised the thought of the images sure to be passing through their heads.

Braesford seated her, then released the company to their own benches with a gesture. The meal began at once as servants came forward to fill beakers, lay trenchers from great baskets of the bread slabs and ladle onto these a savory concoction of sweetmeats flavored with spices, chopped vegetables and cubed bread soaked in broth.

Isabel put out her hand toward the wine goblet that sat between her place and that of her future husband, but immediately drew it back. Sharing a place with one of her younger sisters, as she usually did, it was her right as eldest to drink first or offer the wine, as she chose. Now that she shared Braesford's table setting, this was his privilege.

He noticed her movement, as he seemed to notice most things. With a brief, not ungraceful gesture of one hand, he made her free of the goblet. She took it up, sipped gingerly.

The wine was new, raw and barely watered, so went down with difficulty past the tightness in her throat. That first taste was enough to let her know she could not face food. The smell of it, along with wood smoke, hot oil from the lamps and warm male bodies in stale linen, brought back her earlier illness. It would be enough, she hoped, to merely pretend to eat. The last thing she wanted was to appear to spurn Braesford's hospitality. Meanwhile, manners and common sense dictated that she converse with her future husband, to establish some semblance of rapport that might yet serve her in avoiding intimacy this night.

She could think of nothing to say. Soon enough the feasting would be over, and what then? What then?

"My lady?"

Braesford was offering her a succulent piece of roast pork, taken from the large, golden-brown trencher set on a silver salver between them. She glanced at it on the razor-sharp tip of his knife, met his dark eyes an instant, then looked away again. "I . . . couldn't. I thank you, sir, but no."

"A little crust, then, to go with the wine." Taking the meat from the knifepoint himself with a flash of white teeth, he carved off a piece of their trencher and held it out to her.

She took the bread, nibbled at it and sipped more wine. Even as she lifted the goblet to her lips, however, she realized she was monopolizing it when it must be shared between them. Wiping the rim hurriedly with the edge of the tablecloth draped over her lap for that purpose, she pushed the goblet toward him.

"Your finger pains you," he said, his gaze on what she was doing. "I'm sorry. There is a woman in the village, as I told you before, a healer who can make an infusion of willow bark, which might be useful. I'll send for her at once."

"Please don't concern yourself." She lowered her lashes. "A night of rest will be sufficient, I'm sure."

"Will it, now? And I imagine two nights, or even three or four, would be better."

"Indeed, yes," she began eagerly, but halted as she looked up to catch the silver shading of irony in his eyes, the tightening at the corner of his firmly molded mouth.

"Indeed," he repeated, putting out his hand for the wine goblet, rotating it in a slow turn and drinking from where she had sipped. "Did you never notice that the things you dread are seldom as bad as feared once they are behind you?"

"No," she said with precision.

"It's so, I promise. No doubt the reflection will prove a solace in the morning."

He reached to take her good wrist, removing the bread slice she had been toying with and dropping a light kiss on her knuckles before popping the crust into his mouth.

She sat quite still, feeling the warm, tingling imprint of his lips on her hand, shivering a little as it vibrated through her, watching in peculiar wonder the movement of his jaw muscle as he chewed and swallowed.

"God's blood, Braesford," Graydon called from his place near the dais with Viscount Henley next to him. " 'Tis a habit you caught in France, I don't doubt, kissing a lady's hand. An Englishman can think of more interesting places to put his mouth to work."

Henley, being somewhat less coarse than her stepbrother, coughed and ducked his head rather than joining in the scattered guffaws. His face turned scarlet, regardless, in reaction to the lewd suggestion.

"But not, I think, at table," Braesford answered Graydon, before his tone hardened and he speared Henley and the rest of the company with a look, "and not while thinking of my lady."

Quiet descended, free even of the thump of ale beakers hitting the trestles. In it, the nervous uncertainty in Graydon's snort was plainly heard. Isabel felt suddenly sorry for her stepbrother, reprimanded twice by Braesford in the space of an hour. Though she had endured countless variations on his lewd wedding humor during the past days, had longed fervently for someone to shut his mouth for him, she could not enjoy his discomfiture.

"Aye, no disrespect intended," Graydon muttered. Henley rumbled a similar answer, as did half a dozen others along the boards.

Braesford drank a mouthful of wine and set down the goblet. "I trust not. Her honor is mine now, therefore must be protected by my sword."

"Oh, aye, as it should be," her stepbrother agreed. "Pious Henry would have it no other way, seeing as he gave her to you."

"And I value his gifts above diamonds, plan always to hold them firmly in my grasp."

Her future husband turned his head to meet her gaze as he spoke. What Isabel saw there made her draw a sharp breath. Then she reached for the wine goblet he still held, taking it from him in her two hands before draining it to the dregs.

The meal continued with all manner of dishes, requiring three removes of the cloths covering the tables as they became too soiled for use. Beyond the usual pottages flavored with spices, they were served meat pies, vegetables dressed with vinegar and simmered in sauces, oysters served in various ways, great platters of roast piglet, snipe, lark tongues and even a swan roasted, then clad again in its feathers. The master of Braesford had gone to great lengths to gather such victuals for his bride and honored guests, but Isabel refused to be impressed, just as she ignored the trio of musicians who played from the gallery above her, the dancers who twirled around the tables, the jugglers and mimes who made the men laugh. She was used to such things at court for one thing, but also knew well that ample feasting and merriment often had more to do with status than the appeasement of anyone's hunger or the need to be entertained.

It was some time later that the melodious salute of a trumpet sounded above the clatter and merriment. The signal indicated someone of importance approaching Braesford's outer gate.

The tune played by lute and harp trailed into silence. Voices stilled. Everyone turned toward the entrance doors. The commander of Braesford's men-at-arms rose from a nearby table. He nodded at a half-dozen men and left the hall in their company.

"You are expecting visitors?" Isabel asked in quiet tones as she leaned toward her future husband.

"By no means, but don't be distressed. It

can be nothing of import."

He suspected a neighboring landowner and his men on local business, mayhap, or else a latecomer to the feast. Still, she knew as well as he did that it could also be a command to join the king's army, to ride out to control some uprising or defend a border. Only a mounted troop or king's herald would have triggered the trumpet salute of warning.

They had not long to wait. The clatter of hooves on the stones of the inner court and the jingling of tack came faintly to where they sat. Booted feet sounded upon the tower stairs. Serving men threw open the doors, allowing a cadre of soldiers under the king's red-dragon banner to march inside. They tramped down the open area between the trestles until they reached the high table. The order to halt rang out and their commanding officer stepped forward, saluting with a mailed arm and gloved fist.

Braesford came to his feet with a frown between his dark brows. "Welcome, William, as always, though I thought you settled at Westminster. What brings you this far north?"

"The order of the king." The man addressed as William pulled a paper from the pouch at his side and passed it across the width of the high table to Braesford.

Isabel recognized the newcomer as William McConnell, a man she had seen about the court. Turning over his name, studying his features and something of his manner, she felt the stir of presentiment. He was similar in size and feature to Rand, though McConnell's hair was more badger brown than black, the jut of his nose less bold and his eyes brown rather than gray. Recalling, abruptly, some whispered comment heard more than a year ago, she realized this was Braesford's remaining half brother, the third of three, he who had once thought to inherit the hall where she sat until it was forfeited after their father was executed.

"What is it?" Braesford asked, accepting the roll of parchment, unfurling it so the great seal of the king appeared, impressed into wax as red as blood.

"An unpleasant errand, in all truth." McConnell directed his gaze somewhere above the high table, upon his family banners that hung there.

"Aye, and that would be?"

His half brother cleared his throat with a rasp, speaking in a voice that reached into the most distant corners of the room. "Randall of Braesford, you are charged with the crime of murder in the death of the child born these two months past to Mademoiselle Juliette d'Amboise. By command of His Royal Majesty, King Henry VII, you are directed to leave within the hour for London, in company with your affianced wife, Lady Isabel of Graydon. There, you will appear before the King's Court on the charge lodged against you."

Murder. The heinous murder of a child. Isabel sat unmoving, so mired in disbelief she could hardly take in the implications of the charge.

Even so, three things were blindingly obvious to her.

There would be no night spent in the bed of the master of Braesford, not if she was to leave with him at once for London.

There might never be a wedding if he was convicted of the murder.

The curse of the Three Graces of Graydon had not failed.

3

Fury ran like acid through Rand's veins. It striped his thought processes to such a sharp and raw edge that he was able to order the packing of supplies for his men and his guests, to direct the continued operations for the manse and the coming harvest, all while mentally cursing his king who was also his friend. Or who had once been his friend, in the days of their exile.

What in God's sweet heaven was Henry about with this charge of murder of an innocent? Mademoiselle Juliette d'Amboise's newborn babe, a small mite with Juliette's full-lipped mouth and Henry's pale blue eyes, had been in rosy health when Rand last saw her. He had stood sentinel on the keep wall as little Madeleine, as Juliette had named her, left Braesford Hall with her mother. Henry himself had sent an armed troop to see his mistress to a place of quiet seclusion, so must know full well the baby had not been harmed.

Henry was a secretive man, and who could blame him? When only four years old, he had been taken from his mother and placed in the custody of a sympathizer of the Duke of York. Being fostered in a family not his own was common for the scion of a noble house, as it was thought to promote independence and allow instruction in the art of war without any weakening favoritism, but this was the house of the enemy. Henry had escaped that imprisonment when his doddering cousin, Henry VI, briefly regained the throne from the Yorkists under Edward IV, but was forced to ride for his life when the aging king was murdered. He, with his uncle, Jasper Tudor, barely reached the coast and took ship for France ahead of Edward's forces — who would certainly have killed him, as well.

Blown off course, Henry and Jasper landed in Brittany, where their fate hung in the balance as the Duke of Brittany made up his mind whether more political advantage could be gained from keeping them as his nominal guests or turning them over to their enemies. For the next fourteen years, that cat-and-mouse game had played itself out, with Louis XI of France sometimes taking part in it before his death. Henry had been heard to say that he had been either hunted or in captivity for most of his life. Was it any wonder that he had grown as devious as those who surrounded him?

Understanding could not persuade Rand to overlook the unwarranted interference in his nuptials and his life. He railed against it, cursing the timing and implied threat. He suspected Henry had changed his mind about giving him Lady Isabel. It was always possible the king had discovered a more worthy husband for her, one who would bring greater advantage to the crown.

It was damnable. More than that, Rand objected strenuously to being hung so the lady might be free. He meant to guard against convenient accidents that could remove him, as well; he had insisted that his own men-at-arms must join the king's men, and Graydon's, on this ride to London.

Now he sat his gray destrier, Shadow, in brooding silence. Flanked on one side by his squire, David, a blond and blue-eyed young valiant, and on the other by his own restless soldiery, he watched Lady Isabel emerge from the tower into the court. She appeared pale but resolute in the flare of torchlight, with the hood of her cloak drawn forward, half concealing her face. She was gloved, Rand saw, but the leather was cut away from the injured finger of her left hand.

His splint still held it in place. It gave him an odd satisfaction to see it.

She had not wanted to be wed, had been coerced in the most brutal fashion to accept the match, forced to ride north to Braesford for the marriage. He might have known. She was the daughter of an earl, after all. Why should she be wed to a bastard knight? It was a disparagement to her high birth under the rights granted to nobles by the Magna Carta. She should have been allowed to refuse, might have done so if not for her stepbrother's threats.

A nobody, she had named him.

She had it aright; still, Rand seethed as he recalled that pronouncement in her clear, carrying voice. He was more of a personage now than he had been born to expect, had earned land and honors by his own hard effort. He would have more yet. And when it was gained, he would lay it at her feet and demand her apology, her recognition of his worth and her surrender.

Ah, no.

He would be lucky if he came out of this business with his life. Whatever he was to have of the lady, it must be soon. Otherwise, he might have nothing of her at all.

A horseshoe struck stone as William McConnell, his half brother, reined in close beside him. "A worthy bride," he drawled as he followed Rand's hot gaze. "You almost managed to have her, too."

"You could have allowed departure in the morning, so I might have come to know her better."

"In the biblical fashion, therefore completely? A great pity, that lack of opportunity, but I have my orders."

"And you don't object to carrying them out."

Implicit between them was the knowledge that William had coveted Isabel for himself. He had sighed after her the winter before while cursing his lack of favor with Henry that might have earned him her hand and her fortune. Well understood, too, was the bitterness he harbored for the fact that his patrimony had fallen to Rand. The fortunes of war had dispossessed the legitimate son and rewarded the illegitimate, however, and nothing except another wrenching turn of fate could change matters back again.

"Would you object in my place?" William asked, the words layered with bitterness.

"Probably not," Rand said, "but neither do I honor you for it. More, I have a warning for you. You'd best have a care if you think to profit from this business. For one thing, Henry is more likely to keep Braesford and its rents for himself than return them to you. For another, I will answer to the king for what occurred with Mademoiselle d'Amboise but don't mean to hang. When this is done, I will discover who put about the foul story of child murder. They will then answer to me."

"I would expect no less," McConnell said with a shrug of one mailed shoulder.

"So long as we understand each other."

McConnell swept up his fist, thumping it against his heart. Then he moved off. Rand watched him for long moments before he finally turned back to observe his bride as she mounted her palfrey at the block. He could have aided her, but did not trust himself to touch her in public, not in his present mood.

This was not, after all, the kind of mounting he had envisioned for this hour. Someone had seen to it he was disappointed in his desires. He looked away, his mouth set in a hard line as he considered, yet again, who that might be. Yes, and why.

They rode hard through the night, clattering along the dark lanes with only a fitful moon to show the way, choking on their own dust. No one called out or questioned their passage. They swept through villages and outlying farms where dogs barked and shutters were flung wide as householders leaned out to see who was abroad. Noting the king's banner at the cavalcade's head, the suddenly incurious banged their shutters closed again.

Dawn came, and still they kept the hard pace. Rand turned in his saddle to look back, seeking out Lady Isabel's form near where her serving woman bumped along on her mule. His bride rode with her face set and her cloak rippling along the side of her mount, but her seat in her sidesaddle was not nearly as erect as when they set out. Facing forward again, Rand spurred to join the captain of his guard. He spoke a quiet suggestion.

At the next town, where they stopped to change horses, a narrow-bodied litter slung between mules was procured. Rand thought at first that his lady would decline being carried rather than riding, refuse the luxury of its feather-stuffed cushioning, also its hemp curtains, which shut out the sun's bright rays. Good sense won out over pride, however, and she finally disappeared inside.

Traveling with the litter slowed them down, but was still better than being held up should the lady fall ill from exhaustion.

70

She had just made this wearisome journey, after all, only to turn around and retrace the route.

It was late afternoon when Rand dropped back to walk his horse alongside the litter. Keeping his voice to a conversational tone, he said, "Lady Isabel, would you care for marzipan?"

She was doubtless either famished or bored to distraction, for she pushed back the side curtains at once. Supporting herself on one elbow, she asked, "Have you any?"

She appeared almost sybaritic among the litter's cushions, with the lacings of her bodice loosened for ease and her golden hair escaping the confines of her veil. The sudden tightness in his groin was so intense it was an instant before he bethought himself and leaned to pass over the small drawstring bag filled with the confection that he had taken from his saddlebag. Watching with a rueful smile as she instantly drew it open and took out a piece that was dyed pink and green, it was a moment before he could speak again.

"Are you content in there?"

"Exceedingly. If the idea of the litter was yours, I thank you for it."

"To see to your comfort is little enough. I am to blame for this sudden change of

71

plans, after all."

She swallowed the piece of marzipan, avoiding his gaze as she looked into the bag for another. "It seems a curious business. You are accused of a terrible act, yet allowed to ride as free as you please. I thought to see you in chains."

"You might have, except I gave my pledge not to attempt to escape but to abide by the king's will. William was good enough to accept it."

"How convenient."

"You don't ask if I'm guilty."

"Would you tell me if you were? If you are only going to protest your innocence, then where is the point?"

It was difficult to fault her logic, though it would have been pleasant if she had appeared to care one way or the other. That was apparently too much to expect. And if he did not look directly at her for any length of time, he discovered, he could attend to what she was saying instead of how she affected him.

"What if I'm not?" he asked after a moment.

"Then it will be shown, and all will be as before, yes?"

His every hope depended on it, and every future plan. "As you say."

She looked up at that, as if something in his voice had snared her attention. "You doubt the king's justice?"

It was the king's motives Rand doubted, though it would be foolhardy to say so. The sentiment could become a weapon in her hands, and he had not the least idea how she would use it. "It will turn out as God wills."

"Or as the king wills," she said in tart reply, "which is supposed to be the same thing as he claims divine right. What I should like to know is why I was not told of this charge, was given no hint that you were involved in such a crime."

His smile was grim. "That's easily answered. There was no crime."

"It's all a mistake, then."

He inclined his head as he thought of the tender and helpless babe he had helped bring into the world. "I pray it may turn out that way."

"Who could have accused you? Have you no idea?"

"None whatever."

"But there was a child?"

Rand made no reply. He had pledged to remain silent. He did not go back on his sworn oath.

"Not long after Henry Tudor arrived from

Bosworth last year," the lady observed, her gaze resting on his face, "rumor circulated of a Frenchwoman who had landed in Wales with him for the invasion and traveled in his baggage train. She never put in an official appearance at court, possibly because of his immediate betrothal to Elizabeth of York. Henry would have wanted nothing to stand in the way of his being wed to the daughter of Edward IV as it promised to add legitimacy to his claim to the throne. . . ." She stopped, sending him an impatient frown. "Don't look so hunted, no one can hear us!"

"It isn't your lovely neck that may be stretched if Henry is displeased," he said in dry reproof, "though it could be if you continue in this vein. That is, unless you are offered the ax as a noblewoman."

She ignored that last sally. "What other vein is there? I only speak the truth."

"The truth is what the king declares it to be."

"So cynical. I did not know you were at court long enough for it."

He glanced ahead to where the first riders of their long cavalcade approached the ford for a small stream. In the meadow behind them, a lark sang and a warm wind swept over the wheat awaiting harvest so it waved like a golden sea. The scents of ripening grain wafted around them, along with the dust of their passage and the hint of ripening berries from a distant hedgerow. All was well with their line of march for the moment.

"I was a part of Henry's court long before he reached England's shores last year," he said finally. "It was enough."

"You left it of your own will, then. Could be that's why he has ordered you brought back. Those who wear the crown are often suspicious of men who withdraw from their august presence."

"So it's dangerous to get too close and dangerous to stay away. What is a peaceable man to do?"

She watched him a long moment before she spoke. "You really don't care for court life."

"I prefer Braesford, where my labors make a difference that can be seen, where there is time to watch the sunrise, the rain as it sweeps down the mountainsides and the fat lambs in the fields."

"A farmer in all truth," she murmured, almost to herself. An instant later, she frowned up at him. "Braesford is isolated enough to make a fine refuge. Also, the king would be reluctant to have his wife learn that he had a mistress tucked away in some hidden spot. She is with child, you know. The queen, I mean."

"So I had heard."

"She is due in a couple of months — fast work as the wedding was only in January. The king is greatly wrought, they say, because Elizabeth has never been robust. He might take pains to prevent her from learning his mistress was also with child. That is, of course, if this particular French-woman was your guest when the incident of child murder came about."

He might have known a lady familiar with court gossip would be able to work out the sequence of events. He was not inclined to confirm her thought, however. "There was no murder," he said again.

"Yet someone seems to have done away with the child. It's not too surprising, I suppose, given the many heirs who have died under mysterious circumstances — Edward IV's two boys held in the White Tower, the son of Richard III and so many others. If the baby was a boy, even though illegiti-mate . . ."

"It was not —"

Rand came an abrupt halt, cursing softly before pressing his lips together.

"A girl child, then, and Henry's daughter," she said, leaning back in satisfaction. "It still gives rise to possibilities."

Rand drew up and stepped down from his destrier, tossing the reins to his squire, who sidled close enough to take them. Catching up with the slow-moving litter in a few long strides, he swung inside and pulled the curtain across the opening, closing himself inside with Lady Isabel.

She dropped the bag of confections and scooted back against the litter's front panel. Drawing up her legs, she wrapped her skirt around her bare ankles. "What . . . what are you doing?"

"How can I impress upon you the danger of speaking out of turn?" he demanded, leaning toward her with one arm braced on his raised knee. "You may think you are safe because Henry smiles upon you now and then or because you are a friend of his consort. But Elizabeth is yet uncrowned, and unlikely to be until she has produced an heir to the throne. As a daughter of the house of York, she remains at court on sufferance, so has no power to save you from Henry's wrath. Indeed, she must keep her tongue between her teeth to protect herself from the watchers set around her by the queen's mother."

"Lady Margaret? She would never harm anyone."

"A woman who can scheme for decades, marrying herself off to lay hands on the money necessary to raise an army strong enough to put her son on the throne, is capable of anything — and you'll do best to remember it. Lady Margaret has only one thought in her head, and that is to gain whatever may be best for Henry. Cross her, allow her to perceive you as a threat, only at your peril."

"Why should you care?" she asked so quietly he had to strain to hear. "Why would you warn me?"

"Because I am as devious as they are," he said in grim despair. "I also have only one thought that has nothing to do with kings or queens."

"And that would be?"

She should not have asked. It was all the excuse he required.

Reaching for her, he drew her into his arms so quickly he set the litter to jouncing on its straps. "To show you other uses for a lady's mouth," he answered in low hunger, "and particularly her small, sharp, pink-and-green-stained tongue."

She stared up at him from where she rested against his upright knee, her eyes as smoky green as the northern hills, her flat cap and veil fallen away so her hair trailed in silken fire over his knee. Then her lashes fluttered shut as he set his mouth to hers.

She tasted of marzipan and sweet, warm female, a flavor headier than the finest mead. Rand reveled in it, intoxicated, fascinated by the softness of her lips, their moist inner surfaces, the glasslike edges of her teeth. Her breath feathered softly across his face. She was firmly rounded against him, enticing in her stillness. He released her arm, spanned the slender concave of her waist with hard fingers, skimmed upward until his palm cupped the glory of her breast. The nipple was a small, hard berry under the fine wool of her bodice. As it tightened further, he circled it with his thumb again and again in mindless exhilaration.

A low sound — part moan, part protest — left her. He heard but was beyond acknowledging it, deepening the kiss instead. The retreat of her tongue from his enticed him; the taste of her held him in thrall. The need for more, and still more of her, clamored in his head, his chest, his heated groin. Her wet softness was his grail and he searched diligently for it, sliding his hand back down over her hip and underneath the hem of her gown. He brushed upward over her calf, her thigh and higher, to where she lay unprotected, infinitely vulnerable to his marauding fingers.

She writhed, gasping at his touch, his intimate invasion. His overheated brain presented the image of how easy it would be to roll her beneath him and slide into her hot, moist depths, taking her there in the swaying bower of a litter while their guard trotted before and behind them.

He had forgotten the ford.

The litter lurched forward as they descended the near bank. Water splashed against the curtains, coming through as a drenching spray. Rand drew a sharp breath, returning abruptly to his senses. He sat for a rigid instant, fighting for control. Then he smoothed down Lady Isabel's skirts and set her from him. Not trusting himself to speak, much less look at the woman he had mauled with such fine disregard for their circumstances, he waited until the litter lurched backward as its mules climbed from the ford. He batted aside the curtains then, and stepped down, sweeping them shut again behind him.

Some minutes later, when he had remounted the gray and cantered to the head of the column once more, his half brother fell into place beside him. "Well?" he inquired with a curl to his mouth.

"Well, what?" The words came out with more of a growl to them than Rand intended.

"How was she?"

"Comfortable," he said, and felt heat burn the back of his neck.

"No doubt. But was she, is she, of an accommodating disposition?"

Rand gave McConnell a hard stare. "I have no idea. She deserves better than to be molested while half the men within two counties hang on every moan."

"A sad waste of a fine opportunity, then, especially when you have the perfect excuse."

"Nor does she need to be bedded by a man who may live only as long as it takes to reach the king's Star Chamber. She will have a much better chance at another husband if there's no chance she's breeding."

That was, to the best of his understanding, the reason he had left Isabel alone in the litter. The decision was sudden and in stark contrast to his previous intentions, so he had not been thinking too clearly.

There were, of course, those who would willingly take a pregnant woman to wife since her condition proved her ability to bear children. Most preferred a virgin, however, or at least a lengthy betrothal that would prove she was not with child. Anyway, the likelihood that Henry VII would now hand over the stepsister of the Earl of Graydon to a man charged with murder was so remote as to be laughable.

"Very noble, but will offer little satisfaction while you lie in a prison cell. Besides, if she was with your get, she could well inherit Braesford should you hang."

"Keeping it from your possession? A strong incentive, I must say," Rand answered in dry tones, looking away toward where the wooded copse they had traveled through followed the curve of the burn.

"Or I could offer my aid and support so she might persuade Henry that she requires a new husband to replace my bastard brother. Who knows? He could agree in honor of your memory."

"So he might, but I wouldn't depend on it. Besides, I don't intend to be a mere memory."

Rand kicked the stallion into a fast canter and left McConnell in the dust. If only his doubts and fears could be left behind so easily.

Isabel lay where Braesford had left her. She watched the spots of brightness caused by sunlight striking through the trees onto the hemp top of the litter. She should have been incensed. Instead, she was thoughtful.

Why had he stopped?

It seemed unlikely that a mere dash of water in the face could have had such effect. Had it brought him to his senses, as it seemed, or merely served to remind him of a deeper purpose? Had he really intended an object lesson in the proper use of her tongue or something more? Had he wanted to show her what was to come when they were joined in wedlock, or merely to prove she could be brought to succumb to desire for a nobody?

So this was passion, this languor in the blood and compelling urge toward surrender regardless of the cost. How strange it was, when she resented and half feared the man who caused it. She had heard women sigh after handsome gallants, going into ecstasies over their shoulders, their thighs beneath clinging hose or what lay beneath their extravagant codpieces. She had thought they exaggerated or else were being deliberately silly. All men possessed the same basic equipment, did they not?

Clearly, she had erred. Some men walked in an aura of masculinity far surpassing others. Their bodies were better formed, with muscles that moved like oiled silk under the skin. Their touch could inflame. They were a threat to female peace of mind. Dangerous, too, were their smiles. She would not have believed a man's face could alter so easily from chill sternness to compelling warmth with the mere shift of facial muscles. It began in his eyes, she thought, the sudden rich amusement that she watched for with too much anticipation.

She must be on her guard every minute until they reached London. The Graydon curse had delivered her from immediate marriage to Braesford, and it would be foolish to succumb to his caresses in spite of it. The last thing she needed was to consummate a union she hoped to see dissolved. More, she could hardly claim to fear a husband who was charged with murder if witnesses could swear she had been intimate with him.

That was, of course, if it came to such a pass. It was possible the hangman would deliver her from the necessity.

It crossed her mind briefly that such could be the aim, that the king might have handed her over to a betrothed of lower rank knowing he would snatch her away again. Still, what could be the purpose of such a cruel game of cat and mouse? She could see none that made any sense.

She knew almost nothing about Randall Braesford, of course. There might be all manner of things in his past to cause hidden enmity. The court was a hotbed of jealous intrigue and petty vendettas. Anyone could have decided to play a vicious joke on this baseborn knight of high pride and stalwart courage.

The jest could also be on her. She had rejected a half-dozen offers for her hand while claiming the protection of the curse, turning a near spinster at three-and-twenty. Perhaps someone wanted to show her she was not immune to the fate of most women, of being married without her consent and for what she could bring to her husband. If Braesford knew of the curse and dared to defy it, then it made him the perfect choice. She was sure to be aghast at being handed over to a commoner whose lands were practically falling into the far North Sea. And if they had to see him hanged so she could be snatched back for the greater enjoyment of the joke, then what of it? He was nothing, a nobody.

Those who thought so had, just possibly, failed to take proper measure of Sir Randall of Braesford. This was a fact which could not be ignored, as much as it pained Isabel to admit it. Noble blood ran in his veins, regardless of his birth. He had not achieved his current position by being either stupid or unwary.

Easing to a sitting position, she retrieved the bag of marzipan and tied it closed before tucking it under a pillow. She shook the excess water from the litter's curtain, used the hem of her skirt to wipe her arm where she had been splattered and tidied her veil that had somehow parted company with her hair. She was still tucking in stray tendrils when she heard hoofbeats coming closer.

"Lady Isabel? Are you all right in there?"

The voice belonged to Viscount Henley. It would be like him to make a commotion if she failed to answer. She shoved the curtain aside to gaze up at him with bland inquiry. "As you see, sir. Why should I not be?"

"No reason. I just thought . . ." He stopped, his broad, scarred face turning an unbecoming shade of purple. "I mean, you were so quiet in there."

"I was attempting a nap, if you must know." She crossed her fingers as she voiced that small lie. It was better than explaining her preoccupation.

"Your pardon, milady. Is there aught I can get you, aught you need?"

The man was a champion on the jousting

field and arrogant with it at times. Eldest son of an earl, he had lost everything some three years before when his father was attainted for treason by Richard III, after rising in support of Edward IV's heir, the very young Edward V, who had disappeared into the Tower. His title was complimentary now. What income he had came from sojourns on the continent where he participated in the tournaments held by kings and nobles, gaining ransom from hostages taken after victory on the field. Though lacking the estates which would have made him an acceptable husband, he was persistent in his addresses, with a habit of lying in wait for her in dim corners. Graydon, though standing as Henley's friend, had always discouraged his suit, being unwilling to give up her fortune to a husband. For once, she had been grateful, as it saved her from having to put him off herself. It also meant she could afford to be gracious.

That had been before Henry had decided she should be wed.

"Not at the moment," she answered as pleasantly as she was able. "Mayhap later."

"Aye, milady. I'll listen for your call."

No doubt he would, she thought with a sigh as she dropped the curtain. She would not be making a request of him, however, not if she could help it. She would ask nothing of any man.

So they traveled southward toward London and beyond, down the old north road of the Romans through towns and villages large and small, until they clattered onto King's Street. This thoroughfare, thronged with horses and carts, hawkers and beggars and strolling gentry, brought them finally to the ancient gates of Westminster. Winding through its narrow, fetid streets, they reached the myriad buildings and courtyards of soot-streaked stone known as Westminster Palace.

4

Isabel barely had time to remove her cap and veil before the door of her chamber, one of many allotted to less important personages housed at court, was flung open. A flurry of skirts and flying veils signaled the arrivals of her two sisters with whom she had shared the tiny space before leaving for her wedding journey, and would again for the time being. First inside was Catherine, three years younger at twenty and known to all as Cate, with Marguerite, the youngest at sixteen, following closely on her heels. Laughing, exclaiming, they welcomed her back with fierce hugs and a spate of anxious questions.

"Why have you returned so soon, dearest of sisters? Not that we are not glad of it, you may be sure, but we thought you gone for months, even years."

"What occurred? Did Henry's most loyal henchman reject you? Did you prevail upon

Graydon to turn back?"

"Did our curse, perchance, overcome Henry's decree? Tell us at once, before we run mad with curiosity!"

"No, no and yes," Isabel answered, swallowing on tears as she returned her sisters' welcoming embraces. How dear they were, and how she had missed them, their chatter, their smiles and unquestioning acceptance.

"Provoking jade! Is that all you have to say?" Cate rallied her. "Come, tell all. You know you must, for you shall have no peace otherwise."

Isabel obliged as best she could while her sisters settled themselves on two of the three narrow beds that took up most of the room in the nunlike cell. While she talked, Isabel threw off her travel-soiled clothing and bathed quickly in cold water from a basin.

"I knew it!" Cate exclaimed when she was done. "You consider the curse mere foolishness, I know, but you are wrong. How else to explain the arrival of the king's men at the very last instant? Admit it. You believe we walk in its shadow."

Isabel gave her sister a wry smile. Cate was ever ready to see the best of any situation. Yes, and of people, as well. "Even though I concocted it from thin air?"

"Even so!"

"It's difficult to disagree, I will admit."

"Miracles are possible," Marguerite said, "so the priests tell us. We have only to believe. You are protected, dear Isabel, until a husband is chosen who can love you with all his heart."

"Yes, of course," Isabel said, swooping upon her younger sister to give her a swift hug in passing. Marguerite had wanted to be a nun as a girl, had almost become a novice during their time spent being schooled at the convent near Graydon Hall. She had walked the long stone corridors with her hair tucked into a wimple and a breviary in her hand, rather like the king's mother, Lady Margaret.

The urge did not survive her first infatuation, which happened to be with a French man-at-arms who served their stepbrother. It had been a virulent attachment, but was cut short when she discovered he had bad breath caused by a rotted tooth. She was still quiet, pious and pessimistic, unless the subject under discussion had to do with men. She could be irreverent enough then, though inclined to credit any male in knight's clanking armor with sterling and noble qualities.

The three of them — Isabel, Cate and

Marguerite — were very alike in appearance, all possessed of quantities of golden-brown hair, a little lighter in Cate's case, a little darker in Marguerite's. Cate was taller by an inch or so than Isabel, and Marguerite that much shorter. Where Isabel's eyes gleamed with varying shades of green, however, Cate's were the rich blue of an autumn sky and Marguerite's as brown and sparkling as good English ale. Their features were regular, though Cate's eyes had something of an impish cat's tilt to them, and Marguerite had dark, slashing brows that could turn her slightest frown into a scowl.

Though Isabel and Cate were slender of form, Marguerite had not quite lost her childhood roundness. They could all still fit into the upright armor chest at Graydon, however, their secret hiding place from the wrath of their stepfather when they were children. They knew this because it had sometimes been necessary to avoid their stepbrother's rages, as well. Treated as annoying dependents in spite of the rich inheritance of lands and keeps received from their true father, held as less important by far than Graydon's hounds or hunting hawks, they had banded together from childhood for protection and support. Isabel's wedding journey had been the first time in their lives that they had been apart for more than a few hours.

Their days had been spent in isolation at Graydon Hall and its environs. That was until Henry VII came to the throne. The king had soon sent to command their presence at court, in company with dozens more like them. The royal treasury had been depleted by war and swift means were required to fill it. More, Henry had need of lands and titles to assure the loyalty of those around him. Naming the unmarried women and widows throughout the kingdom as his wards was an ideal solution. He could take possession of the income from their estates, arrange suitable marriages for payment of a reasonable bride price or, at his discretion, accept a handsome recompense to allow them to avoid matrimony.

Isabel had not been given the last choice. She could only suppose it was because she, with her portion of her father's wealth, was Henry's idea of an appropriate prize for his companion in arms.

Who he might consider deserving of Cate's and Marguerite's dowries and their hands was still in doubt. They awaited his decision while putting their trust in the curse.

"Graydon returned with you?" Cate asked,

continuing at Isabel's nod. "He must be laughing up his sleeve at the turn of events."

"As you say. He was quite blithe on the return journey. I heard him humming as he rode."

"Perhaps he will speak to the king," Marguerite said, "saying we are too dangerous to be given in wedlock."

Their stepbrother, having grown up thinking of the vast estates inherited by Isabel and her sisters as his own fiefdom, had been enraged at the idea of losing control of it. He had stormed up and down Graydon Hall, cursing the laws of consanguinity, which prevented him from marrying one of them to preserve at least a portion of it — as his stepsisters, marriage between them was forbidden by the church as surely as if they had been blood sisters. Rather than remain at Graydon while the three of them disported themselves at court, he had journeyed with them to better keep them under his thumb. As the weeks and months passed, however, he seemed to grow accustomed to the idea that they would marry. He was even heard to say that giving up his wardship was a gesture of loyalty to the crown which would redound to his benefit. Falling in with a handful of other malcontents, he spent his time gaming and hunting, drinking and wenching. Isabel could only be glad that he was not expending his energy on more dangerous pastimes, such as plotting sedition.

"Always expecting a way out of dire straits," she teased with a bright look for her younger sister as she lifted her hair and ran a cool cloth over the back of her neck. "You would never agree, I suppose, that we may bend circumstances to our own desires?"

"As to that, you've managed it for us often enough, dear Isabel. Take the way you made Graydon believe it his idea that we should be taught by the nuns, a most marvelous escape." Marguerite caught the edge of her veil, chewing on a corner in a habit from childhood. "But was this the same? I mean, was it also a marvelous escape?"

"Yes, how did this Braesford strike you as a husband?" Cate demanded. "What was he like?"

"Were you glad or sorry to be whisked away before the wedding?" Marguerite added.

"We demand to know all!"

Isabel looked from one sister to the other, trying to decide how to answer. It seemed important, for some reason, to be fair.

"He is an interesting man, and a strong

one," she said finally. "It isn't difficult to see how Henry came to reward him for his service to the crown." She turned away, rummaging for a clean shift in her trunk, which had been set at the foot of the bed.

"That's all very well, but what did he look like?" Marguerite asked with some asperity. "Was he handsome? Did he live up to the description given you before you left? Was he the image of knighthood?"

"Don't be absurd."

"No, but surely you can find more to say than that he's strong and deserving!" Cate protested.

Isabel made no answer as her serving woman swept into the room at that moment, bringing with her a gown of gold velvet that she had taken to the kitchens to steam away its wrinkles. Gwynne, who had looked after them since they were children, as she had looked after their mother before she died, was greeted with nearly as many hugs and exclamations as Isabel had been given. When things had quieted again, and Gwynne was lacing up the back of the gold velvet over Isabel's clean linen shift, Cate gave the serving woman a saucy look. "Saw you this bridegroom of our sister's, dear Gwynne?"

"Aye, that I did." The woman tugged the

laces tighter, so Isabel inhaled with a gasp.

"And what did you think of him?"

" 'Tisn't my place to think."

"But truly, you must have noticed something about him."

"A fine, braw gentleman. Big."

"Big?" Cate turned a gleaming gaze on Isabel.

"Welladay, then," she said, rolling her eyes in mock annoyance. "He is tall and well made, powerful as a man must be who has survived tournaments and battles. He's actually well-spoken, as befits a companion of Henry's years in Brittany. I should warn you that he speaks French as well as the king, so beware of attempting to talk over his head. But you may see for yourselves. He returned with me, or rather I with him." She went on to tell them something of the journey back to Westminster, though leaving out the disturbing few moments spent with Braesford inside the litter.

Marguerite heaved a sigh. "If Braesford is here, then the curse hasn't provided a true escape. It must do better."

Isabel's lips twisted a little. "With any luck, he may be confined to the Tower for years."

"Oh, no, don't say that!" Marguerite was the most tenderhearted of the three, the one who picked up baby birds fallen from the nest and carefully returned them, rescued kittens entangled in vines, bandaged the knees and running sores of the street urchins who clustered at Graydon Hall's back door waiting for the scraps she brought from the kitchen. She could barely stir beyond the palace wall now without a half-dozen scabrous tots clinging to her skirt, calling her their angel. No doubt she was destined to be some great lord's wife, overseeing the welfare of the people of his villages, succoring the aged and the ill and intervening with her husband to better their lot.

"I don't mean it, of course," Isabel assured her at once, which was true enough. There was something about Braesford that made the thought intolerable. "I would not wish such a fate on any man, only . . ."

"Only you don't want to marry him," Cate finished for her with ready empathy darkening the blue of her eyes. Marguerite said nothing, only clasping her hands in her lap with a pained expression on her face.

"Him, or any other man," Isabel said in instant agreement.

"Do you think him guilty? Could he have destroyed this newborn on the orders of the king?"

Isabel gave Cate a sharp look. It was a

question that had occupied her mind often during the past few days. "Why would you think so? Have you heard something in my absence?"

"Not exactly, but Henry has been concerned for the queen's health. I heard one of her ladies-in-waiting say that he and his mother are fretting her past bearing. They worry if she walks out, worry if she stays in, worry if she eats too much, worry if she eats too little. Her constitution is not strong, they say, and he depends on her to provide his heir."

Isabel made no answer. They well knew it was the duty of a queen consort to produce small princes to inherit the throne and princesses to cement relationships with other courts and countries. Some said it was her only duty.

"He would be greatly displeased if anything happened to interfere," Cate went on. "He might consider suppressing any whisper of a child born to his mistress, here so near the queen's time, as being in the best interests of the crown."

Gwynne, twitching folds of velvet into place about Isabel, spoke in a quiet mutter. "The soothsayers, so I was told just now, have promised the king the babe will be a prince."

"I've heard it, as well," Marguerite said.

"Indeed." Cate gave a light shrug, as if it explained everything.

Mayhap it did, Isabel thought. Most men wished to have a son to carry on their name and their bloodline. For a king, it was paramount. Moreover, piety and superstition went hand in hand everywhere, but particularly at court — to pray on bended knee one hour, and visit the astrologer the next, was not uncommon. Henry could easily believe, at one and the same time, that he ruled by God's might and that the gender of his child could be foretold. If he thought the unborn heir to the throne was in danger, there was little he would not do to protect him.

If that were the case, however, what did it mean that he had hauled Braesford to court to answer a charge of murder? Was it mere lip service to the rule of law, a show to quiet the whispers of murder? Or did Henry really intend to execute him for carrying out an order he himself had given? Isabel could not be sanguine either way, not if it meant she was betrothed to a man who could have killed a newborn child.

At that moment, a quiet knock fell on the door. Gwynne moved stiffly to draw it open.

Braesford stood on the other side. He

bowed as Isabel moved forward to stand beside Gwynne.

"Your pardon, Lady Isabel," he said in deep, measured tones. "I would not disturb your rest, but we are summoned before the king, you and I. He awaits us in his Star Chamber."

Rand was more than a little conscious that he and Isabel had been given no time to eat before the audience with Henry. He felt lucky that time had been allowed for bathing and a change of raiment. The concession had been made for Isabel's sake, he was almost certain. Had he been alone, he would have been ordered into the king's presence while tired, hungry, stinking of sweat and horse, and filthy from days of travel. Henry was not a patient man.

Rand had sent to ask that Isabel be excused from the audience. It was not mere concern for her welfare. He would not, for pride's sake, have her witness what might be his humiliation and chastisement. In addition, she could become privy to events and circumstances that might be dangerous for her to know. She was too much the novice at court intrigue for such matters.

His request was denied. Henry required

to see both of them, and that's all there was to it.

Together, they navigated the endless gateways, arcaded courts and connecting rooms that led to the king's private apartments. He escorted her with her hand upon his wrist. Her features were composed as she walked beside him, but her fingers burned him like a series of small brands.

The so-called Star Chamber was a long hall hung with paneled walls that were softened here and there by hangings woven in biblical scenes, and featured a lofty, barrel ceiling painted with gold stars against a dark blue ground. It was here that Henry met with his most trusted councilors to mete out justice on matters of less than public nature. The king stood at a window as they entered, a tall man with a narrow face, flat yet sensual lips and forbidding mien. He was dressed in shimmering gray silk damask over a white silk shirt, with black hose and black leather boots. In token of the confidential nature of their audience, no crown sat upon his long, fair hair, but only a gray wool hat with a turned-up brim pinned by gold rosettes.

As they were announced, Henry left the woman and two men with whom he had been in consultation. Striding across the chamber with a slender white greyhound at his heels, he seated himself on the heavy chair — cushioned and canopied with satin in his official colors of green and white — which rested on a low stone dais at the far end of the room. Lounging at his ease with the dog at his feet, he waited as they came toward him.

"We are glad to see you finally arrived," he said as he accepted their obeisance and waved them to a less formal stance. "We trust the journey was not arduous?"

"If so, Your Majesty, it was due only to our haste in answering your command," Rand replied. He could not quite accustom himself to Henry's use of the royal plural after years of far less formal usage in exile. He often wondered that Henry had fallen into it so naturally.

"Yet you have nothing to fear from it, we hope?"

The king meant to get directly to the point, Rand saw with a frown. It did not bode well for an easy end to the business. "Not in the least."

A small silence fell. Rand glanced quickly at the others who had moved to join them, standing on either side of Henry's makeshift throne. The lady was Henry's mother, Margaret Beaufort, Duchess of Richmond and

Derby, a petite and rather stern figure in her usual nunlike black gown and gable-top headdress with white bands around her face. Her nod of private greeting for him was a token of their many years of working together for Henry's sake. Next to her was the squat shape of John Morton, former bishop of Ely and now chancellor of England. Beyond him was Reginald Bray, a Norman also faithful in the service of the duchess who had recently been appointed chancellor of County Palantine and the duchy of Lancaster. Not one of them smiled.

"I have nothing at all to fear," Rand repeated firmly, "being at a loss for the cause of the charge against me."

Henry pressed his lips together for an instant before making a small gesture of one hand. "You recently entertained a guest sent to you for security and succor in her confinement for childbirth. We are told she is no longer with you. Have you knowledge of this lady you would wish to impart to us?"

Sick dread shifted inside Rand at the pronouncement. He felt Isabel stir beside him, but could spare no attention to discover what she made of the charge.

"Unfortunately not, sire," he replied in tones as even as he could make them. "The lady remained with me for seven weeks and was delivered of her child in due time. When last I set eyes upon her, she was healthy and hearty and on her way to you."

"To us?"

"Under the guard of your men-at-arms sent to escort her to a manse described as a reward for her travail."

The king frowned upon him. "Take care what you say, Braesford. We sent no guard."

Beside Rand, Isabel drew a hissing breath. He could hardly blame her, for he felt as if a battering ram had thudded into his stomach. Glancing down, he saw her eyes were wide and her soft carmine lips parted, though she instantly composed her features to unconcern again as she met his gaze.

She was every inch an aristocrat this evening, he saw, standing with regal pride in a gown of some dark gold velvet almost the same shade as her hair, and which revealed an edging of her chemise that was embroidered in gold thread at the neckline and her sleeve ends. Her cap was the same, as were the edges of her veil, which came down to her elbows. His chest swelled with an odd pride at the fact that she stood at his side, however reluctantly.

"Upon my honor, sire, a troop of men came for her," he answered at last.

"And the babe?"

"Went with her, of course, held in her arms. I would have sent to let you know of their departure, but the message brought by the captain of your guard forbade communication for discretion's sake. Besides, I thought you knew already."

"Yes. We understand what you mean to say. Nevertheless, we have had another account from one who watches over the northern section of our realm. It adds to a rumor reported to us by a second source."

The king paused, his gaze inscrutable. Rand, meeting the pale blue eyes, searching the long, square-jawed face with its small red mole near the mouth, felt his heart bang against his ribs. "If I may ask," he said after an interminable moment, "what would this rumor be?"

Henry sat forward, resting his elbows on the arms of his chair. "On the night this lady went into labor, she encountered difficulties. You sent for a midwife familiar with such complications. Do we have it correct thus far?"

"Indeed, sire."

"The midwife arrived and the child was delivered while you remained close to make certain all was well. In fact, you were in the same room. Is this not so?"

Rand inclined his head in acquiescence,

though the dread of where this might be heading was like a lead weight inside him.

"The midwife, a woman of middle years but with no problem with her eyesight, swears that a girl child was born in due time. She was perfect, in every particular, and cried lustily as she came into the world. The midwife swears that you, Sir Randall Braesford, immediately took the child and left the birthing chamber with it, walking into the next room and closing the door. She says that during the considerable time while she made the new mother comfortable and cleared away the signs of birth, the child was never heard to cry again."

"Young Madeleine, as her mother named her, quieted as I held her," Rand began, but stopped at a regal gesture for silence.

"We are not done," Henry said with precision. "It seems the midwife was not permitted to remain with the lady, but was given a generous reward and hustled away as soon as her job was complete. And she claims that, as she went away, she recognized the stench of burning flesh from the rooms she had just left behind."

Isabel gave a small cry and put a hand to her mouth. The king's mother looked ill, while Morton and Bray stood in grim-faced condemnation. Rand had to swallow on bile before he could speak.

"No! A thousand times, no!"

"You deny the charge."

"On my honor, I burned no child," he insisted. "I cannot say whether the midwife lied or merely misunderstood what she saw and heard, but Mademoiselle d'Amboise's infant daughter was asleep in my arms when the midwife mounted pillion behind my man and rode away. The child suckled at her mother's breast later. She was well and most decidedly alive when she left Braesford. This I swear on God's holy word and the wings of all his angels."

"Nevertheless, we have heard nothing from Mademoiselle Juliette since you sent to inform us that she had been delivered of a daughter. She has not appeared in her usual place, has not been seen since she entered the gates at Braesford. Where, then," the king ended with quiet simplicity, "is the lady now?"

It was an excellent question. Rand wished he had the answer. He swallowed, made a helpless gesture with one hand. "I can't begin guess, my liege. All I can say is that a mounted guard of men-at-arms came and took her away."

"They had orders, we presume? You did not give the lady and her child up without a written directive?"

"I was shown a scroll with your signature and seal," he replied with a short nod.

"You knew the captain of this guard?"

"I didn't, no. But as you surely understand, sire, I've spent many years beyond England's shores and no few months away from court. Not all your officers and men-at-arms are familiar to me."

"Nor to us," Henry said drily. "But why would anyone mount such an elaborate and mysterious charade?"

Rand opened his mouth to speak, but the king's mother was before him.

"It seems clear the intent is evil," she said, her soft, even tones in stark contrast to her words. "The purpose can only be to embroil the crown in an affair with a whiff about it of the dead princes in the Tower."

"Yes." Grim acceptance sat on Henry's face.

It was a pertinent thought. Given the shaky start to Henry's reign, and his tenuous claim to the throne, anything which identified him with the murder of Edward IV's young sons could bring on a ground-swell of contempt that might well harden into opposition. In the right hands, it could even become grounds for blaming that three-year-old murder of the princes, if such it had been, on him, as well. Though he had been out of the country at the time, the members of his faction, including those ringleaders now in the room, had not. They could therefore be blamed for carrying out the deed in his name.

"Another purpose could be to acquire a hostage against future need," Isabel said in clear suggestion.

Rand swung his head to stare at her in his surprise that she would speak for him. She met his gaze squarely, though a flush rode her cheekbones. The acceptance in the gray-green depths of her eyes made his heart throb against his breastbone. Turning back almost at once, he spoke in amplification of her thought. "Certain powers in Europe might be glad of such leverage, should they require allies in the conflict within the region."

"Or it may simply be a matter of ransom," the chancellor of England said, rubbing the extra chin that hung below his jaw.

Quiet fell in which could be heard the distant clanging of Angelus bells. Sunset was upon them. Though the long twilight of summer lingered beyond the tall windows of the room, it was dim inside the palace's stone walls. A candle guttered on its wick, and Rand was abruptly aware of the scents of beeswax, perfume and sweat from Morton's heavy ecclesiastical garments. He breathed with a shallow rise and fall of his chest as he waited for Henry's pronouncement.

"We must not be hasty," the king said at length. "We will send out men to search suitable properties where Mademoiselle Juliette may be held. If she is found, and the child with her . . ."

"I beg the privilege of joining the search," Rand said, speaking past the relief that clogged his throat as Henry paused. "No one could have reason to look quite as hard or as long as I."

"Your eagerness and promise of diligence do you credit, but it cannot be allowed."

"I've given my pledge, and would not break it. Nor would I break faith with you, sire."

"We are aware. Still, the matter is delicate. Say you are correct, and the lady is being held against her will. What is to prevent those who have her from ending her life the instant you are sighted? She would be dead to us and unable to uphold your story, while you would be conveniently at hand to take the blame. More, the rumor which came finally to us is rife at court, so we were forced to make the charge and bring you here for this inquiry. We have also heard whispers that you might be killed in ambush to prevent any denial of it. It is this last possibility that caused us to send so swiftly after Lady Isabel, instructing that you both be brought under our protection." Henry shook his head. "No, you will remain near us, Sir Rand. Besides, it would be unseemly for a new-made husband to be seen searching high and low for a woman not his bride."

"Sire!"

It was Isabel who exclaimed in protest, cutting across Rand's immediate words of gratitude for Henry's thoughtfulness. As the king turned his basilisk stare upon her, she lowered her lashes. "I did not mean to speak. Forgive me. It was the . . . the surprise."

"Surprise, when you have known for some weeks that you will be Braesford's wife?"

"This affair of the child," she said softly, "everyone said . . . That is, we were told it was a hanging matter."

"And so it may be if the lady is not found. Meanwhile, we have directed that you will be properly wed, and so it must transpire. Our fair queen consort looks forward to this day of celebration, of tournament, feasting, mummery and dancing, as the last merriment before she must leave us. She goes soon to her forty days of seclusion before birth, you realize, so there is no time for delay. Tomorrow will be auspicious for your vows, we believe." He turned to the erstwhile bishop of Ely. "Is this not so, Chancellor?"

"Extremely auspicious, sire," Morton said in instant agreement.

"But . . . but the banns, sire?"

"Banns may be waived under special circumstances, Lady Isabel. So it has been arranged. You will sign the marriage contracts when you leave here. All that will remain, then, is the ceremony."

"As you command, sire," she said with a small curtsy of acquiescence, adding under her breath, "though it's all amazingly convenient."

Rand thought only he was close enough to hear that last. He could not blame her for that instant of derision. If Henry had decided to dispense with banns, then there was certain to be strong political incentive for it.

What troubled Rand was what might lie behind the king's determined preparation for this wedding. Sign of high favor or a screen for other things — which was it?

"Excellent," Henry said with satisfaction. "Tomorrow it shall be, then."

113

What could either of them say to that? Rand felt Isabel's tense reluctance, and even shared it to some extent. He had thought to spare her the shame of being wed to a suspected murderer. How soon might she be his widow, therefore ripe for another of Henry's arranged marriages? To command them to the altar now in fine disregard of the outcome was an unwarranted interference in their lives.

Regardless, watching as Isabel inclined her head and dropped into another stiff curtsy of obedience to the royal will, Rand was grateful to have the decision made for him. His own bow was a profound gesture of compliance. And it was all he could do to conceal the sudden firestorm of anticipation that blazed through him, body and soul, as he thought of the wedding night to come.

5

Isabel longed to voice her objections to this marriage as she stood beside Braesford, wished she could refuse Henry's royal command outright. One did not defy a king, however, no matter how galling it might be to bow to his will.

She had been summoned specifically to hear his directive concerning her marriage, she thought. There could be no other reason for her presence. Unless, of course, the king wanted her to know the particulars of the crime lodged against Braesford? A bride should understand precisely why her groom was likely to be taken from her by the hangman.

The case seemed dire. Someone must have arranged for the Mademoiselle d'Amboise's escort and forged the papers presented at Braesford. That person must necessarily have knowledge of the court, of Henry's signature and seals. Well, or have influence with those who did.

That was supposing her future husband had not lied. They had only his word for what had happened. Some few among his men-at-arms might corroborate it, of course. Their loyalty was strong, as she'd noticed during their southward journey, making what they might say of him suspect.

As for the midwife and her suspicions, it was odd that such a piece of gossip had reached the king's ears. It should not, ordinarily, have spread beyond the woman's neighbors. More, by her own admission, the midwife had seen nothing truly damning, had only surmised foul play. Surely the king would have dismissed the matter out of hand at any other time.

Nonetheless, there was the disappearance of the Frenchwoman and her child. Where were they now, if they were alive and well? Yes, and why had this Mademoiselle Juliette not sent to inform the king of her whereabouts? It was always possible the lady thought he knew because Henry himself had arranged for her captivity. Prisoners did not normally send messages to their jailer begging for succor.

So many chances for betrayal. Isabel's head hurt just thinking of them. She could see no clear way through them because she barely knew this man who was to be her husband.

She did not know him, yet they were to be tied together for all eternity.

The king's mother stepped forward then, claiming Isabel's attention, though she spoke to Rand. Removing her hands from inside the belled sleeves of her gown, she gestured toward a pair of bundles that sat beside the throne. "The king and I pray this matter that brings you before us will soon be settled, my good and faithful knight, and in a manner satisfactory to all," she said in quiet precision. "In token of our faith that it shall be, and in honor of your wedding, we extend these gifts to you and your lady. A servant will deliver them to your separate chambers, betimes. It is our dearest hope that you will wear them with joy and the blessings of heaven upon your union."

Rand said everything that was appropriate, and Isabel added her gratitude. Moments later, they were dismissed. Through lowered lashes, as she backed from the royal presence, she spared a glance for the gifts. Their wrappings appeared to be of silk and the contents soft. The king often presented his dependents and favorites with clothing at Christmas or for weddings, christenings and the like. This was, she felt certain, the nature of their gifts.

Nor was she wrong.

When she had returned to her chamber, and her portion of the king's gift was delivered, Isabel hesitated to open it. She had ordered a gown of sanguine-red silk made for her wedding, had transported it northward and back again. This replacement had the feel of a bribe, at least to her mind. To accept it seemed the final submission to her fate. Yet refusing it would be a rather childish bit of defiance. Who would be harmed by it except herself? With stiff fingers, she slipped free the cord that held the wrappings.

Inside was a sumptuous silken costume in Henry's colors of green and white. The gown was beautifully embroidered in a pattern of bracken fronds and gold vines on a white silk ground, with dewdrops among them made of pearls. Its sleeves, attached by ties at the shoulders, were also embroidered and so wide and full at the wrists that they draped nearly to the floor. Included was a girdle for her hipline that was worked with gold and set with a cluster of emeralds, also a fillet of woven gold wire to hold back her hair, which would be left uncovered on this one occasion of her life.

It was necessary to try the new gown and

girdle, so she and Gwynne might make any necessary alterations. None were required, so Gwynne insisted, though Isabel could hardly tell from her reflection in the pie-size round of polished steel held by the serving woman.

" 'Tis a marvel of a gown, fit for a princess, milady. I've never seen silk as soft or as fine," Gwynne said, spreading the sleeves so they draped just so, then standing back with her head cocked to one side to view the affect. "The king did well by ye, he did."

"Yes. I wonder why."

"Ye be his ward, and it's his duty to dress you for your wedding. Should there be aught else?"

"There usually is, I fear."

"You think it a reward? But for what, think you? Unless . . ."

"The ordeal of marrying beneath me, no doubt."

"Yet yon knight can hold his own with any."

This was true, something that caused an odd, heated heaviness beneath the gold mesh of her girdle when she thought of it. He had stood tall and unbowed during their audience with Henry, showing proper respect but no subservience. She had seen nobles of rank display far less dignity in the face of kingly frowns.

Such thoughts were far from comfortable. Deliberately, she said, "But he is only a knight."

Gwynne lifted a brow. "You will receive a third of Braesford as your dower right. What else is needed?"

"You know very well."

"An earl or a duke as husband, 'stead of Braesford? And I suppose ye'd take a hobbling old rake with title attached, instead of yon fine piece of manhood? Indeed, milady, I say 'twould be a sorry bargain."

Isabel gave her a jaundiced look. "You have ever had an eye for a nice pair of shoulders. There is far more to a man."

"So you noticed his shoulders, did ye? And his legs, too, I'll be bound — strong as oaks they be. As for what he's got between them . . ."

"That isn't what I meant!"

"But you won't claim 'tis nay important."

No, she could not say that, though she tried not to think overmuch about that part of Rand, or of what would happen on their wedding night. She was less than successful. In truth, she had tossed and turned in her litter after he left her, trying to forget the strength of his hands, his arms, the way he seemed to fill the small, swaying space

120

they had shared. Yes, and the brief intimation of what it might be like to feel his weight upon her, his power inside her.

His hands had been gentle as he cradled her injured finger at Braesford, before he had ruthlessly pulled the broken bone ends back into place so they might set properly. Would he be the same behind the curtains of their marriage bed, gentle at first but merciless as he possessed her?

With a quick shake of her head to dislodge the disturbing thoughts and the light-headed feeling that came with them, she said, "The richness may also indicate the value of the alliance to Henry."

"What way would that be?" Gwynne inquired with a frown.

"Because of the signal service Braesford performed for him some weeks ago, one that went awry." She went on to explain in full, having no compunction about discussing the matter with Gwynne. The woman had done her best to protect both the girls and their mother during her second marriage, lying for them, making excuses, bringing them food and drink when they were shut away as punishment for some error. She had despised the Earl of Graydon and blamed him for their mother's death, had rejoiced when he died. She was no fonder of his son and heir, their stepbrother.

"Aye," Gwynne said with a wise nod. "I heard some such in the servants' hall at Braesford. All there knew the lady had been the king's mistress, knew men came and took her away."

"And the baby?" Isabel asked sharply.

"The lady carried a bundle when she went. At least, so 'twas said after the charge of infant murder was spouted off in the great hall that night. Some swore they'd seen the babe, though no one went in and out the lady's chamber except the maid she'd brought with her."

Was this something the king should know? Isabel wondered if he would listen, or if, having such a network of spies in various parts of the realm, he knew it already.

"The king mentioned rumors spreading here."

"I heard a snicker or two, though none have said much to me. That's the way of it, see. They fear to say anything to my face, being as you and Braesford have the king's goodwill."

"Do we indeed?" Isabel gave a small, mirthless laugh.

Gwynne shrugged. "Mayhap you can tell what's what by the costume Braesford has from the king."

It was a point, Isabel reflected. The clothing, if it was as fine as her own, might indicate his position as the king's honored friend.

It could also mean nothing more than that Henry would send him well attired to his death. And why that last idea should suddenly be so appalling, she could not say. She barely knew the man. Certainly, his death meant nothing to her. Nothing at all.

Isabel's sisters were out and about the palace somewhere. Though she would enjoy showing them her new wedding finery, there was no time just now. The evening meal was almost upon them. She would much prefer to take a little bread and wine and retire to her bed, but it could not be done. The coming wedding was certain to be on everyone's lips before the night was over. To hide away would make it appear she was mortified or, heaven forbid, fearful of it. Pride was a great failing, but she could not abide anyone believing either of those things. Accordingly, she allowed Gwynne to remove the white silk gown and dress her in the gold velvet once more.

The great hall was an enormous echoing space, the largest unsupported structure in the known world, with walls of cream stone lined with galleries for onlookers and topped by ranks of lancet windows under massive corbelled woodwork. At the moment, it was being set for the evening meal, with long rows of tables laid with ample cloths — plates and cups at the high table under its cloth-of-gold canopy, and trenchers and beakers at the lower ones.

The task was enormous, as the kitchens at Westminster supplied food for several hundred on any given evening, and more were fed by the king's almoner, who passed out the uneaten trenchers and meats to those who begged at the back gate. Menservants moved here and there with jugs of wine that had been decanted in the buttery, setting them out on side tables. Great baskets piled high with more trenchers, warm from the oven and smelling delectable, had been placed on the sideboards beyond. Courtiers and their ladies, diplomats from half a dozen countries, members of the king's new yeomen guard, nobles, families from the country and hangers-on of all kinds lounged around the room. They talked and laughed in a low roar, playing at cards and dice and getting in the way of the servants who scurried about.

Among the throng, Isabel caught sight of the bright heads of her two sisters. Moving easily, nodding and speaking to an acquaintance here and there, she wended her way toward where Cate and Marguerite sat on a padded bench.

A gentleman stood next to them with one foot propped on their seat and a lute resting across his raised knee. His fingers moved on the strings in the faintest of melodies as he made some quick observation that brought trills of laughter.

Cate glanced away from the troubadour just then. Her face lighted in welcome and she lifted her hand to beckon. The gentleman, following her gaze, looked over his shoulder. He straightened at once as Isabel came near.

"Mademoiselle," he exclaimed, sketching a deep bow, "what felicity to see you among us! We thought you lost to us for months, perhaps forever, yet here you are again. I shall compose a madrigal for the event, one to astonish the company and make glad your girlish heart."

It was Leon, Henry's Master of Revels, the gentleman who had so obligingly spread the tale of the Three Graces curse. A Frenchman of boundless charm, he gravitated naturally to the most attractive women in any room. Isabel, like her sisters, enjoyed his extravagant nonsense, but never made the mistake of taking it seriously. She sometimes thought it was the reason he sought their company so often.

"Spare yourself the effort, sir," she answered with wry humor. "My return will no doubt be short-lived, and then where would you be? Possessed of a rare song with no occasion to sing it."

"A smile from your lips would make it worthwhile."

Leon's gaze was meltingly tender. It was no wonder so many ladies succumbed to his blandishments. With dark hair that curled wildly over his head, eyes so black the pupils blended into their gleaming sable-brown and olive skin touched with hints of rose on his cheekbones, he should have appeared effeminate. He was, instead, like some archangel painted by a master, the very epitome of masculine beauty. He knew it, too, but made such a jest of it that it was near impossible to accuse him of vanity. His dress this evening was eye-catching, as always, a doublet of crimson velvet over hose striped in gold, and with a yellow-brown acorn hat on his curls that sported a pheasant's iridescent feather. The lute he began to strum once more was fig-shaped and finely crafted, decorated with inlaid wood of many varieties in the Italian fashion.

"I am desolated, Leon," Cate said in mock chagrin. "I thought you were composing a verse to my lips, comparing them to the sunset."

"So I was, my sweet, and have it still in mind. It will require no great labor, given such inspiration, so will be finished in a trice."

"When you are free from more important commissions, I suppose you mean to say. What a dastard you are."

"You wound me, fair one," he complained, his handsome features taking on a lugubrious look.

"Never mind that," Marguerite said, pinning him with a stern look from her dark brown eyes. "You were telling us of your scheme for a future night of mummery." She turned to Isabel. "It's to be a fine piece with lots of screams and moans and fire."

"Vastly entertaining, I'm sure," she said drily.

"A critic, heaven protect me," Leon moaned. "I must go labor to produce a new and better piece." He tilted his head for a considering instant before resuming his play on the lute. "Or perhaps I will forgo future applause for the sake of present company."

"Forgo nothing on my account," Isabel recommended with an airy gesture, well aware he had no intention of leaving them. Even as she spoke, however, she was aware of a drop in the noise level in the great hall, followed by a spreading whisper, like the sound of wind blowing over bracken. Glancing around, she saw the crowd around them parting, leaving a clear path down which a regal figure made her way. It was the queen consort, followed by a double line of ladies-in-waiting and the queen's fool, a miniature woman no more than a yard tall.

Turning fully, Isabel swept back her skirts and dropped into a deep curtsy. Her sisters did the same, while Leon doffed his hat with a most graceful bow.

"Nor must you neglect your labors on my account, Monsieur Leon," Elizabeth of York said as she joined their small group with the slow and somewhat cumbersome pace of a woman large with child. "The result is always a delight, no matter how onerous it may be to you."

"Your Majesty!" Leon cried in low pleasure, going to one knee before Henry's queen in profound expression of gratitude for the compliment. "No task performed for your entertainment can be a labor. It must always be my greatest pleasure."

"Rise, Sir Rascal," Henry's queen said in her light, musical voice, "and say me no more flattery. I am immune, as you may see from my huge shape." She turned to Isabel, raising her and her sisters with a gesture. "I was told you had come among us again, Lady Isabel. It is good to see you so well."

"And you, ma'am," she replied with perfect truth. Elizabeth was a favorite with everyone, more beloved than Henry, who had not her ease of manner or, in all truth, her naturally royal air. It was not surprising, of course, as she had been trained from birth to be the consort of a king, even if it was meant to be at some foreign court. Some said Henry kept her from public view as much as possible for fear she would become too popular with the people. As the eldest daughter of Edward IV, her claim to the throne was far stronger than his. Though it was centuries since Britain had been ruled by a female, there was nothing in the laws of the land to prevent her from becoming queen regnant.

Divinely fair in true Plantagenet mold, Elizabeth was the very embodiment of the current ideal of beauty, with her pale blond hair, fine skin and fragile bone structure. Her gown of blue damask — though simply made, having only a neckline edged with pearls — was the perfect foil for her blue eyes. The small circlet of gold she wore as a crown was set low on her forehead like a filet to hold the fine white veil that covered her hair. From her girdle, in place of the keys of a chatelaine, hung a small jewel of a book in a bag of silver netting. The beautifully painted wood cover showed it to be De Lorris's story of love and redemption, *Le roman de la rose.* She appeared as blooming as that tale in her advanced state of pregnancy, in spite of Henry's fears for her ability to carry his heir to term.

"But how is it you are among us again?" Elizabeth asked with curiosity on her serene features. "I am sure I was told you had traveled north to marry, though now His Majesty makes other arrangements. Did some unforeseen circumstances prevent the nuptials?"

It was a reminder, if Isabel needed it, that the queen was being kept in ignorance of the charges against Braesford. Nor should she know of Henry's liaison with Mademoiselle Juliette d'Amboise, though it was Isabel's experience that these things were always discovered. A coarse jest here, a laughing comment there, and soon the ladies-in-waiting were whispering in the queen's ear. If the pretense of ignorance sometimes held protection for a woman of intelligence — and Elizabeth was that, having studied with a tutor from childhood so she sometimes translated Latin documents for her royal husband — that was another matter.

"It was the king's request," Isabel answered. "As for why, who can say? Mayhap he conceived a whim to be present for the marriage?"

"Indeed, we are all kept in the dark," Elizabeth of York said in dry response. "I am pleased that I shall see you wed, in any event. Sir Rand is quite a favorite, a fine and loyal companion to the king in his adversity and strong right arm on the battlefield." Her smile softened. "He was also kind to me when I first appeared at court, when many were less so. You could not have a better gentleman as husband."

Isabel hardly knew how to answer such praise, so did not try. "Braesford and I will be honored by your presence," she said, going on at once. "I believe you will absent yourself from the court soon. When do you go, if I may ask it?"

"A few days after your vows are spoken, I believe. Such a to-do as there has been about it. I am to travel to Saint Swithin's Priory at Winchester, as it was built by King Arthur of legend, or so they say. A fine conceit, yes?"

Isabel, meeting the warmth in the queen's eyes, answered it with a smile of understanding. "And shall the child be called Arthur if it is a boy?"

"You've heard it's His Majesty's will, I suppose? I am agreed, though all Lancastrian kings to this day have been called Henry. It is Caxton's fault, you know, for printing *Le Morte d'Arthur* last year as one of the first books brought forth from a press in this realm." She put a hand on her belly in a tender caress. "And heaven forfend it not be a son and heir. Henry has been promised it by his soothsayer, and I dare not disappoint."

The words were lightly spoken, but Isabel thought them serious, nonetheless. Elizabeth of York, for all the crown she wore, was no more mistress of her fate than she was. The queen's marriage was a dynastic union to a man long considered an enemy of her family, one ten years her senior whom she had not met until she was betrothed to him. He came to her bed as a right, his purpose to get an heir on her body. What was that like, Isabel wondered, and how did it feel to carry the child of a man who cared nothing for her and for whom she cared nothing?

It was possible she would soon find out. Her knees felt disjointed at the prospect.

"Does the king join us this evening?" she asked by way of distraction, for herself as well as Elizabeth.

"Most likely, though he has not yet made his will known." The queen divided a smile between them all. "But I must not tarry. My dear mother-in-law waits for me to join her in embroidering a coverlet for the future prince. Until later."

They watched her go, strolling slowly in the direction of the royal apartments and her private solar with the same grace with which she had appeared. Isabel, thinking of Elizabeth's absence from the Star Chamber earlier, frowned a little. There was a reason for it, of course, yet the king's mother had been present as if by natural right. It seemed Lady Margaret might be more in Henry's confidence than his wife. How must that sit with the daughter of a king?

"A noble lady," Leon said, heaving a sigh.

"You should write her story and set it to music," Cate said, her blue eyes serious.

"I may do that," Leon murmured. "I may indeed."

Isabel turned away first, feeling herself unable to watch longer. "So," she said with assumed vigor and a quick glance for Leon, "have you entertainment planned for this evening?"

"A group of Romani that has played before royalty west of the Rhine and which include, not incidentally, a dancer of rare skill, also a *jongleur* who eats fire and, *bien entendu,* the bel canto to your return that plays itself now in my mind."

"Not the last, I beg."

"By no means, if you dislike it," he answered at once, "yet I must have some new inspiration now and then. Henry may grow bored with my songs played a thousand times otherwise, and send me on my way."

"Never!" Marguerite exclaimed.

"The outcry and weeping among the ladies would be insupportable," Cate declared with a roguish look from under her lashes.

"We can't have that, so I shall certainly compose something new soon." He tilted his head, his gaze on Isabel. "For now, I should concentrate on a grand theatrical for your wedding feast. It will be soon?"

"Tomorrow, I fear."

"Fear? *Le diable!* Distraction is in order, then, to banish thought of the bedding. What will serve? A chorus of minnesingers chanting of marital bliss? A martial display of jousting and other games with blood and gore?"

"Neither, and it please you," she said with

a grimace. "Besides, there will be no time."

"It must be my spectacle already planned, then, with only fire and thunder and moving parts."

"Only?"

"You will like it exceedingly, I am sure of it."

No doubt she would, Isabel thought as she smiled at the transports, or pretense of them, of her sisters over the coming treat. The Master of Revels had a genius for constructing machines capable of odd things, and of creating spectacles to amuse and amaze. He had served as an apprentice in Italy to an obscure master he called Leonardo the Procrastinator. Instead of using his inventions for practical purposes, however, Leon dedicated them to entertaining nobility and royal heads of state.

How he had come to Henry's court was something no one knew, not because he did not explain, but because he told so many different versions of the tale that it was impossible to discern the truth. He was the grandson of a dethroned king, he claimed, now forced to make his own way in the world. Or he was a younger son who had fallen passionately in love with the wife of a nobleman and persuaded her to flee with him, though she died tragically in a storm at sea. He had killed a man of influence in an ordeal by combat and was forced to leave his homeland to wander the world. Then again, he was a priest who had loved a veiled novice too well, but not permanently. These were only the ones she remembered.

"I shall look forward to this spectacle," she said, "though I hardly see how you will manage anything very grand."

"Oh, I've worked on it for some time. It will please my heart to have such a fitting occasion to display it."

Cate put her hands on her hips with an air of assumed affront. "See, Isabel? He hints and teases but will not explain what this contraption may be. Yes, and he works in a grain storehouse beyond the palace walls, allowing no one to enter."

Isabel tilted her head. "I am honored, then, that it will be unveiled for me." Even as she spoke, her youngest sister, Marguerite, touched her arm and tipped her head toward something behind her. Forewarned, she gave only a small start as a deep voice, layered with irony and grim forbearance, reached her ears.

"And I also, being the man who will sit at her side to share the spectacle."

Leon, looking past her, grew pale around the mouth while a flash of something cold and hard passed over his face. Isabel turned with a swing of velvet skirts to face Braesford. At the same time, she became aware of whispers all around them, of nudges and grimaces and the shuffle of feet as those nearest to where they stood drifted away.

It was Leon who recovered first, his face clearing as if accepting an accused murderer into their circle was a mere nothing. "And a lucky one you are, if I may say so, for you will have the best seat in the hall — barring the throne, of course — at the side of the lovely Isabel."

"Your pardon, but I put my lower seat over the most high."

"Well spoken!" the Master of Revels exclaimed in approval. "You may even be worthy of her, though that doesn't mean we will not mourn her disappearance into wedded servitude. Alas."

"Oh, but we are still here," Cate said, linking arms with Marguerite as she gave Isabel a meaningful look.

Isabel took the hint and introduced her sisters to her prospective groom. They were all smiles and appraising eyes as they performed their curtsies, though the quick glance Cate flung her way seemed to hold qualified approval. Not that this meant a great deal, as Isabel well knew. Her sister next in age appreciated a strong man. Moreover, any female given in marriage to a gentleman who still had his hair and teeth was to be congratulated, never mind the circumstances.

Braesford acknowledged Marguerite and Cate, asking after their health, before turning back to Isabel. "I regret taking you away from such congenial company, but there is a matter we should discuss."

"Now?"

"If you please."

The words were a mere courtesy. A command lay in the way he offered his arm, Isabel thought. She could refuse to go with him, but it seemed unwise. More than that, given the veiled animosity of those who surrounded them, she was willing enough to quit the hall. She placed her hand upon his sleeve, made her adieus and walked away at his side.

The outer bailey was a tempest of noise and activity in the gathering dusk, of hurrying pages and heralds, swaggering men-at-arms, horses being led to their stalls for the night and priests striding here and there with pale moons of scalp marking their tonsures. Men swore, dogs barked, a minstrel sang a bawdy song from inside the Boar's Head tavern across the way and serving maids called back and forth while leaning from windows above the narrow lanes that led away from the hall.

Isabel and Rand skirted the great open space, making their way past the timber kitchen beyond the great hall, passing through a heavy gate between stone posts that led to a rear kitchen garden. Here, the clamor faded to a distant roar. All was lingering heat, the drowsy hum of bees and birdsong. Thyme, mint and sage gave off their distinctive scents as they brushed against the rampant growth that encroached upon the trodden path. A blackbird, startled from its search among great heads of cabbage, flew up ahead of them with a squawk of alarm. It landed atop an apple tree espaliered against the stone wall, where it watched their progress with a suspicious eye.

"The Master of Revels seems well known to you," Rand said when they had walked a few yards.

She had been waiting for some such comment. That it was rather more subtle than expected did not make it less annoying. Removing her right hand from his arm, she used it to cradle her injured finger at her waist. "He is pleasant company and has proven himself a friend."

"Your brother must have warned you

against such friendships."

"You don't know Graydon if you think so. He takes little thought for the welfare of a mere stepsister. Cate, Marguerite and I have been left to find our own way at court. But if you mean to suggest Leon would take advantage of any of us, you malign him."

"Any man may take advantage under the right conditions."

A vision of the two of them enclosed inside the litter rose in her mind's eye, and she was suffused by the heat of a flush. Through stiff lips, she said, "Your warning is no more necessary now than it was before. I am quite aware of the conduct required of a wife."

He gave a brief nod, and they walked on in silence. Isabel glanced at his set features and away again.

How very imposing he was when measured against Leon. Not only was Rand taller and broader, but he seemed more essentially male, more virile in his aspect. He was also, she had to admit, extremely attractive in a hard-edged fashion. Not only had Cate been impressed, but Isabel had noticed other women turning to stare after him as they left the great hall.

Braesford had paid not the slightest attention. Ego was not one of his faults, it seemed, though it was possible he had been too intent on removing her from Leon's presence. Watching a gray kitten that sat cleaning an outstretched leg at the side of the path ahead, she considered the idea that her groom might be jealous. She abandoned it almost at once, as she could conceive of no reason why he should be. He had no fondness for her, after all. Did he?

"It's late to ask, but it had not occurred to me before," he said after a moment. "Your heart is not engaged elsewhere?"

She gave him a small frown. "Are you still thinking of the Master of Revels? If so, you may rest easy. Leon prefers widows and adventurous married ladies for his amours."

"Wise of him," Braesford said in dry comment, "though you make it sound as if his conquests are legion. God is subject to odd humors in that he makes some men so much more appealing than others."

"Mayhap it is Leon who makes himself appealing."

He turned to rest his gaze upon her again for a frowning instant, but did not contradict her. "In reality, my thought was for a lover of a different sort, possibly some nobleman met here at Westminster."

"There is no one, has been no one, past the foolish infatuations of a young girl. Such attachments are discouraged as they only lead, so the good nuns assure us, to disappointment."

"You are heart-whole, then."

"It could be put that way."

"Amazing, that no one has taken the trouble to draw close."

"There is the curse, you will recall."

He lifted an indifferent shoulder. "Even so."

Such oblique flattery did not require an answer, particularly as she could not be sure what he meant by it. They strolled on, past the kitten, beneath an arbor where a climbing rose released its sweetness upon the evening air, alongside a bed of vivid green parsley. She asked finally, "Is that what you wanted to discuss, the state of my affections?"

"In part." His voice was without inflection as he answered, though he gave her a swift glance. "You are holding your hand. Does your finger pain you still?"

"No more than you might expect." She immediately lowered the injured member to her side. Protecting it had become such a habit that she had hardly noticed what she was doing. That he had been attending was gratifying in some odd manner she did not care to examine.

He stopped, held out his hand. "May I?"

Isabel came to a halt at his side. As if compelled, she surrendered her fingers to his grasp.

His touch was as gentle as when he had set the break with a rush stem, and as impersonal. Regardless, it set her heart to hammering in her chest. Holding perfectly still, she watched as he inspected the bindings, turning her hand this way and that before tightening the ribbon that held that splint in place. The fading light slanted across his face, softening its hard planes, highlighting the curves of his mouth, leaving his eyes in shadow.

With his gaze upon what he was doing, he said, "I wanted to ask if you have changed your mind about the charge lodged against me. After our audience before the king, I mean."

"What does it matter?" she asked with difficulty. We . . . we are to marry, regardless."

"You seemed . . . I would like to know what you think."

It was a novel attitude in her experience. Certainly, neither her stepfather nor Graydon had ever sought her opinion. Wary of the gratitude and warm softness that rose inside her, she answered with care. "I see no reason why you should wish to harm the child delivered at Braesford Hall."

"I am obliged to you for that much, at least," he said with a trace of huskiness in his voice. "And the rest?"

She swallowed, looking away from him. "Men-at-arms must have come for the mistress afterward, as you said, for too many can attest to it for it to be otherwise. As for who sent them, it seems impossible that it was other than by Henry's order."

"Yet you heard him deny it. Do you doubt the king's word? Can you believe him capable of destroying his own flesh and blood?" He gazed down at her with a frown darkening his eyes.

"What a man may do with his own hands and what he may order done by others are often two different things."

"You think I would lend myself to such an act?"

"Many have done worse to retain royal goodwill."

"Not I," he said, his voice like forged steel.

She would like to believe him, yet how could she? The numerous treacheries of the past few years gave her little faith in the sworn word of any man; it sometimes seemed honor and chivalry had died in the bloody battles between York and Lancaster. Nor would she take the easy way and assure him of a belief she did not hold. Let him prove his innocence if he wished to have her good opinion.

Nevertheless, he was such a powerful presence as he stood so close in the waning light that it seemed unbelievable he could be taken by men-at-arms and hung upon some scaffold. A great emptiness echoed inside her at the thought that he could die.

"You are forthright, and that pleases me," he said after a moment, though his voice did not sound like it. "There is another matter I would present, however. The king has offered a chamber not far removed from the royal apartments for our use. It is larger than those either of us occupy now, but puts us under the surveillance of the king's household guard. We could, if you prefer, lodge beyond the palace walls where we might be more private and less at our sovereign's beck and call. The difficulty is that Henry may consider it an insult if we refuse his offer. He could also insist that I accept this billet as a form of house arrest."

"What is in this to discuss?" she asked in frowning confusion. "You seem to have the matter in hand."

"I desire to learn your pleasure, will convey it to Henry, either way."

It was another peculiar pass, being consulted about where she would reside. She was not sure she liked it, considering the responsibility attendant upon it. "I own I would prefer a less public lodging," she said finally. "Yet it seems folly to refuse the king's generosity."

"Shall I accept for both of us, then?"

"If that is what you prefer."

A short laugh left him. "What I would prefer is to set out for Braesford as soon as our vows are spoken, deserting king, court and celebration. Or better yet, never to have left there."

"But you cannot. We cannot."

"No." He held her hand in both his for a moment longer. Then he bent his head to press his lips to her palm in a tingling salute. "In which case," he said as he released her, "it hardly matters where we lie abed tomorrow night so long as it is together."

That last was an important caveat, she thought, one that had lodged in both their minds while they discussed sleeping chambers and the king's will. Hearing it spoken aloud made it seem more real. Her stomach clenched while apprehension swirled in her mind. With it, however, ran a disturbing vein of heated curiosity for what it would be like to lie naked in this man's arms, subject to his will, his touch, his possession.

She wished he had not spoken of the bedding aloud. She really did.

6

A smile spread across Rand's face when he saw Isabel coming toward him, one made up of relief that she had appeared, of possessiveness and, he feared, sheer randy anticipation. She was every inch the beauteous and noble lady in her wedding finery of green-and-white silk set off by gold thread and emeralds, and soon she would belong to him. He almost felt worthy in his matching garments of lustrous fabrics. Almost, but not quite.

By His Majesty's grace, their vows were to be spoken in the king's private chapel of Saint Stephens, as Henry had indicated last evening. The setting could be considered either a high mark of favor or a ploy to make certain their vows were spoken as commanded. The dim and stately space was gilded and painted with vermilion, bejeweled with windows in ruby, sapphire and emerald. Its very stones held the scents of stale smoke, dust, incense and holiness.

Isabel's hand was cool and not quite steady as she placed it in his. Rand held it with firm support as they faced Bishop Morton for the ceremony. Behind them sat the few witnesses — the king, the queen, the king's mother, Isabel's two sisters, Catherine and Marguerite, her stepbrother, Graydon, and his own half brother, William McConnell. That was more than enough in Rand's opinion.

Nothing impeded their vows. There was no armed assault, no divine intervention, certainly no manifestation of the notorious Graydon curse. Rand had not expected it, but was nonetheless relieved when they were done.

Afterward he walked beside his bride along the gallery that led from the chapel to the palace, breathing the fresh evening air as a married man. And he could not stop looking at his wife as she moved beside him, surveying her calm, pale face, the rise and fall of her breasts beneath their covering of soft silk, her unbound hair that made him want to bury his face in its shimmering length. He could not stop the exultation that rose inside him at the night that lay ahead, no matter how insecure his future.

He thought Henry should have included

one of the new codpieces with his gift of a wedding costume. Though an awkward bit of equipment in Rand's opinion, that mock erection could have helped conceal one that was uncomfortably real.

"What is it?" Isabel asked, speaking softly enough to escape being heard by the king and queen and the bishop, who walked ahead of them, or their relatives, who followed behind. "Have I dirt on my face that you look at me so?"

"You are perfection, as you must know," he returned with strained humor. "I am merely admiring my bride. Well, and trying to think how to ask for her favor."

"My favor," she repeated while her eyes widened and wild-rose color stained her cheeks.

A crooked smile tilted his mouth while hot anticipation slid down his spine. "Not that kind, though I will accept it willingly and anywhere you care to name. No, a token to wear for the tournament that has been ordered, or rather the melee."

"Melee?" she inquired, seizing on the subject, doubtless to avoid his suggestion. "Is such mock combat not forbidden?"

"The king has decreed it as a special event. Have you not seen the preparations being carried out in the courtyards?"

"I thought they must be for some military expedition he would send into the country-side."

"I will grant there is not a lot of difference."

The floor-length, bell-mouthed sleeves attached to the shoulders of her gown caught the breeze as she turned to him. "You will not participate? Surely a new-made groom is exempt."

"I am ordered to take the field," he said evenly. "Henry, I do believe, sees it as a trial by ordeal." Rand thought of it, rather, as a good way to speed the long day of celebration that lay ahead so the night might come sooner.

"You can't mean . . ."

One corner of his mouth lifted in mirthless acknowledgment of her amazement. "If I am killed or seriously injured, then I must be guilty. If I live, it will be a sign from God of my innocence. Victory will not, you understand, preclude a legal trial in the King's Court at some later date."

"That is barbaric!"

"It is tradition, though I may be giving myself too much importance, and the royal purpose is merely to provide entertainment for the common folk who will crowd the field to watch. Henry is learning the uses of public display, you see. Nothing so convinces the populace of a king's might as seeing his knights ride out onto the field."

"Or dressing those he favors in silks and satins," she said with a brief gesture toward his wedding costume that, like hers, was a study in Henry's white and green.

"We make a fine pair, do we not?" he drawled. "Like matching tomb effigies."

A choke of laughter left her. At the sound, Henry, walking ahead with his queen on his arm, looked back. Isabel was immediately solemn again but the king was not fooled. He smiled benignly, no doubt pleased at the sign of accord between them.

Rand was also glad to see some of the stiffness leave his bride. Her hands had been like ice in the chapel, and had not warmed during the entire ceremony. Her touch through his silk sleeve was warmer now, almost too warm for his ease of body or mind, and soft color tinted her face where it had been deathly pale before.

They walked on a few steps. Isabel stared straight ahead while the amusement faded from her features. She drew a quick breath after a moment, speaking without looking at him. "Some newly wedded couples, so I am told, observe the custom of Tobias Night."

"They may in the country." Rand hoped Graydon and McConnell, trailing somewhere behind with Isabel's sisters, were not listening to this exchange. It could too easily spread through the court as a coarse jest. Tobias Night was an ancient rite sometimes observed by the devout. In addition to fervid prayers while kneeling on hard stone floors, it involved refraining from intimacy on the wedding night in honor of Saint Tobias, known for his stringent celibacy. The prospect did not recommend itself to him.

"To become used to each other under its influence seems civilized," she persevered.

"It seems very torture to me, if you mean sharing the same chamber, the same bed, without touching."

"Such trials are good for the soul."

"Whose soul would that be, mine or yours?" he asked. "Yours, I daresay, requires no purification, and the blasphemy I'd surely commit would blacken mine. Besides, the king commanded a bedding as well as a wedding."

Her glance would have scalded the hair from a boar's hide, though a flash of something like dread struck through it. "You will obey his will, in spite of the possibility of leaving a child behind should this charge of murder go against you?"

"Or because of it," he replied evenly. "Braesford will be yours if there should be a child of our marriage to inherit it, and I have come to think you will be able to hold it." He had thought, for a short while, of protecting her in that regard. Henry had decreed otherwise. Now he longed to see her large with his child, as serenely beautiful as the Madonna herself.

If she appreciated his confidence in her, or recognized his dream, she did not show it. "So you will not agree."

"I will not." The words were calm, though he could, if required, be more forceful.

"Then I don't believe I can present my favor to you for the tourney."

She thought to reserve her public favor if he would not agree to forgo the private one accorded him by their vows. Anger at the threat heated the back of his neck, pounding in his blood with an odd roiling pain.

It would avail her nothing to spurn his request, or him. He realized she would have misgivings and fears about the bedding, but he was not a brute to take his pleasure while giving none in return. He had waited longer than he wanted to make her his wife. Did she not realize that he could have had her the night before, taking her there in the castle garden in a bed of mint or parsley?

He had delayed for her sake, because he thought she would prefer comfort, privacy and sanctity. He would wait not an instant longer than necessary.

She had miscalculated if she thought to withhold anything from him. He would have her favors this day, all of them, one way or another.

Isabel seethed quietly as she sat in her place of honor at the high table for the wedding breakfast. How she despised being a pawn in the king's game, moved here and there, sacrificed at his royal will.

Properly wedded and bedded.

Those were the words Henry had used during the audience in his Star Chamber, the words which gave Braesford such authority over their wedding night. It was the king's command that the union be consummated. That and tradition, of course. Women were supposed to be accommodating in these matters, giving their bodies into the hands of their husbands without the least protest or repining.

It was insupportable.

Nevertheless, she must support it. What else was she to do? She could not run away, for a woman alone on the streets or roads was at the mercy of every man. If she requested protection, any gentleman strong enough to snatch her away from her new husband could well be worse than Braesford. An appeal to the king was useless since it was he who commanded her to submit.

The only person she could count on was herself. She might yet find a way to avoid what was to come. But if not, then she could at least make certain she was not the only one to suffer.

"Wine?" her husband asked, offering the gold goblet they shared as the guests of honor.

"Thank you, no," she said shortly. It was impossible to eat, and she would not drink on an empty stomach. She needed her wits about her.

"You have not swallowed a morsel. You will make yourself ill."

"I am touched by your concern, however belated."

His smile was as cool as her tone had been. "Your well-being is of great interest to me. I would not have a fainting bride."

"Then mayhap you will look elsewhere for a bedmate."

"Or use extra effort to revive you. I wonder what it would take beyond a kiss. I could, for instance, bare a breast and lick my way from —"

Shock, and something more virulent, coursed along her veins. "Please! Someone will hear you."

"And be entertained, I make no doubt, but what odds? We are wed, after all."

"I require no reminder," she said with an edge to her voice.

"I cannot agree. You seem in frequent need of it. Having Henry's blessing, it will be my great pleasure to supply the lack daily, nightly, morning and noon. Come with me now and I will show you —"

"Nothing! You will show me nothing, for the day has far to run before we must —"

"Not so," he corrected her, his features set and dark. "There is no appointed hour. And it is you who *must,* while for me it is otherwise. I will it. I long for it. I die for the lack."

It was not the morning heat of late August in the hall that suffused her. "Don't be foolish."

"It is you who are foolish for depriving both of us, though not for long. Have you no curiosity as to what you are missing? Do you not crave a taste before the midnight feast?" He reached under the hanging edge of the table's cloth to place a firm, warm hand on her thigh.

The muscle of her upper leg leaped as if

jolted by lightning. She thrust beneath the cloth also, clutching at his wrist. "I . . . I am content to wait."

"Why, when there is no need?"

He was moving his fingers, gathering folds of her skirt under his hand, inching it higher with amazing dexterity. "Stop it," she said in a desperate, hissing whisper.

"Give me a forfeit and mayhap I will," he suggested, the daring in his eyes like the flash of a steel blade. "A kiss would be acceptable."

"Is that a threat?"

"You should recognize the ploy."

She did, though that did not make it more tolerable. He had reached her hem, for she could feel his warm fingertips gliding up her inner thigh. A heated shiver ran over her, along with a species of panic. She caught at his fingers but he eluded her grasp, inching higher toward the juncture of her thighs. It seemed everyone was watching the two of them, smirking a little as if they guessed what was taking place at the high table. They could not see for the overhang of heavy cloth on the side which faced them. Surely, they could not.

"Desist at once!" she said a trifle breathlessly. "I beg of you."

"Kiss me," he said, his voice a low murmur, his eyes holding hers.

She wouldn't. She couldn't. It was too demeaning. And yet he was brushing across the sensitive bend between her thigh and upper body, questing toward the fine curls unprotected by braies in the summer heat, grazing the top of the small mound from which they sprang. Driven by desperation, she made a claw of her hand and dug her nails into his skin.

He smiled. "So you are a scratcher in the throes of passion. Do you bite?"

She could guess what he meant, but had not the knowledge to be certain of it. "No, I could not . . ."

"Kiss me," he whispered, his eyes turning darker as he touched her, burrowed gently into the small cleft he had found, pressing into soft folds with a small, insinuating motion.

She caught her breath, sank her nails deeper. He seemed not to feel the pain. Appalled by the race of excitement in her veins, the peculiar sensation as if her very bones were dissolving, Isabel searched his face. Perspiration gleamed on his forehead and his chest rose and fell in deeper rhythm with his breathing. He was not unaffected by what he was doing under the table. It was some consolation.

Holding her gaze, he probed deeper with a single long finger, there in plain view of the gathering of nobles, mere feet from the king and queen. Isabel could bear it no longer. She closed her eyes, made her decision. With a small sound between a prayer and curse, she leaned to press her lips to his.

He opened his mouth to her, swept her lips with his tongue, slid between her teeth. And his invasion matched the small, twisting movements he made against the very center of her body. She gasped, shuddered, as fire raced over the surface of her skin. An instant later, the sensation coalesced below her waist, seeped in liquid heat against the palm of his hand.

He stiffened beside her, the muscles of his shoulder where she leaned against him going as hard as stone. For long seconds, he did not move. Then his sigh brushed across her cheek. He withdrew by slow degrees, brushed the skirt of her gown back into place. She drew back while shielding her gaze with her lashes.

In that same moment, she grew aware of the low murmur of voices with an undercurrent of laughter. Hot mortification assailed her. She longed to leap to her feet and leave the dais, to be lost among the lowest of those below the salt, to retreat to the chamber she shared with her sisters in virginal security and never think again of marriage or a husband.

It was not possible. Some things must be endured, no matter the cost.

She lifted her chin and straightened her spine, glared directly into the silver-gray eyes of her groom and forced her lips to form a smile. "You have had your forfeit, sir, and may it content you."

"Hardly," he said with a lazy smile. "I fear my appetite has only been whetted for more. Such a tender morsel I discovered, I can hardly wait to taste it entire."

"Sir!"

"Though I do believe, after what we just shared, that you might call me Rand."

He meant their shared vows; that was all. As for what he wished to taste, he could not mean — no, surely not! He was only attempting to discompose her.

She could not permit him to succeed. Or, at least, would not allow him to know it. Controlling her imagination with fierce effort, she turned from him and picked up a small meat pie that rested on the plate between them. She bit into it, intent on appearing oblivious if it killed her. And so it might, she thought as she chewed and swallowed against the knot in her throat. She could not have said what was within the flaky crust. It tasted of nothing in her mouth except ashes and regret.

The wedding tournament was held at Tothill Fields, beyond the confines of Westminster town. An open area set with copses of trees, it was the scene of a three-day fair every year, in addition to bull-baitings, bear-and-dog fights, cockfights and the occasional hanging. A pavilion, canopied for shade against the August sun, had been constructed for the king, queen, their attendants and honored guests, which today included Isabel and her two sisters. The billowing white tents where the knights and their horses would be armored for the contest stretched away beyond it. Everyone else straggled in an uneven row on either side, sitting their horses or perched on the seats of carts. Some few had brought Saracen carpets, stools and baskets of provisions for their greater comfort, also servants with fans to wave away the heat and the flies. Behind these titled personages, the people of the town gathered in a noisy, milling crowd. Ale and wine sellers moved among them, along with purveyors of cakes and pies and wild fruit, and the ever-present cutpurses and doxies.

As Braesford had foretold, it was not to be a civilized joust with knights in plate armor tilting at one another with lances. Rather it was a true melee of a kind forbidden to mere nobles. Armor was restricted to light mail made of steel links for ease and maneuverability. Bodily injury was common in the heat of the contest, and feuds almost inevitable. By common decree, such meetings were restricted to the entertainment of kings in England and throughout Europe.

In this imitation battle, ranks of knights were assigned to opposite ends of a field. At a signal, they would ride toward one another, meeting in the middle ground with a mighty clash. The only weapons allowed were swords blunted at the tip, along with shields to defend against them. A knight retreating from the fray could be chased down, captured and held for ransom. The man judged the bravest, strongest and most cunning in the fight would receive a grand prize from the king. And if bloody wounds and other bodily injury were not inflicted, the crowd would be sorely disappointed.

The sun beamed down with piercing heat, dust rose from the feet of milling horses and the crowd buzzed like a disturbed beehive. Hardly a breath of air stirred under the canopy where Isabel sat as guest of honor. She fanned herself with a sheet of parchment set in a bent willow frame, but still felt flushed. Her most fervent wish was to be elsewhere. She had never been present at a melee, but had heard of them. She did not look forward to seeing who would be jeered from the field for clumsiness or cowardice, who sliced by a dull sword edge, knocked from the saddle and trampled, maimed or worse. That the king had ordered this event in token of her marriage to Braesford might be an honor, but it was one she could have forgone.

It was inevitable, so it seemed, that her new husband and Graydon should be directed to opposite sides of the field. Viscount Henley's bulk was recognizable at her stepbrother's side, while Braesford's half brother, William McConnell, seemed to be assigned to the same troop as Rand. She recognized a few more combatants by their colors and fluttering pennons marked by symbols and devices — such as Graydon's boar, the viscount's bear, Braesford's raven — but could not begin to put names to them all. A part of the reason was that they did not remain in one place, but rode here and there to limber their muscles, to check the security of their equipment or shake the fidgets from their mounts.

She kept Braesford's pennon — of white and blue marked by a black raven with spread wings — in view. Along with his squire, David, he appeared to be examining the ground where the main clash was to occur. He rode with his gaze on the grassy earth, quartering back and forth, though she was uncertain what he expected to find. Perhaps it was merely to guard against surprises in the way of uneven ground or rabbit holes.

He appeared satisfied at last, for a short time later he wheeled his mount, left his squire and rode slowly toward the pavilion. King Henry was just settling onto his throne, and Braesford gave him a formal bow from horseback before turning to her.

"Madam Braesford, my lady," he called out, saluting her with a gloved fist held at the level of his heart, dipping his head, which was covered by his mail coif but no helm as yet. "A thousand salutations to you on this our bridal day! I, a poor knight about to ride in tourney, beg a favor for my encouragement and protection in this fight. Will you not give it me?"

She had told him she would not, yet here he was with a public request. She stared at him with compressed lips and indignation in her eyes, but he seemed unaffected —

165

nay, undaunted — in accord with his personal motto. The man sat waiting, quite devastatingly handsome in his shining mail of metal links that was perfectly fitted to his powerful frame and covered by a pristine white tunic emblazoned with his device. He dared her to deny him, dared her to make him a laughingstock by proving that his bride would not present her favor and her blessing.

She should refuse. It was what Braesford deserved for his stubbornness over her Tobias Night plea, and particularly after the dastardly advantage he had taken at the breakfast table. It was unlikely he required such a boon in any case. Let him do what he might without it.

The king was waiting, as well, a frown congealing his stern features. Elizabeth of York appeared embarrassed. One of her ladies-in-waiting tittered, whispering to another behind her hand, while Cate and Marguerite murmured with their heads close together. At the end of the pavilion, leaning against the corner post, Leon, Master of Revels, strummed his lute and smiled ever so slightly. It was impossible to say, of course, whether his wry amusement was for her dilemma or only at the folly of mankind.

It was in this strained moment that a small boy ran out onto the field. No more than three years old, blond and cherubic, he laughed in high glee at his escape into the open, while his chubby little legs churned beneath his short doublet and his fine curls gleamed in the sun. He looked back over his shoulder as if for pursuit from a woman who called in a high-pitched wail, paying no attention whatever to where he ran. He flashed behind Braesford, dodged a squire leading a stallion half-blinded by its protected armor and pelted straight into the path of a galloping knight.

Gasps and cries rang out. Isabel rose in her seat with one hand pressed to her mouth. The king rapped out a command and half a dozen men leaped to obey.

Too late. Far too late.

Except Braesford was already moving, wrenching his great gray stallion around to plunge after the boy. He leaned from the saddle, one mailed arm outstretched. His fingers gripped the back of the child's doublet and lifted him up, up, up, to fold him against his chest just as his gray stallion slammed into the charging knight.

For a single instant, Isabel thought Braesford had been unseated, thought man and child would be thrown to the ground and crushed beneath the plunging horses.

It didn't happen.

Rand swung his stallion free, regained his seat and trotted a short distance away before halting the gray. He spoke to the clinging boy, who now sobbed against his tunic, bending his head to hear the answer. The child quieted, staring up at Braesford while a species of wonder amounting to awe dawned on his small face.

An odd, choking sensation filled Isabel's throat. She swallowed salt tears, sinking back into her seat with her hands clasped so hard in her lap that her injured finger throbbed with a fierce ache. She hardly felt it, barely noticed as Cate hugged her on one side and Marguerite on the other. With burning eyes, she watched as Braesford rode slowly to the sideline and passed the small escapee down to the woman who ran onto the field to hold up her arms, her face wet with her weeping.

Around her, applause roared from the royal pavilion along with cries of gladness, of amazement, of approbation. A score of women began to strip the veils from the truncated cones of their headpieces, the handkerchiefs from their long sleeves, to tug ribbons from their necklines. "Take this, Sir Rand!" they called out. "My favor! My favor! For good fortune, Sir Knight! For fair fortune!"

Isabel glanced down at her wedding costume. She had no handkerchief, no ribbons. Her hair was uncovered so she was without a veil. All she had was one of her long sleeves that were fastened onto the shoulders of her gown by ties. Tugging the length of embroidered white silk free, stripping it from her arm, she jumped to her feet again. She swirled the length of it above her head as she called out with the others. "Braesford! To me, Braesford!"

He did not look her way, just as he ignored the other trilling female voices. Speaking once more to the child he had delivered into its mother's arms, he swung his stallion away.

"Braesford!"

It was as if he did not hear. He was leaving, riding to join his troop gathering now in formation at the far end of the field. He was going without her protection, without her favor. He had accepted her refusal to present it.

"Rand!" she cried in regret and pleading.

He stiffened, turned in the saddle. A smile rose in his eyes as he saw the sleeve she held. Swinging the destrier's head, he trotted back, rode close to the wood rail of the pavilion. Around them the clamor of high-pitched entreaty died away, as did the rumble of admiration.

Isabel's smile was tentative as she met his gaze. His dark eyes were as sharp as steel, holding hers while she tied the full sleeve above his elbow. When it was done, he leaned abruptly to encircle her waist with a hard arm, dragging her half over the enclosure to pull her against him. The unyielding steel mesh of his mail-covered arm bit into her waist with the force of his embrace, while her breasts were flattened against the shirtlike hauberk of mail that armored his chest beneath his tunic. She felt the steel's heat, and his heated body beneath it, as she put out a hand for support. Then his mouth — hot, possessive and incredibly sweet — captured hers, plundering like a conqueror, demanding acquiescence as his due.

For the space of a single second, she gave it. She pressed against him, allowing him entry, twining her tongue with his in surrender. The noise around them faded. A red haze appeared behind her closed eyelids. She forgot to breathe under the assault of purest need and half-acknowledged longing.

With a wrenching movement, he set her back on her feet, steadied her for an instant.

His gray stallion reared a little, curveting as he backed away. Clapping his fist to his heart in hard salute, Rand stared into her eyes for an endless second, his own silvery with some vivid purpose. Then he wheeled and thundered away with her white sleeve fluttering like a private pennon from his arm.

Isabel, watching him go, was suddenly afraid that her favor would not be enough to keep him safe and whole. It might be no protection at all from the curse of the Three Graces.

7

The melee was vicious, a maelstrom of blows clanging against shields, of dust and sweat, screaming, neighing horses, shouts of agony and cries of rage and despair. For long moments, in the middle of it, Rand was overtaken by the red-hot heat of battle fury and the shuddering conviction that this was Bosworth Field again, that all depended on killing before he could be killed.

It was the thought of Isabel in the king's pavilion that shook him from it. She was watching, and unlikely to appreciate seeing bodies littering the ground. He wore her favor and must bear it with fairness, with honor and gallantry.

She had changed her mind. Why had she done that? Why?

He could hardly believe it when she had called him back, so sure had he been that she despised being tied to one of his low birth, hated him for his insistence on taking his rights as her husband. Had she changed her mind about him? Was this her way of saying she looked forward to the night to come?

It seemed unlikely. What, then, had moved her? Henry's order, the queen's distress, the knowledge that the crowd watched? She was not so hard of heart as she wished to appear. It was also possible she was reluctant to spurn him publicly.

Or her change of heart could have been because of the toddler on the field and his effort to save him. It had not been done for her approval, but only because he had been there. Yet mayhap she saw that he valued young lives.

Then again, it could have been jealousy that spurred her, the disinclination to allow her new groom to wear the favor of another woman. Not that he had intended to accept the pledge of any except his wife. He would not so dishonor her in front of the court, no matter her conduct toward him. It was a matter of principle.

High principle was his guide. He had demanded her favor because it was his right to have it and her duty to provide it. It had no special meaning, no extraordinary power, carried no importance as a talisman. The silken flutter of it from his arm did not gladden his spirit or make his heart swell with pride. No, not at all.

Hooves pounding behind him dragged his attention back to the fray. He swung his great gray destrier, Shadow, to meet a rear attack. Graydon and Henley came at him, one on either side. They swung their swords, whistling, at his head, and he saw the glint of Graydon's point, knew in grim acceptance that it had not been blunted.

Defending with his shield against Graydon's thrust, he could not avoid a blow from Henley that slammed his steel helm against his skull. He twisted away from a second thrust from Graydon, blocked another. Henley, burly veteran of tourneys that he was, spurred his mount so it shouldered into the gray while Rand was busy with Graydon. Instead of slashing with his heavy blade, however, he lunged forward in the saddle, reaching with a gloved paw, trying to tear away Isabel's favor.

The blazing ferocity of war seized Rand once more. He slashed and feinted with feral cunning and the surge of limitless strength. His muscles glided with the hot, well-oiled precision of one of Leon's infernal machines. His sword clanged against Henley's with such force it seemed both would shatter from the impact. Somewhere on his right, he was aware of his half brother thundering toward him to join the one-sided battle. He had no time to acknowledge him, no time for more than vague surprise when McConnell drew up in a cloud of obscuring dust, changed directions and rode away again.

Immediately he executed a backhand swing that took Graydon, howling, from the saddle. The man's horse reared, catching his rider's foot in the stirrup so Isabel's stepbrother bounced heavily, head down, as it raced away. Henley, cursing, withdrew and thundered after his friend to keep him from being dragged to his death.

And Rand, his rage boiling, scourging his veins, fought on. He charged, slashing right and left, laying low the opposing force until, suddenly, he and his troop held the far end of the field and the roar of the crowd penetrated, finally, the haze of his blood-lust.

Cheers, shouts of approval and cries of victory — none of it meant anything. Rand's ears rang, his skin felt scorched inside his sunstruck mail and he ached in every muscle of his body. None of the men around him were more than dimly familiar. His half brother was chasing an errant knight of the opposite camp into a copse of oaks, intent on ransom. With sweat pouring into his eyes, he turned toward the knights' tents on the far edge of the field.

A chorus of trumpets sounded before he was halfway there. The king's herald stepped forth and called his name. He must come forward and claim his prize as champion of the tournament.

Rand did as he was bid, though the honor meant nothing. He had already been given the only prize he valued. He had taken Isabel to wife, and would claim her as his own if the devil himself sought to prevent it.

The prize was a gold ring set with a carved carnelian, one taken from Henry's own hand. Rand sat looking at it for long moments. It would be something to hand down to his son one day, along with the tale of how it had been won, by fighting for his life against his wife's brother. Would he say his wife had wanted him to die? That was something he must discover.

Meanwhile, it was the custom to present any prize won in the tourney to the lady whose favor the champion wore. A brief smile tugged at his mouth at the thought. He kissed the ring and handed it over to his lady wife with his deepest bow. Putting spurs to his mount then, he rode from the field.

It was his squire, David, who found him sometime later, wandering half-blind from a headache amid the combatants' whooping celebration around a butt of ale. The lad led him and the gray back toward Westminster and the destrier's stable. There he helped Rand from his mail, discovering in the process that the blow to his helm had left it so misshapen it could not be removed. A blacksmith was his only recourse and they wended their way there. The great oaf and his hammer nearly deafened Rand as he clanged the metal back into the round while he knelt with his head on an anvil in a pose far too similar to a beheading for comfort.

Afterward, David, carrying the helm under his arm, guided him to the new quarters allotted to him and his bride. It was there they discovered Isabel awaiting them with anger and impatience in her pale face.

"Where have you . . ." she began, then came to a halt with her gaze on his temple. "You are hurt. I feared it."

"Feared?" he asked, made dim-witted by surprise and the pulsating agony in his head.

"When I saw Graydon and Henley attack you. It was a dastardly trick, to come at you together and from behind."

"All is fair in a melee," he said as he touched his fingers to his head, saw they came away smeared with blood.

"It was a dastardly attack, two against one, unworthy of knight or noble."

"But one I'd have thought you wouldn't mind watching."

She stared at him a long moment while her eyes turned more storm-gray than green. "How can you say such a thing?"

She had been alarmed for him. It was an astounding notion when he had half feared the attack might have been at her request. He felt the agony in his head begin to ease.

How very cool she appeared, there in the quiet of their chamber, so far removed from the violence of Tothill Fields that he might almost have dreamed she had been there. Her serving woman had removed the white silk sleeve that had been left to her after she gave him its mate, replacing both with new ones of pale green samite woven with strands of gold. They were not a perfect match but close enough. Isabel must have dismissed the woman afterward, for she was not in the chamber. That was, unless she was hiding behind the bed curtains.

The bed curtains in the chamber allotted to them on Henry's orders were of dark blue wool embroidered with field flowers. The bed was so large it took up a good third of the floor space. His gaze slid away from it, but returned against his will.

Isabel paid no heed to his confusion. Turning to David, she frowned upon him. "Why are you standing there? Bring warm water and bandaging at once."

A smile passed over the lad's firm, regular features, no doubt because concern disguised as annoyance was more familiar to him than solicitude. Abandoned at the gate of a nunnery on Saint David's feast day some two decades before, reared by its sharp-tongued inhabitants, it was what he had known for most of his young life. Shielding the blue of his eyes with his lashes as if determined not to offend, he dipped his guinea-gold head and went to do Isabel's bidding.

Rand did not make the mistake of thinking her anxiety on his behalf was personal, no matter her tone. He was her husband, and he had been injured while wearing her favor. It was her duty to tend him and she would see to it. It was only to be expected.

He had little use for impersonal assistance. What he longed for, suddenly, was her compassion, her womanly softness, womanly succor in its most basic form. The cause of that virulent desire, he knew, was the furor of battle. All men, when the fight was over and they discovered they still lived, demanded that ultimate affirmation of life. If he took her now, it would be a driven, mindless rut.

She deserved more. She required a gentle and most mindful initiation into the intimacies of the marriage bed. Knowing that did not prevent him from swaying toward her with the pull of instinct so strong that denying it brought the acid burn of tears to the backs of his eyes.

"Sit down before you fall down," she said, taking his arm and leading him to a stool. Standing before him, so close he could reach out and clutch her softness if he dared, she lifted a hand to push her fingers through his sweat-flattened hair.

It felt so good that a low groan sounded in his throat. He closed his eyes, the better to savor it.

"Did I hurt you?" She took her hand away. "I'm sorry, but something must be done. The cut on your head is bleeding."

"No," he said, a husky sound of protest for the removal of her touch. He yearned for it even if it had not been a caress.

"You cannot leave it as it is."

He could, of course, often had after a tourney. The slow trickle of wetness he felt was more a nuisance than a danger. "David can tend to it later."

"Your squire is unlikely to have skill with a needle, and I believe that is required."

"You would be surprised at his skills." Bright-haired, bright-minded David had made himself indispensable in any number of ways since Rand had rescued him from a mauling by street thugs the winter before. Though Rand named him his squire, the lad had little ambition to be a knight, calling himself a servant instead. That he would not always be one was a certainty for Rand. In token of it, he had taught David all he knew of manners, courtesy and gallantry, in addition to the practical skill with sword and lance that he might require to stay alive.

"There is still the feasting and mummery to be got through before you can rest," she insisted. "You will have to change into your wedding raiment again, and you cannot bleed all over the silk."

"No," he said on a sigh. The shirt, thin wool doublet and padded chausses he had worn under his mail for the tourney were rough garb more suited to a peasant than a gentleman, though appropriate for the purpose. They smelled to high heaven of hot metal, sheep grease, horse and randy male, but there was nothing he could do about it until David returned. She would have to endure it, as she would endure other things in their marriage. "I'm sorry."

"For what? It isn't your fault you were bloodied. I cannot understand what Graydon was about. He has no need of ransom."

"I doubt that was his aim," Rand said with a wry twist to his lips.

"What, then?"

"Henley may have wanted to see me bested, or dead."

Her lips compressed in a most enticing fashion while color spread upward from her breasts. She began to pluck at the knot which held her silk sleeve, much soiled, to his arm where he had insisted David secure it as his mail was removed. "It would avail him little since the king claims the right to choose my husbands for me."

"Or else Graydon could see himself taking charge of Braesford and its rents in your name." He caught her wrist as she released the silk sleeve and started to toss it aside. Removing it from her grasp, he folded it with care, keeping it in his hand.

She barely glanced at what he was doing. "My stepbrother may also bear you a grudge for calling him to account over my broken finger at Braesford. He is not a complicated man."

The implication was that others were. Was he among them in her estimation? he wondered. It was encouraging to think so.

"On the other hand, my half brother," Rand said deliberately, "cannot be called simple. I misdoubt he would do anything as obvious as attempting to have me hanged. Nevertheless, it could be instructive to discover if he and Graydon are on terms of friendship."

"You believe . . ."

"He could have joined me in fighting off Graydon's and Henley's attack. He did not."

"He may have thought you capable of handling them on your own," she said with a frown.

That was true. "Mayhap."

"It must gall him to see you in his place."

"Not his place but mine now," he answered. Her breasts were so close, their tender curves above her bodice more enticing than honey mead. He watched with some bemusement as his hand lifted of its own accord, cupping the fullness, brushing with a calloused thumb where he thought the peak should lie hidden. It was satisfactory beyond reason to feel it harden instantly under the fabric, to see the small, tight outline poke against it.

She inhaled softly through parted lips. Her eyes turned sultry as they met his. It seemed she inclined toward him, leaning into his clasp.

Footsteps, light and quick, sounded in the corridor outside. Her lashes swept down and she stepped away from him. "Don't."

He allowed his hand to fall away. "It seems I must bow to your wishes once more," he said quietly as David pushed open the door with an elbow to deliver two cans of water, hot from the kitchen cauldrons, into the chamber. "But it will not be so forever."

She left him to David's ministrations, which was no more than he expected, also what he wanted while he was so vulnerable to her nearness. Though he could not be sure the time would come when he would actually be stronger. His trusty squire put three stitches into his brow with no more fuss than mending a tear in his hose, and was considerably less distracting while he went about it. The lad then brought an infusion of willow bark for his headache and a tankard of ale to wash down the sourness, and then dressed him anew as a bridegroom. By the time the trumpets blew to announce the midafternoon dinner, Rand was ready to take his place at the high table in Henry's hall.

David served them, seeing that he and Isabel had fresh water scented with mint and cardamom with which to wash their hands and clean toweling to dry them, pouring their spiced and watered wine, bringing them platters of meats and delicacies. They ate their way through smoked eel, roasted beef with broth, venison in red wine, pig knuckles with dumplings stewed in their juices, stuffed crane in its plumage, plovers in pies, cress sallet and peas cooked with honey and saffron. Meanwhile, the boy's choir from the abbey sang a cappella, followed by a juggler who performed with a multitude of precious oranges. An Egyptian gave them wild music on the viele while dancers spun and stamped behind him. Marzipan and nougat were passed along with wild pears, soft cheeses, nuts and more spiced wine.

Halfway through the meal, Rand noticed Henley among the lesser nobility at one of the side trestles, just down from where Isabel's sisters shared a cup and plate. Graydon was nowhere in sight, not surprising as David had reported him laid up in bed with his tourney injuries. McConnell was apparently so far away as to be hidden by other diners, for he could not glimpse him either above the salt or below it. Regret touched Rand for that removal when his half brother should be among the nobles. Still, there was nothing he could do about it.

Surfeited at last, he and Isabel washed their hands again in a stream of herb-scented water poured by David, dried them on the cloth provided, then leaned back in anticipation of the mummery. This acting of maskers in some allegorical play and other comical nonsense would no doubt be the final entertainment of the evening. Thank heaven for that small mercy.

Leon, Master of Revels, introduced this offering of his own devising, standing with grace and confidence before them in a costume of stark black and white sewn with brilliants and hung with bells at the edges of his silken tunic and the seams of his sleeves. His bow to the king and Lady Margaret, Henry's mother, was profound; that to his queen, Elizabeth of York, even deeper. His voice pitched perfectly to reach to the far corners of the echoing hall and the ears of every diner, he begged for their attention. He had created a special tableau for the occasion, one popular at the merry court of young Charles VIII of France under the regency of his sister, Anne. It had been improved upon somewhat, but time for preparation had been short. He asked their indulgence with its imperfections. Turning toward the end of the hall where a curtain closed off that section of entrances and exits to the buttery and pantries and timbered kitchen beyond, he swept an arm toward it with the discordant jangle of bells.

"Your Majesties, noble gentlemen and lovely ladies," he called in sonorous announcement, "I give you *La danse macabre!*"

The curtain swept back, pulled by unseen hands. Behind it was revealed a group of men and women backlit by fat candles in floor stands. They were dressed all in black and white and wore mantles with hoods that covered their heads like shrouds. One was dressed as a pope, another as a king. Some were attired as nobles, some as merchants and some as freemen or peasants. Some had suffered gaping wounds while others appeared thin and wasted by disease. Among them were old and young, even children. Each one had a face washed with solid white, with black painted ovals for eyes and round circles of woe where their mouths should be.

"The dead . . ."

The whisper came in half a dozen voices, including that of Isabel. Rand, glancing at her, saw her face was as pale as the figures provided for their amusement. Following her wide stare, he saw why. One of the females was a new mother. She was identified by the stuffed doll she carried, one that dangled in her grasp with the limp nakedness of a stillborn babe.

Looking beyond Isabel to the queen, Rand realized Elizabeth of York had not missed the implications of the piece. She held a hand to her mouth as if to prevent protest or illness, and her long, aristocratic fingers were not quite steady. Lady Margaret, on her far side, sat with an air of austere sufferance and her lips pressed together in disdain.

Henry's eyes narrowed as he turned them upon his Master of Revels. He threw himself against the high back of his throne while tapping its arm with a fingertip in a slow, steady beat.

Now the sickening tableau was moving, forming a line, swaying to the slow and even cadence of a drum. A third of its members shuffled forward between the rows of tables, dragging their winding sheets behind, while several of the heftiest among them pulled and tugged at a boxlike affair that rolled with a dull rumbling and squeaking. As they got it moving, following the others, the last section of mummers followed behind it.

This was hardly the joyous romp usually reserved for a wedding. The hair on the back of Rand's neck tingled. Frowning, he came erect in his chair with every nerve alert.

Lute, harp and psaltery picked up the drum's dreary pace with a whining melody in a minor key. The morbid figures began to caper, to embrace and cavort in slow and lascivious parody. Some pretended to feast, smacking their lips. Some mimicked love-making. Some stabbed at one another repeatedly. A man toward the rear appeared to remove his head and tuck it under his arm.

At one of the lower tables, a woman moaned. Isabel's sister, Cate, grasped the hand of her younger sibling so hard her knuckles were white. Somewhere beyond them, a man mumbled a ribald comment and his companion gave a nervous laugh.

The mummers approached the high table, stumbling, almost tripping as they bowed and curtsied in such exaggerated homage to the king and queen that it was mere parody. Henry's mouth flattened, yet he stayed his hand.

Rand could guess at the reason. The king had been called humorless in the past, and would not care to have it proven. If French royalty were able to find some vestige of entertainment in this ghoulish display, then Henry's disdain for it would be suspect, charged to his dour nature rather than the play's failure to amuse. Besides, it might yet change in midact to some tasteless yet humorous satire on wedded bliss.

For his own part, Rand saw nothing comical in it. It did appear to have a point, however. All were equal in this pageant of the dead. Young or old, rich or poor, none escaped the reaper of souls, none found perpetual life. It was a sentiment that found resonance in his mind, though he could not think it fitting for a wedding feast. Nor was it suitable to present before a king whose reign was uncertain because he could prove no descent from a legitimate royal ancestor.

It would be easy to see a Yorkist plot in it, or at least the hand of Yorkist sympathizers.

Leaning a little toward Isabel, Rand said in soft query, "What think you?"

"Vulgar," she breathed so quietly only he could hear, "and quite horrid. I cannot think what Leon is about with it."

"It should be stopped, but I don't see the Master of Revels."

She scanned the mummers, the tables and beyond. "He seems to have gone. I think . . . I believe Henry should take Elizabeth away."

"Suggest it to him," Rand said in a fierce whisper.

She did as directed, reaching to let her

fingers hover just above the king's taut hand without quite touching to claim his attention, whispering into his ear after he had given her leave to speak. A moment later, Henry gestured to his mother, who rose and swept away without a backward glance. He then stood and offered his arm to his queen. They began to turn away.

The mummers had reached the cleared area before the high table, spreading out so the large box that trundled along with grinding, clanking metal wheels was directly in front of the throne. As the king turned his head to look, one of the burly tenders of the box stepped forward and flung open the double doors that closed it.

Flames roared and leaped high inside the makeshift firebox. The king fell back, taking the queen with him, though he seemed spellbound by the fiery interior of the contraption. Swinging his head, Rand saw that within the conflagration were tiny figures made of metal — men, women and children. The rumbling mechanism caused them to writhe as if in agony, tortured by the searing heat.

The box was a miniature hell, and its flames blazed higher and higher still.

"Be gone, sire!" Rand shouted at Henry. "Now!"

Henry backed away a long step, then another. He swung about, pressing the queen to move ahead of him into the rear passage that led to their apartments. Even as he moved, Rand grasped Isabel's arm and pulled her to her feet, sweeping her around to follow the royal couple. Glancing over his shoulder, he saw David ushering Isabel's sisters from their places, drawing them back from the high table.

The firebox exploded with a great, muffled thud. Fire blossomed from it, reaching out toward the high table. Rand kicked out at the heavy board. As it fell, he caught Isabel and carried her with him as he plunged to the floor behind its protection.

Screams of pain, shrieks of horror and moans of terror erupted on all sides. Shouts, oaths and desperate prayers rang under the high ceiling. Benches were overturned, more tabletops shoved from their trestles. The thud of running feet made a dull roar, while beneath it all was the crackle of flames.

Rand leaped up, sparing a single glance to see that the king and queen had vanished down the back passage and Isabel was dazed but unscathed. "Halt!" he shouted at the panicked crowd. "Don't run! Strip the cloths from the tables to beat out the fire. Bring the butts of wine and water. Stamp out where the rushes are ablaze. Set to! Do it now or the palace will go up in smoke!"

Some few men paused, tried to turn back. It was not enough. Dragging Isabel to her feet, he commanded her to follow the king and queen, saw her slip away in that direction. He shouted to David where he had Cate and Marguerite safe against the wall, commanding his aid. Bending, he snatched up the royal tablecloth from where it had fallen. He leaped from the dais and began to beat at the crawling inferno.

8

Everything was ready. Steaming water filled the oaken tub with its lining of linen cloth. The screen to protect the bather from drafts stood nearby. A container of soap, scented with precious sandalwood, sat ready. Watered wine in a silver jug occupied a table near the bed. A clean linen shift of large size was draped near the fire to remove any dampness. All that was missing was the man for whom these preparations had been made.

Isabel sent Gwynne away after the serving woman had helped with the bathing arrangements, then undressed her and made her ready for bed. David had also been dismissed. She would tend to Sir Rand alone.

The role of handmaiden was not one she relished, yet was her obligation as a wife. More than that, she owed Rand some small recompense for saving her from fiery pain, and she paid her debts. He had spent a long, weary day in mock battle, sustaining at least one injury she knew of and perhaps more, then had single-handedly protected Henry, the queen and their unborn child from injury or death. He had then saved Westminster Palace's venerable walls from the conflagration. The least she could do was see that he bathed away the smoke and grime, that his wounds from the melee and the fire were soothed and that he wanted neither for wine nor comfort.

She would not think of how he might prefer to be comforted on the evening of their wedding.

She had not seen him for hours. Once the fire had been doused and the servants set to putting the hall to rights again, he had attended the king in private audience. What had passed there none could say, though Isabel supposed Henry had expressed his gratitude in some manner. Afterward, Rand had joined in the search for the Master of Revels that was already taking place, fanning out from the palace into the streets of Westminster and its river landing, and even as far beyond the gates as London.

At least this was the report David had brought her, along with the news that her sisters were unharmed and safe in their beds. She had received no word from her husband, nothing to show he remembered he now had a wife.

She had bathed earlier, lathering away the stench of smoke and hot metal from her hair and her person. Dressed in her voluminous shift with its long, full sleeves and rounded neckline, as befitted a private chamber, she paced while a thousand thoughts ran through her head.

Why had Leon devised such a gruesome exhibition? Was it connected in some way with the charge against Rand? Did it speak of murder by fire? Yes, and retribution for it?

Had Leon intended his mechanism to blow up or had it been happenstance? If constructed as a weapon, who at the high table had been its intended victim — the king, the queen, Rand or herself?

Yes, and why? Where was the logic in it?

The Master of Revels was a purveyor of wit and song, a troubadour who moved from place to place at the behest of his patrons and his own whim. He had little interest in crowns, dynasties or power. The king of the moment was of no importance except that he provided him room, board and occasional largesse in exchange for entertainment. No reason existed for Leon to harm anyone, Isabel thought. To remove Henry would be to remove his livelihood, and she could not believe he would deliberately bring peril to Elizabeth of York.

If the explosion was an accident, however, why could he not be found? Why had he not stepped forward, explained the error and begged forgiveness? The only explanation Isabel could see was that he feared to be accused, regardless of his innocence, feared to be hanged out of hand for endangering the king.

It was possible he had reason. The prospect of hanging was too easily bruited about these days.

Impromptu judgments of all kinds were common. Take the tournament this morning. Henry had commanded it as an ordeal by combat. Had he hoped Rand might be killed, putting a convenient end to the question of his guilt or innocence?

It had not happened. Instead, Rand had won the tourney with his skill and courage.

Her husband's prowess on the field — the unrelenting strength of his arm, the force of his tactics, his command of his destrier and of the forces which fled before him — seemed imprinted upon Isabel's brain. She had thought him a warrior when he appeared before her for the first time. He had proven her right. It was not something she would soon forget.

Not that she was thrilled to mindless ecstasy by the sight of a peerless knight on the field with his opponents in flight before him, but she must give him his due. It was only fair.

A quiet scrape at the door startled her from her reverie. She swung around in a billow of linen as Rand stepped into the chamber. He paused with his hand on the latch, his gaze moving from her unbound hair that cascaded over one shoulder, down her shift to her feet in slippers of samite embroidered with beads. Weariness and pain etched his face and lay in dark shadows under his eyes. His fine clothing was wrinkled and streaked with grease and soot. In spite of these things, or even because of them, he had never appeared so powerful, so armored in muscle and sinew.

She opened her lips but could find nothing to say, could not make a sound for the tightness in her throat.

"Why are you still up?" he asked in hoarse surprise. "I expected to find you abed."

She swallowed, found her tongue. "How could I sleep when everything is so unsettled? What said the king? Did he . . . did he offer you pardon?"

"For the sake of a few words of warning, you mean? No." He closed the door, moving forward as he lifted a purse from the belt at his waist. "He did bestow this upon me for my efforts."

Upending the bag, he poured a gold chain into his hand. It glittered as the candlelight shimmered over it, highlighting its evenly spaced medallions in the shape of roses that were enameled in white and red, combining the symbols of York and Lancaster. Taking its weight in both hands, he stepped close to pass the chain over her head, settling the heavy gold links upon her shoulders so it lay upon the curves of her breasts.

"It looks better on you," he said with a smile lifting one corner of his mouth.

She picked up a medallion of the chain. Frowned at it. "But is this not . . . ?"

"The Order of the Garter made to Henry's new design? So it is, though I am not yet invested. Nor am I like to be unless Mademoiselle Juliette and her child appear soon."

"Henry must expect it," she said almost to herself.

"That may be, though with him it's impossible to be sure. It could also be a boon that will cost him nothing if I am judged guilty."

"Don't say that!" The protest was instinctive.

He gave a short laugh. "Spoken like a true wife. Would that you meant it."

For that, she had no answer. She looked away, searching her mind for a distraction. "Were many injured by the fire?" she asked finally.

"A dozen or so were burned, those nearest to the contraption, though they should thank God to be alive. By His grace, none were killed."

"Yes, a great mercy," she said, her memory alive with the blast of fire, the roar of flames. She pushed the images away with an effort. "Come, water for bathing is ready. Allow me to help you undress."

He studied her face for an instant, his features without expression. Looking away, he scanned the chamber. "Where is David?"

"Gone to his quarters," she said shortly. Reaching for the belt that spanned his doublet at the waist, she unfastened it, slid it free. "What a shame that the king's gift is ruined."

"Is it?"

She had spoken without thinking, a symptom of her disturbance of mind. Rand's costume of green and white had become him to a nicety, as she had discovered with the advance of this day, lending him a more polished appearance so he became less the farmer-knight and more the courtier. "Given the cost of it, I mean to say," she added in haste.

"Aye, the cost."

He watched her with a species of bemusement on his face. His regard made her clumsy, so she let the belt fall too soon as she set it aside. It slid from the stool where she intended to place it, but she left it where it lay. Turning back, she began to tug at the closures of his doublet.

"I will admit that you make a more pleasant servitor than David, but I would know the reason for it," he said with a gruff note in his voice.

She gave him the briefest of glances. "It's no more than I must do for your guests once I am installed as chatelaine at Braesford."

"Who says so?"

"My mother before she died, also the nuns who trained me in my duties."

"But not while you are in the same state of undress, I hope."

"No."

"Good." He caught her hands, stilling her efforts. Making short work of the fastenings, he shed the doublet with a shrug of his shoulders. He tossed it on top of the belt, then stepped to where a stool sat next to the tub. Without pausing, he dropped down on it and stretched out one leg. He waited with a challenge in the silvery depths of his eyes.

He meant to see if she would slip free the points that held up his hose, Isabel realized. They were threaded into eyelets at the bottom of his shirt, so lay in the bend between his body and his hard-muscled thighs. The only way to reach them was to kneel.

She had begun this, so must go on.

Steeling her nerves, she sank down in front of him. Immediately, he guided her between his spread thighs with a hand on either elbow. He pulled her nearer so she hobbled awkwardly on her knees with the heavy gold chain shifting back and forth between her breasts.

She was enclosed, surrounded by the not unpleasant scents of smoke, warm silk and male musk. Oddly enough, she felt supported instead of threatened. She should not linger, however. The best way to escape was to finish her task. Accordingly, she began to pull free the series of slipknots that held the hose tops.

The chamber was quiet except for the fluttering of a flame on a candlewick and, somewhere beyond the walls, the clatter of horses as a party of horsemen went about the king's business and drunken singing from a tavern in this town overrun with drinking establishments. Her heart beat so strongly that it seemed to shake her body, making her fingers unsteady at their task. Her elbows brushed the taut musculature of his thighs covered by his hose. She could feel their heat even through her shift.

How many points did it require to hold up a man's hose? It seemed there must be a thousand of them.

Reaching out in a casual gesture, Rand rubbed a fingertip over her nipple that pressed against the soft linen of her shift. "So this is for my benefit alone."

Her body betrayed her by tightening under his attention, the nipple forming a small, hard knot. Chagrin at that involuntary response colored her reply. "Hardly. It's usual to discard excess clothing while in the privacy of the chamber."

He withdrew his hand, his look of amusement fading. "I don't believe I care to share your wifely attentions. It should be enough to send a maidservant to attend my guests."

"She would not be safe, whereas a guest would not dishonor the wife of his host."

"Send an old and ugly maidservant," he said.

She would be glad to obey. The prospect of tending all and sundry had no appeal. "As it pleases you."

"For now, I smell like a boar being singed over the fire. Are you not yet done?"

He knew very well that she had yet to release the points under his backside. Setting her jaw, she reached to unfasten them as he lifted from the stool. Then she stripped away his hose inside out, like skinning an animal, and sat back on her heels.

He smiled at her with a wicked gleam in his eyes as he studied her hot face. An instant later, he crossed his arms and skimmed his shirt off over his head.

Suddenly he was almost naked, might as well have been for all the loosely wrapped braies worn low on his hips did by way of concealment. She was close, so close. The hard planes of his chest were like a wall in front of her, the rippled surface of his upper abdomen, his flat belly and the sculpted turns of his legs were mere inches away. A light-headed sensation invaded her mind. All she had to do was drop his hose and put out her hands . . .

"I have a thirst like the devil's own minions," he said, his voice harsh. "Is that wine in the pitcher there?"

Relief washed over her at the prospect of moving away from him. Setting her hands on his thighs, she prepared to push upward, so glad to be released that she barely noticed what she used for support.

He drew a hissing breath. She met his eyes, her own wide with distress as she feared she had hurt him.

He looked tormented. His jaw was clamped tight, and beads of sweat stood out on his upper lip. The cut on his forehead appeared swollen as it lay across the vein that throbbed at his temple. He glanced down.

She followed the direction of his gaze to where her fingers grazed the front of his braies near the juncture of his thighs. She turned fiery hot all over as she recognized the firm length outlined there, realized that her thumbs bracketed it on either side.

With an abrupt shove, she regained her feet. Turning swiftly, she moved to the wine tray. Her hands were so wildly unsteady that the jug clattered against the lip of the silver goblet as she poured.

She required something, anything, as relief from her embarrassment at what had just passed between them. "Did you find Leon?" she asked without looking at Rand. "Has he said what went wrong?"

It was a moment before he answered. When he spoke, however, the words were even, without inflection. "What makes you think something went wrong?"

She put down the jug, picked up the full goblet. "It's inconceivable to me that it should be otherwise. He would never harm the queen."

"So Her Majesty said, as well. Henry is not convinced."

As she turned with the wine, she saw he had dropped his braies and was just stepping into the tub. The goblet wobbled in her hand before she steadied it. She breathed deep, once, twice. What was the matter with her? There should be nothing in the sight of a naked man to so discompose her. Other women sustained the sight without being stunned to idiocy by it.

Oh, but he was magnificent in his nakedness, more perfectly formed than any statue of a martyred saint, and as hard in body as the carved wood of such images. He was as marked by suffering as such saints, however. A white streak that ran at a diagonal across one arm had the look of an old sword cut, and his legs carried multiple scars. His back was marked by an ugly bruise the size of a shield, while beneath it was a multitude of white, crisscrossed lines that could only have been made by a whip.

Isabel felt a peculiar shifting sensation inside her at this evidence of past battles, past pain, past hardihood. He was so different from the feminine company she knew best — her sisters and the nuns who had taught her Latin and sums and writing, embroidery and the art of preserving foodstuffs. He was larger, heavier, with long bones that must be made of steel that they had not broken as a result of his other injuries. He was angular and hard where she was rounded and soft. He could summon furious concentration as required, fighting with brutal will and every ounce of his considerable power. He lived by a stringent code that made few allowances for human weakness.

Because he had given his word, he had walked into the prison of Westminster Palace and would, if requested, submit himself to the will of his king and the unkind hands of the hangman. He would die without protest because he had pledged his honor as a knight.

It was a horror in her mind to think of him dying for no reason other than to save a kingdom for the man with whom he had shared exile. For that was his purpose in

London, Isabel was almost sure of it. He was to be the scapegoat if the Frenchwoman and her child were found to have been murdered. Rand would be condemned for the crime so no blame would fall upon Henry VII.

The injustice of it was more than any man should be asked to bear. It seemed, in that moment, more than she could bear.

Rand sank into the tub, though his legs were so long that his knees rose above the water. He lathered his hair, rinsed it with a great deal of splashing and slicked the long strands back with fingers that plowed glistening black furrows. Squinting a little against the water that threatened to run into his eyes, he reached for the wine she held.

"You should not have wet your stitches," she said as she put the goblet in his hand. While he drank, she reached for the toweling and blotted the wound dry, as well as the hair around it.

"I doubt it will matter."

"Because . . ." She stopped, unable to form the words.

"Because it's a piddling cut, and I'm fast to heal," he said. "Did you think I meant aught else?"

"You could have," she said defensively. She had thought he meant a cut could not matter if his life's breath was stopped at his neck.

He tipped the last of the wine into his mouth and handed her the goblet before leaning back against the side of the tub. He rested his arms along the linen-draped edges and closed his eyes. "I've not lost faith that Mademoiselle Juliette will be found. And would have more if allowed to join the hunt."

It was no doubt madness, but Isabel wished most fervently that the dratted woman would turn up. "Have you any idea at all where to look?"

"In the countryside. Her presence would have been easily marked in town, I think. The curiosity of some servant, yeoman guard or merchant must have been aroused and word brought to the palace." He paused, glanced at the cloth she held. "As long as you have that to hand and are being dutiful, you could use it."

It was permission to bathe him, or possibly a request. She could hardly protest as the task was expected of her. Something in his tone, the faintest rumble of anticipation, made her wildly conscious of the intimacy, however. Ignoring it as best she could, she went to one knee beside the tub and dipped the cloth in the warm water. She soaped it well as she considered where to start.

"Don't wet your splint," he said in soft warning.

He was watching her through the slits between his eyelids while a corner of his mouth tilted in something perilously close to a grin. He knew how she felt, she was sure of it. Inhaling with fortitude, she smacked the cloth into the center of his chest and began to scrub in tight circles.

He grunted, and a rash of goose bumps beaded his skin, flowing over his shoulders and down his arms. Regardless, he made no protest. His lashes flickered, and his eyes closed completely. His chest rose and fell as he breathed deep. After a moment, the goose bumps faded. The stiffness began to leave his muscles.

He was enjoying her ministrations, or so it seemed. That pleased her in some ridiculous fashion. Her movements slowed. She eased her pressure to a gentle glide. After a moment, she put her hand inside the cloth and slid it over the taut musculature of his chest, working the soap into its coating of hair. His nipples tightened when touched just as hers did, she discovered, though their color was like tanned leather.

While he drowsed, unaware, she was able to study his features more closely than before. How long his lashes were, how firm the curves of his mouth. It was not a brutal face for all its strength, but was limned with sensitivity and fierce intelligence. A thin scar bisected one brow and crossed his cheekbone, but he had newer injuries. His hair on the right side of his head was singed on the ends, and angry red burns ran from his jaw down his neck to his collarbone. The discoloration on his side had now spread over most of his upper back.

Easing him forward with slight pressure from her injured hand, she began to wash the area between his shoulder blades, though she used extra care on this section. "This big bruise came from Graydon's attack, did it not?"

"Probably." The single word was a low rumble of sound.

"I am sorry."

"So is he, I'll be bound, as he'll have plenty of bruises of his own. I would not be greatly surprised if his leg turned out to be broken."

"It was only sprained and his knee wrenched, according to David," she replied, "not that he didn't deserve worse." When he made no answer, appearing half-asleep, she went on. "And these scars, what of them?"

"Scars?" He arched a brow, though he didn't open his eyes.

"Just here," she said, running the cloth over the mesh of fine white lines.

Rand twitched a shoulder. "It's nothing."

"They don't appear nothing to me." She eyed the marks as she rubbed carefully across them. "You must have had them a long time. They are hardly raised at all."

"Since I was ten."

"Ten! Who would do such a thing to a child?" She could not keep the indignation from her voice.

His laugh was mirthless as he finally gave her a quick glance over his shoulder. "A half brother not a great deal older, as it happens. William was thirteen, and none too happy with our father for having me trained as the estate's future steward. Until then, I had been living with my grandmother and an uncle in their croft hut, but they had died of the fever. McConnell — William — thought to show me my place, so had two villeins hold me down while he used his riding whip on me."

"He was jealous," she said.

"Mayhap, though he had no need. He was the legitimate son, after all. Anyway, it was a mistake, as it turned out. Our father came upon him in the act. To illustrate the error of his ways, he brought me into the house to share William's privileges and his tutor. Though not, of course, the McConnell name."

"You took it, anyway," she said in dawning understanding. "Or at least assumed the name of your father's estate as your own."

"It seemed fitting."

He had taken Henry's gift of his dead father's confiscated lands and the designation of Braesford that went with it. Yet he preferred to be called by his given name, as he had so aptly proven this day. Was that because it was the way he thought of himself, still?

"You appear to deal well with McConnell now," she said in tentative tones.

"He learned to tolerate me, as our father's goodwill depended on it. We even became companions, of a sort, when we were both fostered at Pembroke."

"Where Henry was kept a prisoner after the estate was taken from his uncle, I think. Was that where you met him?

"As you say. We struck up a friendship, Henry and I. When he went into exile, he asked me to go with him as his squire."

"And not your brother?"

"William remained behind with his mother's people. After a time, he made his peace with Edward."

"Even though Edward IV executed your father?"

"And his," Rand agreed with a nod, "not that McConnell forgave him. But like many a nobleman's son in the years just past, he made accommodation with his conscience. He joined Edward's army to make his way in the world, and in hope of gaining favor."

"The return of Braesford, for instance."

"Just so. He respected Edward's younger brother, Richard of Gloucester, as a general, and served under him readily enough. After Edward died, he couldn't stomach Richard's grab for the crown. He bided his time, then changed York's white rose for the red of Lancaster again. He thought Henry would be grateful enough for the support that he might return Braesford to him. What he failed to take into account was my return with Henry."

"But not as a squire."

Rand gave a small shake of his head. "Being outcasts together in Brittany for over a decade allowed me to gain Henry's friendship as well as a higher place in his service. The time spent on the fringes of foreign courts, with little to do except spar with sword and lance or compete in tourneys, were ample to turn a squire into a soldier."

She paused, spoke in dry disbelief. "You are quite sure that's all you had time for?"

"Almost all, if you must have it." He snorted in dry humor. "It was not a monkish life with our hosts being a Breton noble and, later, a French king, both known for the luxury of their courts. There was wine and dancing, lessons in French and Italian and for the lute and harp, also country expeditions in the company of ladies fine and not so fine. Yet Henry was then, and is now, a pious man with weighty matters on his mind. We gave more time to prayers and political maneuvering than to debauchery."

She believed him, strangely enough. What was even more peculiar was that she was gratified by the picture he painted of his exile with Henry. "So you were knighted on Bosworth Field and given Braesford Hall. Your half brother must have resented that."

"And resented Henry for giving it to me. Now he must resent the bride I gained, as well."

She paused in the act of squeezing water over his shoulders, watching it run in a path down the long, lean pathway where lay his backbone. "What?"

"William had a fancy for you last year when you first came to court, and still does. Had you not noticed?"

She wished she could see Rand's face, but all she viewed was the stiff cords at the back of his strong neck. "No."

"It's there. I saw how he looked at you then, as well as at Braesford and this morning. He is eaten alive with envy, also with the certain knowledge that he would have been a more worthy groom."

"He's said nothing of it," she insisted.

He gave a soft snort followed by a sigh. "Maybe I'm wrong. Maybe I resent him for being born legitimate and first in our father's affection. Maybe he was coming to my aid on the field today, instead of joining Graydon in his attack."

"How can you think otherwise?"

"Easily, when I consider that any personal attack was forbidden, but I met one, anyway."

She skimmed her cloth over the great bruise that was shaded with purple-and-blue tints and centered by a long line of red. His mail must have been all that saved him from more permanent injury due to that blow dealt from behind. "You defeated Graydon and could have ridden him down and demanded ransom," she said in meditative tones. "Yes, and Henley, too, I expect. Why didn't you?"

He hunched a shoulder. "I feared I might

kill rather than capture. I preferred not to add to the sins of the battlefield that weigh my conscience."

"Sins of the battlefield?"

"The killing at Bosworth Field," he said in quiet strain. "Men become — I become — an animal in the midst of a fight, a beast that fails to think beyond the moment. A king's knight whose only purpose is his orders and the need to stay alive no matter the cost to other men."

She brushed over the bruise again, deeply disturbed by the self-loathing she heard in his voice. "Yet you had the presence of mind not to kill Graydon."

"That was different."

She weighed the iron in his tone, spoke, anyway. "How so?"

"The melee was relatively bloodless compared to . . ." He halted, said again after a moment, "It was different."

"Or you are less an animal than you think."

"A more calculating one, most likely. But never mind. Tell me how dutiful a wife you intend to be on this our wedding night."

She didn't care for the deliberate change of subject when she had meant only to ease his needless self-blame. His derision that went with it, and the determined light in his eyes as he glanced over his shoulder, were also unwelcome. Tossing the cloth she held into the soap-clouded water that covered his lap, she put her good hand on the side of the tub and began to rise.

He closed one hand on her wrist, reached to catch her waist with the other. A cry of outrage caught in her throat as she was pulled off balance. Water splashed in bright droplets as she landed in the tub with her legs draped over the side and her bottom pressed firmly into the cradle of his thighs.

"What are you doing?" she demanded. "My shift will be soaked. I'll have nothing to wear tomorrow."

"You may need nothing," he said, placing a hand on her abdomen to hold her down as she struggled to rise. With his other arm, he reached around her and held her firm by clasping the fullness of her breast.

She redoubled her efforts, shifting, kicking to gain purchase. "My hair will be wet, too. Let me up."

"I'm trying to keep it dry, but you're making it hard — making other things hard, as well," he said, speaking against her temple while laughter threaded his voice. "If you don't be still, you may be bedded in a tub."

Her every muscle stiffened as she felt the shaft of rigid flesh that lay beneath the curves of her bottom. Her heart thudded against her ribs. Her chest rose and fell with the swift tempo of her breathing. "What . . ." she began before her throat closed. Swallowing hard, she tried again. "What do you want?"

"Oh, Isabel, how can you ask?" He shook his head, even as he held her down with his elbow while delving under the water, his long fingers skimming, grasping and squeezing her curves. "Though what I really want at this minute is to find the cloth you threw at me —"

"I didn't!" she protested.

"That you threw at me," he continued implacably, "so I may serve you as you have served me."

"I've had my bath, thank you." She made a small lunge toward escape, but desisted at once as he pressed upward with her, somehow nestling himself more firmly into the space where her upper legs came together.

"To my regret."

"You aren't supposed to bathe me. It's not seemly."

"I am your husband and you are my wife. To serve each other in divers small ways before we take our pleasure, and take it merrily, is just as it should be."

"Merrily," she repeated with a catch in

her voice.

"Just so." Finding the cloth, he drew it out, dripping, then compressed it in his fist so water cascaded down, wetting the fabric over her breasts. The rose-pink of her aureoles bloomed under the wet linen, while her nipples became as beaded as plump, ripe berries. Bending his head, he sucked the wet cloth over one, and the flesh beneath it, into his mouth.

Her gasp turned to a moan of shocked gratification. Without intending it at all, she lifted a hand to his wet hair. She threaded her fingers through it to hold his head in place as he laved her, suckled her, breathed hot against her and circled her tight, tight nipple with his tongue before taking it into his mouth again. She forgot that she wanted out of the tub, forgot her fear of what he intended. All she knew was the hard strength of his arm that supported her, the firmness of his chest where her shoulder rested against him, the warm water that pooled around her lower body and the intoxication that raced in her veins.

Rand lifted his head, taking her mouth with the same sure possession as her breast. She met his tongue, accepting its glide, its marauding exploration, its friction against hers. The taste of him urged exploration of her own. She accepted the enticement, sweeping the curves of his lips, their smooth surfaces where his pulse throbbed, thrusting inside as she felt the gentle adhesion of his welcome.

He slid his hand under her shift before she knew it, slipping it between her legs, clasping, holding. A shiver raced over her at his intimate incursion, and she held her breath an instant, releasing it into his mouth with a low sound of unwilling enjoyment. Liquid heat flowed from her, warmer than the water that cooled around them.

He growled, released her mouth and lifted her to balance on the rim of the tub until she could sit upright. Surging to his feet, he caught her against him while he stripped off her wet shift and let it fall. Lifting her in his arms then, he stepped from the tub. Dripping water that made wet tracks across the rushes, he carried her to the bed and fell onto the feather mattress with her.

She turned to him as he stretched out beside her, over her, half burying her in the feathered softness. Trembling, aching with the need to feel him against her skin, she clung, and almost cried out when he drew away. But he only rolled her to her back again and buried his face between her breasts, brushing aside the heavy gold chain of his reward before kissing his way downward over her navel, down to her damp curls. He threaded his tongue among them, found the small, most sensitive bud hidden there. While she thrashed, turning her head back and forth on the sheeting, he tasted her like some succulent August pear, drinking her sweetness. And when she was mindless and gasping, near desperate with need, he slid upward, spreading her thighs wide to accommodate his hard hips, and filled her in a single, fluid glide. The barrier inside was found and breached so swiftly she had no time to resist. It burned, a stinging pain, yet faded almost before it began.

He went still, every muscle clenched. She thought his jaw muscles creaked a little as he opened his mouth to whisper against her hair. "Is all well with you?"

She gave a small nod. It was the most she could manage while he filled her to such completion it was almost more than she could sustain. He withdrew a little, and she inhaled as if he had left breathing room. Yet she wanted him back again, reached with spread fingers to smooth her way down the firm line of his back to his backside. Grasping the tight curves, she drew him toward her once more while reveling in the heat, the slow friction.

He pressed forward on a glide of hot, strong muscles, then set a rhythm that made her choke on a moan of bone-deep surcease. She met it, matched it, twined her legs with his to urge him on, drew up her knees to take more and more of him. Her very being opened to him, clung to him with deep internal contractions. All consciousness of who and what she was vanished. She wanted nothing more than this, the endless sounding of body and mind, the close and elemental connection.

Surcease wound its way up from somewhere deep inside — burgeoning, mounting, spreading — until there was nothing else in the universe except the hot, blood-red glory and the man who held her. Her throat ached with tears that spilled from her eyes, draining into her hair.

"Rand," she said, a low cry of amazement mixed with some primal mourning.

He opened his eyes, looked deep into hers while his face contorted with an expression like agonized grief. She felt the pulsing of his heartbeat deep inside her, the first swelling force of his explosive completion. She closed her eyes and buried her face in his shoulder then, unable to bear the thought of what might come to them, unwilling to witness his final surrender.

9

Rand came awake with every sense suddenly, acutely, alive. He did not move but lay staring into the early-morning dimness inside the bed curtains. After a moment, he relaxed, smiling to himself as he absorbed the feel of full arms and warm, feminine curves pressed against him. He was replete, and why not? He had taken his bride not once or twice but any number of times between dark and this dawn, the last time at cockcrow. How aptly named, that first daylight hour when man and beast began to stir and to rise.

His body was on the verge of readiness again at the mere thought. It seemed his hunger for the woman he held could scarce be sated. She was so very responsive in her ladylike fashion that it fueled his hunger beyond imagining. Who would have dreamed such reservoirs of passion lay beneath her cool and distant demeanor? It would be his pleasure to plumb them one by one until she was free and easy in her expression of them, until she could look him in the face when together they reached *la petite mort,* the little death of love's apogee.

That was, if he lived to have her again. The fear that he would not was what had driven him to use her so sorely. She had been a virgin, unacquainted with bed sport, unused to its rigors. He should have exercised more care and concern, should have given her time to become accustomed. The devil of it was that time was far from certain.

His body was as unruly as a rutting ram. One thought of Isabel's moist, hot softness and it sprang up, waving in search of it. 'Twas best if he quitted the bed before he did something he would regret, such as use her yet again in spite of her soreness. He should give her respite, at least until night came again.

Easing away, he slid from under the sheet that covered them. Half-off the mattress, he halted. Isabel was turning, stretching in sybaritic languor, one hand reaching out as if in search of his warmth against the early-morning cool. Dear God, but she was lovely, a vision of heaven with her hair spread over the pillow, her lashes lying like silken feathers on the faint shadows under her eyes and the milk-white globe of one breast, capped by its peak the color of a sun-blushed peach, rising above the cover.

Hot need clawed at him. With a silent oath, he sprang away, jerking the bed curtains closed behind him. Naked but far from cool, he strode to the small window let into the stone wall of the chamber. He knelt on the window seat built into its recess, opened the heavy wooden shutters and leaned out, breathing deep.

He was bewitched; he must be, held in the thrall of one of the accursed Three Graces of Graydon. Yet the last thing he wanted was for it to end. The very last thing.

Isabel had given him absolution for the injury to her stepbrother. Did it mean she truly saw him as a man instead of a senseless destroyer like one of Leon's infernal machines? Or only that she despised Graydon more than she disliked him? Either way, he was more grateful for the heart's ease of it than he cared for her to know. He honored the impulse in her as highly as he honored her as his wife.

His wife. At last.

He closed his eyes while he breathed a small prayer that there would be no end to this miracle. Or at least not yet.

The scents of the morning came to him

on a stray breeze, those of horses and hay, baking bread, roasting meat, fermenting hops, animal dung and too-human humanity. Brought to the present, he saw that the window looked out over the stables and, beyond them, to the mews for the king's hunting hawks. Sparrows chirped and sang from where they lined the near stable's rooftop ridge or scratched in the loose hay that filled the spaces between the cobblestones of the frontage yard. A cat stalked from the stable door and birds flew up like leaves blown before a gale. One spiraled higher than the others, fluttered an instant before Rand's face and then landed on the windowsill in front of him.

"And a good morning to you, too," he said in a base rumble. "Someone must have been feeding you their bread crusts."

The sparrow cocked its head and pecked at an imaginary crumb. Rand put out his hand, half expecting the creature to fly off. Instead, it hopped upon his thumb and sat there, waiting.

He chuckled quietly, charmed against his will. At that instant the bells of the abbey began to ring. The small bird paid no attention. His feathered friend had either greeted the dawn with a thankful heart already, or else was inured to the clamor that called those less blessed to their morning prayers.

A whisper of sound came from inside the room. Rand turned his head toward the bed. Isabel had pulled aside the bed curtains and lay watching him. A faint smile curved her mouth, warming her eyes to the color of summer leaves. A strange sensation invaded his chest, constricting his heart in a grip so tight that its beat altered.

Before he could speak, a scratching came on the door. Rand thought he knew who to expect, but called out in question, anyway, though his gaze never left Isabel's face.

"It's David, sir. With bread and wine to break your fast."

Isabel snapped the bed curtains shut, closing herself behind their protection. Rand made certain no slit between them remained before he strode to the door. As he swung it open, David entered with a laden tray. He flashed a single glance toward the bed as he placed his burden on a table, then turned strict attention to setting off the basket of bread, jug of wine and silver goblet it held. That done, he reloaded it with the half-empty jug and wine-stained goblet from the night before. The untouched cheese, nuts and apples, he left behind.

"Excellent," Rand said. "Come back in an hour."

David inclined his fair head. "As you command, though you may wish to hear what passes."

"And that might be?"

"The queen left the castle at daybreak. With her traveled her mother, her sisters and the king's mother, the Duchess of Richmond and Derby, along with a guard of a thousand men-at-arms. Official word is that they journey to Winchester, where the queen will remain for the forty days of seclusion before childbirth. Court tittle-tattle says the king is near out of his mind with worry for her safety and that of his unborn heir. He believes last evening's *La danse macabre* was an assassination attempt."

"And so fears they may try again."

"As you say."

Rand rubbed a hand over the bristles on his chin as his thoughts moved like quicksilver through his mind. "And the Master of Revels?"

"They still seek him high and low. He is nowhere to be found."

"Too bad," Rand said with a frown. "I suspect there is much Leon could tell us."

David's smile was grim. "So thinks the king. He will not deal lightly with him if he shows himself."

"A fine reason for staying out of sight."

"Guilty or not," David replied in dry agreement.

A rustling sound came from behind the curtain. Both he and David heard it, Rand knew, though both pretended otherwise. "Where could he have gone?" he asked. "Who might he know that would hide him?"

"No one can say," David said. "He knew everyone, was beloved by the ladies, but had few friends."

"He can't have disappeared, not unless he made for the coast and a fast ship for the continent."

"Not impossible." David, without appearing to give it a moment's thought, moved to the tub where sat the cold, soap-scum-ladened water from the night before. Bending, he picked up Rand's hose, his doublet and shirt, draping them over his arm.

"No," Rand said thoughtfully, "but is it likely? Would he abandon all he knows here?" His thought was for the people the troubadour had known, especially for Isabel. In the Master of Revel's place, he would not have left her without some attempt to clear his name.

"You think he tried to kill the king?" David asked, tipping his head so he watched from the corners of his eyes.

"God alone knows. Any at the high table could have been the chosen victim."

"Or all of you," his squire said.

To that Rand made no answer. It was too true to require one.

"So we will spend the day searching, along with the others?"

"Would that I could, but the king will not allow it. Mayhap I can direct some manner of search party from the hall. I know naught else to do."

His squire picked up Isabel's shift from where it had landed near the foot of the bed. Shaking it out, he held it up a moment, then draped it across his arm. Rand thought he must intend to deliver it to Isabel's serving woman for washing, but refused to ask.

"You are certain you are equal to it?" the lad inquired, his gaze on what he was doing.

Rand glanced involuntarily at the bed. "I am certain."

"I meant because of the bashing you took during the melee, and your burns."

"Of course you did," Rand said on a growl as he walked to the door and held it open. "You will not return, after all, but meet me at the stables betimes. You may send my wife's serving woman to her, but not now. In an hour will do. Mayhap two."

"Aye," David said, his face without expression, though an imp of humor lay half-hidden in the blue depths of his eyes.

Rand slammed the door behind his squire. Turning away, he poured wine, added water, picked up the basket of fresh baked bread and approached the bed. The bed curtains opened and Isabel reached out one hand to take the wine. With the other, she caught his wrist and drew him into the haven within.

It was just before the midday meal, long hours after Rand had left her, that the message arrived for Isabel. She read it with some disbelief. Leon asked that she meet him in the abbey. He would await her coming.

She could guess why he had chosen the church. He could claim sanctuary if discovered, like so many others in recent years, notably Edward IV's queen and her children on the takeover of the throne by Richard III. Isabel wondered if the erstwhile Master of Revels remembered that Henry's men had violated sanctuary after the victory at Bosworth Field, and might do so again if hard-pressed.

She should not go. To be discovered with a man wanted by the king could be embarrassing, if not downright dangerous.

Nevertheless, Leon was a friend. Behind his flirtatious banter lay a kind heart. He had given her and her sisters a measure of security at court, had been their bulwark against rapacious scoundrels well before she was promised to Rand. Isabel could not believe he had attempted to harm anyone, especially her or Elizabeth. He was a lover of women, and valued them more than most men. He also protected them. That he would send word to her could only mean that his need was great. And why would it not be when every hand was turned against him? Now, of all times, he required loyal friends.

Added to that, she had a fearful need to see what he might have to say about the explosion. If she could discover from him what had caused it, who had set it off and why, would that not be beneficial?

Rand seemed to think the blast had been directed at all who sat at the high table. She could not agree. It was an unfortunate accident. That was all. Given the chance, Leon would explain it away and all could breathe easier.

The Master of Revels was no threat to her. Should she be seen with him, she could surely explain it to Rand. Her new husband had no cause to doubt her fidelity; he must know he was all the man she had use for at the moment. Not that she cared for him beyond the powerful allure of his body, of course, but she certainly had no strength to expend on another.

As for what Rand felt, she could not hazard a guess. He desired her, seemed enamored of her kisses and her touch, but men were a mystery in that regard. They took what they wanted and went about their affairs as if it meant nothing. Mayhap it didn't, and Rand would not care if she consorted with Leon.

She prayed that was so. She had seen his rage in battle and did not care to be the focus of it.

Oh, but surely no one would see her with Leon. No one need ever know she had spoken to him.

The abbey was deserted when she entered as everyone made ready for the main meal of the day. The stained-glass windows glowed in the dimness. Candles flickered, barely piercing the gloom, their smoke spiraling upward to form a blue-gray haze below the vast ceiling. Isabel genuflected, knelt to pray, then eased back onto the bench and sat in contemplation.

No one awaited her. No one came to seek

her out.

She sat staring at an image of the Virgin while her mind wandered to her wedding ceremony in the king's chapel. How distant it seemed, she thought, though it had taken place only yesterday. So much had happened. She recalled with heated cheeks the couplings she had shared with Rand behind the bed curtains. That was before she banished it with a guilty flush as being unsuited to her pure surroundings.

She wondered if the queen was well enough for the journey undertaken at the king's command. Did she fear the birth that was to come? Did she regret being parted from Henry as her time drew near, or was it a relief to withdraw from his solemn, demanding presence?

The women around Elizabeth would surely send for him when her labor began. Would he ride to her side, offer comfort to the woman he had married out of expediency and the need to solidify his reign? Or would he wait until he heard she had been delivered of the son he craved?

The child brought into the world would be Henry's heir, but it would also be the heir of its mother, Elizabeth of York. Did it ever occur to Henry, Isabel wondered, that he had usurped the throne from the woman who would bear his child? Did he ever consider that his son, if such was brought forth as promised him, would be the only truly legitimate male claimant to the throne in a direct line?

If it occurred, now and then, to gentle, fragile Elizabeth, she never mentioned it.

How long Isabel sat in the silent abbey, she did not know, though it was long enough to become weary of the hard seat. Once, a priest passed through, smiling at her with a gesture of benediction before he went on his way. An elderly woman entered, prayed and went away again. Two nuns came for ritual prayers, between which they whispered back and forth.

Leon did not appear. He had changed his mind, or else been prevented from coming.

Isabel rose to leave, making her way toward the great front door. She was some yards from it, just passing a darkened alcove, when a voice spoke from the shadows.

"Well met, milady. Stand where you are and listen. No! Do not turn."

That voice, she would swear, was not the melodious baritone of the Master of Revels. She strained to identify it, but the timbre was no more than a rough whisper. "Who are you?" she asked, staring straight ahead as directed. "What do you want?"

"I bear a message. If you would free yourself from your unwanted marriage, you must act. Someone will tell you what is required. Be vigilant. Wait for their coming. It will not be long."

The speaker did not linger for an answer. Footsteps receded, moving quickly. Though she whirled at their echo, she saw only a shadow flitting away in the gloom. A side-entrance door creaked open and closed again with a solid thud. The abbey was quiet once more.

Isabel shivered as if with a winter chill. She took a step, and then another. Abruptly she broke into a run. She did not slow until she was through the great doors of the abbey and out in the late-afternoon sun.

"Sweet Saint Catherine, Isabel! Where have you been? You look as if you've seen a ghost."

It was Cate who called out to her as she came toward her down the palace corridor with Marguerite on her heels. She moved swiftly to catch Isabel's uninjured hand, holding it between both her own. Marguerite hastened to her other side, putting an arm around her waist.

"What happened to you?" her younger sister echoed. "You were not at dinner just

237

now, nor was Braesford. We wondered if he was keeping you prisoner."

That possibility, being so far outside the mark, surprised a small spurt of nervous laughter from Isabel. "No, no, he would not stoop so low."

Immediately, she wondered how she could be so sure. She knew not, but she was sure indeed.

"He need not stoop at all, as far as I can see," Marguerite said in tones of gloom. "He has broken the curse now so has nothing to fear. Nor has any other man."

Isabel put her arm around Marguerite and began to walk again, gathering Cate on her other side. "Something has happened, it must have. Surely marriages have not been arranged for you already?"

"No, but nearly as bad," Marguerite complained. "We are being besieged, I do swear it. I have had six invitations to share a place at table. Never was I so glad to have a sister to fall back on as an excuse to refuse."

"Two ballads and a chanson have been dedicated to me, and four gentlemen have said they mean to speak to Graydon." Cate shook her head.

"We are doomed," Marguerite said with a moan, lowering her head to Isabel's shoulder and closing her eyes.

Isabel touched her cheek to her younger sister's head, resting it an instant against the small cap under her veil. "I wish there was something I could do, but . . ."

"You can't protect us forever, though you have watched over us like a ewe guarding her lambs since Mother died," Cate said with a sigh. "We must give thanks that we escaped being married off for so long."

"Or thank Graydon's greed," Isabel said with some asperity. "But really, I would think the rumors surrounding Rand would make your suitors think twice."

"He still has the freedom of the palace, which is no discouragement at all." Marguerite scowled. "Unless you believe he will soon be taken to prison?"

"No," Isabel said sharply, and was surprised at how painful the idea was to her. Had she not been half wishing for the same thing not so long ago?

"What has become of Braesford?" Cate asked. "Has he been taken ill, perchance? Were his injuries worse than they seemed? That might put off the others, you know."

"He has great powers of recovery," Isabel answered, avoiding her sister's eyes as she considered the proof she had of that statement.

"Or could we say, at least, that the curse

resulted in a Tobias Night?"

Isabel shook her head.

"You mean — Oh, Isabel!"

"We are truly wed," she said with a small shrug.

"I told you we were doomed," Marguerite said to Cate with grim satisfaction.

"Not entirely, not yet." Isabel went on to tell them what had occurred at the abbey.

"It almost sounds as if this man, whoever he may have been, expects you to do something to be rid of Braesford," Cate said with a scowl. "Has he bothered to look at him? Can he really think you able to harm such a fearsome knight?"

"Even if I would!"

"Does that mean you would not?" Cate leaned to search Isabel's face. "Do you like him as a husband?"

"Nothing of the kind," Isabel said stoutly. "It's only that there are worse fates." The memory of Rand as he hovered above her slipped through her mind, the sculpted perfection of his shoulders, the dark fastness of his eyes, his fierce concentration as he made love to her. To be denied that closeness, or the magic of his heat and power inside her, would be a loss. Not that it meant anything. Of course it did not.

Cate pursed her lips, but made no reply.

"What has this odd message you were given to do with Leon?" Marguerite asked. "Or had it anything at all?"

"I think it unlikely."

"So do I, for what would it avail the Master of Revels to remove Braesford? The king would never allow you to marry a mere troubadour."

"Nor would Leon expect it, which makes me think the request to meet was sent by someone else in his name."

Isabel squeezed her sister's slender waist as they walked. Though youngest of the three of them, Marguerite often had the clearest vision of people and the reasons for their actions. "Indeed, someone who noticed our friendship with him."

"Unless Leon thought he might be doing you a favor by making you a widow," Cate pointed out.

A frown crossed Isabel's face before she waved away the suggestion. "Neither of you have seen him?"

"He has quite disappeared," Cate said. "It's worrisome."

"I think he has been imprisoned," Marguerite declared.

"Oh, come."

Isabel gave her second sister a quelling look before turning back to the younger.

"By Henry, you mean?"

"Or someone acting under his authority. It stands to reason, does it not? Leon could be prevented from saying what happened to his machine and who may have tampered with it. It could be made to appear he is in the pay of the Yorkists who want Henry deposed. And it would keep him secure, betimes, should he be required as a sacrifice."

A sacrifice, a scapegoat.

That was precisely what she had thought about Rand, Isabel remembered. But if this was the way the wind blew, then did it not follow that the business of the fiery explosion and the disappearance of Mademoiselle Juliette were somehow connected?

What possible link could there be? Yes, and what could be the point of two scapegoats?

She and her sisters had reached an antechamber from which opened a number of the small chambers given over to courtiers, among them the one Isabel now shared with Rand. She glanced in that direction.

Her husband lounged in the open doorway with his back to the jamb and his arms crossed over his chest. His dark eyes rested on her, and his features had a grim cast.

"Oh, dear," Marguerite said under her breath. "He looks none too pleased."

Cate lifted a brow. "He looks hungry, I would say, as if he missed his dinner and expects you to make up for the loss, one way or another."

"Cate!" Isabel murmured in protest, though she could not gainsay her. A tremor of disquiet moved over her. Or could it be anticipation?

"Whatever his purpose, I believe we should only be in the way," Cate said as she dipped a small curtsy in Rand's direction. "Marguerite and I will leave you here, and hope to see you in the great hall this evening."

"That is," Marguerite added, "if he doesn't eat you before then."

Isabel made a small choked noise as the memory of Rand's mouth upon her sent hot blood pounding through her veins, making her breasts swell against her bodice. Her sisters turned inquiring looks upon her, but she ignored them. "I will be there betimes, but . . . but you need not leave us."

"Oh, I think we must," Cate said hurriedly as Rand shifted his tall form, coming erect.

"Heaven preserve you," Marguerite whispered.

Her sisters gave her a quick hug each and turned back the way they had come. Isabel moved on alone.

"Been saying your prayers?" Rand asked as she drew near, his voice like stone grating over stone.

"What makes you think so?" She entered the chamber with some wariness as he stepped back to permit it.

He followed her inside and closed the door. "Someone saw you at the abbey."

How could she trust him to believe she had gone to meet Leon, a man he knew as her admirer, from mere friendship and concern? Oh, and how could she tell him that she had been promised her freedom without him asking whether she would seek his death to gain it?

She could do neither. The anger of men was to be avoided at all costs. She had learned that lesson long ago. Removing her cap and veil, rubbing at the soreness where their weight had pulled at her scalp, she spoke a half-truth over her shoulder. "I missed mass from lying so long abed."

"It's to be hoped that you did not say a prayer to be spared the attentions of your husband."

His voice was close as he followed after her. He put his hands at her waist, halting her forward motion by pulling her against him. As she spoke, her reply came out in a gasp. "No. Why should I?"

"Because it is destined to be unanswered," he said in a low murmur, his breath warm against the side of her neck.

Shivering with reaction and what she barely recognized as remorse, she turned into his arms, slid her hands up the hard wall of his chest and twined them around his neck. He pulled her close and set his mouth to hers while smoothing his hands down over her hips to fit her against the hot, velvet-over-iron firmness between the columns of his set legs, hidden behind his doublet.

Neither partook of supper in the great hall during the long evening that followed, but it did not prevent them from feasting.

10

The court was not the same without Elizabeth of York, Rand thought as he bent over a lute he had found discarded on a bench in the great hall, plucking quietly at the strings. Though a gentle presence, she had exerted a beneficent effect that extended to its every corner. In her absence, the king was morose and short of temper. Courtiers exchanged sharp words over matters of procedure and precedence. Servants were slack in their duties and snappish with one another. The kitchen did not send forth its best efforts, whether to high table or low, and the silver and gold plate which graced the chests of the great hall had lost their sheen, turning dim with dust and fingerprints. Add the lack of a Master of Revels to arrange entertainment and the difference was complete.

Not that Rand blamed Henry for instantly removing his queen. She was meant to go, anyway, and who knew what tale someone might pour into her ears if she lingered? The king could give her some simplified version of the mystery of the missing child in future, but she did not need it now. Some said hearing of such an evil event could mark a child in the womb. That was without the fright caused by the explosion during the mummery.

A sense of strained anticipation lay over the palace. All waited for news from Winchester, of course, to learn whether Henry would have his heir or must undertake the onerous task of trying again. Still, it was more than that. Leon had not been found, though troops of men spread through the town and countryside, almost tearing it apart. No one had discovered how or why his hellish machine had belched flame and smoke, or who was meant to be the victim. No man came forward to accuse foe or friend. Whispers about plots to overthrow the king always drifted about, but no serious evidence of such a coalition had surfaced.

The more Rand considered the matter, the less he liked it. The machine had been a clumsy and uncertain method of eliminating the king. Far more deadly means of assassination had lain to the Frenchman's hand, if such was his intention. Poison was one, and a favorite at the French court. The thrust of a well-honed knife was another. A harquebus shot from a tower, an asp in the royal bed, a stray arrow from a longbow during the hunt — any of these could have accomplished the deed if a man had no care for his safety. The Master of Revels might have escaped any whiff of blame with them, while his *La danse macabre* pointed squarely in his direction.

On the other hand, someone who wanted to be rid of the king could have seen the potential for destruction and acted accordingly. Leon, a man of swift intelligence, may well have discerned the plot as it unfolded and made his escape to save his neck from stretching.

There was one other possibility that Rand could see. The death dance of small souls within that fiery maw of steel and gears had borne a disturbing parallel to the newborn's death by fire that was laid to his account. Had Leon thought to flay him, and by extension the king, with a reminder of that supposed destruction? Did Leon, a Frenchman, know Mademoiselle Juliette d'Amboise well enough to have a care for her fate and her child?

Rand, frowning over a complicated run of

chords in the melody he played, considered how best to discover the answers to these questions. They must be found, else it could mean his life. Henry had stayed his hand these many days from past friendship and gratitude, but that could not last forever. If Mademoiselle Juliette and her child did not appear soon, the king would be forced to act.

A prickling awareness raised the hair on the back of Rand's neck. He looked up, his gaze settling unerringly on Isabel as she traversed the great hall in the company of her two sisters, as usual. She inclined her head as she met his gaze across the room, but did not smile. It was not a slight, regardless of how it felt, but only recognition of court etiquette which said a lady should not publicly favor her husband. Nor did he smile, though it was hard to prevent the tilt of his mouth in secret pleasure as he surveyed her from top to toe, lingering on all the divers curves in between.

He had watched her dress just that morning, lying back in bed while Gwynne arrayed her for the day in sea-green samite over a linen shift with a ruffled neckline. It was he who had chosen the sleeves the color of an autumn sky that she wore with it, also the knots of blue and green ribbon that held them in place. Blue for fidelity, he had selected, a private conceit and secret pleasure.

He also knew precisely what she wore underneath her pristine splendor, and that was nothing whatever. He knew because he had dismissed her serving woman and taken advantage of that fact, taken his lovely wife by simply flipping up her skirts and draping her knees over his arms while she lay back upon their bed. He had made the bed curtains sway as if in a high wind, and felt still the imprint at his waist where she had clamped him to her with her slender legs.

She was stronger than she looked.

God's blood, but when would he have his fill of her?

He could not think it would be anytime soon. It was all he could do not to rise up this instant, in imitation of his unruly rod, fling down the lute and take her straight to their chamber.

She fascinated him. He could watch her for hours, absorbing the way she moved, the tender curve of her cheek, the grace with which she sipped from their wine goblet or pushed her veil back from her face. The sheen of her skin, like the luster of a pearl, was amazing to him. Her soft yet firm curves, her warm, damp hollows, drew him as if by unseen bonds. Her mind was a mystery he yearned to solve. Steeped in reserve and private deliberations, she seemed cool, proud, given to calculating her every move. Underneath, however, she was warm and caring, quick to sympathize with the pain of others, fair and intelligent in her judgments. She had not a mean-spirited bone in all her fair body, nor did she speak ill of any soul.

She honored her vows, both in word and deed, coming to him in bed without shrinking or protest. And once there, her response to him was sweet beyond imagining, springing from a vein of sensual delight so wide and deep he had yet to find its limit.

He had sought it. Indeed he had, and, pray God, soon would again.

Without conscious thought, his fingers found the tune of a lascivious French ballad about a lad and lass who go a-berrying on a fine summer's day, and all the ways they found to enjoy their berries, all the places they managed to stain with juice while resting in the shade. And he grinned as he saw a flush rise to Isabel's cheekbones, saw the hot, leaf-green flash of her eyes, before she turned away.

He wondered if there were berries to be had in the pantries of the palace.

Isabel's sister Cate, Rand noticed, leaned to whisper a comment as they strolled. On her other side, Marguerite smothered a laugh. They passed quickly through the room, though Rand noticed that their footsteps matched the tempo of the notes that trickled from his fingers. And as they reached the doorway that led to the queen's solar, where the ladies of the court were still embroidering a bedcover for the much-hoped-for young prince, Isabel stopped. With one hand on the door frame, she turned, looked back and smiled into his eyes.

Rand half rose from his seat to follow her. He might have, might have taken her arm and walked her to their chamber, if not for a slurred voice that came from behind him.

"Lucky bastard, you are, for all ye don't deserve her."

Rand turned to see Viscount Henley gazing with glassy fixation at the place where Isabel had stood. His lips were loose and his eyes watery as he raised an ale tankard to his mouth. Sweat made circular stains under the arms of his shirt, the device of a bear embroidered on the tabard he wore was spotted by the remains of more than one meal and a sour, animalistic smell indicated that he had either been drunk for days or else had no affection for bathing.

Rage boiled in Rand's veins and he straightened, took a step toward the viscount.

Henley slewed around toward him, took a hasty step back. A bench caught him behind his knees. He sat down with such a solid thump that ale sloshed into his lap. He looked, suddenly, as if he would cry.

Rand's anger faded as he considered the man's drunken misery. His first impulse had been to let holes into the big oaf's skin with a few well-placed sword thrusts. Being the wedded husband of Lady Isabel, however, he could afford to be generous.

Added to that, Henley was seldom encountered when not at Graydon's side. He was doubtless alone now because Isabel's stepbrother was laid up with his tournament injuries. He would be at loose ends, and ripe for someone to share his drunken grievances.

"I could not agree more that I don't deserve my lady," Rand said in smooth urbanity. "No man could, as she is without peer."

"She'd have been mine but for Henry's interference." The words were brooding, laced with impotent fury.

"Would she indeed?"

Henley wagged his great head. "Graydon gave me his hand on it. It was set in all but deed. Then . . ." He trailed off, buried his face in his tankard again.

"No contract had been signed, surely." Propping his foot on the bench beside Graydon's companion, Rand flipped Isabel's favor that he yet wore tied at his elbow out of his way and began to finger the berry song from the lute once more. He listened intently, however, for marriage contracts could be binding, making any later ceremony null and void.

"No time to draw it up, so he said to me. He was talking to Henry behind my back, even then."

Rand allowed himself a breath of silent relief. "But you remain comrades, the two of you. You rode to Braesford with Graydon, after all, as well as in the tourney. Truly, you have a generous spirit."

Henley looked owlishly wise. His mouth worked for a moment before he found words. "Graydon said all I'd to do was wait. The curse of the Graces would get you, then 'twould be my turn."

"Your turn to be done in by it? No great honor, that," Rand commented as pleasantly as he was able.

"My turn with Lady Isabel. But the curse

254

has not got ye yet, damn your eyes. Mayhap you've beat it." Henley laughed, a rough, mocking sound, and flicked his fingers toward Isabel's sleeve tied to Rand's arm. "Or not. You wear your wife's favor still. Could be you're under her spell and don't know it. Could be you're to die by inches."

Henley was swaying where he sat. Rand stopped playing, put a hand on the man's shoulder to steady him. "It may well be that I am in her thrall," he said in grim sincerity. "If so, I pray it continues. Well, and that no one decides to help this curse along."

"Oh, aye, best watch out," Henley said with a wink that made him look cross-eyed. He laughed again.

Rand put the lute aside. "So Graydon proposed the match between me and the Lady Isabel. It was not Henry's thought."

"Wouldn't say that. 'Twas the king's will, right enough." Henley was silent a moment, lost in ponderous thought. "Graydon liked it, though. He'll get more from Braesford's rents, see, than from her inherited lands."

The only way Isabel's stepbrother could lay hands on the rents from Rand's estate was if Isabel was left a widow with a child. As her nearest male relative and head of her family, Graydon would take control of her inheritance from a dead husband, at least until she remarried. If he gave her to Henley betimes, it was unlikely the viscount would challenge his continued use of the income, or at least so long as he shared it.

And if she was left a widow without a child, she would still inherit a portion of Braesford, though she must return to Graydon Hall and another marriage arranged by stepbrother or king. Braesford Hall and the majority of its lands would descend to Rand's next of kin. As he had none other than his half brother, what were the odds that William would be handed the prize and the lady's hand with it?

These thoughts were not new, but were less comfortable now than before he had taken Isabel into his bed.

A widow with no close male relative could claim much more independence. Barring interference from the king, she could collect her own rents, buy and sell property, invest in commerce and other such ventures. If he was to hang, Rand thought, it might as well be for a death he had caused. Perhaps he would see to it that Isabel was minus a stepbrother before he was gone.

"Graydon is unlikely to enjoy the income he covets," Rand said. "You might tell him so."

"Aye, and I have. Told him, too, that this

curse of the Three Graces is a false tale made up among his sisters. He didn't like hearing it."

"Was that," Rand asked in his softest tone, "when he broke Lady Isabel's finger?"

Henley frowned. "He did that?"

"Aye, and took joy of it, used it to force her to marry."

"Shouldn't have." Henley attempted to drain his tankard but found it empty. He sat staring into it for long seconds. Shaking his head, muttering something about more ale, he pushed himself off the bench and shambled away.

Rand let him go, though his gaze rested on the retreating figure. It was possible he had done more harm than good with his revelations.

No matter what came of them, the results would not be allowed to touch Isabel. He would see to that.

The morning passed with excruciating slowness. Rand chafed at the enforced inactivity. He might as well be shut up in the Tower prison as to be kept kicking his heels about the palace. He ached to be in the saddle, to be riding out with the men-at-arms that still quartered the meadows and marshes, hills and valleys outside town, searching for Mademoiselle Juliette and

Leon. It almost seemed instinct would lead him to one or the other of them if he was allowed to join the hunt.

Midday arrived, tolled by the abbey bell. Dinner would not be long in coming. He made his way toward the chamber allotted to him and Isabel, in part to make sure his hands were clean before sharing food and drink with her, but also because he expected her to do the same and hoped to steal a kiss. Or something more if she was so inclined.

He whistled as he approached, trilling the self-same air he had played earlier. It lingered in his head, maddening him with its sprightliness and the images of playful lovemaking it brought to mind. His thoughts were running once more to the use of berries when he emerged in the antechamber that led to the chamber.

A man straightened from where he hovered in the shadows on the far side of the long room, a somberly dressed figure in black and white. He adjusted the wide hat he wore with its fan of swan feathers, tipping it at a jaunty angle that concealed much of his face. At a sauntering pace, he moved off toward another door that gave onto a maze of corridors and the rabbit's warren of the old palace's back reaches.

The walk was familiar. Rand frowned,

undecided. It couldn't be. No, surely not. Leon could not be here in the palace when half the soldiery in Henry's service rattled up hill and down dale on his track. Could he?

Rand turned his footsteps in the direction taken by the other man. The gallant of the big hat stepped up his pace, reaching the far door and passing through it. Rand broke into a run. The next moment, he heard racing steps ahead of him. Bursting through the half-open door, he glanced right, glanced left, heard the faintest jingle of bells and caught a flash of white and black descending the squeaking treads of a servant's stair. He gave chase.

Cat and fiendishly agile mouse, he and his quarry sprinted along passages, swirled through chambers made jewellike with tapestries and Saracen carpets, crashed through storerooms and lumber rooms. They slid across a court slick with water and old soap scum, slapped through dangling laundry and ducked down a narrow alley. Emerging in a courtyard that had been turned into an abattoir, they dodged around menservants armed with cleavers, circled each other about vats where hogs' heads were being rendered and leaped gingerly through a far corner given over to eviscerating chickens. The clatter of wings marked the Master of Revel's bypass of a pigeon roost.

Moments later, the figure clad in black and white sought the dusty shadows of a stable where rows of horses, destriers, palfreys and rounceys lifted curious heads over half doors. Rand knew his way now. He swerved toward the rear doors of the long building. Plunging to a halt, he flattened his back against a gate shaped like a horseshoe. As Leon whipped through it, he caught his doublet in a hard grasp, slinging him into the wall at his side with a solid thud of flesh meeting stone. Then he bore him down to the ground.

They breathed with the wheeze of a blacksmith's bellows. Sweat streaked their faces and matted their hair. Leon looked half-dead, with a lump like a hawk's egg forming at his hairline and blood trickling from his nose. His eyes were glazed, and in his olive skin lay a blue-tinted pallor.

Rand had pig's blood on his shoes, chicken feathers on his sleeve and a complete lack of mercy in his soul. Hovering above the fugitive with a knee pressing into his heaving chest, he slipped his knife from its sheath and held the point to Leon's throat.

"What were you about near my lady's

chamber?" he asked in hard demand. "You have the space of a single breath to answer before I carve you a new airway."

"Nothing, I swear . . . swear it."

Rand increased the pressure of his blade point. "What did you there, then?"

"The lady is gracious . . . kind."

"How kind, exactly?" he inquired while his heartbeat drummed in his ears.

"She speaks . . . understands . . . Does not hold herself above me. I thought . . ."

This did not have the sound of assignation. Rand eased the pressure of his knee a bit, also his knifepoint. "Thought what?"

"That she might tell me . . . tell me what you and the king have done with my Juliette."

Rand sat back on his heels. Whatever he had expected, it was not this. "Your Juliette?"

"Mine," Leon said in strangled certainty. "Mine before Henry turned her head with jewels and fine clothes, before she thought she might be his lady mistress or even his queen. Mine, even as she warmed his bed and his cold heart."

This was lèse-majesté, indeed, to bed the mistress of a king. "You could be hung for admitting such a thing, or made to disappear without a trace."

261

"I don't care, never did. Juliette felt . . . otherwise."

"So I would imagine. Unlike with the Saracens, an English king doesn't sew an unfaithful concubine into a sack and toss her off a sea cliff but may still be less than kind."

"Ah, she never feared for herself."

"For you, then?"

Leon managed a nod and a smile that was both sickly and whimsical. "For the father of her babe."

It was beyond belief, the smiling duplicity of women, Rand thought. He had played host to Mademoiselle Juliette for six weeks or more, had sat with her at his table, spoken with her during long evenings while she sat stitching on small garments. He had walked with her in the first throes of labor, and stood beside her while she was delivered of a daughter. Never in all that time had she breathed a single word to indicate the child she carried was not of the king's get.

"You think Henry discovered the dupe and has done away with her?"

"I don't know. I can't find out, can't find her, and it's driving me mad."

It would. Rand could imagine how he might feel if it was Isabel who . . . He pulled up short before the thought was complete.

"What did you and Juliette expect," he asked in strained patience, "a nice stipend to live on while you continued the affair? Or were you supposed to come and take her away?"

"What chance had I of removing her? Or that you would let her go except at Henry's command?"

"She went so willingly when the escort arrived, as if she expected it."

"We had made no plans, lacked the money for it," the troubadour insisted, speaking more evenly as he caught his breath. "She may have thought she could evade Henry's attention and come to me once she was back at Westminster."

It was vaguely possible. People were able to convince themselves of almost anything. Except Juliette had never reached the town.

"That mummery the other night, *La danse macabre,*" Rand said, "the woman with the dead child was meant to be Mademoiselle Juliette instead of the queen."

"I wanted to make Henry think. That is, if he is holding her somewhere. As for the queen, it should have caused no more disturbance than any priest's homily on the fires of hell. Yet I do pray there have been no ill effects."

"Even as it's Henry's child Elizabeth carries, his true child this time?"

"You think I wish him ill?"

Rand gave him a straight look. He had felt murderous with jealousy himself just moments ago. He could hardly imagine what it must be like to suffer it for months on end. "Don't you?"

"I meant to present a lesson in humility, to show him that life is weak and death is strong. My dancing dead were to say to all, *As you are, so we once were. As we are, so you will be.*"

Rand grunted in recognition of the sentiment before he went on. "You did not take the role of grim reaper upon yourself, then?"

"Never! The mechanism was not meant to burst apart. It was supposed to pass by the high table as a reminder of what rumors say happened to Juliette's child. Someone tampered with it."

"Mayhap someone who wanted the king to have a more desperate lesson. Who could have done it? Who had access to your workshop?"

Leon closed his eyes and shook his head. Whether it was from despair or reluctance to speculate was impossible to say.

"You're quite sure? There is no one who came by while you worked on that contraption, no one who asked more questions than usual?"

"Many were curious, but none more so than others, as I recall. And I was not always there."

"You have no wider reason to want the king and his queen dead? Or if not that, then warned they might be?"

The Master of Revels lifted his lashes to meet Rand's gaze, his dark chocolate eyes opaque. "What are you asking? Do you want to know if I am an emissary of some foreign government, a tool for their bidding? There are diplomats enough at court for that role."

That much was certainly true, Rand thought. He gave a short nod.

"My concern is for my daughter, tender new babe that she is, and for her mother, who is my love. I will not rest until I know what the king has done with them."

"And if he has done nothing, if he is as much in the dark as you are as to their whereabouts, just as afraid for the child he believes to be his?"

"Then I will discover who had taken them, and where. If they have suffered hurt, if they no longer live, then I will not rest until I have returned pain for pain, death for death."

It was a vow Rand could understand.

"Should it prove you speak the truth," he said deliberately, "then I will join you in it."

"And be a welcome ally," the Master of Revels said, his eyes clear at last.

Rand rose to his feet, held out his hand to help the other man to his feet. Leon took his arm at the wrist, grasped hard. He began to pull himself up.

Abruptly, he jerked Rand off balance, shoved him against the stable wall. Then he was gone, speeding like a parti-colored shadow in black and white, vanishing into the maze of outbuildings that served the palace.

Rand watched him go with no attempt to chase after him. He had much to think about, much to do to discover the truth of the story he'd heard. It would be time enough to lay the Master of Revels by the heels if it was shown that he had lied.

For now, he had another need altogether, one that flayed his mind raw and shriveled his heart in his chest, though he would not shrink from it. He required to hear just how much his lady wife knew of what he had learned, how much she had been keeping from him.

11

Isabel roused from a ravishing dream to feel an exquisite caress on the very peak of her breast. So sensitive had she become to such things of late that she was instantly awash in desire. She made a small sound deep in her throat and tried to turn toward that touch. She could not. Rand lay with one elbow propped on the mattress beside her and a heavy knee across hers, so she was wedged between his arm and his lower body.

She slept without clothing, as most did in summer. He had eased the sheet from her so her breasts were bare. Now he touched her with only the sword-calloused surface of one palm, brushing in small circles above her nipple so he barely skimmed the tight and tender bud.

She lifted her lashes by slow degrees, still not fully awake. Her husband's face was serious, absorbed. He watched what he was doing, and her reaction, as if nothing had ever been so fascinating. To be touched with such attentiveness was stirring beyond any mere caress.

"You are late to bed this night," she said with the beginning of a smile.

"I had things to do."

"Did you?" she asked, but with little curiosity. There was heat in the depths of his gaze that she had learned to recognize. Sleeping was not his intention, she thought, now that he had joined her on the feather mattress. He had discarded his clothing, was completely, rampantly, naked.

"I needed to go a-berrying."

A small frown pleated the skin between her brows. She wasn't sure she had heard aright. "Berrying?"

"For these." He took his palm from her breast and reached to take up a small crock that sat on the mattress near her shoulder.

The crock held raspberries. Their sweet, mellow scent drifted to her. A faint inkling of his intention touched her as she recalled his earlier song, though she could scarcely credit it. "Hardly a task for a knight," she said, her voice a little husky.

"Oh, I didn't pick them myself, but only searched them out in town."

Reaching into the bowl, he took a handful. Gaze intent, he placed the ruby-red berries, one by one, in a deep semicircle from one collarbone to the other, so the line curved just above her nipples. Some few berries would not stay in place on the milky-pale hillocks they traversed, but tumbled down into the valley between them. He bent his head to pick up the truants with lips and tongue and crunch them between his white teeth.

A drawing sensation invaded her lower body. She squirmed a little beneath him. "Rand . . ."

"Shh," he said, his warm breath drifting over her breasts.

"What are you doing?"

"Making a necklace to replace the Order of the Garter you put away." Another pair of berries fell from their places and he followed them, leaving a trail of kisses along their path.

"It isn't necessary," she protested on a gasp. "Only let me up, and —"

"Do not deny me, I beg. I have been thinking of this all day."

"Have you?" The surface of her chest felt on fire. Pulsing heat swirled in her veins. Her heartbeat throbbed under her breasts, adding to the instability of his effort at edible jewelry.

He tipped his head in solemn assent as,

abandoning the raspberry chain, he made a small pyramid of berries in the valley where the fallen had congregated. "Since I saw you in the great hall, my mouth has been parched for the taste of these, and of you."

What woman would not be seduced by such an admission, let alone the sweet suction of his mouth upon her as he captured a berry and her nipple with it? She closed her eyes as intoxication flowed in her veins and the tender, feminine core of her grew overheated, swollen. Though one of her arms was trapped between their bodies, the other was free, and she lifted her hand, threading her fingers into his hair.

He groaned in satisfaction, or so it seemed. A moment later, she felt him shift, reach for something, perhaps more berries.

The next sensation against her skin was different, a sprinkling feeling, as light as a feather. Through her lashes, she watched pale gold sugar drift down from his fingertips, falling onto the berries he had placed. It must have required considerable effort with mortar and pestle to grind it so fine, she thought in near incoherence. Or mayhap it had been David who had been put to that labor. Pray God he had no idea what his master intended with it.

"They will stain, the berries will," she said

with tried reason. "What will Gwynne think?"

"I care not. If she says aught, send her to me." Rand went on in the same pensive, conversational tone, his gaze rapt as he took another pinch of sugar, watched it drift over her skin. "I saw a friend of yours today."

"Did . . . you?" she asked with a catch in her voice as he began, quite gently, to crush raspberries into the sugar-sweetness with a single hard fingertip.

"Leon, Master of Revels."

Her eyes flew open. "Truly?"

"He seemed quite well. Did you know he was still in the palace?" He spoke against her skin, just before the velvety warmth of his tongue lifted a droplet of sweetened raspberry juice from her nipple, then harried the sensitive bud for more.

"How . . . how should I?" she answered on a ragged whisper.

"He was not far from our chamber here. I thought you might have been expecting a visit."

She gave a small shake of her head. "I had no idea he was near."

Rand pushed another raspberry to the peak of the same rose-red nipple that held his attention. "He wanted to speak with you, felt you would be sympathetic. He

271

seemed . . . reluctant to accept me as confidant in your stead, but was finally persuaded."

Her head was beginning to clear, caused in large part by the hint of steel she heard beneath the quiet timbre of Rand's voice. Ignoring the throbbing between her thighs as best she might, she said, "You fought?"

"How could you think so? Your Leon spoke freely, as he had questions for me in his turn. He wished to know, you see, if I could direct him to Mademoiselle Juliette."

"Mademoiselle — but why?"

He looked up, his gaze bleak. "I thought you knew. He is troubled over her health and well-being — given that he is her lover and the father of her babe."

"No," she whispered, her eyes wide as she searched his face. It was quite impossible, she was sure of it.

"I have his word on it."

"But that would mean . . ."

"That he has been unfaithful to you."

"Not at all," she said in distraction. If Leon wished Rand to believe such a tale, he must have reason. She should know what it was before she said more. "I told you there was only friendship between us. I was thinking of the king, of how he will feel if he hears of such betrayal."

"And what if," he asked in contemplative tones, "Henry has heard it already?"

She sat up, pushing Rand away from her so suddenly that he was thrown back, half off the bed, before he came upright again with the flex of stone-hard stomach muscles. "Then he may have sent the men for Mademoiselle Juliette, after all," she pointed out. "He could be keeping her shut away until he can be certain to whose child she gave birth."

"Or he can be preventing her from making a claim against the royal purse for her bastard."

"While you are suspected of its murder. That's infamous!"

Instead of an answer, he supported himself on one elbow again, reaching out with his forefinger to follow the trail of raspberry juice and bits of sugared berries that ran from between her breasts to her navel. Eyes shuttered, he smeared the juice down her abdomen and into the triangle of soft, gold-brown hair between her closed thighs. With a soft sound of disapproval, he said, "Just look what you've gone and done."

"I didn't do anything!"

She came to a breathless halt as he probed among the fallen berries with insinuating thoroughness, raised his finger and licked it.

He closed his eyes, groaning with pleasure.

"Rand?" she said in a different tone altogether, one strained in its softness. Heat flared through her, scalding her like the hot, sweet moisture that seeped between her thighs. She forgot to think, forgot even to breathe.

"What?" He felt for the crock of raspberries without taking his eyes from her. Locating it, he emptied it into the small V-shaped opening where her legs came together.

"I don't see . . ." she began a little incoherently.

"I do, but no matter. More important business is at hand." He dipped again into the cluster of crushed and sugared raspberries that bejeweled her soft curls, and sucked the results into his mouth.

"You mean . . ."

He heaved a sigh of long suffering and turned to his stomach above her, shifting his weight until she opened her legs so he could lodge his upper body between them. Resting on his elbows, he sighed again, blowing his warm breath across her belly, against the center of her being, as he drawled, "It appears I must go a-berrying again."

Isabel roused as Rand left their bed at

daybreak. She watched him covertly as he moved about the shadowed darkness of the chamber, bathing in cold water, dressing without David's aid in the clothing he had discarded the night before. His bruises from the tournament were fading, she saw as he pulled on his hose, the cut on his forehead almost healed. He had threatened to remove the stitches with his knife tip yesterday, desisting only when she said he would leave more of a scar.

He reached for his shirt, turning it right-side out. She watched the muscles that rippled in his back and along his sides as he pulled it on. She could almost feel them under her fingertips, between her legs. Memories of the night before drifted in her mind and slow heat moved from her curled toes to her hairline. Had she done those things, made those noises, pleaded in such abject need?

She must have. She felt sticky with sugar, berry juice and other liquids she did not care to name. She was incredibly tender in various places due to his fervent attention there. And she could feel, almost certainly, the prick of a raspberry seed under one hip.

Dear God in heaven, were all lovers so tender yet insatiable, demanding yet careful? She could not think so. Husbands, from what she had gathered, most certainly were not.

The mere thought of him tasting her, filling her, plunging into her with a cadence that matched the hard, swift beat of her heart sent a rash of goose bumps shivering over her skin. Almost, she called out to him, reached out for him.

She held back with stringent effort. She must not cling. The desire that had moved him the night before seemed forgotten this morning. He had not touched her before sliding from the bed, did not glance her way now. His mind bent on whatever task or errand taking him abroad, he left the room without a backward glance.

Or it might have been from consideration, because he preferred to let her rest now to be ready when next he desired her, she thought with a sigh. That was acceptable.

Instead of sleeping again, she rose at once. Moving quickly, she flipped the sheets up over the berry stains, and then used the cold water Rand had left to wash the stickiness from her skin. With that done, she turned to her chest to search out something to wear. She hoped to be away from the chamber before Gwynne arrived with her bread and watered wine, before her serving woman found the evidence of how she had passed a part of the night. It was not that she cared overmuch for what Gwynne thought, but she was in no mood to hear her scold.

She was not swift enough. She was still kneeling in front of the chest when Gwynne swept into the chamber with tray in hand. There was nothing to be done except wrap a cloak around her against the early-morning coolness and settle upon a stool to receive her breakfast.

Gwynne bustled about the chamber while Isabel ate. She picked up Rand's discarded clothing, took away the water left from where they had bathed to dump it down the stool of the garderobe. Returning, she laid out a fresh shift, also a gown of plum silk with a wide and heavy band of rose embroidery at the hem, and a cone-shaped cap, a truncated hennin, for Isabel to wear with her veil.

"My hair," Isabel began as Gwynne turned toward the bed, but it was too late. The serving woman flung back the sheets Isabel had pulled up and stood staring. Finally, she turned.

"You had your monthlies just before the wedding, milady. Are you injured? Is there aught I can do?"

Isabel felt hot all over, but also knew a

mad desire to crow with laughter. "It is not blood."

"But, milady . . ."

"Sir Rand had a powerful craving for raspberries, and brought them to bed with him. They . . . spilled."

"Ah." Gwynne turned back to the bed, but not before a flash of understanding passed over her face. "You failed to notice the accident, I see, so lay in the berries. No doubt you were busy with other things."

"Yes." Isabel allowed a moment to pass before she spoke again. "Are all men dedicated to bed sport?"

"It's my belief they think of little else."

"But do they . . . ?"

"What they do about it depends on the man, and on his lady," she answered with stolid practicality.

Isabel let that dry assessment pass while watching as Gwynne stripped the feather mattress of its sticky sheets, then covered it again with fresh ones brought from some linen press. She tried to think of any other man of her acquaintance who might give lovemaking so much attention as Rand, but could not imagine it. Their aim seemed to be for their own pleasure in most things, which would surely carry into the bed-chamber. The only one who appeared at all likely to view it as a time of endless mutual joy was Leon. But though he might be a tender and even inventive lover, he appeared to lack Rand's hard strength and stamina.

It was a conundrum, that someone with no claim to be a gentleman should display so surely the gallantry of a courtly knight.

"Do you believe, Gwynne," she asked after a moment, "that the love of a knight for his lady as shown in the tales of the troubadours is as pure as they pretend? Did a knight, good and true, never bed the lady who held his devotion?"

"Faugh!" the serving woman answered with disdain while fluffing a feather pillow. "As if that would be enough for either of them. No, no, the service a knight offered his lady did not stop with throwing down his cloak to protect her dainty feet from mud or even laying down his life. He laid her down, too, mark my words, and followed his lady's every command thereafter."

Her command. It was an intriguing idea. What might she command from Rand?

By all the saints, what ailed her? She wanted nothing from him. She was not interested in her husband's services, had no desire to initiate them, certainly none in prolonging them.

That someone seemed intent on removing

him from her life should be a secret joy. She should be out spreading news of it, extolling the power of the curse of the Graces and predicting its triumph. It had not saved her from marriage as before, but that was not, in all truth, what it promised. It only foretold disaster for any who took a Graydon bride without love, and so it had transpired. The outcome of that happenstance might yet free her.

Free, she longed to be free. She wanted to have charge of her life, to be able to come and go without answering to any man. She yearned to live without worrying about the censure of others, without having to account for where she went and what she did there, what she spent from her purse and how she would use it. Yes, freedom was her dream.

At the same time, she was contrary enough to long for a place where she belonged by right, where she was safe, protected, cherished. Could she ever have both? It seemed unlikely.

Yet she did feel safe while Rand was near. More than that, the passion she discovered in his arms was a constant amazement, one she had not yet tired of exploring. Nor had the novelty palled of seeing him gloriously naked in bath or bed, touching him, taking him inside her. Though some small resentment lingered at being forced into wedlock, she could not bear the thought of him being hanged. Nor could she see any freedom in his death, as it would only mean her return to Graydon's power once more.

She had not seen her stepbrother since her wedding day. He was better now, or so she had been told. Thinking of him was a reminder that he had an explanation to make for the attack on Rand, and answers that he needed to supply.

It might as well be this morning.

Graydon was having his morning bread and wine in his chamber when she arrived. At her request to speak to him, sent in by his manservant, he joined her in the antechamber. He had pulled on a doublet over his shirt and hose, but that was the end of it. It appeared he had not bathed, shaved or combed his hair in days. He walked with a stick and had no boot on his left foot. His groan, as he dropped onto the bench beside her, was followed by a strangled oath.

"How do you fare?" she asked, running her gaze over the purple-and-yellow splotches that still decorated his face, and the scabbed skin at his forehead. "Are you recovering from the tournament?"

"Well enough," he said with heavy sarcasm, "though you've taken your time coming to find out."

He was right; she had been remiss. It had simply not occurred to her that he might expect more than common courtesy. He had always been older, rougher, with no inclination to linger in the women's solar with her and her sisters even when residing in the same house. Hunting was his passion, and fighting. As far as she knew, he had no others.

"Cate and Marguerite visited, I believe, and I sent Gwynne to deliver such comfits as might aid you."

"Calf's feet jelly and chicken broth. What good was such swill to me?"

"Not a lot, as you threw them at her head."

"Bloody-minded old witch. She's more likely to poison a man than cosset him. You brought better to a sickroom when no more than twelve. I well remember from when I had my head split open by a staff."

So did she. Her mother had sent her to him with a spiced-milk-and-wine posset. He had exposed himself to her and laughed when she ran away.

"I am here now," she said evenly. "Are you in pain? Do you think your leg permanently injured?"

"It should be well enough in a day or two,

no thanks to Braesford. It's my belief he wanted to kill me."

Isabel did not flinch from his hard stare. "From where I sat, it appeared you and Henley struck the first blows, and those from behind. I don't believe you would have minded if he had died."

"He escaped by the devil's own luck."

"So it was a deliberate attack."

"It was a melee," he countered with a scowl directed at the end of his stick. "Your husband was on the other side. Though I'll admit to being of a mind to cut him down to size with a well-placed whack or two."

Down to whose size? she wondered. In that instant, her husband seemed both a bigger and better man. "And that's all?"

"What else should there be?" he asked, his eyes narrowing under bushy brows while uneasiness flitted across his coarse features.

"According to Rand's squire, his mail shows that your sword was not blunted." It was Gwynne who had passed on that information, received as she and David went about their tasks together.

"These things happen."

"Particularly when they are planned." She hesitated before going on in careful neutrality. "Did you arrange it, Graydon? Or did someone else suggest what a fine comeuppance it would be if Braesford fell during the contest?"

"Think you I need someone to do my brainwork for me?" he asked in growling disdain.

"What I think is that you have made your resentment of Braesford too clear. There are those who might find it convenient."

"And it bothers you that they should? You've gone over to the enemy." A sneer lifted his upper lip. "Trust a woman to favor the man who gets under her skirts."

Hot color rose to her face. She clenched her hands in her lap to control her urge to slap his face. "That is uncalled for, particularly as you forced me to marry."

"A bad bargain it was, too, scraping together a dowry for you when I should have had the lot. But I'll have it back, see if I don't."

"What are you saying?" she demanded while alertness tingled in her veins.

" 'Tis a matter beyond the ken of a female. Best you go back to warming Braesford's bed for him and leave such things to men."

"You meant Braesford will soon be dead, and you able to enjoy my widow's portion."

"I don't depend on it, though I'll not deny it would suit me."

"What do you hear of the accusation

against him? What is the word in the town or among the men-at-arms?"

He shrugged. "Nothing much. All await the king's decision."

And what was the king waiting upon? First, it had been the wedding, she thought, and mayhap the outcome of the melee. But now?

Henry could be delaying until after the birth of his promised son. In the celebration over that event, with its promise of security for the realm vested in a child with both York and Lancaster blood in its veins, he might feel the disappearance of a mere country knight would go unnoticed. So it might, she saw with a sinking feeling in her chest.

She had no special fondness for her marriage, yet this did not seem a fair way to be done with it. That was naturally her only concern, the fairness of it.

"Hear you anything of the mistress gone missing or . . ." She paused, trying to think how much she might be giving away. Graydon had been present when the indictment against Rand had been read, however, so knew full well that it was the disappearance of both mother and child that was laid at his door.

"Or the king's get? Not a word. I wager

the woman knew her days as Henry's whore were over and has found another to tup her, royal or not."

To tup her. What a telling phrase that was, Isabel thought, as a tup was any heavy, swinging object such as a pendulum or battering ram. It was also vulgar in the extreme, an aspect she chose to overlook in her relief. The king's get, Graydon had said, rather than Leon's. That possibility, however inaccurate it might be — and she had compelling reason to believe it false — was not yet common coin.

"But then Braesford could have sent the woman away himself," her stepbrother went on with sly cunning in his eyes. "He may be sneaking off every day to enjoy the king's leavings."

Her glance held a full measure of scorn. "At the risk of hanging? I somehow doubt it."

"But he might think it worth the chance, being so given to pleasing the ladies," her stepbrother said. "I've heard he had a reputation for such *plaisance* while across the channel."

Her chest felt as if a rope constricted it, closing off her breath. She tried not to picture Rand with other women, noble, sophisticated ladies of a foreign court. Yet it would explain his dedication to her pleasure, his slow and careful tending of it.

Plaisance, a word that meant pleasure . . . worldly, physical pleasure. It sat ill on Graydon's tongue — *tup* was far more his style. Her stepbrother had little French, and scorned to use what he had. English was good enough for him, he said, and if he had need of fancy speech, well, that's what scribes were for. Someone had put the word in his mouth, just as that person had fed him the gossip of Rand's activities while in exile with Henry.

That did not make the informant wrong.

"Who said that to you?" she asked with an edge in her voice. "Who wants Braesford out of the way?"

"Don't distress yourself, my fair stepsister," he said in rough contempt. "Some things you don't need to know. Go back to your embroidery and wifely duties. When they are over and another husband found for you, someone will send to tell you."

To argue was useless. He would tell her nothing more, possibly had nothing more he could tell her. But he was wrong about what she needed to know, also about what she must do.

Isabel was weary unto death of being kept in the dark, sick of being ordered against her will, disgusted with having her decisions made for her. She would accept these things no longer. She would not sit embroidering while her fate was decided. She would learn everything there was to know.

Afterward, she would choose for herself what she would do about it.

12

"Blue for keeping faith with thy lady wife," the courtier said with a lisping accent of some country beyond England's coast as he paused in front of Rand. "Next you'll be playing drone to her queen bee, with her stinger in you instead of yours in her."

Rand glanced up from where he reclined on a bench in the great hall, making one of a group of six or seven knights and men-at-arms, old comrades who had cleared a place in the rushes to cast the bones. The man seemed familiar, though he could not place him. Had he seen him with Leon last year, or was he merely one of the hangers-on at the court? Whatever his position, the words spoken were sheer provocation, he thought. To rise to it before he discovered its cause would be ill done, though his blood simmered in his veins at the suggestive parlance.

"If you speak of my doublet," he drawled, "the color is gray."

"It appears blue to me."

It was, in fact, the soft gray-blue of a cloudy sky, and chosen for exactly the purpose the courtier proclaimed. The lady for whom its message was meant had not yet seen it, he thought, and was unlikely to recognize it when she did. "Mayhap, but some men have no eye for color," Rand said with negligent ease.

One of his fellow players, a grizzled mercenary and veteran of wars in a half-dozen countries, snorted as he cast his one good eye over the newcomer. The man's costume consisted of a rust-red doublet paired with hose striped in green and black and a yellow wool hat stuck with a purple plume. "Braesford has ye there, milord."

The courtier's face turned mottled red and white. His scowl was fierce and his hand strayed to the hilt of his knife. "I say it's blue. I say he's a man-hen bound to become a cuckold."

It was too much. Rand sighed, tossed down coins for his debt and pushed to his feet. "Outside in the courtyard," he said. "Which shall it be, staffs or swords?"

"Here now," the man exclaimed, his eyes going wide. "I'll meet you at dawn, like enough, but not before."

The answer came so quickly that suspicion

touched Rand. He studied the courtier. He was not of impressive stature but appeared wiry and compact of form. Of mingled Spanish, Moor and Italian blood, he carried himself with the arrogance of one familiar with clashes over matters of honor. Still, he had no stomach, so it seemed, for an impromptu meeting. That was telling in itself.

Summoning a guileless smile, Rand asked, "You and who else will meet me?"

"Say you it would not be a fair fight?"

"Now what gave you that idea?" He slapped the courtier on the shoulder before draping an arm about his neck and walking him away from their audience. "Come, let us have a drink and decide how best to settle the business."

His erstwhile challenger tried to pull away, but Rand would not allow it. Behind them the dice players, cheated of what they had expected to be a fine show, went back to their game in disgust. A few others watched, however, perhaps having nothing else to relieve their ennui.

"I won't drink with you," the courtier said, half strangling on the words as Rand twisted a hand into the back of his shirt.

"Nor I am inclined to tipple with you," Rand said in a hard undertone, "but I can, if necessary, arrange it so wine never flows down your throat again. Who put you up to this masquerade? No, don't bother to lie. Only go back and tell them it did not serve. And if crude words about my lady wife ever pass your lips again, I will stop them beginning at your miserable neck."

They had reached a passage that led from the hall and past various antechambers to fetch up eventually at a rat's nest of sleeping chambers well away from the king's apartments. With a hardy whack between the shoulder blades, all boisterous companionship, Rand sent his would-be opponent stumbling into its obscuring shadows. The man caught himself, straightened his doublet with a jerk. With a malevolent look over one shoulder, he turned and walked away.

It had been a mistake, mayhap, to shame the courtier in front of others. Men were never quite so vicious in retaliation as when they had been made to look the fool. Still, it was hard to see how it could have been helped. The last thing Rand needed just now was to be forced to a meeting he could not win. If he suffered a fatal blow, Isabel would become a widow. If he struck one while a charge of murder hung over his head, he would be twice damned.

Was that what was intended? Had the courtier been sent as a sacrifice in hope of a hangman's noose for the master of Braesford? Or was it possible he was seeing complications where there was only an ambuscade in which he was meant to receive a fatal wound?

"What was that about?" Isabel asked, coming up behind him so quietly that he started like a squire at his first tourney before turning to face her.

"Nothing," he said, "only an idiot with more pride than sense." To prevent further questions, he went on the offensive. "What have you been doing? I looked into the queen's solar, but did not see you embroidering with your sisters and the other ladies."

"I go to join them now. But did you not linger to play them a French air or two as entertainment? I *am* surprised."

She had turned his tactic against him. A smile of appreciation curled one corner of his mouth. "I save my best airs for my wife," he said lightly. "I wonder if she appreciates it."

"I have it on the best authority that she is not unappreciative," she answered, her gaze resting on the gray-blue damask of his doublet, "just as she has a regard for your declaration of faithfulness. But she would as soon not be the butt of jests because of either."

"She prefers staid boredom in her married state." He waited with a suspended feeling in his chest for her answer.

Deep rose color suffused her face. "Not . . . not entirely. But some things are . . ."

"Too risqué to be mentioned?"

"Private," she finished while giving him a glance from under her lashes that threatened to scorch his soul. "Much too private."

"And require solitude for their further discussion," he said in a deep-voiced hint as he leaned to brush his lips along the curve of her neck, then flick her earlobe with his tongue.

"I doubt it would be wise." She placed her hand on his chest to prevent him from moving closer. "Though an intriguing invitation, it excites more interest than need be."

It did indeed, he saw with a quick glance from under his brows. Their exchange seemed to fascinate any number of the men and women who lounged about the hall, holding their attention as much or more than had his brief confrontation with the courtier.

The matter was wiped from his mind on

the instant. The minx that was his wife found his flat nipple unerringly through doublet and shirt, squeezing the nub between her fingers with the lightest of pinches. Fire shot to his groin like the blast from a Chinaman's harquebus. He thought his mouth might have fallen open as she released him and turned swiftly to walk away. Did her hips sway more than usual? He would swear they did, swear, too, that it was for his benefit, because she knew he watched.

A stunned chuckle vibrated in his chest. He would let her go for now, he decided. The retribution later would be sweeter for the wait. Though having a sheep's brain himself where his lady wife was concerned, he yearned to have her both now and later.

It had been torment to leave their chamber this morning. The taste of her mingled with raspberry flavor had lingered long on his tongue. It was maddening, a more powerful aphrodisiac than any unicorn's horn. He had gathered his scattered clothing and dressed without glancing at the bed, since the sight of her bare shoulder or smooth, white calf thrust from under the sheet might have undone his good intentions. He would certainly have thrown off his clothes and taken her again. He might not have risen from their bed the whole day long.

He could not afford such distraction. Forces were gathering that boded ill. He could sense their import in the distance Henry had placed between the two of them since the wedding, also in the sly glances of those he passed in the corridors, the watchfulness of the guards as he moved in and out of the palace. It was there, too, in the isolation in which he moved. Nobles who had been his companions in arms in France and at Bosworth Field avoided him as if he was plague-ridden. Few dared chance the taint of friendship with a murderer or the possibility of sharing his fate if he fell so far out of the king's favor that Henry allowed him to hang.

Isabel was a part of his fate, regardless of her wishes. He regretted it, but it could not be helped.

That was a lie. He could have sworn to Bishop Morton, who had heard their vows, that he was unwilling to wed her. That would have ended the matter, for the church did not condone forced marriage, not even at the behest of a king. He had been too intent on his own desires for the sacrifice. More, he would have had to perjure himself and confess the sin later, for he had wanted nothing in this life so much as to take Isabel to wife.

He had half expected her to speak up at the service, stating her own unwillingness. He had steeled himself for it, had bethought himself of how he would support her should Graydon attempt to force her compliance as he had before. Almost, he wished she had dared it. As it was, he had no idea whether she had married him because she was truly willing or because she feared to refuse.

And yet, and yet . . .

For a short, shining hour at Braesford Hall he had felt complete. It seemed his poor, wandering bastard's heart had finally gained a place and position where it belonged. He would have a family where he was accepted, welcomed, valued in spite of his birth. He and Isabel, so he had dreamed, would build something together that was strong and lasting.

Before, when handed Braesford as the king's gift, he had expected to glory in his possession. He had thought being able to call himself Sir Randall of Braesford, master of lands as far as the eye could see, would satisfy him all his days. The honor had soon worn thin. Something had been missing. He had known what it was when he saw Isabel of Graydon dancing in the great hall at Westminster. He had watched her smile with the light of a thousand joys in her face and had longed for her, suddenly, as a starving man longs for food and drink. He had thought he would pay any price to have her, any price at all.

The possession might yet cost him his life, but what odds? It had been worth it, if only for the dream.

The Angelus bell was ringing, the day far gone, when David found him in the palace stable where he had gone to check on Shadow and feed the destrier a windfall apple. The lad was flushed and out of breath, his eyes dark blue with worry. Seeing Rand there in the dim interior of the great, echoing building, he broke into a run.

"Sir! A message, come an hour ago. I've been looking everywhere for you."

"Lady Isabel?" he asked, his voice sharp.

"No, no," David assured him in quick comprehension of his alarm. "I saw her in the solar just now. She sent me to seek you here."

How had she known, Rand wondered, unless she was more aware of his habits than he thought, or had watched him from their chamber window? He would have to think on that later. "From Braesford, then?"

David gave a quick shake of his head that sent evening light glinting across the waves of his fair hair. With a quick look around to be certain they were not observed, he took a rolled piece of parchment from his tunic. "It was a villein that brought it to the servant hall."

A villein — slave to his master, though a freeman to all others — could be ordered to do almost anything, Rand knew. Nor would he speak of it later for fear of maiming punishment. "Brought to you, rather than to me?" he asked with a frown.

"Someone may have pointed me out to him as your squire. I'd not seen him before, I'd swear to it."

The parchment crackled as Rand unrolled it. The writing straggled across the page, an uneven script embellished with flourishes, dashes and inventive spelling for all its correct French. Rand angled it toward the light.

"Cher ami . . ."

A stinging prickle of alertness ran down his spine as the first words leaped to his sight. His fingers tightened to a death grip as he swept his gaze down the few lines.

The writer begged his indulgence that she addressed her message to him, but she knew not where else to turn. She dared presume on his kindness that had been shown to her during her recent travail by begging for succor. The keep that had been represented to her as a sanctuary had become a prison. Escape was imperative as she feared for her life and that of her child. It was her earnest plea that he attend upon her without delay. He was to take care on his journey for enemies were everywhere. She would await his coming with fervent prayers for his safe arrival. She was his grateful and affectionate Juliette d'Amboise.

Rand whispered an oath. The note was like the lady, a shade dramatic but polite and concerned for others. It was also a quiet essay in terror.

"Sir?"

Rand told his squire what the message contained, while a frown drew his brows together. "There was nothing else," he asked, "no directions given?"

"The villein who brought it waits on your convenience. He grunts instead of speaking, but indicated he is to guide you."

"Does he now? And who might he serve?"

"He wears no livery but only peasant's clothing, gave no sensible answer when asked for the name of his master." David shook his head. "It doesn't feel right."

Rand agreed wholeheartedly. He longed to find Mademoiselle Juliette, yes, but to go harrying off into the night with a guide he had never laid eyes on would be foolhardy.

"It may be a trick to get you to break your pledge to remain in the palace, so give the king cause to send you to the Tower."

"So it may," Rand answered, tapping the parchment against his thumb, "but what if it is not?"

That was the question, one his squire did not attempt to answer. "The man seems to have traveled many leagues. You'd need to leave soon if you would go and return before dawn."

Before he was missed, David meant. It left little time for contemplation. But what was the point of that when all was said and done? He could not ignore the possibility that Mademoiselle Juliette had need of his aid.

"It seems you could not have found me in a more appropriate place," he said in dry approval as he reached to thread his fingers through Shadow's forelock.

"We are going, then."

"I am going. You will remain." He hesitated. "You said nothing of this to Lady Isabel?"

"Nay, never."

David sounded insulted, as if his loyalty had been impugned. Or else it was the refusal of his services as a squire that set him on his high horse. "I prefer that you

301

stay by my lady," Rand said, placing a hand on the lad's shoulder. "I cannot protect two gentlewomen at once."

David sighed, then squared his shoulders. "As it pleases you, sir."

"Excellent," he said, infusing his voice with assurance. But in truth he was not pleased at all.

Where was Rand?

Isabel had not seen him since their exchange earlier in the day. The time since had dragged past with leaden slowness. She had pricked her finger so many times while embroidering that she feared the wall cloth under construction by the queen's ladies would forever bear the stains of her blood. The tunes played on lute and clavichord for their pleasure as they worked had seemed off-key and insipid. She dined with Cate as a companion of the plate and goblet, but had expected to sup with her husband. That he had not appeared as evening drew in was worrisome, raising suspicions that he stayed away because she refused to be bedded at his convenience.

When the long, mist-laden twilight turned slowly to darkness and still he had not appeared, she began to fret in earnest. Where could he be? On the king's order, he must not leave the palace and its environs. He was not in the great hall, not in the tiltyard, not in any of the taverns snug within its commodious walls, for she had sent David to look. He did not attend upon Henry, for everyone knew the king had been meeting with his council for most of the day. What did that leave?

Rand had gone to another woman, that was surely it. She did not doubt any number of them would take delight in stroking his injured pride along with his manly parts, but how could he go from her bed to theirs so blithely? How could he strip naked and caress some other female with the same hands, lips and tongue he had used to stall her heart and turn her bones as liquid as melted wax?

She did not care, of course she did not, she told herself as she paced up and down their chamber. It was insulting, all the same, that he made no distinction. She had thought she was something more than a body to be used for his pleasure. She was his wife, after all.

Why did he not return? How long could it take to — what was that word? — *tup* some compliant female? But no, she would not think of that. It could take all night, as she had learned to her amazement. It was not a question of stamina but of dedication to the task, of deliberately tended responses and infinite caring allied to insatiable need. Rand had been so . . .

She wouldn't think of that, she would not.

David, being Rand's shadow, must surely be aware of any adulterous affair. That such a thing could be kept from him was unlikely even if his master wished it. Add the lad's extra attentiveness to her in the past few hours, as if to make up for lack of her husband, and the thing became painfully clear.

The palace had grown quiet for the night, though revelry could still be heard from the town taverns and chanting from the abbey, when Isabel sent for David. Gwynne opened the chamber door to him, then busied herself brushing a velvet bodice and changing its lacings. Isabel stood at the open window, staring out into the thunderous night, until she was certain her features were composed. She turned then to face Rand's squire.

"Where is he?"

"Milady?"

"Don't act the simpleton with me. I know well you were searching for him this afternoon. Did you find him?"

"Aye, milady."

"Where?"

He told her but added no details, nothing that might allow her to guess what her husband did now or what he intended. He set his jaw when he finished speaking, his blue gaze focused somewhere over her head.

"Did he leave the palace?"

Uneasiness brushed the lad's features, as if he realized any answer he might make would plunge him into deeper trouble. "I can't say, milady."

"Can't or won't? Never mind. Why did you not go with him?"

"He said I was to stay and look after you."

"Did he now?" She clenched her teeth, trying to think how to dislodge information held in loyalty's grip. "Did he venture out to see another woman?"

"Milady . . ."

She pinned him with a stern gaze. "Did he?"

He folded his lips in a firm line, saying nothing. It was as damning as any admission.

She had not thought it of Rand, not really. She realized that now as pain swept in, surrounding her heart. She had thought him steadfast and true, chivalrous, loyal, kind — the very reflection of all the knightly virtues. It was devastating to be proven wrong.

She had been naive. It was a mistake she'd not make again.

Her voice a rasp in her throat, she asked finally, "Have you any idea when he will return?"

"Nay, milady."

"You may go," she said, lifting her chin, turning away before Rand's squire could see the tears that stung her eyes, threatening to spill over her lashes.

"He had to go, I swear it," David said softly, "but he will come back, milady. He will come back."

Yes, of course he would. He would come back and she would be waiting. He would slide into their bed and reach for her, pretending all was as it had been before. But he would be wrong.

He would be so very wrong.

13

Purple-gray banks of clouds covered the evening sky, and the air had a damp feel to it. The gathering darkness was not as apparent while Rand and his guide wound their way through Westminster town where candles and lamps had been lighted. The glow from taverns or houses that leaned so close together that neighbors could whisper secrets across the narrow streets was sufficient for their needs. By the time they reached the open fields where straggling trails led off the road to scattered villages, however, it had grown dark indeed.

Smells of ripe grain and damp earth drifted on the night wind. A fine mist blew into their faces, though it never quite turned to rain. Dogs barked and a cow lowed now and then as they skirted the looming, humpback shapes of thatched cottages. They rode through the forest — land of some nobleman's domain where the rustling, sighing leafiness closed above them like a tunnel. An owl called, a fox barked and then all was quiet again but for the thud of their horses' hooves. That sound echoed back from the encroaching trees with a muffled echo like the distant sound of some mounted troop. It was an hour, maybe more, before they left the woodland behind. Afterward, the road stretched ahead, empty, deep trodden between hedgerows, absorbing the shadows and their hoofbeats into its soft mud.

The guide did not speak. Rand thought him the usual taciturn countryman at first, with his grunts and abrupt gestures. He soon realized his mistake. The man, of early middle age, square built and lumpish in his hooded tunic of weed-dyed wool and rough-cobbled shoes, had no tongue.

A man's tongue could be cut out for talking treason, for spreading false rumors, slandering his neighbor or at the whim of his master. The tragedy of it was the same, regardless. Rand felt for his companion, but could not allow it to make a difference. What was important was that the villein knew where he was going even if he could not give the direction.

He did not say where that was, of course. Nor could he explain why he appeared reluctant to start out when Rand had first come upon him in a low tavern. He had jumped up, waving his hands and making sounds of protest. It seemed he had not expected Rand before midnight when everyone slept, felt they should wait until that hour to depart.

Rand lacked the patience. Mademoiselle Juliette had asked that he come without delay. He would not sit kicking his heels while danger closed in upon her. Besides, the sooner he and the guide were off, the sooner he could return.

He was troubled in mind over going back on his pledge to Henry. It was not something he undertook lightly; his word was sacred, not to be broken. But neither could he fail someone who depended on him. If he had to do penance to king or priest for riding to a lady's aid, then so be it.

Leaving the palace had been no simple thing. As he could hardly mount Shadow and ride out the gate, some subterfuge had been necessary. He had loosened one of Shadow's shoes as an excuse for taking him from the stable. David had then led the gray outside the palace gates, grumbling every step about a master too high-handed to wait for the palace blacksmith to manage the task.

Once the lad was away, Rand made for his chamber where he changed into his darkest, most sturdy clothing. He thought to see Isabel, perhaps to steal a kiss to see him on his way, but she was still occupied in the solar. Disgruntled, he left again, making his way through the maze of rooms to a rear servant's stair. He skimmed down this, slipped through the kitchens and along an alleyway to the kitchen garden. With the aid of an ancient apple tree, he scaled the stone wall that surrounded it. When he dropped down on the far side, he was loose in the streets of Westminster town.

A number of servants spied him as he made his escape. Most of them being female, he had winked and smiled in hope they would think his intentions were dictated by the needs of his crotch. With luck, he would be back before he was missed so they would not be called upon to recount his movements.

David and Shadow had awaited him at the stable attached to the tavern and inn where Rand was to meet the guide. The two of them found the man deep in a tankard of ale. Rand had arranged with David to return to the tavern stable in the early-morning hours, in case of need. Then he had forced an immediate departure.

Riding through the darkness now, Rand was as jumpy as a hart in rutting season. He cursed the lack of moonlight while squinting against the dampness and wishing for a torch to light their way. Now and then, he drew up, staring back along the distance they had come while he listened for pursuit.

Nothing.

That did not mean he could let down his guard.

He had no idea how far they had to travel and could not extract the information from the man who slumped in the saddle beside him. The longer he was away, the more certain it was he would be missed. David would not raise the alarm if he did not return before daylight, but he feared Isabel might. His dependence was on his squire to prevent it, though he had no idea how the lad might go about it.

It was a little after midnight, he thought, when they turned off the main road, meandered some distance along an overgrown pathway and emerged before a stone gatehouse. It belonged to a darkened building that loomed above it, appearing to be a smallish castle so ancient it was falling into ruin. It had a stone curtain wall set on mounded earth and a drawbridge that spanned a dry moat. No one challenged them as they rode forward, no trumpets sounded and no one came out to greet them.

Their hoofbeats rattled across the loose planks of the drawbridge, and they ducked under a snaggletooth portcullis that seemed as likely to impale a friend as a foe. The fitful blaze of a single torch lighted their way into the bailey with its rough stone walls. Centering it was a great, battlemented pile of stone two stories high, with arrow slits instead of windows. Towers with conical roofs anchored each of its front corners and stone steps mounted to a center entrance. No attempt to soften its nature as a defensive bastion had been made, no gesture toward making it a comfortable place to reside. It was a fortress to hold against all comers, or one to imprison those its master wanted to keep.

The torch that shed orange-and-yellow light over the bailey was fixed in a ringed holder beside the solid entrance, gleaming on the wide door's bronze nail heads and the sunken places on the tall stone steps where thousands of booted feet had trod. The place dated at least three hundred years back, possibly more. It might have served as a refuge at some time during the wars of the past thirty years, but the village it had no doubt protected seemed to have vanished, wiped out by plague or famine, so the castle no longer had a purpose.

Rand pulled up so sharply inside the bailey that Shadow reared back on his haunches. Settling the stallion with a firm hand, he stared around him. Nothing moved — not a sentry, not a single man-at-arms or bond servant. No pennon flapped to show who owned the keep, nor was there sight or sound of an animal of any kind.

His heart rattled against the walls of his chest. His every sense narrowed to near-painful alertness.

It struck him then, the question that had lain half-formed at the back of his mind from the moment he had opened Mademoiselle Juliette's message. If she was a prisoner, and had been one since leaving Braesford weeks ago, how had she known to direct her plea to him at Westminster?

"Where is everyone?" he asked, turning in his saddle to seek counsel of his guide.

The man was no longer behind him. He had stopped just inside the gate. Swinging his mount now, he galloped back under the portcullis with his elbows flapping against his sides. The hooves of his horse pounded on the drawbridge, then thudded away into the dark.

Calm settled over Rand. He sat staring around him for a moment more, noting the crumbling state of the keep's defenses, the sagging wood of a postern gate set in the rear wall, the litter of old leaves, moldering straw and ancient horse droppings that had settled against the bottom of the steps. Dismounting, he passed the bridle over the gray's head and led him to a horse trough half-full of rainwater. He left him there as he eased cautiously up to the heavy entrance and knocked on its door.

No one came.

The place was far too quiet, as if no one had been there in years. Regardless, the torch that burned near his right shoulder, dropping soot and rosin down the wall, flared like a signal. Rand's every instinct shouted that this was a trap. His best course, he knew with absolute certainty, would be to take to his heels in imitation of his guide.

He couldn't do it. If any chance existed that Mademoiselle Juliette and her babe were imprisoned in this dismal ruin, then he could not desert her.

The door shuddered as he pounded upon it again. With the last blow, it bounced out of its frame, then creaked open a few inches. Rand hesitated with his fist still upraised.

Giving it a quick push, he slid inside and moved at once to put his back against the near wall.

It took a moment for his eyes to adjust to the gloom. He was in a vestibule of sorts, he saw, one devoid of any kind of welcome other than a stone bench formed in one wall. Doors opened on three sides, the larger being straight ahead. He moved forward, his footsteps grating in the dirt that lay over the stone floor.

The torchlight behind him shed a muted, wavering glow through the open doorway, casting his shadow into the cavernous blackness of what appeared to be the keep's great hall. Just inside, he paused again to listen while he scanned the hollow, echoing void.

Not a sound, at least nothing human.

He eased past the area from which opened the pantry, buttery and kitchen passage. Here, too, all was silent. No men-at-arms cast dice by the light of a tallow candle, no manservant snored on any of the trestle tables left set for a last dinner, no hunting dogs scratched fleas among the rushes. All he saw was a nervous mouse that skittered away, pausing only once to look for crumbs in a cracked wood platter. Nothing existed here except emptiness and the smells of stale ashes, moldering rushes, rancid grease and mice droppings.

Or was there something more, after all, some metallic, too-human odor? Rand's stomach muscles contracted as his mind registered, belatedly, the scent of fresh blood. Bile rose in his throat and he swallowed it down again, swearing in a savage whisper.

Retreating back to the entrance, he snatched down the torch from its holder. With it gripped in a hard fist, he retraced his footsteps.

Juliette d'Amboise lay crumpled at the foot of the stairs that led to the private chamber of the keep's master directly behind the great hall dais. Her eyes were glazed with death. Her head lay at an odd angle, but she had not fallen by accident, had not died of a broken neck or head injury. Her throat had been cut, sliced so viciously that her head was half severed from her body.

Her hair seemed alive, shining with coppery highlights in the flaring light of the torch he held over her, while her skin took on its rosy glow. Rand, remembering her laughter in the early summer, her courage as she gave birth and her joy and pride in being a mother, felt his throat close. He coughed, almost choking on rage and raw, unexpected grief. She had been so young, so cheerful in her awkward, uncertain situation, and had lived so briefly, so briefly.

The torchlight glistened also on the ends of her tresses where they trailed in a pool of blood. And though her skin still retained a faint trace of warmth, it made no difference. He had come too late.

He had come too late.

That was, he was too late unless this had been a fool's errand from the start. Had her plea for aid been real, smuggled out of the keep in some fashion? Or had it been penned at the behest of whoever had killed her? These were questions that might never be answered.

Rand could do nothing for the lady. He might yet aid the child she had borne.

Rising, stepping over the body, he searched the chamber behind the dais. He found nothing, but did not despair. With grim endurance and rigorous method, he ranged through the remaining rooms of the keep, first those on the lower floor, then those above. No chamber, no chest, no armory built into the stone walls — no smallest nook or cranny — was left undisturbed. He found divers small items of clothing fit for a babe, found a crude oaken cradle of the kind used by villeins in their

317

cottages, but no tender suckling babe called Madeleine.

It was as he crossed an upper passage, which had an arrow slit at its far end, that he glimpsed the flare of light. Reaching the slit in a few long steps, he held his torch low, standing to one side as he peered through.

A troop of men rode toward the keep, their heads bobbing in unison with the torches they carried. The flames gave a lurid, sulfurous glow to the dust that hung on their heels. They were armored, for metal cuirasses shone copper and gold with reflected light. Their lances and pikes bristled above them like the fur of some great beast.

The ancient keep was a trap indeed, and it had been well baited.

Rand shoved away from the arrow slit, slung himself from the passage and down the shallow stone stairs. Leaping into the great hall, he strode for the entrance.

He was almost there when he heard a mewling cry like that of a half-drowned kitten. Rushes skidded and shattered beneath his feet as he plunged to a halt. Lifting his torch high, he stared around.

A pale shape beneath a trestle table leaped to his sight. In an instant, he was on his knees beside it, dragging it from under the planks held up by rickety supports. It was a small, hard board, broader at the top than at the bottom and wrapped by yard upon yard of white linen. Attached to it was a weak and unhappy babe.

There was no time to lose. Drawing his knife from its sheath, he slashed through the linen bindings, dragging them from around the child, casting them aside. Juliette must have been carrying the baby when she was caught from behind, he thought as he worked. The swaddling board had protected little Madeleine from real injury, but she might have been stunned into silence by the jarring fall. Either she had been overlooked by the killer or left behind to die if no one answered her mother's plea.

With the baby free of its awkward wrappings, he tucked it inside his doublet, grimacing a little at the smell that came with it. Supporting the small head against his shoulder, he refastened his doublet but left it open at the neck for air. Perhaps his body heat and the thundering of his heart provided some comfort, for the baby ceased its feeble cries.

Rising to his feet with his burden, Rand stamped on his torch to extinguish it, then crossed to the entrance in a few bounding strides. He clattered down the stone steps, half falling into the bailey in his haste. Shadow stood where he had left him. He snatched up his reins and dragged the great destrier toward the postern gate he had noticed earlier by rote, the result of too many prisons, too many battles against superior forces.

He did not mount once outside the keep, but led the stallion down the embankment that gave the outer wall its height. Using the enormous stone bulk as cover, he forced his way through the shrubs and bracken that crowded around the place, dodging limbs, tripping over briars, until he reached the cover of the forest. He mounted then, but resisted the urge toward swift flight. Keeping to the deeper darkness of the tree line as much as possible, he held Shadow to a slow walk. Only when he was certain the troop of men had reached the bailey and were well inside did he kick the gray into a gallop. Leaning over his powerful neck then, holding the baby to him with one hard arm, he rode for London and Westminster.

The rain that had threatened all night came when he was halfway there. Rand welcomed it, for the gray curtain would make it that much harder to pick up his trail. He also cursed it, for it foiled his attempts to hear any pursuit, turned the road into a river of mud that made slow going and soaked him through except where he hunched over the child. Little Madeleine was reasonably dry and warm, however, and that was all that mattered.

What was to be done with her? He could hardly appear at the palace with a babe in arms. Her crying and need for a wet nurse would draw attention and inevitable questions among the servants. Henry would hear of it before good light.

Isabel would know sooner than that. What would she think if he showed up with another woman's child? Would she be glad of the proof that he had not done away with the small mite or outraged that he dared ask her help in hiding her? Would she take little Madeleine in gentle arms or scream until someone came to take the baby away?

Of course, he could turn the child over to Henry. But what if the king discovered she was Leon's daughter, what would become of her then? Or what if Henry knew it already and Mademoiselle Juliette's death had been the price for her betrayal? If Madeleine had been left once to die, what was to keep it from happening again?

No, some temporary sanctuary for this little one was required, and soon. It must be hours since she had nursed. She could not go much longer without it.

There was only one solution that he could see, try as he might to find another while the miles thundered away beneath the destrier's hooves. Rand despised it, felt he failed Juliette by considering it, yet it was better than delivering her baby to an enemy.

David waited at the stable next to the tavern, as had been arranged. When applied to for his advice, the lad at once suggested the convent of Saint Theresa. It was all Rand could do to unclench his jaws enough to agree. Coward that he was, he gave the warm weight of the baby into his squire's young arms, then walked away so he need not see her delivered to the nuns.

Isabel was asleep when he let himself into their chamber. Or he thought so as he stood listening to her soft, even breathing from behind the bed curtains. He sighed, grateful for that one small boon. Moving with great stealth, he stripped to the skin, washed with a goodly lathering of soap, sniffed at his chest where the baby had nestled and washed again. He rubbed some small amount of heat into his body with a length of linen toweling, then tossed it aside and eased toward the bed.

"You may go and sleep with the horse you smell like," Isabel said in stringent anger.

"There is no room for a fornicating husband in my bed."

Did he smell like a horse? Rand held his right hand to his nose, thinking he had neglected that possibility. As he could catch no trace of it, he suspected the odor was in the clothing he had left piled on the floor. He would not argue, however, as he had noticed long since that women had more sensitive noses. Still, the injustice of it acted like a goad after the betrayal, the grief and difficult decision of the night. Outrage lent force to his movements as reached the bed in a single stride and swept the curtains aside.

"My bed," he corrected, "and the only one I use for fornication, the only woman in it that I'll have this day."

She sat up so the linen sheet that covered her slipped down into her lap. He could just discern her outline in the dim room, a shapely and warm figure that made his hands itch to touch, to feel, to hold. That he could see her at all told him dawn was near, particularly as it approached through the steadily falling rain.

"You expect me to believe such a tale when you have been gone the whole night through?" she demanded.

"I don't care what you believe as long as

you lie down and let me hold you." He had not meant to say such a thing, but realized he needed it with an ache that verged on desperation. Snatching back the sheet, he slid in beside her, lofted it over them both.

"Don't," she snapped, fending him off as he reached for her.

It was too much. He was tired, cold and heartsick at the death of a young Frenchwoman who had done nothing except allow herself to be loved. His proud, disdainful wife had refused him once already this day, and now he had been falsely accused on top of it, as he had been falsely accused since she first came to him. She would not gainsay him now.

With a swift lunge, he rolled above her, trapping her thighs beneath his long legs. Catching her forearms, he slid his fingers upward to pin her wrists to the mattress beside her face, though with a care for her injured finger. He pushed his knee between hers and spread her legs while he pressed down with his chest, absorbing the softness of her breasts, the flutter of her abdomen. The heat radiating from her skin sent a violent shudder over him from head to toe.

He expected her to struggle, to gasp and threaten before she turned to pleading. He thought to force her to lie still, accepting his right to lie beside her, if nothing more.

It did not happen.

"You are frozen," she said in tones of wondering discovery as his shivering was communicated to her. "How did you get so cold?"

"Rain," he said with difficulty, "and a long ride for next to nothing." He could not open his jaws for more without his teeth chattering. He felt palsied, almost ill. It was not merely cold, he recognized abruptly, but the aftermath of danger, the violent surging in the blood that stayed with a man after it was past. As with battle frenzy, it had at its heart the need to defy fear, to deny human frailty, human mortality.

He wanted to tell Isabel what he had seen and what it meant, to talk away the guilt that he had been too late to prevent Juliette's death, to explain that he had no part in it and hear her absolve him of responsibility. It was impossible. Once begun, he might never stop. Besides, she did not need to hold such horror in her mind, would not if he could help it.

He kissed her instead, blindly seeking the warm depths of her mouth, her sweet sanity and sweeter surcease. And miracle of miracles, she met his lips, opened to him, took his tongue into her precious heat.

Suddenly he was rapacious, a ravening beast who could not get close enough to her, could not fill his hands with enough of her body, her softness, her moist and glowing heat. She moaned, rubbing against him, as ferocious in her need as he. They came together with grasping, squeezing hands, skimming over mounds and hollows, dipping into sensitive valleys, following with lips and tongues and mindless intent. They rolled over the bed, legs entwined. He shifted to heave her above him, pressed her down upon his strutted flesh while he spread his fingers over her hips, urging her, silently demanding her encompassment. She took him in, gasping a little at the depth of his reach. Then she arched her back, sinking upon him still more, eyes closed, a low hum in her throat with the sound of gratified need.

He raised his head and upper body, sought her breast with desperate hunger. The nipple was so sweet on his tongue, so tender a morsel. He suckled her, sliding his hands to her rib cage to hold her close for his pleasure. She rocked gently upon him, then stronger, and stronger still until he was forced to release her so she might move freely.

She leaned forward then, shaking the

thick, sweet-scented curtain of her hair around them. He felt the ends of it whip his face as she moved, felt the hard clutch of her hands as she braced herself on his shoulders, gripping the bones beneath them as she slid in the hot moisture that poured from her now. He surged against her, ramming upward, seating himself so firmly inside her that he felt her heartbeat, felt her quick, hard breathing, felt the tremulous flutters deep inside her. He felt the swift flow of her life's blood, her warm and vibrant life, and was deliriously glad.

Suddenly she tensed, holding him with the hard possession of a rider, stronger than he would have thought possible, triumphant in her possession. He gave her what she wanted, his quiescence, his acceptance. Gave it until she sighed, until she relaxed and keeled forward to lie upon his chest.

He turned with her then, raising her knees to accommodate him completely as he stroked in steady rhythm as endless as the rain that poured from the roof to stream into the stable yard below. He took her, sounding her, molding her to his form, basking in her heat, her acceptance that held nothing back. And still he strove with every muscle as hard as stone, every intention like steel, every iota of his will awaiting, needing, her surrender.

Her eyes flew open, and she stared into his face as her body tensed again, throbbing against him, around him, drawing him deeper. He redoubled his efforts, took them both spinning into insanity and beyond, to a place where they were two no longer, but only one. She was his and he was hers, whether she wanted him or not. She would not sleep separate from him, would not escape him, would not, could not, never, not ever. . . .

Unless . . .

Unless he was forced to let her go.

It was some time later, as he lay in stunned sleep with Isabel held in the curve of his body, her bottom against his belly and her breast captured in his hand, that booted feet tramped into his dreams. In the way of such things, he could not move, though he knew what the sound portended. He was seized by near-superstitious awe for the way things happen, of fatalistic submission to the will of his God and his king.

It was always meant to be this way. He had known it from the first, had fought against it with all his might and will, but to no purpose. The end had been there in the beginning.

The curse of the Three Graces had come to him.

The door of the chamber crashed open, slamming against the wall behind it. Isabel cried out, sat up. She swept back the bed curtains with one slender arm while holding the sheet to her breasts. She was tousled, lovely with her hair streaming around her, curling over one shoulder to shimmer in the morning light through the window as her chest rose and fell with her swift breathing.

Rand was reminded for a fraction of an instant of Juliette's bloodstained tresses shining in the torchlight. Forcing the image from him, he pushed up in the bed, sat with his knees drawn up and his share of the sheet draped across his lap.

The chamber filled with men-at-arms fitted with mail and armed with halberds. They tramped inside, broke formation and took positions on either side of the door. With the way secured yet clear, a trio of nobles stepped through. Two of them were Graydon and Henley. To their fore was McConnell, Rand's half brother, his expression almost sorrowful as it rested upon him.

"Rise, brother, and dress yourself," he said as he came forward, stopping less than a yard from the bed with his hand resting on his sword hilt. "I regret to be the bearer of ill tidings yet again, but you are ordered to the Tower."

"No," Isabel whispered, her gaze moving over the men as if unable to accept the meaning of their presence.

"The edict is signed in Henry's own hand and set with his seal, Lady Isabel. That's if you care to see it."

She put out her hand on the instant. It was a brave gesture, Rand thought, for a woman lying barely covered in a room crowded with men-at-arms who pretended to look straight ahead but cut the corners of their eyes in her direction. Her gaze was imperious, however, her manner as stately as if she had been gowned in velvet sewn with jewels. Taking the heavy parchment, she ran her gaze down the closely written lines, making short work of the Latin phrases. The color drained from her face. She closed her eyes, and it was a moment before she looked up again.

"But this charge is not the same. It says here . . ."

Rand knew what it must say. Regardless, the knowledge that she had seen it was like acid scalding his heart. His fists clenched on the linen that covered his thighs. A soft, ripping sound fretted the silence.

"Indeed," McConnell answered, his face

grave as he continued in gruff tones. "The charge now is double murder. I regret to tell you that Mademoiselle Juliette d'Amboise, mother of the child your husband is accused of burning to death, has also been killed. She died last night at a place some distance from Westminster. Her body was discovered after a man answering Braesford's description was seen fleeing the place of the murder."

As McConnell spoke, Graydon limped forward a step. He leaned on his stick while he plucked from the floor the sodden shirt, doublet and wrinkled, wet hose Rand had discarded. "Aye, and here is proof he was outside the palace. 'Twas late when he came to bed, I think, as his squire has not dealt with this mess."

McConnell shrugged. "It is all that's required to set the seal on it."

Isabel made a gesture of dismissal, though she was so pale her skin appeared almost transparent. "Withdraw, all of you. Withdraw and allow my husband to be dressed." She glanced from Graydon to Henley, who stared back with an avid look in his eyes, then to the open door where David had appeared, hovering with desperate worry in his face. "He will join you when he leaves his squire's hands."

"We cannot risk it, I fear," McConnell said in grim tones.

"But you have Rand's pledge . . ." she began.

"Which he has broken, as he was seen outside Westminster. You should realize —"

"Have done," Graydon interrupted, slinging the wet clothing at Rand so water splattered as it hit his chest. "He can wear what's to hand or go without. It's all one to us."

McConnell looked pained. Rand wondered if it was an act. He had not the time to consider it, however. Graydon and Henley would be glad of an excuse to drag him naked from the bed and the chamber, and he would not give them that pleasure. Nor would he shame Isabel by such an undignified departure.

He slid from the bed and quickly donned the wet shirt and hose, tied up enough points for decency and pulled on his doublet. No sooner had he tugged it down than a pair of men-at-arms advanced on him. He was jerked around and his arms pinned behind him. They started toward the door, hustling him between them.

With a single hard wrench that pulled both men-at-arms with him, he turned back to face Isabel. "I killed no one," he said, speaking fast and low for he knew not how much he would be allowed to say. "Trust to David. Have a care for yourself alone. Believe nothing that doesn't come from me."

"I will go to the king as soon as may be," she said, the words hardly more than a whisper.

"You can try," he said. "But if it's to no avail —"

"Don't!" she cried, putting a hand to her mouth while tears gathered along the rims of her lashes.

He was stunned to see that evidence of concern for him, so caught in disbelief at the sight that it was a moment before he could find his tongue again. "If it avails nothing, remember this. I have no regrets."

They wrestled him around again then, half dragging, half marching him from the chamber. David scooped up his boots and hurried after them. Rand looked back, trying to see between the armored guards that fell in behind him and his captors. Isabel sat where she was, upright and stiff with shock in the bed they had shared, the linen sheet and her cascading hair her only protection from the glances of the detail. It seemed she hardly noticed their lascivious interest. She looked appalled, horrified.

But Rand saw one thing more, something

he had learned to recognize since making Lady Isabel his wife. It was a thing that caused a low laugh to shake him and his heart to leap high in his chest.

It was the dawn of fury, elegant, ladylike, yet deadly, in the rich green fastness of her eyes.

14

Few men returned from imprisonment in the Tower.

Isabel, sitting upright in bed while the tramp of booted feet faded away, was struck to the heart by fearful rage. She could not catch her breath. Her hands trembled where she clutched the sheet to her. That Rand had been taken away to be lodged in that prison by the Thames, once an ancient palace, was a devastating blow. At the same time, it seemed inconceivable. There had to be some mistake.

Henry and his mother had known Rand for years. He and the king had shared the misadventures of exile and the triumph of winning a crown on the field of battle. Henry would not permit this new accusation to stand, would not allow Rand to hang.

Surely he would not?

Recalling the doubt in Rand's eyes as she said she would go to Henry, and the acceptance in his low-spoken words, she sensed he lacked faith in royal intervention. No matter. It would be forthcoming.

She would see to it because she could not bear that whoever conspired against Rand in this despicable way should win out over him. It was neither fair nor just that he should suffer for a royal transgression and its results. Her intentions had nothing to do with what she might or might not feel for him. Certainly not. They would be undertaken out of the loyalty due a husband. That was all.

For a single instant, she felt a near-desperate urge to sling the bed curtains closed, pull the sheet up over her head and seek oblivion in sleep. Surely the arrest would be revealed as a nightmare when she woke again.

No, and no again. There was no time for sleeping or hiding away. She must be up and doing. Rand's life could depend on it.

An hour later, she left the chamber. Dressed in sea-green damask and wearing a lace-covered headpiece from which hung lace veiling that lifted like wings behind her, she strode toward the king's apartment. Her time had not been wholly spent upon a toilette fit for a royal audience, however. She had also set David and Gwynne to collecting every comfort she could think of to soften her husband's imprisonment, from dry clothing and boots to books, pen, parchment and a cake of ink, also a lute, wine and sweetmeats and coin to purchase more substantial food and drink from his guards.

It meant nothing that she took such care, of course it did not. Simple kindness required it.

The king was not receiving. He had taken his hawks and a favored few gentlemen and gone hunting.

Anger sizzled along Isabel's veins at the news. Her footsteps were brisk with it as she left the royal apartments and made her way toward the great hall. How dare Henry behave as if this was a day like any other? He must be as cold of heart as everyone claimed that he could ride afield while a friend faced death.

Hunting, forsooth! Flinging a great raptor with talons like knives into the sky to dive upon defenseless doves and larks was scarce fair hunting in her view. It was, of course, typical of a royal sport wherein anything, and anyone, could die at the king's pleasure.

She very nearly strode past William McConnell without seeing him where he sat in conversation with another gentleman outside a cabinet room. It was only as he rose from his bench, bowing low, that she came to a halt.

"Lady Isabel, a moment of your time, I beg you."

Her curtsy was so shallow it barely caused a fold in the hem of her gown. "Another time. I am upon an affair of importance, as you must know."

"Yes, unfortunately. You are acquainted with Derby?"

She had barely noticed the man with McConnell. It was Thomas Stanley, Earl of Derby, third husband of the king's mother. He received a deeper curtsy and a smile as she acknowledged the introduction. He paid her a handsome compliment, but excused himself immediately, pleading business elsewhere.

"A fine man," McConnell said as they stood watching the earl's portly form retreat down the passage, "and one of excellent understanding."

"Oh, indeed. He apparently understands that it's best not to be seen with the wife of an accused murderer."

"You are bitter, and who can blame you? But no, I meant because the earl allows his good wife to live apart from him, attendant upon her son. It is said she speaks of petitioning the court for separate domicile.

A strong step, you must agree."

To agree would be unwise, particularly if she wished to remain at court. Such slips of the tongue could mean instant exile. "I am sure," she said evenly, "that you did not accost me to speak of Lady Margaret's marital arrangements."

He gave her a faint smile as he gazed down at her. "Only in that they might reflect your own."

"Mine?"

"If you so choose. You are free to return to the chamber you shared with your sisters, if you like, or even to Graydon's protection."

"Why would I do either of those things?"

"You are alone now," he said gravely. "No one would think ill of it if you chose to leave the court."

He meant, she thought, to discover if she was grieved or relieved by Rand's arrest. She would not give him the satisfaction. "Except, mayhap, the king, who seems to have made living apart from my husband a necessity."

"His royal prerogative. Have you come from scolding him?"

"His Majesty was not available," she said with a lift of her chin.

"Oh, yes, I had almost forgotten. You may,

if you like, vent your ire on me."

"On you?" He had to be fully aware that Henry was hunting, she thought. It would be his duty to know it. The wonder was that he had not gone with him.

"I am sure you resent me for Rand's arrest."

"If not you, sir, then certainly the part you played."

"I was but obeying Henry's will, you know, when I invaded your chamber this morning."

A flicker of expression in the blue of his eyes made her suddenly aware that her husband's half brother had seen her naked in her bed. She had been covered in part by a sheet, it was true, but he must have realized her state of undress. It was possible the scent of lovemaking had lingered around her, in token of how she and Rand had been disporting themselves only a short while before.

Her cheekbones stung with uncomfortable heat. The feel of it annoyed her so she spoke without thinking. "As you performed your duty by interrupting the wedding at Braesford Hall?"

"I rather thought you thankful at the time."

So she had been, though nothing would

compel her to admit it at this moment. "It seems less than sincere to deplore a duty which may allow you to regain Braesford Hall and its lands."

"My position is not comfortable, I will admit. To fear for my half brother even as I escort him to prison, to pity his probable fate, though it may benefit me?" He spread his hands in a helpless gesture. "And yet Braesford holds all my childhood memories, has been the seat of my family for generations."

"Which your father lost due to his mistakes."

"Or for his loyalty to another Lancastrian king. A different thing, you will agree?" McConnell gave a wry shake of his head. "I suppose Rand has been before me with his version of the tale. I misdoubt it is precisely the same as my own, but cannot argue with the facts."

"Yet you served Edward IV, who ordered that king killed, and Richard of Gloucester, who may have done the deed."

"What would you? I was a penniless youth when Edward came to the throne. Even a nobleman must eat. Edward was strong and had sons to found a dynasty from his line. Who could guess he would die young, or that Richard would snatch the crown."

"Or kill his nephews to keep it."

"That, too, sadly enough," he agreed with a sigh.

"But then you abandoned Richard on Bosworth Field."

"But I did choose the right man to follow, so gained my present position."

It was true enough, though where the man's loyalties truly lay was anyone's guess. It was possible that, like others who swayed with the wind, he had none except to himself. "But you did not recoup your family lands," she pointed out.

"There is yet time for that."

"You must surely realize that even should they be taken from Rand, nothing guarantees they will be handed back to you," she said with deliberation. "Ownership will revert to Henry, who may prefer the income over buying your loyalty."

If he caught the sting in her words, he did not flinch from it. "I must make myself more valuable to him, then."

"Doubtless you will find a way." She sidestepped as if she meant to move around him.

"Wait, please," he exclaimed, setting a hand on her arm to halt her progress. "I would not have you look on me as an ogre in this business."

She lowered her gaze to his hand, standing stiff and silent until he had removed it. "How else am I to view you," she asked, "especially after seeing my husband's scars?"

A puzzled frown appeared between his eyes, but cleared abruptly. "His scars, yes. That was so long ago it almost slipped my mind."

"As it had his, though I find it difficult to forget."

"It was ill done, I agree. But I was young and proud, and not used to sharing my father's affections. Did Rand tell you the old man took the whip to me as punishment?"

"He told me he was brought into the house to share your tutor."

"Also my chamber, my clothing, my hunting equipment and my dogs." McConnell gave her a wry smile. "I was not happy, but grew accustomed. In time, we made up our differences, Rand and I. It was necessary to survive our tutor, who had a great fondness for the birch rod, also to survive Pembroke's master of the tiltyard, who enjoyed seeing noblemen's sons thumped by the quintain."

She caught his quick look that seemed to ask if she was familiar with this man-size practice target, one which spun around when struck by a lance, dealing a hurtful blow to anyone too slow to avoid it. Of course she knew it from her father's tilt-yard. Ignoring his sally, she said, "Yet you relegated your half brother to the lowly position of your squire the while."

"Really, Lady Isabel," McConnell said with a shake of his head. "He was baseborn, after all."

It was so simple in his mind, she saw. It was difficult to fault him since it had been the same in hers not so long ago. "In spite of which Sir Rand won his knighthood, the friendship of a future king and the right to call himself Braesford of Braesford Hall."

William McConnell lifted his brows a fraction, possibly at her championship. "True, Lady Isabel, but now he is a prisoner in the Bell Tower, one of the more secure keeps on the Tower grounds. If convicted of the charges lodged against him, he will forfeit whatever he owns as well as his life. There is only one thing he can hold by God's laws which any man must envy."

"And that would be?"

He inclined his head. "You, fair lady, as his bride."

"Oh, please," she said with a gesture of repudiation. Hovering at the edges of her mind was Rand's assertion that his half brother had desired her. Did McConnell think to be given a wife to go with the family estate should it be returned to him, perhaps his half brother's widow? The thought chilled her to the bone.

"You are offended and I respect that. Nay, I honor you for it. I would have you know, however, that you shall not be deserted in this travail. I pledge to stand by you in all things."

"For Rand's sake, I suppose," she said, and did not trouble to hide her disbelief.

"As I've seen to his welfare in his Tower chamber, ordering his confinement to be as lenient as possible."

"For that, at least, I thank you." Her voice was quieter as she made that concession. Almost, she could be in charity with him.

"I could do no less. His imprisonment may be long before trial is set."

"Or not, if Henry can be prevailed upon to see reason."

McConnell frowned. "Have you not heard? Henry leaves on progression in a day or two. He will be moving slowly westward for some weeks, fetching up at Winchester in time for the queen's confinement."

Fear sliced through Isabel. "Surely he will not . . ."

"See Rand hanged before he goes? Unlikely. My half brother could, like Sir Thomas Malory and many another like him, enjoy the king's hospitality for decades."

"He could also be released."

What he might have answered went unheard, for she moved away from him at a swift pace. He remained where he stood, though she felt his gaze on her back until she passed out of his sight.

Isabel slowed, fighting an odd desolation, as she passed from the king's apartments into a long colonnade that led from one section of the palace to another. The king was leaving Westminster. He might well go without seeing her. What was she to do then?

One moment she was alone, and the next David appeared at her side. He made no great business of it, but simply slid from behind a post and fell into step with her.

She glanced his way, noting the grimness that sat on his handsome young features. Her spirits dropped lower than they were already.

"You saw him?" she asked, keeping her voice low so as not to be overheard by the courtiers who came and went around them. There was no need, with David, to say whom she meant.

"Aye, milady."

"And he was well?" In the back of her

mind was the fear that Rand might have been beaten, even tortured, to gain his confession to the accusations against him.

"Aye, milady."

"You were able to give him the things I sent?"

"Aye, milady," he said, then catching the fulminating look in her eyes, answered more fully. "I gave them into his hands but was not allowed to speak to him. His chamber is small, though not a windowless cell, nor is he obliged to share it."

Relief caused her footsteps to falter for an instant. It was possible McConnell's influence had been to some purpose. As long as Rand was treated as something above a common criminal, there was hope.

They walked on a few yards before she spoke again. "Did he —"

"Nay, milady. No messages."

A wan smile twitched a corner of her mouth at his perceptiveness. "How did you guess what I would ask?"

"Sir Rand wanted to know the same thing."

The knowledge sent a wave of pain over her. Rand had asked for a message and she had sent none. Her mind had been on other things, of course, but it would have been easy enough to offer a few words of encouragement.

"Did he ask anything else?"

"Nay, milady."

No, he would not have, she thought. It was too early for there to be news. Glancing at the lad again, she saw that he strode beside her with all the grace of a courtier, also something of the same long and powerful stride Rand used, or as near as he could come to it. Mayhap it was time she began to look upon him as a young man instead of a lad, she thought with a peculiar tenderness around her heart. He must be nearly the same age as she was herself, after all.

"I know Sir Rand said you were to stay by me," she continued after a moment, "but you need not spend all your hours on guard. If you have other tasks to perform, I will be perfectly fine on my own."

Rand's squire lifted a muscled shoulder gained, no doubt, from sword practice with his master. "I have nothing else to do, milady. I returned Shadow from the town to his palace stall. I also gave Sir Rand's wet clothing to the laundress, the things he passed to me after changing."

She was glad to know he had been allowed to use the fresh clothing she had arranged for him. It was a reminder, however, that she knew not where he had been the night before or exactly what he had been doing on his foray outside the palace.

How very cold he had been when he slid into bed beside her. She had meant to withhold her favors after his desertion and midnight absence, but it had been impossible in the face of his need. Moreover, she had ignited like black powder the instant he touched her, clinging to him in a fury of desire so strong she had shuddered with it, as he shivered with cold against her. The passion that leaped between them had been devouring, enflaming, so they grappled on the mattress, clinging, crying out like warriors in extremis. It had been extreme indeed, a fierce and pounding consummation, and she had the soreness this morning to prove it. Yet she could not believe the man who had held her, who had urged her to ride him like some creature of witchcraft, could have come to her directly from murdering Juliette d'Amboise.

She refused to believe it.

Clearing her throat of an unaccountable tightness, she spoke without looking at David. "Do you know where Sir Rand went last night?"

David sent her a flashing cobalt glance before looking away with a quick shake of his head.

"But you do know how. I assume taking Shadow to the blacksmith in town was a ruse, so Sir Rand might have use of him once he left the palace."

A modicum of something that might have been respect for her perception shone in his eyes before he gave a reluctant nod.

"You must also know when he left and when he returned, as you supplied his means of travel. Do you also know why he went?"

"He had a message."

"Of what kind, pray?"

David folded his lips and did not answer, but Isabel did not desist. In a short time she knew exactly what kind of message Rand had received and the fact that it was in a lady's hand.

"So he went to meet this lady. Yes, and was seen near where Mademoiselle Juliette died. It seems obvious, then, that the message must have been from —"

"She was dead when he got there. This he swore."

"Yes," Isabel whispered. She believed it without question, oddly enough. To have it otherwise was simply unthinkable.

"It appears someone did not want him to speak to her."

"Or didn't want her to talk to him."

"Isn't that the same thing?" she asked with a frown.

"Nay, milady, not if she had something important to tell him."

It was an excellent point. What might it have been if she had? "Was it . . . could it have been something about the baby?"

"I can't say."

The flat sound of his voice sent dread skittering through her. Holy Mother, what if the little one had been with her? She moistened her lips. "Please . . . please don't tell me the child was killed, as well."

A sheen of light slid over David's bright head as he shook it. "She is safe, for now."

Isabel sighed with relief at this corroboration that the baby had not died at Braesford, that Rand had not lied. It hovered on the tip of her tongue to ask how David knew the babe was safe, also where it was being held and by whom. Such questions were banished as he spoke again.

"There is one last reason why Sir Rand might have been summoned."

"Yes?"

"Aye," he said, his young face grim. "They could have wanted the lady dead, and thought it convenient to blame him for it, same as for the other."

It seemed so likely there was no point in

answering. The ache of it was too sharp to make words possible, in any case. They walked on in silence until David left her at the door of her chamber.

The king remained elusive. Isabel presented herself outside his audience chamber the next morning, and left that evening without being admitted. Henry could not spare her even a minute as he strode past between one chamber and another with his yeoman guard and his retinue. She might have been a stranger for all the attention he paid her.

Gossip was rife in the meantime, a growing whirlwind of conjecture, snide laughter and incredibly vicious accusations. Isabel was spared the worst, perhaps, as few cared to be seen speaking to her, but she heard enough from her sisters, from Gwynne and from David to guess the rest. What she could not avoid were the whispers and snickers behind her back. Within them lurked veiled hostility, or so it seemed, as if she shared the guilt credited to Rand.

It made no difference. She would not give up. She refused to slink away without being heard, without at least some plea for an explanation of the charges leveled at Rand. She needed someone to tell her what was going to happen to him, and to give her permission to visit him.

No audience was forthcoming. Her questions went unanswered. Early on the morning of the third day after Rand's arrest, Henry prepared to leave on royal progression.

The great multitude who would travel with the king on his slow journey gathered in the courtyard outside the palace. Honored noblemen, men-at-arms with their great armored chargers, courtiers, minstrels, dancers, capering fools, priest and servants all milled around the baggage wagons in hopeless confusion. Finally, Henry's guard appeared with the king walking among them. They mounted up. Order was established as the procession moved out. The noise and confusion faded into the distance. Westminster grew so quiet it was as if all life had drained from both town and palace.

The days slipped past, one after the other, with little purpose and less pattern. Isabel felt caught in a civilized purgatory, of the court yet outside its circle, wed but not a true wife in Rand's absence, bereft of purpose and privilege. She slept but did not feel rested, ate though she was never hungry. It seemed she waited for something and feared both that it would never come and that it would come too soon.

At sunrise a week after Rand had been taken away, she stood at the window of her chamber. She shredded the bread that had been intended for her breakfast, dropping the crumbs onto the windowsill. A half-dozen small birds twittered and chirped as they accepted the bounty she spread before them. One, a sparrow, came close, regarding her with its head cocked to one side.

Isabel was assailed by the memory of Rand standing at the window, magnificently naked while he held a sparrow perched on his thumb. Wonder had been in his face for the trust of that small creature, and he had turned to share it with her. He had appeared so much younger then, as he might have before court intrigue and affairs of state had caught him in their toils.

"No, Sir Rand isn't here to feed you this day," she said quietly to the small winged creature that watched her with such bright eyes. "Yes, I'm sure you miss the way he whistles for you. Mayhap you might fly about the Tower later in the morning. I'm sure he would like to see . . ."

Tightness closed around her heart as if it was being squeezed by a giant fist. She breathed deep against the pain. She had not been married long enough to miss her groom — of course she had not. Why, then, did it hurt so much to think of him shut up in the old castle beside the Thames?

A knock sounded on the bedchamber door. Light as it was, it set the birds to flight. Isabel turned to bid whoever was outside to enter.

"You are up. Good," Cate said, pushing the door open a crack and putting her head around the edge. Her gaze took in Isabel's reddened eyes. "You aren't sickening for something, are you?"

"Nothing so convenient," she said with a wan smile. "Do come in, dear sister, for I have need of company. Have you breakfasted?"

"Long ago." Cate, the early riser among the three sisters, spoke with a virtuous air as she whisked inside and closed the door firmly behind her. "And a good thing, too. I was taking a turn along the outside passageway just now when a boy came up to me. He asked was I not your sister, and when I said I was, he gave me this."

From the string bag that hung at her waist, she took a parchment square sealed with wax. Dread seized Isabel at the sight of it. It was very like that which had bid her come to the abbey so many days ago.

"What kind of boy?" she asked, making no move to take the missive.

"Just a street urchin from the look of him. He had no connection to the palace, I dare swear. I gave him a shilling, though he said he had already been paid for the delivery."

It did not have to be a communication from the same unseen man, need not be the instructions he had promised. Hundreds of messages were delivered about the palace every day by street boys eager to earn a coin or two. It was, in fact, the way Rand might contrive to send word, should he be allowed the opportunity.

Stepping forward in sudden decision, Isabel snatched the parchment and broke the seal. She shook off the pieces of wax into Cate's outstretched hand, and her sister moved to the window to fling them out. Isabel unfolded the message.

There was no salutation. The few lines were brief and to the point.

To win free of your hateful marriage, as was promised, you have only to take courage. You will appear before the King's Court where you will swear that Rand of Braesford was absent from the palace from before vespers till after the midnight bells on the date of Mademoiselle Juliette d'Amboise's demise. The outcome will be more certain if you speak of the blood upon his hands when he returned to your bed.

No signature, title or seals marked the bottom of the page. The handwriting was precise, as if it might have been penned by a paid scribe. That precaution could have been because the writer feared his hand would be recognized, or simply to make certain whoever had commissioned it was never connected to its results.

The page crumpled under the shuddering force of her grip upon it. She wanted to tear the thing into a thousand pieces. Yes, or else to leave it conspicuously in the garderobe's basket of hay kept there for cleansing, that someone might use it for a more proper purpose.

"What is it, Isabel? Are you all right? Is it bad news? Is it . . . is it Rand?"

"No, no," she said, giving herself a quick shake. "It's nothing."

"Yes, and I suppose an announcement that the queen had been delivered of triplets, all male heirs, would also be nothing."

That comment earned a brief smile. "It's not that momentous, certainly, only a request that I help to hang my husband by testifying against him. And with false information, if you please."

"You are reluctant?"

"Astounding, is it not?" At the edge of her mind hovered the intimation of an idea concerning that fact, though she could not quite grasp it.

"Hardly. You have ever had a tender heart, dear Isabel, though you try to hide it. What shall you do?"

She smoothed the paper and refolded it. "Nothing, as I know not where to send a refusal."

Cate looked pitying. "That is your only thought, to refuse?"

"I could send a messenger to the king with the missive if I thought he would trouble to read it."

"Which he has fairly well proven is not his pleasure. Too bad his mother is not here."

"Lady Margaret?"

"She likes Rand, has made use of him for years. She is also the person who spun the scheme that put Henry on the throne, the one who holds her son's heart in her tiny hands. She who comes closer than anyone to understanding him, though they did little other than write back and forth for years. She whose blood gives him the nearest claim he has to being of royal lineage and so —"

Isabel held up her hand to stop the persuasive flow of words. "I understand, thank you. But Lady Margaret is unlikely to return from Winchester until after the queen is delivered, even if it doesn't turn out to be triplets."

"I suppose." Cate heaved a sigh.

"Unless . . ." Isabel said as hope began to rise inside her.

Her sister's head came up. "Yes?"

"Unless she may be persuaded the crown, and Henry, are in danger."

Alarm leaped into Cate's face. "Isabel! You wouldn't."

"Would I not? She may deign to see me, though her son refuses. As for the danger . . ."

"It is two days of hard riding to Winchester, at the very least."

"A mere nothing compared to the long journey to the north and back again. If Henry will listen to anyone, it will be his mother." She began to construct a mental list of things she should pack, things she must do.

"This time I shall travel with you," Cate declared.

"I think not. You will be required here. You will hover around my chamber, visiting often and reporting my decline into melancholy to all who may ask."

"But you won't be — Oh."

"Or possibly an attack of the sweating sickness that has struck down so many, if you think that will better serve the purpose. Gwynne will assist you by bringing meals that the two of you may eat so the trencher doesn't go back untouched to the kitchen. David will procure a mount for me, also one for himself since he must ride with me."

"No, really, you will need more protection than —"

"Please, Cate, I would have you and Marguerite out of this business. I could not bear it if danger came to either of you because of it."

"Yet you chance it. Suppose Rand learns of it. What will he say?"

He would be angry, Isabel thought, or more likely enraged that she meant to entice David into aiding her. And he would be wroth beyond bearing that they would set out minus a full complement of men-at-arms. "Nothing I need heed since he is safely shut away for now."

"And Graydon?"

"Our dear stepbrother may never hear of the journey, with any luck," she said in prompt reply. "If he does, what of it? I am a married woman, by His Majesty's grace, so need no longer answer to a mere relative.

No, do not go on putting obstacles in my way, sweet Cate, for I have no time for them. Go now and send David to me, and Gwynne, too, if you will. There is much to be done and no great time for it."

Her sister did as she asked, though not without more objections and dire warnings. When Cate finally left her, Isabel stood in the center of the chamber with her hands clasped in front of her. She should be filled with dread for the ride ahead of her, imagining all manner of disasters. Her knees should be shaking at the thought of the audience with the king's mother, for she was a severe and pious lady who did not suffer fools with good grace. Instead, pure exhilaration ran in her veins.

She was free to do as she chose, to seize this, her own path. The truth of it was as intoxicating as unwatered wine. There was no one to gainsay her, none to demand or expect obedience to their rulings. She could come or go at her own behest, in response to her own desires and intelligence.

It would not last. If anything happened to Rand, either Graydon or the king would again control her person and whatever wealth she owned. If Rand survived, that right would return to him. But for now, no one governed her. No one.

She would take what pleasure she might from it for as long as it lasted.

15

Rand lay on his narrow bed set against one wall, the main piece of furniture in the small chamber allotted him. He propped his head on one fist while fixing his gaze on the coffered ceiling high overhead. From that time-blackened wood hung the silver-lace splendor of a fine new spiderweb. An industrious lady spider was busily expanding its width with another draped section. Now and again, she descended on a fine line of silk as if to test the danger from the prisoner who shared her domain, or else his edibility. Discovering little chance of either, she continued with her labor.

The mattress beneath Rand had been stuffed with careless handfuls of straw, so was comprised of lumps in various sizes. The sheet and thin blanket that covered it were neither of them particularly clean. He barely noticed. He was, in memory, in his bed at the palace with Isabel in his arms.

Amazing, how accommodating she was in his imagination, taking him into the hot, sweet hollow of her mouth, tasting him, pleasuring him, while smiling into his eyes. He flung his free arm across his eyes. He should think of something else, of anything else, other than his wife's untutored yet deeply sensual beguilement.

It couldn't be done. He was sick with need of her and pure, unbridled rage that he had been taken from her bed, her company, her solace. What else mattered compared to such a loss?

He had not meant to be so besotted. Once she was his, so he thought, he would have his fill of her and be troubled no longer by the hot lust of unrequited longing. Instead, his lust and longing had increased a thousand times over. He wanted her now, here beside him, close in his arms. He wanted her tenderly compliant, utterly naked and ready for him.

He was the king of fools. All that was wanting was the cap with its tinkling bells.

Footsteps roused him. With them came the jingle of keys rather than the bells of his imagining. He rose with lithe strength and stood alert, feet slightly spread for balance. He had not yet been shut up so long that despair and bad food had taken his pride, though he feared it would come to that in the end. Or perhaps not, if the hangman came for him first.

The lock rattled. The door swung open. A slender figure stepped inside.

"A half hour, no more," the jailer said, and slammed the door, locking them in together.

David.

It was David and not Isabel. He might have known. He drew a hoarse breath, pushed aside his disappointment before stepping forward for the handclasp of greeting.

"What news?" he asked. "I'm told nothing, have heard nothing since last you were here."

David shrugged. "The court is the same, though without the king, who has left on progress. The babe you saved thrives. Leon has not surfaced again, in spite of rumors which say he has been seen here or there. Nothing of great import."

Nothing, the lad meant, that might lead to his release. It was what Rand expected. Nothing might be heard until he was taken before the King's Court and from there directly to the hangman. The next news he had might be his last.

"And how is your mistress?" he asked

without inflection as he turned to measure the six paces to the far wall and back again. "Have you a message from her this time?"

"She bids you be of good heart. She journeys soon to gain your release."

"What?" It made no sense to Rand's brain, which seemed to have slowed to the pace of a spider's crawl. "How?"

David told him, his voice tight as if he feared to be blamed. When he was done, he remained standing near the door with his hands clasped behind him.

"She goes to Winchester," Rand repeated, while the mixture of dread and hope inside him gave his heart a ragged beat.

"Your lady knows you have been useful to the king's mother in the past and that she holds you in affection. It is all that's left, for the king would not see her."

"She tried for an audience?"

David's gold curls swung forward at his short nod. "Aye, and waited for hours, for all that nothing came of it."

Rand sent his squire a sharp look as he heard the trace of fervor in his voice. Another conquest for the lady, it seemed. Something about her inclined males that way, and that included her husband. It also made what she planned impossible. Winchester was a weary long ride away from

Westminster over roads rife with all manner of dangers.

"She must not go. I forbid it."

David tilted his head, a scowl pinching his brows together over his nose. "Even if it could save your neck from being stretched?"

"What good is it if we both die? No, I refuse to chance it."

"She has asked that I go with her."

"Even so."

"We need not worry about thieves and cutthroats if a few mercenaries were hired for protection."

Rand reached to put a hand on the lad's shoulder. "There is more to this business than meets the eye. One woman has died already. Nay, my lady must not leave the palace. Go back and tell her I will not have it."

"And if she won't listen?"

It was possible Lady Isabel would not. By all the saints, it was almost certain she would not. "Tell her to come to me. Arrange it through McConnell, in secret if need be. I must see her at once. Tell her."

His squire executed a stiff bow. "I obey, sir, but doubt the lady will do the same."

"She will. She must, or I shall . . ."

"Yes, Sir Rand?"

He looked away from the interest and

sympathy in the rich blue of the lad's eyes. "Never mind. Only give her my command," he said, and added various other orders as would serve to ease his mind.

His squire bowed his acquiescence once more, began to turn away.

"Wait."

"Sir?"

Rand hesitated, asked finally, "You have my sword? You've kept it safe?"

"Indeed, sir."

"If, by chance . . ."

"Yes, Sir Rand?" The patience in the lad's face remained steady.

"Take it for the protection of my lady. Keep it close in case of need." He turned away again, unwilling to see the rise of pity in David's eyes.

"But, sir, I am only your squire."

"You have trained well and long so have the skill for it, and the strength. You are ready."

"If you say so," the lad replied, the words fretted with pain, "though I would rather you carried it in my place."

Rand turned to him, meeting his gaze for long moments. They had been through much together in this past year. Pray God, they would weather more before David earned his spurs as a knight. "So would I," he answered with a ghost of a smile. "Since that isn't to be, use it as I would."

David bowed again. The chamber door with its iron grille clanged behind him.

Rand ordered water for bathing and shaving, drawing out the process to fill the time. Then he sat down to wait. He waited all that day, and the next, and the one after. Finally, he ceased to shave himself each morning, ceased to demand more clean water, clean clothing or frequent emptying of the foul *pot de chambre* that stood in one corner. He lay on his bed and stared at the ceiling.

Sometimes he spoke to the spider that diligently spun her web above him. He accused the creature of all the sins of females, all the self-centered vanity of one who weaves webs in obedience to her own wayward caprice and in defiance of her mate. He cursed all women who did the same.

She would not obey Rand's summons, Isabel vowed. For one thing, there was no time. For another, she resented being commanded from behind a prison door. She was also incensed that he could suppose she would drop everything and scurry to his side for dalliance in his Tower chamber. She did not doubt it would come to that. And if she avoided him because she feared she might succumb, that was her secret.

The time to depart on her quest was now, while the court was in turmoil. News had arrived of a minor uprising in the West Marches. Heralds had come and gone all day and far into the night, pounding the road between the king on progression and his counselors and nobles left at the palace. A few weeks on campaign should see the matter settled, or so said those who pretended to knowledge. When it was in hand, Henry would turn his attention to the charge of murder lodged against his former companion. His assessment of the facts in the matter would be stringent, as would his directions to the justices of the King's Court. No one would be able to accuse him of favoritism.

What was wrong with a little favoritism? Isabel asked in indignation as she set out for Winchester. Did loyalty and service count for nothing? Henry might not be king this day if men such as Rand had not made his cause their own, sticking to the course against great odds, tramping at his side from the landing for invasion in Wales to the carnage of Bosworth Field.

A veritable cavalcade streamed out of the town with her on this fair dawn. In addition to David, Isabel had with her two courtiers on business with the king's mother, the Spanish diplomat sent by Isabella of Castile and Ferdinand of Aragon with orders for a written report on the birth of Henry's heir apparent, the men-at-arms attached to the courtiers and six mercenaries recruited by David with the aid of Rand's purse. Extra horses had been bespoken, as well, and awaited them at taverns along the road. So the column traveled along the road to Woking and beyond, toward the priory attached to Winchester Abbey where the nuns would attend the queen in her labor. They swept through villages, past farms with paddocks of sheep, beside hedgerows where wildflowers were going to seed and along the edges of fields studded with shocks of grain. And Isabel felt, no matter Rand's command to remain in her woman's place, that his protection went with her.

They reached Winchester in late evening of the second day. Isabel decided to wait until morning before going to Lady Margaret. She had not slept for many a long night for the anxiety that gripped her, and was overtired from the journey besides. Rest might sharpen her wits, something she would have need of when she faced the king's mother. Besides, she did not care to appear in all her travel dirt, as if desperate in her mission.

For all the sleep she got, she might as well have pounded on the palace door at midnight. Heavy-eyed and heavy of heart, she sent off her request for an audience the instant she had breakfasted next morning. That it was granted at once earned her fervent gratitude.

She was received in a solar made cozy by pastoral paintings of gigantic size and the liberal use of Saracen carpets instead of rushes. Henry's mother was dressed in her usual black and white and with her small face topped by a gabled headdress. She sat in a large armchair with her feet propped on a stool to prevent them from dangling without touching the floor. Putting aside her breviary as Isabel was shown into her presence, she tucked her hands into her full sleeves.

"What pleasure to see you, Lady Isabel," the Duchess of Richmond and Derby said in her softly modulated voice. "I trust you bring no unwelcome news from Westminster?"

Unease lurked in the lady's pale blue eyes, Isabel saw. It was the natural fear of a mother who had seen kings come and go in her five decades of life. "None, Your Grace," she answered in prompt reassurance. "All is well with the king save a small insurrection that I believe he has well in hand."

"Yes, so I have it from the dispatches brought by the courtiers who rode with you. And everything at the palace is as it should be?"

"Close enough, I believe."

"I delight to hear it, and would speak more on it later. Meanwhile, I pray thee tell me what brings you, for I cannot suppose you are here without purpose."

Isabel knew precisely what she wanted to say, having had ample time to think while cantering toward this audience. She plunged in at once with the death of Juliette d'Amboise and Rand's arrest for her murder. "We spoke before, Lady Margaret, of the attempt by the king's enemies to draw a parallel between the death of the French-woman's child and that of the princes in the Tower. What His Majesty may not realize is that many at court know full well the lady was sent to Braesford Hall for the birth. It was done for the queen's sake, of course. . . ."

"A king does not worry about the effect of his amours on his consort," Margaret said severely.

It would be well if he did, in Isabel's

opinion, though it could hardly be useful to say so. "Indeed not, but what of the effect on the child carried by Elizabeth?"

The king's mother slid from her chair and walked away down the length of the solar. Turning with such force that the small silver crucifix on a chain at her waist swung in an arc, she paced back again. "My son is surely aware of the implications of his order of arrest," she said as she passed Isabel on her way to the chamber's opposite end.

"He may be. Or he might not realize that people, knowing Rand acted for Henry in concealing the Frenchwoman, must believe he also acted for him in removing her. By allowing Rand to hang, he would be implicating himself in the murder."

"You are assuming Sir Rand is innocent."

"Yes." Isabel could not have said what made her so certain, unless it was the way he had saved the small boy at the tournament. Yes, or the way he had held the toddler afterward, as if his young life had infinite value. He had also felt the pain of her injured finger even as she had, for she had seen it in his face. No man so tender in his concern could take the life of a newborn or its mother.

"Such loyalty is commendable, but you imply that my son might allow such a miscarriage of justice."

"Would he not, to retain his crown?"

Margaret flung her a cold glance. "He may well believe, or know on good evidence, that Sir Rand is guilty."

"Then why did he not put him in prison the moment he arrived in London? Why wait? Nay, Your Grace. The king has been constrained to act against his better nature, or so I believe. The death of Mademoiselle d'Amboise was designed to embarrass him and force his hand. Someone wants Sir Rand to stand his trial so the evidence against him can be manipulated to besmirch the king. Once Henry is suspected of ordering the vile murder of his own flesh and blood, and that of the baby's mother, then he can be reviled for child murder as completely as Richard III, and toppled from power as easily."

Lady Margaret paused in her pacing to stare at Isabel. "The idea is not new."

"But the manner in which Rand was lured to the scene of Mademoiselle Juliette's murder adds weight, do you not agree?"

"If only we knew who came for her. Yes, and where she was taken."

This was the point Isabel had been waiting for. "You could discover it, Lady Margaret," she said, hiding her fisted hands in the folds of her gown. "You are the king's mother and most beloved by him. No one can or will deny whatever you request. More than that, I am told you sometimes hold council on minor matters with the king's blessing, that you hear petitions and make judgments so His Majesty may direct his efforts toward more weighty matters. Could you not hold a tribunal on this affair?"

"A tribunal." The older woman's face turned thoughtful.

"With your influence and under seal of your orders, the captain of the men-at-arms who spirited the Frenchwoman away from Braesford might be located. The midwife who delivered the babe could be brought before you to be questioned. The owner of the keep where Mademoiselle was killed could be produced so he might explain how she came to be lodged there, or at least why she died in that place and not some other."

"You are suggesting I undertake this while Henry is absent from Westminster. Yes, and otherwise occupied with this insurrection."

Isabel flushed. "I had not intended anything quite so . . . so devious. It's only that the time is now."

"As you say," the king's mother agreed with a dismissive gesture before turning away again, allowing her gaze to rest on her prie-dieu of black oak with a velvet-covered kneeling bench, which sat in a corner. Her voice dropped to a whisper. "But what if the answers turn out to be . . . wrong?"

"I dare not think they will," Isabel answered. "But if so, you must make the matter right, Your Grace. You cannot be who you are and bear in good conscience that it should be otherwise."

Silence descended between them. Somewhere men chanted in voices low and serene yet thrumming with restrained power. A dog barked and earned a reprimand. Hens cackled in alarm, then sang into quiet. Isabel stood so stiff and straight that her knees hurt. She began to sway, a faint movement that grew more pronounced with every passing second.

"No," Lady Margaret said at last, "I refuse to believe Henry can be guilty. Nor can I accept it of Sir Rand. If something is to be done, it must be soon and it must be in Westminster. There is where I have access to account rolls showing who was paid, when and for what service, also to heralds to send here and there and to the official seals that will force answers."

It was full agreement, Isabel saw. She had won. The relief was so intense that her knees sagged with it, forcing her to recover with a jerk.

Lady Margaret gave her a swift glance. "Of course, I would have to leave Elizabeth."

"Yes, but the queen consort has some weeks yet before her time, I believe?"

"So does everyone else, counting back from the wedding. I am not convinced. But no matter. We must depend for her security on her doctor and those who hover around her like wasps around ripe fruit."

"I am certain all will be well. Her Majesty may not be . . . of a robust nature, but neither is she a weakling."

"As you say." Lady Margaret drew a deep breath, forcing the air from her lungs in a rush. "I will require aid if the business is to be done in good time. Once back at Westminster, you must remove to a chamber near mine and become my scribe for the messages that will go out under my private seal. We want no chatter about this business. If all goes well, we may be able to sort out this madness and keep safe the lives of the men we love."

The king's mother thought she loved Rand. Isabel opened her mouth to refute it, but closed it again. Allowing the suggestion to stand might be an advantage. With a lift of her chin, she said, "If you will recall, Your Grace, the chamber I shared with Rand was near the king's apartments."

Lady Margaret gave a nod. "So it was. Excellent. Go, then, and make ready. We leave for Westminster as soon as everything is in order."

Isabel accepted her dismissal with a deep curtsy. A moment later, she was outside the solar with the door closed behind her. She stopped there, staring at nothing.

She had won.

The concession she had thought to extract had been allowed her.

She should be joyful. Euphoria should flood like a millrace in her veins, filling her heart to bursting. Instead, she was suddenly tired, so tired. And repeating endlessly in her mind was the question the Lady Margaret had whispered to the God she consulted at her prie-dieu.

What if the answers discovered in tribunal turned out to be wrong indeed?

Preparations for the return from Winchester took forever and a day, or so it seemed. Servants ran here and there with stacks of folded linen. Menservants knocked beds apart to be loaded, and packed silver and gold plates, cups, basins and ewers. Horses and mules, carts and wagons, were gathered.

Heralds were sent flying ahead to arrange changes of horse and announce their coming at the tavern where they would rest the night. Squabbles among Lady Margaret's attendants over who would go and who would stay had to be settled.

Isabel waited in a fever of impatience. She would have liked to harry the servants, forcing them to move faster. She wanted to mount up and gallop away as swiftly as she had come. Neither course was within her power. The servants were not hers to order and she could not offend the king's mother by leaving ahead of her.

It was on the third day of packing, as Isabel sought patience in the priory garden, that she came upon Elizabeth of York. She had seen her in passing and at meals, of course, but Henry's queen was usually so surrounded by ladies-in-waiting, nuns and courtiers that it was impossible to speak to her. Now here she sat, gilded by spangles of summer sunlight falling through an arbor of roses, reading a book with marble covers. She looked up, her face apprehensive, at the sound of Isabel's footfall.

"Ah, Lady Isabel, it's you," she said, her features relaxing into a smile.

"Forgive me, Your Majesty," Isabel said quickly as she dropped into a curtsy. "I did not mean to intrude."

"By no means, you are most welcome. I only thought it might be . . ." She paused, drew a quick breath. "Suffice it to say it is not you I seek to escape. Come, join me here on the bench. It is more than wide enough for two, even considering my present size."

To refuse a royal request was not possible. With a murmur of gratitude, Isabel complied. They sat exchanging the usual pleasantries for a few moments.

"You are anxious to be off, I expect," Elizabeth soon said with the glimmer of a smile in her fine sea-blue eyes. "The requirements of royalty can be tedious, can they not?"

"Oh, I would not say so."

"No, being much too polite. I say it for you, who suffer it every day."

"In truth, I wonder that you can support it, especially just now."

The queen's gaze turned wry. "Your departure may make it easier."

Warm color suffused Isabel's face. "I apologize if I have caused difficulties for you by coming here."

"No, no, I only meant that you take my mother-in-law when you go, a great boon." She moved a gently rounded shoulder. "Lady Margaret is a strong woman, stronger than I for all her small size. Her ideas of what is required to bring a royal child into the world clash with those of my mother, who gave birth to eight while married to my father so considers herself an expert. Their endless arguments, their conflicting rules and instructions, quite overset me."

"I can see how they might."

"I do carry a future king, of course, the progenitor of a new Tudor dynasty, as we are told. My lady mother-in-law is accountable to Henry for his safety, and so I must abide by her strictures above all else."

"I wonder that she has agreed to leave you."

"As do I, believe me. I can only suppose the need to be severe."

The faintest intonation of a question was in the gentle comment. It was on the tip of Isabel's tongue to relate the cause and the events that had brought it about, but she caught the words back in time. How horrifying it would be if she so upset the queen that she went into early labor. "I am sure Lady Margaret will tell you everything if you ask."

"And I am sure she will not," Elizabeth of York said. "I am cocooned against all unpleasantness for the duration. Or forever, as the case may be." She put a hand on her swollen abdomen, rubbing it in a gentle caress. "I don't repine, knowing it is for the good of the child I carry, which is also my father's heir, and my own."

Isabel met the queen's gaze, her own softening as she understood the daughter of Edward IV was well aware that the royal Plantagenet line of her family would continue, on the distaff side though it might be. After a moment, however, the true force of the words spoken by Henry's queen consort struck her. Her brows drew together in a frown as she said, "If you know the matter is unpleasant, then . . ."

"Oh, I know far more than that."

"Ma'am?"

"I am aware that Henry, naturally enough, brought a mistress with him from France, also that the woman had a child. I've heard whispers that the babe did not live, and am inclined to believe it after the mummery at your wedding to Sir Rand."

It made sense, as Isabel had thought before, that Elizabeth would learn these things at a court where anyone who resented her connection to the Yorkist regime might take revenge by disturbing her peace with gossip. Compassion for the lady, set about with those who were less than friends if not downright enemies, shifted through Isabel.

"I am truly sorry," she said in quiet sincerity.

"You have a kind heart, Lady Isabel, but I beg you won't refine upon my circumstances too much. I am where God and my fate intend that I should be. I only mention the small discontent in order to explain my gratitude for the respite you are providing. For that, as well as for the friendship you have so freely given, I should like to offer a boon. If ever there is anything I may do for you, you have only to ask."

It was a precious gift, and Isabel knew how to value it. Elizabeth of York did not scheme or pretend to influence in her husband's court, but that did not mean she was ineffective. The woman who slept with a king and bore his children would never be without power.

Isabel expressed her appreciation as best she might. Afterward, the two of them sat long under the arbor with the scent of roses surrounding them and petals drifting down like gentle rain. And in the two days that followed, she and Elizabeth of York met often in that same place, speaking there of a thousand things, including men and their foibles, of being wedded with reluctant consent, of learning to live with a strange husband. Isabel was briefly sorry, after all, when the time finally came to go.

Depart they did, however, on a hot day as August came to an end. When the walls of Winchester were left behind, the column of outriders, guards, courtiers, servants, baggage wagons and provision carts moved with the slow and majestic state. Isabel, reining in her mount to the deliberate pace preferred by Lady Margaret, soon had a headache from heat, dust and improving lectures on everything from how to wear her caps and veils to the frequency of her prayers. She must act the smiling companion for the sake of future favors and, above all, be grateful that the inquiry into the death of Juliette d'Amboise had been set in motion, even if at such a deliberate pace. Never in her life had she been so glad to draw near the great sprawl of London and the shining ribbon of the Thames, or to turn with a great clatter of hooves into King's Street, which led to Westminster Palace.

She was soon installed back in her bridal chamber near the king's apartments with her sisters near at hand. The next few days saw messages imprinted with Lady Margaret's seal speeding in all directions. But though various nobles and king's soldiery tramped in and out on the order of the king's mother, no one could say who had commanded the detail that traveled north to take the Frenchwoman away from Braesford. No one had any idea who had served in it or where they had gone afterward. Some hinted the men-at-arms might have been mercenaries pressed into service and fitted out with royal accoutrement, but not a soul ventured a guess as to who had supplied them or for what reason. What could it matter, after all? The woman was only the king's mistress, little better than a whore, so hardly worth the time it took to answer questions about her.

Isabel, noting the attitude, could not but wonder if those questioned imagined they were protecting the king's interest, and that of the house of Lancaster. It would explain much.

But no, that was unacceptable, for if Henry was guilty, what did that say for Rand?

In due time, the midwife who had been at Braesford was brought to Westminster, surrounded by the escort dispatched to find her. She was hustled directly to Lady Margaret's council chamber, a long room fitted with paneling and wall hangings embroidered with a portcullis, the badge of her Beaufort family.

Anticipation hummed along Isabel's veins

as she stood at Lady Margaret's right hand, next to a discreet scribe who knelt with pen and paper resting on his bent knee while he recorded the proceedings. It seemed they might learn at last what had actually occurred at Braesford.

The midwife, a plump woman with wide hips, round face and soft, almost shapeless nose seemed frightened out of her wits. Her face was pasty white, her eyes bulged and her lips trembled. Her clothing was rough and travel stained, and the plain linen scarf that covered her head had slipped to one side so she appeared half-tipsy.

Isabel felt a pang of sympathy for the woman's weariness and terror, but hardened her heart against it. The more in awe the midwife was of her surroundings and the person asking the questions, the more likely they might finally hear the truth.

"Your name?" Lady Margaret asked as a preliminary.

The midwife went from white to fiery red. She pushed at her head covering, though without improving its appearance. "Dame Agnes Wellman, milady."

The questions went on, establishing the woman's status as the widow of a freedman, where she resided, how long she had lived there, if she had children, how long she had been a midwife, how she came by the trade, how many babies she had delivered and how many had lived and a dozen other things. Finally, the crux of the matter was reached.

"On a night this July last, you were summoned to a lying-in at Braesford Hall. Is this correct?"

"Aye, milady."

"You arrived in good time to find a woman in labor, I believe. Tell us what happened then."

The woman looked as if she might faint. Her throat worked as she swallowed and she blinked so constantly the movement was like a tic. "I did me duty as best I know how. The lady was having a hard time of it."

"She was a lady?" The expression on Lady Margaret's face as she put the question said plainly that she doubted it.

"Aye, that she was, though a foreigner. She screamed out, praying in words I couldna understand."

"She was delivered of the infant?"

"That she was, though it was a long, wearisome business. 'Twas a breach birth, see, but was finally turned. The babe was a girl child, such a pretty little thing."

"It was alive and healthy?"

"Oh, aye. It cried and all, for I cleared the wee throat so it might. 'Twas a bit weak from the long birthing, but right as rain."

"What happened then?"

"I showed her to her mother, didn't I? And right proud she was, too. But the afterbirth was coming, see, and I had to tend to it. The gentleman who was there, Braesford himself, took the baby and walked away into the next chamber. I was that surprised, most men not liking to touch the wee ones. They fear to hurt them, see."

"Yes, yes, and then?"

"Well, the poor babe hushed its crying, sudden, like. Which I didn't think too much about, as the mother was bleeding something fierce. It was only later that I —"

"The mother's bleeding stopped?"

"Aye, for I had herbs and simples and clean linen by me for such."

Lady Margaret nodded in satisfaction. "And how long before you thought about the baby again?"

"Nigh on an hour, it may be. Braesford came back to ask about the lady. He said the lady's serving woman had bathed the girl child and wrapped her in swaddling, and she was fast asleep."

"So then you left the manse. You were not asked to remain to look after the mother and child?"

"Nay, milady. The serving woman, a

foreigner like her mistress, knew a thing or two about birthing. She must, for she'd tried to deliver the babe before I was brought in. I was paid me fee and sent on my way." The midwife's lip thrust out as she spoke, as if in resentment at her dismissal when she had no doubt expected several days of nursing service with extra coin for it.

"And then?"

"Well, I went away down the stairs, didn't I? I was met outside by the man who would take me homeward. It was while I was mounting pillion behind him that I smelled the stench."

"Stench?"

" 'Twas like flesh burning, I vow. I looked up then, and black smoke was pouring out the chimney pot of the room I'd left."

Lady Margaret frowned. "Could it not have been something else you smelled? A kitchen fire, say?"

The woman shook her head, almost dislodging her head covering. "I'd say not, milady. 'Twas nothing like it. 'Twas more . . . more —"

"Quite," Lady Margret said, cutting her off with a regal gesture.

Silence fell in the chamber except for the scratch of the scribe's pen on parchment. It stopped as he caught up with what had been said. Isabel waited for the king's mother to continue. When she did not, she cleared her throat with a small sound.

"Yes, Lady Isabel?" Lady Margaret said drily.

"If I might speak?"

Assent was given with a wave of one small hand. Isabel turned immediately to the midwife. "Was a fire burning already in the fireplace?"

"Aye, and it was. 'Twas a night of misting rain, damp, like, and chill, for all 'twas coming on summer. Lovely, it was, to have a fire in the chamber like that. I like to have hot water handy, see, to warm my hands before I set to work."

"So it was burning the whole time. You removed the afterbirth, I believe you said. What did you do with it?"

"Why, nothing. It was got out of the way, left with the bloody rags and such. 'Twas the serving woman's job to tidy the chamber. Afterward, I mean."

"Might she not have thrown rags and all on the fire? Could the smell have been the afterbirth burning?"

The woman opened her eyes wide. "Well . . . well, I suppose it could have happened that way. But I never heard the babe again."

"The baby was supposed to be asleep. Would it have been so unusual not to hear it?"

The woman gave a slow shake of her head. "Not really, when the birth was so hard. It was the gentleman coming and taking it away that was not as usual, see."

"Were you given any cause to think Braesford meant harm? Was anything said between him and the lady to make you believe injury might befall the newborn?"

"I can't say so, now I think on it."

"Still you immediately thought, on smelling cooked flesh, that the baby had been killed? What of the man who brought you? Did he notice it, too?"

The woman's face cleared. "Oh, 'twas not the same one as brought me. It were young Tom Croker, son of Old Tom, who came for me, you know. The man who took me home was another I'd not seen before, a gentleman, like. But he smelled the stink, right enough. He caught it first, asking what did I think, saying was it not a funny smell. It brought to his mind a time when his young servant boy fell into the fire pit, so he said, and was sore burned before he could be snatched out again."

16

Rand finally trimmed the beard he had grown. He bathed because he could no longer stand himself. The miserable half pail of cold water provided by the guards at high price was a far cry from the sumptuous bath Isabel had prepared for him after the tournament. He missed the full, big tub with its comfortable linen liner, missed the scented soap, missed the linen toweling, missed, most of all, the tantalizing touch of the lovely female who had knelt to bathe him and that he had dragged into the water with him.

God, but Isabel had been warm and tender, her skin like satin over ivory. If he closed his eyes, he could escape the stone walls that enclosed him, could imagine himself in their chamber once more with her in his arms. Her mouth had been so sweet, her hair a silken wonder, so soft he wanted to bury his strutted length in it. And he had, yes, he had.

Wrenching from the rough mattress and coming erect, he shook himself, cursing viciously in English, in French and the lingua franca of the mercenaries in European armies. If he didn't find something to do other than torture and titivate himself with memories, he would go mad.

Lost in the violent fight against too-vividly remembered sensation, he failed to hear the key grating in the lock. He swung toward the door only as it opened. For a wild instant, he thought he was fevered or mad indeed, for it seemed Isabel swept into his cell-like chamber in a great whiff of fresh air, Saracen perfume and splendor.

She was lovely beyond belief in a summer cloak of golden-yellow linen embroidered in red over a red gown of summer linen, a small red cap and a veiling of palest orange over her hair. In her hands she carried a covered basket from which came aromas so delectable that his stomach growled in virulent anticipation. It was she he wanted to devour, however, every single inch of her without let or hindrance, stopping only when he was sated enough for eternity.

"Well, sir," she said, coming to a halt just inside the door while the yeomen jailer locked it again behind her. "You sent for

394

me, I believe. Am I not welcome?"

"Aye," he answered, his voice husky with disuse. Tightness invaded his chest even as he spoke, and black anger surged through him like a lightning strike. "Where in God's name have you been that it took so long?"

She observed him as a bird might eye a coiled snake, wary yet confident in the knowledge that she could fly away. Skirting him with gliding footsteps, she placed her burden on the small table under the high window, moving aside a book he had been reading, his lute, a few sheets of parchment, his pen and cake of dried ink. He turned slowly to follow her progress, helianthus to her sun, watching with every fiber of his body in perilous strain. His stomach muscles clenched and the back of his neck grew hot as she slipped her cloak from her shoulders and draped it over his single stool.

"I have been about the business of discovering the truth concerning Mademoiselle d'Amboise," she said.

Her voice was meant to be soothing, he thought. Instead, it acted upon him like a siren's song so he took a step toward her. Annoyance for that involuntary movement lent an edge to his answer. "I sent word that you were not to concern yourself."

"What was I to do instead? Sit stitching

on pretty flowers while waiting to hear you had been hanged?"

"Waiting to hear, rather, that the curse of the Graces had been fulfilled and you were free."

Her lashes swept down, but not before he caught a flash of stark consciousness in the vivid green of her eyes. "I lacked the patience."

"Or the obedience you swore to before the priest."

"A mannish conceit, I think. At mass on Sunday last, the same priest declared women to be base creatures of overweening passions and no honor. If we are to be denied honor, then why trouble about a vow not of our choosing?"

"Are your passions overweening, sweet wife?"

He was rewarded by the lift of her eyes in a fulminating glare. "It was the priest's description, not mine. Do you wish to hear what I have been about or not?"

He did, but it was secondary to other wishes that crowded his brain. Lifting a hand in a gesture of accord, he turned away, the better to hide the evidence of what his ruminations on her passions had done to his body.

From the corner of his eye, he caught

sight of his narrow bed and the length of white silk that lay at its head. It was the sleeve from Isabel's wedding costume given as her favor at the tournament. Running it through his hands, sleeping with it draped over his face, had become habits after he found it packed among the items David brought for his comfort. It still bore the stains of his blood, pale brown against the white silk, but it also held captured in its weave the faint perfume of Isabel, the scent she wore and her innate sweetness. Holding it to his nose calmed the beat of his heart, or so it seemed, and sent him into satyr's dreams.

It did not suit him to have her guess how dependent he had become upon its consolation. Moving without haste, he stepped to the bed and pretended to straighten the grimy sheet while sweeping the silk rectangle beneath it. Turning again, he gave her an ironic bow as he offered the low bed as a seat.

She glanced at the lumpy mattress, then away again, before shaking her head. "I would as soon stand."

It was wise of her to avoid that rather obvious step to perdition, he thought. He might easily have joined her there and put an end to all discussion.

"Did you know," she asked, bracing her fingertips on the table beside her, "that the man who returned the midwife to her home after Mademoiselle Juliette d'Amboise was delivered of her child was not from Braesford? That he was, in fact, a gentleman?"

"A gentleman?"

"So the woman said. He was not known to her, nor did he give her a name. It seems it was he who put the idea of child murder into her head."

Rand had not known. Even if he had his ideas of who might have set the business in motion, however, there was little to be done about it. "What would you? I fear the thing has gone too far for causes and stratagems to matter." He paused, brushed the subject aside with a gesture. "I see the splint is gone from your finger. It's healed, then?"

"As you say." She glanced down at it an instant, then met his gaze, her own unguarded and so soft with remembrance that it wrung his heart. "For which I must thank you yet again."

He could think of ways that might be accomplished, but choked back the words as he inclined his head. "Not at all."

"No." She took a swift breath that pressed her breasts higher against her bodice. "Where was I? Lady Margaret's council and

398

what has been discovered. Allow me to tell you, if you please?"

She went on to relate a good many things as he faced her in the small chamber, most of them unknown to him. Hope, that bastard emotion that tied men's souls in knots, awakened inside him as he listened, particularly as he realized the scope of Lady Margaret's entry into the business.

Ruthlessly, he choked it off. It would not do, not while he lay behind lock and key, unable to provide the least modicum of protection for his wife.

"You do realize," he said with deliberate scorn, "that a woman has died to prevent the knowledge you are seeking from being made public? You can understand, can you not, that you may be killed if you continue?"

"I am not stupid, however much you might prefer it," she answered with a lift of her chin. "But I abhor unfairness, cannot abide that whoever has brought this upon you should profit from it."

"So it's the unfairness of it that moves you. You have no concern for my life."

"I did not say so. What manner of wife would I be to show myself content that you should die for a crime you did not commit?"

"One forced to wed against her will," he

drawled in tried reason. "Some pray to be released from such unions. But if you have any respect whatever for the tie that binds us, you will heed my command in this matter. Return to Westminster and keep as still in our chamber as you are able. Forget what took place at Braesford because the truth will not change what is to happen. Preserve yourself and, just possibly, the child we may have created between us. That is the best thing you can do for me."

The look she gave him held only scorn. "I had not expected you to be grateful, but did think you might have some appreciation for what I am about."

"Oh, I appreciate it, my dear wife, far more than you know. But I object to lying here in terror of your death while I can do nothing to prevent it. I have no wish to discover, when I am hanged, that you are already on the other side to greet me."

Her eyes, dark green with concern, searched his face even as color drained from her face. After a long moment, she sighed, lowered her gaze to a point past his shoulder. "You think," she said in the barest of whispers, "that Henry is really behind this thing. You believe he did away with his mistress, meant to be rid of her baby."

"A kingdom is a hard thing to lose."

"All because he bedded a woman for some few weeks or months before he took a queen, yes."

"Or for the sake of another man's child," he answered with a snort of disdain.

"Another man's . . . ?"

"Did I not tell you before? I have it on good authority that Mademoiselle Juliette had more than one lover. It seems she was also the mistress of the king's Master of Revels."

"That is clearly impossible, as I would have told you before if you had allowed me to know what you were about. Yes, or taken the time to hear what I would say."

He remembered the incident, remembered also the crock of raspberries he had brought to their chamber on the night of his interrogation on the matter. That he had been so distracted as to miss the knowledge she held did not aid his temper. "You say so because you know him so well? You feel he was so entranced with you that taking another woman would not occur to him? Few men are so single-minded."

"I say it because it would be incest. I say it because I know well that Mademoiselle Juliette is, or was, his sister."

Shock and confusion struck Rand like a double blow. He stared at Isabel, seeking the truth in the clear, gray-green depths of her eyes. It lay there, like a new-minted coin at the bottom of a well. "You know this . . . how?"

"He told me months ago, when I first came to court. It was a slip of the tongue, I think, as he spoke of a song he had written about a sweet young girl seduced by a king's idle desire. He said he could never sing it at Henry's court, but should earn renown with it later, when he returned to —"

"To Brittany," Rand supplied, as that was where Leon had joined Henry's retinue as a minstrel and, later, the architect of his entertainment.

"To France," she corrected.

To France. Of course, to France. Leon and Juliette no doubt were, or had been, in the pay of the French crown. The French crown that had been trying for centuries to wipe out all trace of English dominion over French soil.

God, how could he have been so blind? The child was Henry's, after all. It must have been conceived during Juliette's liaison with him for the sole purpose of becoming a hostage for his favor toward French policy.

How very maddening it must have been for Anne, regent for young Charles VIII, and how lethally inconvenient that Henry had so quickly gotten another babe upon his new queen.

The usefulness of Juliette's child might be lessened if Elizabeth of York produced a royal heir, though not neutralized entirely. Henry would still have a care for his flesh and blood. Who had spirited the baby away, then, and why? Had it been done to prevent Henry's small daughter from being used against him? Was it so she could be held by those who would best know how to use such a tender captive?

Yes, and had Juliette died trying to protect little Madeleine, or had she been killed for another reason altogether? A dead woman could not identify her child, and a child without a mother could be claimed by any female. It would not have been necessary to kill the little one.

"I had her," Rand said, the words stark in the quiet room.

"Had who?" Isabel asked in sudden coolness.

The fleeting thought struck him that she thought he referred to Juliette. Could she, just possibly, be jealous of his acquaintance with the dead lady? It was laughable on the face of it, since Juliette had been hugely pregnant during her time at Braesford, but he was not amused. "The baby Madeleine,

Juliette's child," he said in gruff explanation. "I discovered her at the rendezvous on the night I was arrested."

His lady wife was not dull-witted; she took no more than an instant to grasp what he was saying. "The baby was with her all along? She truly was removed from Braesford with Mademoiselle Juliette?"

He heard the gladness in her voice and allowed himself a moment of irony. "Oh, aye, as I've said all along."

"David told me she was safe, but not how it came about or who had her. What happened? Where were they taken?"

"A message was delivered asking for my aid, as you may know."

She gave a quick nod. "Go on."

"I was told where to meet Mademoiselle Juliette, at a ruined keep deep in the country. The idea was that I should be discovered there with her body, and with the baby. By good luck, I was early to the meeting place. I found Juliette newly dead and the baby lying where she had fallen, so it appeared, as Juliette died. She was such a small mite. I tucked her into my doublet and escaped through the postern gate. Once back in town, I —"

He stopped abruptly, appalled at his near mistake.

"You what? Where did you take her? What did you do with her?"

He refused to tell her. Once Isabel learned where the child was, she would not rest until she had the small one in her keeping; it was how she was made. Who could say what might come of that? Murder had been done because of this birth, as he had told her, and might well be again.

"It isn't something you need know. Suffice it to say she is well and well hidden."

"You are quite sure of it? You know this in spite of being shut away here since Mademoiselle Juliette was killed?"

"As sure as any man may be."

She paced away from him, turned with a swing of linen skirts and retraced her steps to halt in front of him. "Few places are truly safe. Any person may weaken, in spite of everything, if the bribe is large enough."

"And some have no need for riches," he said with certainty.

"What if you are wrong?"

If he was wrong, then the child would become the pawn she was intended to be. Those who had possessed her would achieve their ends. Either France would force Henry to stand aside while it annexed former English territories, or the Yorkists would create a scandal that, like the deaths of the princes in the Tower, might doom the Tudor reign before it had well begun.

It was not impossible, of course, that whoever was behind it intended to accomplish both aims. Or that an extra one could be to see Isabel widowed and a new master installed at Braesford Hall.

"If I am wrong," he said deliberately, "it will make little difference. Henry either will or will not acquire new allies, new alliances. He will or will not keep his throne. You will either be the mother of my heir, therefore empowered to hold Braesford in our child's name, or else a childless widow available to be married again to Henry's advantage, with or without Braesford as your dowry. Your life will go on and mine . . ."

"What?" she demanded, searching his face.

"Mine will not."

"For the love of heaven, Rand, do not be such a martyr!" she cried, clenching her fists as she moved closer to him, raising them toward him while anger flashed like green fire in her eyes. "Does your motto of Undaunted mean nothing?"

"It means everything."

"Why will you not fight? Do you not care to live? Have you nothing worth living for?"

Rage, trapped deep inside him for weeks,

sprang free to meet hers. He reached for her, grasping her arms and pulling her against him so she was melded to him from breast to knees. "You," he answered, the word so harsh it scraped his throat. "You are the reason I would live."

He kissed her as if he meant to devour her, plundering her sweetness, licking the tender, quilted inner surface of her mouth, the polished edges of her teeth, capturing her tongue. He enclosed her in the circle of his arms and still could not get close enough. Swinging with her, he put her back to the wall next to the door so anyone peering through the iron grille could see nothing. Pressing close, he moved into the soft juncture of her thighs, glorying in the feel of her against him, in the sensation of her breasts flattened upon the hard planes of his chest.

She did not resist, but met him in a fury of her own, sliding her arms around his neck, clutching his hair in her fingers. He shuddered with the scrape of her nails on his neck and his scalp, groaned aloud as he felt her arch against him and move sinuously in her own need.

She was temptation and beguilement, comfort and every promise of surcease he had ever known. Half-crazed by the feel and the scent of her when he had feared never to touch her again, he had no thought of restraint. Nothing, nothing mattered except to have her, take her, fill her, become lost in her, never again to be found.

He framed her breasts with his hands, teasing the nipples while he licked and sucked the fragile skin of her neck, took her earlobe between his teeth until she gave a small cry and turned her mouth to his once more.

He smoothed one palm downward and around, kneading the fullness of her hips, grinding her slowly against his aching body, lifting her to the tips of her toes for a better fit. Blind, deaf, uncaring of where they were or who was near, he gathered folds of her skirt in his hand, grasping for more, dragging it up until he reached the hem. Burrowing underneath, he skimmed the warm, firm flesh of her thigh, found her softness.

God, she was wet and hot, so hot, burning tenderly into the palm of his hand as he cupped her. He used the heel of his hand and wrist to stoke her desire, felt the tight bud of it harden against his pulse that throbbed there. She gasped on a tried sound of need, shivering in his hold. He loosened it a fraction, enough to bend his head and tongue the neckline of her gown, find the strutted nipple that pushed up beneath the fabric. And with a sudden thrust, he pressed a long finger home.

She clenched upon it in abrupt, hot reception, while internal muscles caressed, invited in liquid surrender. He needed nothing more. Raising his doublet, ripping aside points, he pushed down his braies to free himself. Lifting first one of her legs and then the other, he draped them over his arms while bracing her against the wall, and then he drove into her.

It was perfect entrapment. She surrounded him, absorbed him, took him deeper than he had ever gone, deeper than he had dreamed. Mindless with the delirium of it, he ground against her, plumbing her velvet softness. His skin felt on fire. It was too tight, too full, too sensitive to her every movement, her every contraction.

She sobbed against his neck, a small sound that carried his name. That was all it took.

He possessed her with furious strokes, each harder and deeper than the last. He couldn't stop, wouldn't stop, wanted to go on forever until they were one flesh once more, one body, one soul. He felt her hands upon him, grasping, holding, while her breath, her small gasps and cries, grew ever louder. He took her mouth again, mocking his movements with his tongue, drinking her sweet desperation, until abruptly she keeled forward, pressing her forehead into his shoulder with a guttural moan.

He exploded with the force of an overcharged harquebus, shuddering as his life, his hope and every dream pumped into her. He held her, chest heaving, heart thundering against his ribs, head pounding with the sudden return of blood, while tears burned the backs of his eyes.

"You," he whispered against her hair, "you are the reason I would live. You are also the reason I would die. Undaunted."

17

It was said by those who should know that a woman only conceived if she took pleasure in the act of procreation. Isabel was not convinced. Couplings witnessed in and around the barnyard, swift mountings protested by she-animals, gave little weight to the idea. So it had been as well with an incident at Graydon, where a serving woman had been set upon by drunken louts and left near death but still bore a child to one of her attackers.

Yet her pleasure had been fierce during the time spent with Rand. She had whisker burns on her face to show for it, also discolored splotches like bruises on her neck and wrinkles across the front of her gown.

Who could have guessed how much she would miss his touch or how easily he could prove it. His strength, his sure caress, had melted her will like a tallow candle in the sun. The ferocious concentration he brought to what he was doing, the powerful glide of his muscles as he moved against her, were reminders of his terrible prowess on the tournament field. He had taken her against the wall of his Tower chamber with the same determination to prevail.

And what incredible abandonment she had known at being held there like some servant girl coupling with a randy man-at-arms. Her face burned to think of how open she had been to him, how uncaring of anything except the fierce, hot joining. She had surged against his force, taking all of him she could get, wanting more, needing more still.

She could not help thinking she might be with child. A part of her viewed the possibility with dread; a woman with child was always at a disadvantage, restricted even more than usual in where she could go and what she could do, forced to have a care in all things for the life growing inside her. Regardless, she hugged the thought to her as tenderly as she might a newborn itself.

Rand had her wedding sleeve as his token still. He had tried to hide it, but she had seen. He kept it by him, one of a handful of personal items brought to relieve the tedium of imprisonment. It pleased her in some way she could not quite grasp.

As for what he had said as they made love, she would not think of it.

She had not asked his meaning. She knew full well that he meant her to understand he preferred to die rather than that she should continue with what she was doing. To hear a fuller explanation would have been more painful than having the simple thought lodged in her mind. Though how it could possibly hurt more, she could not imagine.

To leave him had been a wrenching agony. It was only made bearable by the knowledge that causing a scene might make it impossible for her to return.

David waited for her at the end of the passage that led away from Rand's prison chamber. Isabel pulled the hood of her lightweight cloak closer around her face as she caught sight of the lad. Though she had worn it to protect her gown against street offal and discourage unwanted attention, she was glad of the concealment it provided. She regretted nothing of the moments just past, but neither did she care to display the results to all and sundry.

David glanced at her and looked away again as he fell into step beside her. They walked on for several yards before he spoke. "What had he to say?"

The question was gruff. Rousing from her

introspection, Isabel glanced at the young man beside her. He had grown taller and broader in the passing days, gaining a greater air of confidence. Time and responsibility had that affect, she thought, and worry.

"Much as you predicted. I am to tend to my embroidery and leave him to die."

"But you won't."

He spoke as if there was no doubt. In all truth, how could there be? "I shall not."

"Have you any idea of what you will do now?"

"I must seek a person or persons who cannot be bribed."

His blue gaze was keen. "Is it a riddle?"

"You could say so."

"But you know the answer?"

She walked on for several steps, her mind moving in swift thought on that question. As she came to a simple, inescapable conclusion, she halted.

"David?"

"Milady?" He stopped beside her, his expression watchful as he glanced around them then looked back to her.

"Who holds Sir Rand's confidence beyond all others? Who would he trust with what he values most?"

"You, milady," he answered without hesitation.

She flushed a little, but shook her head. "You, I think. And that being so, tell me, where were you reared before Rand came upon you on the streets? Where were you brought as a foundling?"

"A convent, milady."

"Of which there are any number hereabouts."

"Aye."

"Aye," she repeated, her voice soft, "so which convent?"

He paled and uncertainty darkened his eyes as he gazed down at her. In the distance could be heard the moan and mutter of prisoners and the unlovely calls of ravens. A draft blowing down the corridor where they stood stirred his hair, lifted her veil. Finally, he sighed. Inclining his head in acquiescence, he told her what she wanted to know.

David left her at the gates of the palace. Isabel was pensive as she made her way toward her chamber, trying to decide what must be done with the knowledge she'd gained. She well knew her first instinct, but not what was best. So deep were her thoughts that she failed to notice Gwynne approaching until she was almost upon her.

"Milady, I came to warn you," she called.

"A visitor awaits in your chamber. Viscount Henley declares he will not leave without a word with you." Hectic color flared in the serving woman's face. She breathed in huffing rhythm that seemed as much from annoyance as from hurrying.

"Does he indeed?" Such a visit was highly irregular. The only reason her stepbrother's great oaf of a friend dared breach her privacy was because Rand was not able to call him to account.

"I told him you would not see him, milady, but he insisted. If you care to stay away until he leaves, I will come tell you when it's safe to return. Or I can summon one of the king's guards."

Isabel was in no mood to endure a commotion or to be kept from her chamber and its amenities. "Did he say what was so important?"

"No, milady."

"Mayhap it's to do with Graydon." It was also possible his purpose might have bearing on the inquiry she and Lady Margaret were pursuing. Though she had said nothing of it to her stepbrother or his friend, she was sure the activity had not escaped their notice. Indeed, the entire court, or what was left of it in Henry's absence, must be aware of it.

"And mayhap it's not," Gwynne said darkly.

"We had better go and see, I think," Isabel said, and walked on with militant firmness in her step.

"Lady Isabel," the viscount said in a bass rumble as he rose from a stool near the chamber's single window to sketch a bow. "Forgive the intrusion, I beg."

"Certainly, if you bring no ill news." Gwynne reached to untie Isabel's cloak and take it from her, but she hardly noticed in her preoccupation with her visitor. That was until she glanced down and noticed again the wrinkles that marred the linen of her gown. The light in the room was dim, however, due to the leaden skies that hovered beyond the open window. It was possible her visitor would not notice. "Have you, perhaps, come from Graydon? I've not seen him in this age."

"Nay, milady, though he is well enough, up and about his affairs as usual."

"I am pleased to hear it," she said, though with a mental grimace for what manner of affairs her stepbrother might have in hand. "And you, sir? What affair brings you here?"

"A request, you might say."

"Of what nature, if you please?"

He shifted in apparent discomfort, putting a foot forward, securing his hat closer under one arm. "I would that you might speak to the king about my suit when the time comes."

She stared at him for a moment. "Your suit."

"For your hand. I have wanted you to wife for long years, milady, and would not lose you again."

"I have a husband," she said in sharp rebuke.

"But not for long."

"You can't know that!"

A stubborn expression closed over the viscount's battered features. "It's plain enough, I think."

She would not argue with him. It would serve no real purpose, and might seem to admit doubt. "Even should I be in need of another groom, you must know I have little say in the matter."

"Nay, but ye have the king's favor and that of his lady mother, the Duchess of Richmond and Derby. Only see how you are consulted by Lady Margaret, a mark of favor indeed."

Something in his tone made Isabel think, suddenly, that the viscount might be curious about the association. He had not asked directly, but could be hoping to hear how it came about. Perversely, she was not inclined to tell him. "It means nothing."

"Yet tongues clack, saying the two of you hold your private councils as Henry does in his Star Chamber. With your sisters beside you, betimes, it becomes a womanish version of the same."

"I vow it's no such thing. Lady Margaret seeks to aid her son by taking the burden of some minor judgments from him. You will grant, surely, that she has that right."

"As she put him on the throne, I daresay she can claim any right she chooses," he answered, his deep voice as dry as tomb dust.

Isabel's smile was brief. "Just so. But nothing we have discussed in such councils has bearing on my future. Now if you will excuse me, I have had a tiring morning and would like to rest."

He scowled, making no more move to go than if he had been attached by roots growing into the stone. "Have you discovered aught? In these councils, I mean?"

"Such as?" It might prove instructive, she thought, to know what he expected of them.

"Why, who killed the Frenchwoman, if 'twas not your husband, and what became of her babe. Is that not what ye want to know?"

Did he mock her? She had doubted he was capable of it. His stolid face showed no glimmer of it now. "On these things," she said carefully, "we have made little progress, to be sure."

"You being so close to the business, could be you've heard when Braesford will come before the King's Court for his crime?"

She was forced to swallow before she could reply. "Certainly not until after Henry's heir is born and he returns to Westminster."

"Nay, but I suppose you'll know how to answer when they ask where your husband was the night the king's whore died, and how he appeared when you saw him later."

Isabel turned sharply away to hide her shock. Her gaze met that of her serving woman for an instant of silent communication. As she kept nothing from Gwynne, both knew the viscount's words were amazingly like the instructions in the message she had received. Was it a coincidence, or did he have knowledge of it? If the last, was Graydon involved as his close companion? Had her stepbrother learned discretion, at last, that he thought to persuade her to do what he wanted instead of bullying her into it?

Yes, and what did either man know of Mademoiselle Juliette's death? Were they behind that terrible business, or only attempting to take advantage of it?

It made no difference. She could not be cajoled or forced into helping convict Rand with lies. "I know exactly what to say," she answered with perfect truth.

"Ah, well. Then I expect all will turn out as God intends," Viscount Henley said, sweeping the floor with his hat as he bowed. "Until next we meet, Lady Isabel."

He left her then, striding away out the door as Gwynne sprang to hold it open for him. Moving with the crude swagger of some hulking animal, he clapped his hat on his head and stamped along the corridor. He did not look back.

Isabel stood unmoving as a multitude of thoughts and images swarmed in her head. Abruptly, she swung around, calling for Gwynne to hurry and bring bathing water so she might change her clothing that still held the Tower's prison stench in its folds. The king's mother must know of Henley's and Graydon's attempt to ensure that Rand hanged. It could make a difference, a dangerous difference.

Hurrying along the corridors toward the king's apartments a short time later, she frowned at the tips of her shoes as they flickered from under her skirt with her every step. Really, what was she to make of the viscount? He had always been there like a stool or settle before the fire, seldom noticed but made use of at need. Somehow she had seen him only as the bumbling friend of her stepbrother. Now, she wondered. He might be craftier than he looked. His awkwardness could be mere discomfort in her presence, or even artifice.

Voices raised in babbling commotion made her look up. All thought of Henley was wiped from her mind as Lady Margaret turned a corner and swept toward her. She was dressed for travel in a serviceable gown of fine black wool covered by a dust cloak of the same that was embroidered in silver thread. Behind her came a gaggle of ladies and serving women, as well as her confessor, her steward and her personal guards. She threw orders over her shoulder as she walked, pulling on embroidered leather gloves at the same time.

"Ah, there you are, Lady Isabel," the king's mother said as she caught sight of her. "I had begun to think I would not see you before my departure."

"You are leaving Westminster?" she asked in trepidation as, receiving a regal gesture, she rose from her curtsy and turned to walk beside Lady Margaret. Though it had been clear from the beginning that she could not be long away from the queen consort's side, the plan had been for her to remain at the palace at least another week.

"News has come from Winchester. Elizabeth's physicians expect her to go into labor at any moment. She may be delivering as we speak."

The baby was coming early, by all accounting. Though August had turned into September while they held their councils, it was still no more than eight months since the king had wed Elizabeth of York. "You must go, of course. I trust there has been no accident, no difficulty?"

"None in the least."

The rumors which said Henry had bedded his bride between the betrothal and the wedding had apparently been true. That, or else Lady Margaret was putting a good face on the news.

"I am delighted to hear it," Isabel said. "Please extend to the queen my profound wishes for an easy confinement, also my warmest felicitations when her child is born."

"I shall."

"The king has been informed?"

"A herald was sent with all speed to where he wends his way toward Winchester in progression. No doubt he will be there before me."

Isabel hesitated, hardly daring to speak yet afraid to be silent. "And . . . and this matter we have been looking into here?"

"I shall surely put it before him," Lady Margaret said with a brief, harried glance, "later, after the heir is born and duly christened. My son and I will then pursue it with all the vigor at our command."

It was as much as she had any right to expect, Isabel knew. She bowed her head in acceptance. "You are kindness itself to keep it in mind."

They were nearing the front entrance. The majordomo stood holding the front door through which opening could be seen a spirited white palfrey surrounded by members of the king's yeoman guard in their distinctive livery.

Isabel came to a halt, curtsied and moved to one side. "I must not delay you. Godspeed, Your Grace."

"May He hold you in His hands," Lady Margaret said in quiet answer. She moved swiftly on, gliding out the door and down the steps with her cloak flapping, blowing back from her narrow shoulders. A few moments later, she was gone.

Left alone, Isabel was not certain what she should do. Lady Margaret's impromptu council was ended for the moment, and there was little she could achieve on her own.

Or was that strictly true, she thought, remembering the information she had received so short a time ago. Rand's arrest had prevented him from doing more than hide Juliette d'Amboise's child away. If little Madeleine could be brought forth and shown to the public, might that not aid his cause?

Why had Rand not delivered her to Henry? What reason could he have for hiding the child from its father now that Mademoiselle Juliette was no more? Was it possible he didn't trust the king not to make a permanent end to the threat posed by this small babe?

Child murder. The words had such an ugly ring.

Some said it was not Richard III but Henry who had arranged for the deaths of the young sons of Edward IV. Did Rand know it to be true? Was that why he had hidden the child away?

There was one other possibility. Rand had traveled from Brittany with the king's forces, had been with Henry every step along the path of invasion. From the victory at Bosworth Field he had come to court, remaining long enough to be awarded the prize he sought. Afterward, he had left London and Westminster, burying himself at Braesford until forced to return by the king's command. What if he had been Mademoiselle Juliette's lover and the father of her child? Suppose it was he who had spirited the lady away under guard and later murdered her?

Oh, but why would he destroy the one person who could swear that the babe had been alive and well long after the midwife left Braesford? No, no, Isabel refused to accept it. He could not have made her his wife so thoroughly, could not have held her, loved her so well, if another woman had been in his heart.

Could he?

Rand had been suspected of the death of the baby, but arrested for the deaths of both child and mother. The charges had been fabricated for the dual purpose of embarrassing the king and putting an end to Rand's life; it could be no other way. If the baby was produced, proving the first crime never took place, surely his guilt in the second must seem less certain?

If it was not safe to take the baby to its father, to Henry, there was still one other who could be depended upon to hold tiny Madeleine safe from harm, also to see that the implications in her being alive was presented in Rand's defense when he appeared at the King's Court. Lady Margaret, Duchess of Richmond and Derby, would serve admirably. She would keep this baby safe because it would benefit her son, but also because, like it or not, she was the child's grandmother.

By the time Isabel had worked her way around to that conclusion, she knew exactly what she must do. She also knew where she must go. For the first, she had to trust to her heart. For the second, she need merely persuade David to take her to the only persons in Henry's wide realm who had no need for riches.

18

The Convent of Saint Theresa, on the outskirts of London, was a complex of buildings in cream stone kept safe behind walls of the same mellow material. A world within itself with its chapel, kitchens and cloister from which opened scores of small rooms no larger than cells, it had also a wall garden replete at this season with vegetables and ripening fruit, the trills of birds and hum of bees. It looked a warm and welcoming place in the late-evening quiet, but the abbess was less than convivial.

Upright and proud, she stood before them with her hands tucked into the wide sleeves of her habit and her features under her wimple set in lines of stern authority. By what right did Lady Isabel seek possession of this child? she demanded. Young David there at her side was well-known to them, yes, but that counted for little. He had brought the child to the convent on guidance from God, one more orphan to join all the others. He had denied being the father, asking only for succor for her. The little one had been well fed and put back into swaddling. She had begun to thrive. To give her over to just anyone might not be in her best interests. The abbess must first be certain of His will in the matter.

It was dusk-dark with a ghost moon rising by the time Madeleine was handed over to Isabel and David at last. It might not have happened then except that Isabel had invoked the name of Lady Margaret. The duchess, it transpired, was a patron of the nunnery, and honored the abbess from time to time by staying within the convent walls for a few days of prayer. A most holy and gracious lady she was indeed. Why had Isabel not said at once that she had come from the king's mother?

"Sir Rand chose well for a place to see Mademoiselle Juliette's child safe," she said to David when he had held her palfrey while she took the swaddled infant he passed up to her.

"Aye."

"At your suggestion, I suspect."

"There was no time to think long on it, and few places to turn." He stood gazing up at her in the pale light that turned the world to shades of gray, in no hurry to mount Shadow, Rand's destrier that he had taken for his use. The abbess had insisted on sending the woman who was Madeleine's wet nurse with them, and they awaited her coming.

"You could — he could — have brought her to me." That Rand had not trusted her enough for it was an ache deep in her chest.

"Not without everyone in the place knowing of it. It seemed best to hide her among many like her."

"But to tell me nothing of where she might be," she began in protest.

He shook his head. "I gave my word not to speak of it. As for Sir Rand, he feared you would not rest until you found some reason to . . ."

"To have her in my arms, yes." It seemed Rand might know her better than she could have guessed. "I am grateful you answered my plea to know where she might be found, even if it went against your vow. To search every convent would have taken far longer."

"I kept guard outside when you went to him today," David said with a shift of one shoulder. "I heard Sir Rand tell you how he'd found the babe and made away with it — though did not stay to listen to the rest." Color darkened his face, an indication that he had heard enough to know what she and Rand had been about.

"You realized then that I could guess the rest, so felt freed of your vow of secrecy," she said to prevent added embarrassment for him. "I do understand. Thank you." She had no right to be angry that he had not told her before, though it would have saved much time and trouble. A man's word was sacred, or should be.

He made no answer. As silence fell between them, Isabel turned her gaze to the stone walls of the convent, considering their age and solidity before glancing down again at the sleeping babe. "Are there really so many like her here?" she asked.

"It's the way of the world. People die easy." At the sound of a squeaking hinge, he looked away toward where a plump, fresh-faced woman, the wet nurse without doubt, emerged from the convent gate on her way to join them. His shoulders lifted in a shrug that was not as careless as he might have wanted it to appear. "Those left behind live as best they may."

"You were brought here like her." Though Rand had mentioned the bare facts in passing, she knew no more than that.

"Not quite. I was older by some months, almost walking, when brought here from some country convent."

"The abbess must have been paid for your keep as you were educated instead of being sent out early as an apprentice."

"A small sum, mayhap, though I was finally put to learning the tanner's trade." He gave a short laugh. "Living hand to mouth on the streets, where Sir Rand came upon me, breathing that stench."

"You've no idea who brought you, then?"

He shook his head so his curls gleamed in the light of a rising moon. "I was never told. Sometimes . . . sometimes I pretended to be the son of a king."

He could have been a Plantagenet, she thought, as he had the same fine, strong body, the same clear blue eyes and fair hair. He might well be one of the many by-blows sired by Edward IV, or by his brother Clarence, who was equally prodigal with his embraces. It was a harmless fancy.

"You would have made a fine prince," she said quietly, then looked away from the color that suffused the lad's face because it hurt her to see it.

They rode out at last. Their pace was slow, in part because of the baby but also because the wet nurse sat her mule like a sack of grain. The animal she rode was not happy with the panniers fitted on either side of the saddle, either, one of which held provisions for the baby while the other was meant for the infant.

The woman offered to take the baby in her charge at once, but Isabel refused. She was by no means sure the wet nurse could control her mount and see to the baby's safety at the same time. Besides, the feel of the small body in her arms satisfied something deep inside her. It pleased her to cover the small, sleeping face with her cloak against the cool night wind and hold her close.

It wasn't, she would swear, that she actually hungered for a child as did some women. Regardless, she was aware, once again, of the small hope for one. It had nothing to do with Rand and his imprisonment or with the likelihood that his line would die with him otherwise. No, it was simply nature's way. That was all, nature's way.

"Halt!"

Two horsemen came at them from behind a copse of trees. Helmeted, wearing unmarked surcoats over chain mail, they crowded in from either side. They jostled against them, shouting, snatching for their bridles as if to drag them to a standstill. Isabel felt the baby she held start, straining against its swaddling bands as it woke with a strangled cry. In the same moment, she heard the hiss as David drew the sword he wore.

Rage poured through Isabel in a wild surge like nothing she had ever felt before. She jerked her palfrey's head away from the grasping hands with such force the mare reared up, almost unseating her. As she came down, the way ahead was clear and Isabel kicked her into a run, bending over the precious burden she held.

Behind her she could hear the wet nurse screaming amid the curses of the two assailants, hollow behind their concealing helmets that had no identifying devices. Metal clanged on metal and horses whinnied in panic. Ringing above all was David's hoarse shouts as he cleaved the air with silver flashes of the great blade he wielded with two hands.

"Ride, idiot woman!" he called out in angry demand. "Ride!"

He spoke not to her, Isabel saw as she stared back over her shoulder, but to the lumpish wet nurse, who ducked and wove on her saddle as one of the horsemen grappled with her, trying to pull her from her mule. David meant the attackers to believe the nurse had the baby strapped into the mule's pannier like a peasant's child. He whacked the animal's flank with the flat of his sword so it bucked free and took off at a panicked gallop.

Isabel had the baby instead, held close to her breast with one firm arm. The wee thing was crying, but the sound, muffled by the cloak that covered it, could barely be heard amid all the rest.

She would keep her, too, with luck and David's valiant efforts. But though Rand's squire was brave and strong, he had no chain mail and little skill to match against the blows of heavier, more experienced men-at arms. All he had was Shadow and the destrier's strength and swiftness to aid him. She could not help him, though her soul shriveled with the knowledge. To honor his effort, she must take advantage of every second he gave her.

Isabel lowered her head and rode like a Viking goddess of old, plunging through the night with her cloak flying out behind and her hair, torn from its veil, streaming in the wind. She had meant to take the babe to Lady Margaret, but rode instead toward Winchester, where it was less likely she would be attacked in plain view of passersby. In moments, she could barely hear the tumult behind her. Soon all was quiet except for the thudding of her mount's hooves, the squeak of leather and rattle of the bridle.

And in that quiet, with the echo in her mind of the shouts and curses hurled by the men who had appeared from nowhere, she understood two things with stunning clarity. Most paramount was the purpose of their attack, which had been to take the baby at all costs. Just as important was their identity. One of them had been Henley, the other Graydon.

It was on the outskirts of Westminster that David caught up with her. He rode with one hand while the other dripped blood. Still he grinned as Shadow drew even with her palfrey. Gladness that he was there and reasonably unscathed tilted her own mouth into a smile, though she sobered almost at once.

"The wet nurse?" she asked.

"They went after her, though they may regret taking her as she was screeching as if demented. I expect they will let her go when they discover she has no charge with her."

"Pray God," she answered.

"The baby?" His gaze rested on the bulk beneath her mantle.

"Asleep again. I believe she likes riding." She paused. "Will you be all right until we reach the palace?"

He gave a nod. "And after. 'Tis nothing."

"I will tend to it when everything is settled."

David grimaced but did not argue. He had, it seemed, learned more from his master than how to handle a sword.

It was impossible to enter the courtyard where lay the king's apartments without the steward on duty noticing that she had brought an infant with her. If the man was surprised, he kept it to himself. He even offered his assistance with arrangements. Within the hour, a cradle and every other accoutrement for tending a nursing baby had been supplied, including a scrupulously clean young wet nurse with a three-month-old child. Gwynne took charge, seeing that the new nurse was comfortable in a corner of Isabel's chamber and the baby settled in her cradle while Isabel tended David's injury.

It proved to be a slash down his left arm. Though ugly to look at and likely to leave an impressive scar, nothing vital had been touched; he could open and close his hand, raise and lift his arm. When he had been stitched, he murmured his excuses and left her. Isabel did not expect to find him sleeping across her threshold in the morning, but neither did she think he would be far away. He was faithful in pursuit of his duty. It was a trait she valued, especially as it had served her well this evening.

Exhaustion caught up with her before the door had closed behind the squire. She thought of sending to tell her sisters she had returned, but was simply too tired. Stifling prodigious yawns, feeling suddenly as if she might drop in her tracks, she allowed Gwynne to seat her on a stool so she could remove the veil that had become entangled in her hair. While she worked, Isabel slipped off her shoes, removed her garters and rolled down her hose. The serving woman had picked up a comb of carved horn to bring order to her long locks when a firm knock fell on the door.

Gwynne looked at Isabel, who simply shook her head. She put down the comb and moved to answer the summons.

It was the steward who stood outside. He stepped forward into the chamber as Gwynne backed away, then executed a precise half turn, coming to a halt to one side. Avoiding Isabel's questioning gaze, he drew himself up as he intoned in quiet solemnity, "His Most Royal Majesty, King Henry VII."

The quiet that descended was feathered

by a single gasp. It was a moment before Isabel realized it came from her own throat. In that instant, Henry stepped into view.

He was resplendent in green silk sewn with pearls, white-and-green striped hose and shoes of bleached leather. His sandy hair was restrained by his favored acorn hat in green felt with a dagged brim like the points of a crown drawn by a child. Though he appeared to be dressed for an evening of merriment, no smile softened his features. His pale blue eyes expressed only the most deadly calm as he watched Isabel slide off her stool and drop into a curtsy.

Behind him, the steward jerked his head toward the door while staring at Gwynne and the wet nurse. When they passed through into the corridor, the man closed the door after them. He stepped in front of it as if to bar entry and crossed his arms over his chest.

"Rise, Lady Isabel," Henry said, but added no gesture to ease the formality, much less to indicate friendship. "We trust you are happy to see us despite the lateness of the hour."

"Certainly, Your Majesty," she said, her voice made uneven by the frantic beat of her heart. "If . . . if I seem surprised, it is because I thought you on your way to Winchester."

"We were constrained to take an alternate route," he said without emphasis.

"I dare hope it is nothing which . . . which threatens the crown or your safety?"

"That remains to be seen. Intelligence brought to us indicates you have been busy on an errand outside these walls. We are certain you would wish to present what you have discovered, and this without delay."

"Discovered, sire?"

"Perhaps we should have said *whom* you have found?"

She had known it would be impossible to keep such a thing from him. Her dependence had been on his being too far away to hear of it before she made the arrangements she planned.

Anguish crowded the walls of her chest until she ached with it. She wanted to protest, to snatch Madeleine from her cradle and rush from the chamber with her, speeding away into the night. Instead, she moistened her lips, searched wildly for something, anything, to postpone the moment when she must present her.

"It is only a girl child, sire, hardly worth your valuable time."

"We shall decide what is worth our time, Lady Isabel. Show us the child."

There was nothing for it but to obey. With muscles so stiff with reluctance they felt as if they belonged to someone else, she turned to the cradle, picked up the baby. Young Madeleine woke at the movement, opening her eyes to fix her trusting, gray-blue gaze on Isabel's face.

She touched her cheek, a brief brush of the fingers, while tears burned the back of her nose. Turning, she walked to Henry and knelt, holding the baby on her swaddling board carefully balanced on her forearms.

Henry took her, holding her up before him. The baby stared at the king, essaying a small smile that turned into a frown when it was not returned.

"Her name is Madeleine, we believe?"

"As you say, sire."

"Madeleine," he repeated. "It will have to be changed."

She wanted to protest, wanted to take back the baby as she began to fuss at being held out so stiffly.

"We are pleased, Lady Isabel. You have done well."

"I did nothing, sire. It was Sir Rand —"

"Your modesty does you credit, but we are aware he did not cause the return of this child."

Isabel gathered her courage, lifted her

chin. "But he did rescue her when her mother was killed. You will grant, I hope, that the fact that Madeleine lives proves him innocent of child murder."

The king did not remove his gaze from his daughter. "That is merely the first charge. There is another."

"If the first was false, then why not the second? Others had ample reason to harm Mademoiselle d'Amboise. My husband had none."

"We approve your fidelity, as we said before."

Anger flared inside her, exacerbated by the rising cries of the baby. "It is justice that concerns me! Rand should not be in the Tower. It is only just that you free him."

Henry lowered Madeleine and placed her in the crook of his arm before giving Isabel a curious look. "Such intemperance might almost lead us to suppose a fondness for the husband we chose for you."

"Sire?" she said, not quite certain she had heard correctly.

"Or even that you love him if your exertions on his behalf are included."

"Love? Oh, no, it's only that —"

"Such a thing is not beyond the realm of possibility. The love of a wife for a husband, or a husband for a wife, is greatly to be treasured, despite those who frown upon it. We are human, you know, have human feelings, human needs."

Was he speaking of himself with his royal plural, of the two of them together, or of human beings in general? It was not possible to say, even less possible to ask for clarification. Still, she could not prevent the fleeting notion that Henry might have fallen in love with his queen. She was young, lovely and royal in a way that he was not. After years of lonely exile, she had given him legitimacy as a ruler and hope for the future. It would require a hard heart and immense ego to be unmoved by these things. Whether he could express them was another question. Kings could seldom afford the luxury of such weakness, could not risk being unloved in return. If Henry yearned for Elizabeth's wifely affection, it could only add to his determination to keep the knowledge of his mistress and her child from her.

Being a man and undeniably human, it would not occur to him that some secrets could not be kept. Being a king, he might well believe that nothing was as important as retaining the queen obtained with his crown. Any sacrifice would be considered well made, even the life of a friend. If it was a choice between Rand's life and the throne of England, which would Henry choose?

There was, in reality, no question.

Oh, but did she love Rand as Henry suggested? Was this longing she felt to be close to him, this sickness inside at the thought of his death, the pangs of true love? How could she tell when she had been brought up to suppose only peasants and troubadours enjoyed such tumults of feeling? Yet she would gladly admit to the fault if it would soften the king toward her husband.

"Mayhap I do love him," she said as heat burned its way to her hairline. "My husband is a good and honorable knight, and tender in his care of me."

Henry watched her with a smile in his eyes, though it faded before it reached his narrow lips. "We will overlook your outburst for the sake of the avowal, also for the service rendered us this day. We recommend, however, that you not try our patience further."

"If you truly believe that I have served you well . . ."

"Do not presume. It is unbecoming."

She lowered her gaze. "No, sire."

"We cannot allow you further liberty to interfere in matters of the realm. You will remain confined to your chamber while you reflect on the wisdom of keeping to your woman's place. When you understand its limitations you may apply to rejoin the court, but will not be seen until then. Do we make ourselves clear?"

A curtsy was her only answer, for she did not trust herself to speak. It seemed to be enough. Henry swung on his heel and stalked toward the door. The steward leaped to open it, and then followed Henry from the chamber. Outside, the king made a royal gesture and the wet nurse came to him, trotting obediently after him as he disappeared along the corridor with the baby in his arms.

Isabel felt for the stool behind her and sank down upon it. Bending her head, she put her face in her hands while her whole body shook with violent tremors. She hated it, hated that anyone, even a king, could so discompose her. It was the power he held, she knew, the power to decide the life or death of others in an instant, to extend pain or joy, to shut someone away from the light forever or to set them free. No one should have such arbitrary control over another soul.

She was confined to the four walls of this small chamber. She could do nothing more to help Rand, nothing to help herself. What happened now was in God's hands.

The baby was alive, but Rand was still in the Tower. Henry had not the time to order his release. Would he ever find the time? Did he intend that Rand, like so many others, should be left there, forgotten and alone? Or would he, some fine day, quietly decree that Rand should be tried for his crimes and, just as quietly, hanged in some hidden court?

The king had Madeleine and there was nothing she could do about it.

Should Henry decide it was best that the babe disappear again, never more to be seen, if he determined that his reign as King of England would be safer if she did not exist, then that would be the end of it. Isabel could not quite believe he would make such a decision, but neither could she be certain he would not. Between the two possibilities lay abject fear.

Such a sweet, beautiful child to cause so much grief, so tiny and so helpless against the forces around her. How could anyone harm her? How could they?

If she had not taken the baby from the nuns, Madeleine would be safe. She should have left matters as Rand had them. The guilt of it was like a knife blade in her heart.

The king thought her efforts to save Rand sprang from love. The grief and dismay she felt, now that she was forbidden to do more for him, made it seem he was right.

How had it happened? Was the intimacy of bed sport enough to cause this pain of longing? Was it his smile, his kisses, the panting joy he brought her, the feel of him hot and hard inside her? Was it his concern for her comfort, his air of command, his strength that he expended for everyone except himself? Was it the hard musculature of his body with its scars from old battles and old loyalties well served? Was it because he had taken David as his squire and turned another baseborn lad into a man? Was it because he risked injury, therefore his chance at victory in the melee, in order to save a small boy who was so full of reckless joy that he ran into danger on Tothill Fields?

Was it all these things?

Or was it simply that something inside him drew her, the lost, tormented, illegitimate boy loved by no one who had somehow become a man deserving of respect and affection calling out to an orphaned girl left to fend for herself and her sisters in a brutish household? Was it in the hope that he might, one day, come to love her?

Reasons, all good, all true, yet what did they matter? She loved him. She knew it for the truth in this moment. She knew because of her grief-stricken horror at the thought he might die for her sake, after all.

It could not happen.

Isabel lifted her head and used the edges of her fingers to wipe the wetness of tears from under her eyes. No, it could not happen. She refused to stand for it, though it might require a miracle to prevent. A miracle or a grand, royal boon.

There was one hope left, only one.

Isabel rose to her feet, straightened her veil and smoothed her skirts. With a lift of her chin, she moved to the door, put her hand on the latch and pulled it open.

A man-at-arms stood outside. No doubt he had been assigned the post to see that she did not leave the chamber. It made no difference; she would not contest with him.

Lifting her voice, she called out for David.

19

The pealing of the bell in the belfry directly above his Bell Tower chamber dragged Rand from the table where he sat trying to write, composing his last will and testament on a sheet of parchment. It was melancholy work, and he had no great objection to being interrupted. Moving to the high window, he leaned one shoulder against the stone beneath it, listening.

This was no ordinary tolling, nor did it seem an alarm that might cause the Tower drawbridge to be raised upright and the portcullis to come down. Every bell tower in the city seemed to have taken up the clanging, as if a legion of mad bell ringers had invaded them all. The clamor grew louder, raising dissonant echoes from far and near, while beneath it could be heard cries and cheers.

Abruptly, the probable cause struck him. Elizabeth of York must have given birth to a son.

Henry had his heir. The Tudor dynasty was secure.

Rand gave a low laugh. How pleased Henry would be, though his long and solemn face might never show it. A son and heir. A legitimate claimant to the throne of England, which, even more than the marriage of this new male child's parents, signified the true merging of the houses of York and Lancaster.

No wonder people cheered in such noisy jubilation. It meant stability, prosperity, the final end to the warfare of the past thirty years and more. Yes, and of the hundred years before that. An end to the constant battle carnage, the beheadings and hangings.

Except his hanging, of course.

Past kings had been known to pardon certain criminals to mark a royal marriage, birth or death, sometimes emptying whole prisons. It seemed, in Rand's rather prejudiced view, a fine custom. Not that he dared hope for it.

Rand was glad for Henry, truly glad. Indeed, he was. Even if, given half a chance, he would like to knock the royal idiot on his royal ass.

As his hand fisted, he looked down to see

that he had closed his fingers on the dangling end of Isabel's favor that was tucked into his shirt cuff. He pulled it out, drew it across his palm with sensual pleasure in the silken glide, like the slide of her clothing under his hard hands. But no, he must not become lost in such things again.

With a few practiced, one-handed moves, he tied the long length around his upper arm where it had been on the day of the tournament. He had mangled the piece of silk until it was little more than a rag. Originally white, white for purity, it was no more than a grubby gray now.

He knew what it was supposed to be, however. Oh, yes, he knew. If he wore it always, they must surely bury it with him.

Sweet Isabel.

His mouth watered for the taste of his wife. She had come to him in a hundred dreams, sat beside him, let him put his head in her lap while she ran her fingers through his hair. He had listed a thousand things he wanted to know about her, and a thousand more he wanted to do with her. He had undressed her in imagination, piece by piece of clothing, tasting every inch of her skin, filling his hands with its satiny resilience.

Imagination had to suffice for she had not come to him since that one, vividly remembered visit.

Where was she? What was she doing? Was she even alive? And what had she done to David that his squire did not come to relieve the bastard fancies that tormented his idle mind?

So deafening was the sound of the bells that it covered the noise of approaching footsteps, the scrape of the key in the lock. It was the draft from the window as the door opened that made him turn.

David stood there like the answer to a prayer. He seemed to have grown taller, broader and even older since his last visit. He was travel-stained, or so it appeared, his shoulders and the folds of his doublet coated with dust while brown tracks of sweat streaked his face. Weariness was in his eyes, yet they were bright blue with pleasure and his lips tilted in a grin.

Gladness propelled Rand toward him. He clasped the lad's shoulders for a moment, before buffeting him on the arm. "Where have you been, you son of Satan? I thought you had gone off on some quest and forgotten me."

"I've been to Winchester and back again, sir, among divers other places."

"Then you may know if the bells ring for Henry's heir. Am I right in thinking so?"

David inclined his golden head in assent. "A fine boy it is, who will be named for King Arthur of legend. At last report, both newborn and queen were in good health. The king is in high spirits, as you may imagine, and has ordered all manner of celebrations for the christening."

Rand smiled with a shake of his head before his amusement faded. "But Winchester, you say? What took you there at such a time? You cannot have had cause to await the birth with the rest of Christendom. That is, you couldn't unless . . . Is my lady there?"

"Nay, sir. She is here."

He sighed, unaccountably glad to know it. "And Henry's daughter, the small cherub Madeleine? How does she fare?"

"She is well also," the lad said, shielding his gaze with gold-tipped lashes before shifting his shoulder in a shrug. "She is with her father."

"Her father, the king?" Rand asked, while his heart flailed his ribs, making it feel bruised.

"Aye, sir."

Dread mingled with rage threatened to close off Rand's breath so it was a moment before he could speak. "And how has this happened when she was meant to be safe elsewhere?"

David said nothing. A woman's voice answered instead, coming clear and strong from the door of his prison chamber. "She is with Henry because he took her from me."

Isabel.

Isabel, lovely beyond his most fervent dreams in a scarlet mantle trimmed in blue over a blue gown and with a pale blue veil over her hair. Blue for fidelity. Blue, though he refused — would not allow — that it might carry the message he craved. She might have donned it as a whim or, more likely, to persuade the constable of the Tower of her devotion so she was allowed to visit him again.

She was so clean compared to his bearded, unwashed, unkempt state, so very fresh and serene that he wanted, suddenly, to pull her into his squalor and force her to share it. Base though it might be, he longed for her to comprehend his futile, despairing rage at its deepest depth, and to join him in that, as well.

Instead, she seemed above it, uncaring for the long days he had spent with little word of where she was or what she was doing. Careless of the fate of a baseborn child, one upon whose small existence might hang the fate of a realm, she had just announced

454

what might be its death sentence. That, above all, he could not bear.

"And how did it happen that you had her?" he asked, his voice like a sledge pulled over gravel. "What mad caprice made you take her from her hiding place when you were told to let matters lie?"

Hauteur descended over her features, though not before he saw a flicker of pain deep in her eyes. "My own caprice, sir," she answered, "and why not? What difference can there be between a widow able to go her own way and a woman with a husband so willing to die that she might as well count herself bereaved? But we have no time for this. Your squire has been to Winchester and back again in the past several days, has ridden through the night to deliver the order for your release. It has been duly presented and accepted, so you are free to go. You have an hour's leave at the palace to make yourself presentable, and then we must make haste to Winchester for an audience with the queen."

It was too much to take in at once. Rand put his spread hand on the nearby table for the sake of something solid to support him in what seemed a dizzying fog of delusion. "You mean . . . . You can't mean Henry has signed a pardon."

"A most official document, one affixed with a great deal of frippery and stamped with the privy seal."

"But why? How?"

Her smile was brief. "It was the boon asked for by Elizabeth of York in exchange for presenting him with a son. Are you not honored to be so valued? But come, there is no time to waste. We must be away."

"Elizabeth, the queen consort. Not Lady Margaret."

He sounded stupefied to his own ears, which was not surprising as it was exactly how he felt. He had accepted his death, taken its likelihood so deep within it was almost impossible to accept that it could be otherwise.

"The king's mother may have spoken on your behalf. But it was Elizabeth of York who bargained for your life."

He shook his head. "I don't understand. She barely knows me."

Color rose in Isabel's face that might have been from anger but had the appearance of embarrassment. "She knows me, which is enough."

"And I am to hasten to kneel before her for what reason? Other than a chance to express my gratitude, of course."

"She wishes to see for herself that you

have been released unharmed, as promised. It comes, no doubt, from others disappearing while locked away within these walls."

He knew not how to reply to that, being unable to equate himself with her brothers who had entered here, never to be seen again. While he made coherent sense of his thoughts, David began to unfasten the sword belt at his waist. Taking the sheathed sword in his two hands, he stepped forward.

"You must have this, sir. It stood me and your lady in good stead, as you intended, but belongs now at your side."

Rand took the blade, clasping its scabbard in a hard grip to still the tremors that shook his hand. For a second he stood unmoving, staring at the sword, symbol of his pretense as a gentleman and a knight. Yes, and of his return to that status.

"Strap it on, good husband, as is your right," Isabel said with a small clap of her hands. "But then gather what you require and let us go before Henry sends to say he has changed his mind!"

It was an excellent point.

Rand's few belongings made only a single parcel — his precious books and his lute, the parchment sheets he had covered with writing, his best doublet and hose that he had been saving so he need not go to his trial looking like a villein. He left the cell without a backward glance, striding forth with single-minded determination. His pace along the corridor was so swift that Isabel had to run a few steps now and then to keep up with him, though he could not make himself slow for her comfort. His every sense was painfully alert. He feared a shout to halt, dreaded a yeoman jailer coming after them to demand his return. Yes, or some official puffed up with self-importance stepping forward to claim a mistake had been made and he was not free, after all.

They passed beyond the walls and through the various courts. Suddenly, they were outside the gates. The town surrounded him, its noise too loud, the smells too strong, the milling throng too dense, the smoke-hazed sunlight too bright. He felt like some creature exposed by the removal of a stone, so rattled by the sudden change that his one thought was to scurry into hiding.

The impulse faded within moments, yet remnants remained. He was not entirely free of their taint even after they reached Westminster Palace. It clung to him while he bathed in the hottest water the servants could bring, then shaved and changed into raiment suitable for travel. When they set out for Winchester, it mounted to Shadow's saddle with him. It was there in a prickling at the back of his neck, the itchy feeling between his shoulder blades, the urge to ride as if the hounds of hell were on his trail.

If Isabel was aware of such misgivings, she kept them to herself. She was not a chatterer, the sort of female who felt it her duty to fill every moment of silence with inane observations and questions to which she already knew the answers. She rode with her face set and her gaze turned forward, did not even speak to her maid Gwynne, riding on her far side, much less him. David was much the same, though he had the excuse of fatigue.

There was little chance for conversation in any case, for the three of them did not travel alone. They were accompanied by outriders in the livery of the royal household, an honor escort of yeomen guards sent by the king's order. They were welcome protection from trouble along the way, though their true purpose, Rand thought, might well be to prevent him from hying off in the opposite direction.

By degrees, the sense grew upon Rand that he was actually free. The sun upon his shoulders felt like a benediction, the wind in his face like a caress. The scents of curing hay, drying hops and Michaelmas daisies blowing in the hedgerows had never seemed sweeter. Isabel, riding at his side, was so lovely that it wrenched his heart to look upon her. The fugitive gleam of her hair under her veil, the curve of her cheek, the sweep of her lashes, the shapes of her arms under the dust mantle and the way it fell over her breasts, the line of her thigh where her leg hooked around her sidesaddle — everything enthralled him.

His wife.

His wife, who had come for him, had somehow arranged his release from prison. Or was it, perhaps, his escape?

She had yet to answer his questions. The turmoil of making ready for their departure had prevented it before, and the presence of the king's men made it impossible now. Besides, he was in no mood to shout back and forth over the noise of hoofbeats and saddlery and the wind in their ears. He wanted quiet and privacy so he could be sure of the answers he desired.

Among other things.

The need to be alone with her was a desperate ache. He longed to hold her, to touch her, to feel her beneath him, around him, clutching him as he buried himself in her to the hilt. He wanted to sleep for a year with her held close in his arms.

So strong was the urge that he resented her distant air and the way she did not quite meet his gaze. He was also annoyed by the faint assumption of authority about her, as if he was her prisoner now, one she meant to deliver whether he willed it or no. These were matters that could be adjusted.

As the day passed and the miles fell away behind them, he began to long for nightfall and whatever place they might find to take their rest.

It was a small tavern used by the drovers, wool traders and other merchants who plied the roads. Of brick construction on the lower floor, mud daub and cross timbers above that and a thatched roof over all, it was rustic without being a hovel. The main room featured trestle tables set around the center fireplace, from which smoke spiraled upward in a gray plume to make its way out a hole in the roof. Beyond this was a private parlor for the gentry that was fronted by a stairway that led to a quartet of bedchambers. These chambers were mere boxes, being without fireplaces, bathing screens, armoires or glazing on their single windows.

Rand cared not a whit for extra comforts. It was enough that the chamber he meant to share with his wife had no guard and no iron grille let into its door through which anyone could watch his movements. Yes, and a bed.

Eager though he might be, he had a care for Isabel's reluctance, expressed weeks ago, to be the subject of ribald humor from the men-at-arms. He remained below for a tankard of mead while Gwynne prepared her mistress for bed. He took note when the serving woman descended the stairs, supped on ale, soup and bread and rolled into her cloak in a corner of the common room to sleep. Still, he waited a good half hour before draining his tankard and mounting the stairs.

Though he knocked with all politeness, he stepped inside with scarcely a pause. Isabel must know full well who asked entry. If she did not realize asking for admittance was a mere courtesy because he intended joining her whether she willed it or not, then it was time she understood it.

She sat propped on pillows against the head of the bed. The sheet was pulled high and locked under her armpits, and her hair cascaded around her in shimmering, golden-brown waves.

Rand stopped for an instant, too stupefied to move. Dear God, she was everything beautiful he had ever seen or wanted.

Recovering with stringent effort, he paced forward with footsteps timed to the hard throb of his heart, and did not stop until he reached the end of the bed. Framed by the bed curtains that draped to either side of the end posts, he braced his hands on the heavy oak footboard. He gazed at his wife, noting the quickness of her breathing, the rise of color like the blush on a peach that stained her skin from the curves of her breasts to her hairline. The ache in his groin made his eyes water at the corners.

"Welladay, my lady," he said in quiet reflection, "you have saved me from hanging. Now what would you?"

Green fire flashed in her eyes and her chin came up. "You sound as if you would prefer I had not bestirred myself."

"I did tell you to refrain."

"Forgive me, but what happens to you concerns me, as well. I have had enough notoriety as one of the accursed Graces of Graydon without becoming known as the widow of a man hanged for murder."

"You prefer being the wife of a bastard."

"Aye, I do indeed. That's if you mean instead of coming under Graydon's thumb again. Or being handed over to another man Henry may feel like rewarding."

His smile was sardonic. "I am, after all,

the devil you know."

"You could put it that way."

"One you disobeyed by seeking out Mademoiselle Juliette's babe."

"I meant to take her to Lady Margaret, I swear it," she said, swallowing with a noticeable movement in the fine line of her throat. "She would have been safe with her, even . . . even from Henry."

She was right in that. Why had he not considered it? "Possibly."

"Besides, if I could surmise where you had her concealed, others could do the same."

"As I said, the devil you know. Others might not have understood him so well."

Her lashes fluttered at that. "But the fact remains that she was not safe at the convent. You should be glad that I . . . that I . . ."

"Disobeyed me?"

"If you insist!"

Passionate anger was in that capitulation. It acted like a goad. "I do insist," he answered in grim implacability, "though it seems we are well matched, you and I." Straightening, he began to unfasten his doublet. "Would you not say so?"

"Unaccountably."

She moistened her lips as she watched him, in a movement that made the lower part of his body feel on fire. "What troubles me," he went on, removing his sword and laying it across the end of the bed's mattress, shrugging from the doublet and tossing it aside, "is what you had to do to secure my release. With Elizabeth banished to Winchester, Henry has had little to do except brood over the business with Mademoiselle Juliette. I trust you were not required to, shall we say, raise his spirits?"

"You think I would sleep with the king to save your stiff neck?"

Other parts of him were the same or worse, if she only knew. "He is a man, and not beyond temptation. In his place, I might have demanded it."

Her eyes narrowed, though she did not look away as he jerked hose points free in a fast series, then skimmed off his shirt over his head. "You seem to believe every man at court wants to . . . to tup me."

"Am I wrong?" That word on her lips was absurdly stirring. Who would have guessed she would use it?

"The question is whether I am willing to oblige them."

"And are you?" he asked, the words a rasp like drawn steel in his throat.

"By no means, having other things on my mind! As does the king, I dare swear, since he has been somewhat busy with a royal progression, an insurrection and the birth of his heir."

"Unlike your husband, you mean, who has had little to occupy him of late. Or little else besides . . . tupping." He struggled with the need to laugh at the way her eyes widened when he shucked out of his hose and braies, then rounded the end of the bed in flagrant nakedness.

Her hot gaze lifted from his strutted erection to meet his eyes. "Apparently!" she snapped.

"But there lies the difference between us. I am able to give my attention to two things at once, in this case your delectable body and your disobedience."

"I am not a servant to bow always to your will!"

"No, you are my wife and sworn to obey me. And it is my right to chastise you as I choose."

Catching the sheet in his fist, he pulled it from her grasp with a single, hard twist of his wrist, leaving her naked as Eve. An instant later, he caught her arm and dragged her to her knees, pulling her close until her every curve was plastered to him and his heated flesh rested exactly where he wanted it, in the cradle between her firm, white thighs.

466

"Rand . . . please," she said as a tremor ran over her, leaving goose bumps in its wake.

"Please what?" He was lamentably distracted by the way she twisted in his arms, straining against his hold so he was forced to slide a hand down her back and grasp a hillock of soft flesh to hold her close.

"I did nothing to shame our wedding vows, this I swear before all the saints. I only . . ."

"Tell me later," he said, lowering his head until his lips brushed hers with every word he whispered against them. "Right now, my mind is divided between whether to kiss you into submission first and tup you later, or tup you into submission first, then kiss you."

Abruptly, she ceased to fight him. The fearful tension drained from her, though another shiver beaded her flesh and tightened her nipples into small, hard knots against his chest. She moistened her lips with a flick of her small, pink tongue. "And that's your idea of punishment?"

"It's all I can think of at the moment," he confessed, his gaze upon her mouth before he took it like a man slaking thirst in a desert, drinking from it in a frenzy, driving his tongue into that sweet well again and again while she twined around it with her own, taking it deeper.

"You could," she said with a gasp when he finally paused for breath, "do both at the same time."

"Both of what?" he asked in husky bemusement while bending his head to lick the curves of her breasts, then draw the warm and tender firmness of a nipple into his mouth.

"Tup me and kiss me, kiss me and tup me." She let herself go boneless while clasping his neck, which she had circled while he was busy elsewhere, taking him with her as she fell back onto the straw-filled surface of the mattress, pulling him between her thighs.

How could he resist such an invitation? It was selfish, he knew, but she was so open, the core of her so damp and heated, that sinking into her seemed as natural as breathing. He groaned aloud at the tight perfection of the fit, the bliss of burying himself in her pulsating depths. He reveled in it for long moments, until the need to move, to increase the pressure, the friction, became too powerful to resist. He stroked into her then, filling her, stretching her to accommodate him, molding her to fit his most fervid desire. And it was rampant glory, delirious beguilement, the most heartrending and joyous of possessions.

At its height, he whispered many things into the fragrant mass of her hair, among them the words that confessed his love, but his heart was beating so hard he could not tell if he said them aloud, could not know if she heard them above the soft cry of her completion.

Afterward, he rolled from her, then gathered her close, tucking her into the curve of his body, turning her so her hips fit against his groin. The sensation was so satisfying that he heaved a deep sigh and was asleep in an instant.

He woke once to the sound of hoofbeats passing on the roadway. The riders were abroad late, he thought in bemusement. The speed of their travel suggested they had come from Westminster on the king's business, as he was almost certainly with the queen and his new son at Winchester.

Poor Henry, ever destined to be harassed by the problems of ruling a kingdom. It was unlikely he ever enjoyed waking with a warm wife nestled so enticingly, and conveniently, against his body. Gently questing, Rand captured a breast in his hand, using his thumb to brush it into arousal. Isabel murmured in her sleep, pressing against him. It was all the invitation he needed.

Well before the first light of dawn, they were on the road again. It was Rand who rousted them all out. He awoke consumed with impatience to spring to horse, to put the miles behind them and make his bow to Henry's queen. He could guess what she wanted to know, for though a princess all her life and now a queen, she was also a woman. He was not quite sure how he would answer her, but wanted the interview behind him. Only when it was over could he take up the reins of his life and guide it in the direction he wanted to go.

They rode through the day and into the early evening, stopping only to rest or change horses. The days were growing shorter as September advanced for it was well after dark by the time the outskirts of Winchester appeared. The town was silent save for the barking of dogs disturbed by their entrance. The clatter of their hoofbeats on cobblestones echoed off the walls of buildings, carrying ahead of them. It almost seemed to Rand that they echoed behind them, as well, but he put the notion down to weariness and imagination caused by too little sleep.

Time and again, he had slid into the softness between his wife's tender thighs, slaking an insatiable need for the solace he found there. She had not protested, had seemed to revel in the elemental friction almost as much as he. Yet lavender shadows circled her eyes when morning came, and she seemed half-asleep in her saddle now.

The walls of the palace loomed ahead of them. Though Henry's child had been born at the priory of Winchester Abbey, Rand could not suppose that the queen had remained there. She would not take up her public duties for forty days after the birth, and then only after the blessing of the church, but the comforts of the palace would be far superior to those in the priory. Accordingly, he sent the leader of the king's guard to inform the queen's steward of their arrival. He had no expectation of being received; in truth, he was not sure they would see the queen in anything under several days. She must be less than half a week out of childbed.

They had not yet selected the tavern for their domicile while in the town when a messenger came galloping after them. The queen would be pleased to receive them at once.

They were met by the queen's steward, who asked that they follow him. Elizabeth of York awaited them in the privacy of her solar. Their retinue, including David,

471

Gwynne and the king's guard, could wait in the great hall outside the queen's apartments.

Rand exchanged a glance with Isabel, who only shook her head. "Mayhap," he said so softly only she could hear, "she prefers to have done before Henry discovers the required proof of my release."

"Or else she would know more from you of Mademoiselle Juliette without him being present," Isabel said in agreement.

They were both wrong. Elizabeth of York was not alone when he and Isabel attended her in her solar. With her was her newborn son, asleep in his large and ornate royal cradle. Lying next to Henry's son and heir was a small girl child of surpassing beauty, small Madeleine, not quite three months of age. The pair had been placed near to the thronelike armchair on which the queen sat. Not far away stood a young woman in cap and apron, no doubt the nursemaid to both infants. And standing behind the queen, richly dressed in burgundy brocade sewn with gold thread set off by garnets, was His Majesty, Henry VII.

Rand was aware of Isabel's swift-drawn breath as she halted beside him and dropped into a deep curtsy. Conscious that he might be in the queen's apartments without the sanction of his king, he went to one knee with bowed head.

"Well met, Sir Rand and Lady Isabel," the king said in dry tones. "You are surprised to see us?"

"I thought . . . that is, we expected an audience with the queen," Rand answered.

"Which you shall have, though she invited us to join her for the occasion. May we say how much we rejoice to see you free again?"

"Thank you, sire."

"Rise, then, so we may express our regret for your time in the Tower. We thought to protect our queen, you perceive, but have learned not to underestimate her powers of discernment, her wisdom in coming to us with her knowledge or her generous absolution. It makes —" The king broke off as the door through which they had entered crashed open behind them.

A hulking figure burst into the solar. The light of the oil lamps burning atop their triangular stands illuminated the device of a bear emblazoned on the tabard he wore. It glittered with flashes of silver-blue from the blade he lifted like an executioner's sword high above his head.

"Nay, don't rise, Sir Rand," Viscount Henley said, his voice mounting to a hoarse shout of triumph. "Kneel and meet the end you deserve!"

20

The blow aimed at Rand's bent neck should have severed his head from his shoulders. He was not there.

With fierce power, he plunged aside, catching Isabel so she was flung, crying out, beyond the danger area. She heard the whistle of the blade, felt the hot whiff of its passing as it sliced air near her shoulder. She saw in shivering horror the instant when it seemed to slice into Rand's arm, but caught instead in the knotted rag of white silk he wore around it. In that brief moment of entanglement, he snatched free and leaped erect.

Then she was scrambling farther out of Rand's way while behind her the nursemaid screamed, the queen rose to her feet with a shaky cry and the king, earthy in his rage, bellowed curses like a Breton sailor.

Rand snatched his knife from his belt even as he ducked away from another two-handed sword slash, swirled like blown smoke from where a third singed the air. The table blade was his only weapon as he had surrendered his sword before entering the queen's presence. He seemed not to recognize its inadequacy as he steadied his gaze on the man intent on killing him.

"Sir!"

The shout came from David, most faithful of squires, who had followed after them. Beyond him lay the bodies of the yeoman guards, still in bloody death, the guards that should have stopped the armed invasion of the queen's private chamber. In the lad's hard right hand was Rand's own trusted sword David must have taken from them. In his other was a second blade taken from a fallen guardsman.

Hard upon his forewarning, he sent the first great, long weapon in a glittering arc, straight toward his knightly master.

Rand tossed his knife to his left hand, caught the sword from the air with his right. In the same movement, he whirled to face his attacker as David eased deeper into the solar, his young gaze fiercely alert as he waited to see if his further aid was required.

Isabel drew a sobbing breath so deep it tore at her throat. The sound was drowned out by the harsh clang of metal on metal, like the first toll of a funeral bell, as Rand blocked a hammering blow on a cross of steel made by knife and raised sword. He threw Henley stumbling back.

Immediately, he skipped aside to allow a wider field of play. He dropped into a swordsman's crouch, his face set in grim lines as he faced a new threat.

His opponents had multiplied.

Surging through the door, they spread to either side of Henley, forming a semicircle around their target. They numbered only two more, though they seemed in the first onslaught to be twice as many. And Rand faced them with hard purpose and not a tremor in his sword hand.

Undaunted indeed, Isabel thought in aching remorse for the jibe about his motto she had thrown at him in his Tower chamber. Her heart shuddered in her chest and she blinked away burning tears of despair as she stared at the dangerous tableau. She should have told Rand of Henley's attempt, along with Graydon, to take Madeleine from her. Their clumsy effort had almost slipped her mind, in truth, swept away by the loss of the baby to Henry. With the distraction of Rand's perfect punishment of her the night before, she had not recalled it.

The newcomers stalked their prey, their

creeping forms casting grotesque shadows that shrank and grew like beasts of legend. Their features were brutally clear as they faced the lamplight. With no great surprise, she recognized Graydon and William McConnell.

The trio had joined forces, the three men who had reason to want Rand dead. Or had they been confederates from the first, each with his part to play in bringing him down, and his king with him? They must have followed from Westminster, she thought, recalling the ghostly sound of horsemen in the distance and Rand's listening attitude. Had they claimed to be with their party that they had gained entrance to the queen's apartments?

Her stepbrother and McConnell must have thought Henley to be in control while Rand was unarmed. They had hung back to watch the slaughter. Now, all three moved around him with the caution of weasels facing their prey, watching for any sign of weakness, depending on their numbers to overpower the quarry. Rand moved in counterpoint, his gaze vigilant as he waited for their move.

In that moment, the king's majesty vanished and he became the knight he had surely trained to be in his exile. He stepped forward, placing himself between the struggle and his queen with the cradle beside her. Gems gleamed on his short velvet cloak as he whipped it aside to free the pommel of a ceremonial sword. The fine blade sang as he unsheathed it from its swinging, jeweled scabbard.

The three were traitors. It was not just Rand's death they sought, but that of the king, as well. The die had been cast. They could not withdraw now, could do nothing except play it out.

A brief glance of communication passed between the intruders. Faces set, they leaped to the assault.

At the same moment, Henry stepped into the fight with a ringing clash of steel. He deflected a hard thrust from Viscount Henley, engaging him, drawing the wild-eyed peer away from Rand. His jeweled sword hilt shone with red, green and blue fire between his two hands as he parried in tierce, in prime, his tall form moving with strength and grace. Driving his opponent before him with skill as well as power, he forced him back step by step, back away from the cradle and the queen. And it was easy for Isabel to think, watching him with wide eyes and breathless disbelief, that he had come armed to the confrontation with

Rand because he did not trust his friend after holding him prisoner, might not trust him even now.

Moving in concert on the far side, David challenged Graydon with a shout. Isabel, trying frantically to follow this action, saw her stepbrother turn with a guttural oath, saw his eyes light with confidence in his ability to squelch this lesser threat. Her heart doubled its crazed beat as fear he was right scalded her chest. David had been wounded in the clash with Graydon and Henley over Madeleine. It had been his left arm that was slashed, yet how fit was he for this terrible contest?

Rand was left facing his half brother. They circled each other, watching for an opening, two men almost perfectly matched in size and strength. The only difference Isabel could see was that McConnell appeared a trifle more burly in the upper body while Rand had the longer reach. The concentration on their features was the same, and the determination.

McConnell lunged into a lethal advance with every ounce of his strength behind it. Rand met and matched it, his sword catching the lamplight with the flash of a beacon. They settled then into a fury of beating, clanging attacks and parries, slashing at each other with whistling blades and grunts of effort. Sweat shone on their brows, made them blink as it ran into their eyes. McConnell tried a desperate stratagem, plunging into an assault of such power it seemed he thought to beat Rand down with it, to take advantage of his old injuries from the tourney and the weakening affect of prison. But Rand executed a parry that sent his half brother's sword point sliding harmlessly past his shoulder, then whirled into a riposte that tangled his blade, nearly springing it from his hand. McConnell leaped back, disengaging, while his chest heaved with his hard breathing.

"Unfinished affairs, William?" Rand inquired holding his guard position. "You overreach yourself, it appears, trying to remove not only a pesky half brother who stands between you and what you consider yours, but a duly crowned king. Ah, no, allow me a correction. You meant also to dispose of the newborn heir and his mother so as to eliminate all threat. Otherwise, you accomplish nothing."

"It can yet be done," McConnell answered, leaning into another advance.

"Without losing your head for it?" Rand parried with swift grace and a bell-like chime of blades. "I'd have said differently.

To take the blame for your crimes, yet again, is no part of my plans."

McConnell gave a breathless laugh. "Why not, when you make such a perfect whipping boy?"

At that snide reminder of past pain, Rand sprang forward to drive his half brother back. His words were as sharp-edged as his sword. "My part in this game is paltry. If Henry did not send the men-at-arms — or mercenaries, rather — to Braesford for Mademoiselle Juliette, then it had to be you. Naturally, you could not afford to come yourself, but the thing was easily arranged. Who else had the authority to use the king's livery? Who had access to such directives as could be forged for your purpose, or to mercenaries who cared nothing for how they earned their pay?"

"The advantages of rank are many," McConnell answered, with arrogance layering every word of that platitude.

"It was always you from the first, hanging about when Juliette's baby was born, making trouble by suggesting to the dull-witted midwife that the small mite had burned to death, taking the rumor of it to Westminster so Henry's hand was forced and he had to recall me to the palace. You even pushed your men like a devil's spawn so they reached Braesford on Isabel's heels, in time to stop the wedding."

"Are you just now seeing it? I thought you sharper than that."

"Or less trusting, mayhap? Would that I had been! Poor Juliette. Was she frightened when she realized your men were not taking her to a retreat arranged by the king? Did you visit her in her prison? Was she trying to escape when you threw her down the stairs, then cut her throat?"

"Why should I do that? The little whore was quite accommodating, as you may imagine." McConnell snorted. "She thought to gain her freedom with a bedding or two, expected to be released when I tired of her."

"Because you told her so, I don't doubt, and she expected a nobleman to stand by his word."

"More fool she, when it was given to one so worthless. But it was Henley who ended her life. He was annoyed, you see, as she refused to accommodate him."

It was said so easily. Isabel put a hand to her mouth to hold back a cry of disgust laced with sick rage. Behind her, she heard the king's growl of fury, the queen's strained breathing, the nursemaid's moans. Above all these rose the crying of the babies in their shared cradle, a frantic rasping brought on by the tension in the chamber, the raised voices and the clamor of blades.

Rand seemed beyond it all as he narrowed his gaze on the man before him. "You allowed Henley to kill her," he said in grim accusation.

McConnell twitched a shoulder. "You were to have the blame, after all. All was in order — the message to you written as I stood over the French strumpet, the men-at-arms led at a fair distance behind as you rode gallantly to her rescue, her death at the appointed hour so you might be caught with a warm corpse. But you came early, so outdistanced us. You found her before we arrived, must have seen us coming."

"Thus slipped through your careful trap. Such a disappointment for you."

"These things depend on dame fortune. Your escape was temporary, however. Dear Henry signed the order for your arrest almost before I could present the story of Mademoiselle's death. You should thank him, as the Tower can be a refuge as well as a prison. My next move, had you been available, would have been to stir up the common folk so they hanged you out of hand."

The words were shortened by McConnell's labored breathing. Rand, his features grim and hair wet with sweat in the gold-

and-orange glazing of lamplight, gave him no time to recover but bore in with another advance. The snick and slide of the blades was like an accompaniment to the harsh clash of their voices. Beneath both, like an obbligato, was the clang and clatter of the other matches and nerve-shattering screams of the babies. The smells of sweat, hot metal and lamp oil hung heavy in the thick air.

"Enterprising," Rand commented. "Still, the effect of your plotting was failure, as with the tampering with Leon's firebox."

"Graydon's stupidity, that. It was to have been a fiery death for Henry, Elizabeth and the heir she carried. And you, too, had He not ordained otherwise."

"To what end? A Yorkist king on the throne again? Did you expect Braesford as your reward for bringing it about?"

"Why not, as you were so disobliging as to avoid death twice on your wedding day. Did you actually believe I was coming to your aid at the tourney? No, no. It was for the coup de grâce."

"After I was unhorsed by Graydon and Henley, of course."

"So simple a thing in the dust and confusion, yet the clumsy idiots could not manage it."

Grim acceptance was Rand's only response that Isabel could see. "And the courtier who thought to entice me into a dawn meeting?"

"Another unworthy instrument too easily vanquished. But I still had hope then of seeing you hanged for the death of the French whore's bastard."

"But the baby lived," Rand said, constantly harrying his adversary.

"Henley misplaced her in the dark. You had the luck of the devil, laying hands on her so quickly. No doubt it was borrowed from your accursed wife. I expect to enjoy the like myself one day."

"You intend to have her along with Braesford Hall."

McConnell grunted. "Oh, aye, her above all."

"Above all, indeed, as she is and always will be forbidden to you," Rand returned in accents like the breaking of thickest glass. "As the widow of your half brother, she would fall within the forbidden degrees of consanguinity."

"Who said aught of marriage? The curse of the Graces should be avoided if I merely bed her. But you, as her duly wedded husband, must die for daring to be wed in defiance of it."

"No!" Isabel cried out in half-mad anguish. "No, he need not! There is no curse, never was a curse."

McConnell gave a harsh laugh, his gaze raking her before he snapped his attention back to Rand. "She lies for you, is that not fascinating? She ignored my whispered persuasion, my enticements to turn false for our purpose. She would not agree, even under threat, to perjure herself at what should have been your appearance before the King's Court. Did you know?"

"It was you who accosted me at the abbey," she called in trembling recognition. "You assumed too much — my willingness to join your scheme, for one thing, my silence for another." She was distracted, briefly, by the match between Henley and the king. It had come to an abrupt end as the king disarmed Henley. Shoving him backward so he stumbled on the solar's Saracen carpets, Henry caught the viscount's blade as it spun from his grasp, clutching the hilt in his free hand.

David, squared-off against Graydon to her left, fought on with the dissonant clank of beating swords and the scrape of blades, edge to edge, that showered blue and orange-red sparks to the floor. Graydon tried again and again to overpower the younger man, as if hoping to beat him down with sheer might. Still, between attacks and attending to David's lightning ripostes, he exchanged a crafty glance with McConnell.

David, his movements armed with grace and economy, frowned to see it. And it almost seemed to Isabel, aching with fear for his safety, that the lad might have defeated her stepbrother handily except for the curb he put on his skill. It occurred to her that he could be reluctant to defeat Graydon in front of her, for fear of how she might react to his death.

Before she could fully grasp the impression, the struggle between Rand and his half brother reclaimed her attention again.

"Your lady wife will refuse me no longer when you are gone," McConnell was saying with malignant satisfaction. "She will do exactly as I say or join you in your grave."

"I believe not," Rand replied, his face like iron.

Hard on the words, he whirled into an attack that drove his opponent back and back again, well away from Isabel. McConnell stumbled, recovered, though the move was jerky, almost uncoordinated. Regardless, there was no defeat in his face. It registered cunning instead. He seemed to drop back faster and farther than was necessary.

Isabel saw the trap in that instant. David

had only tenuous control of his fight against a swordsman less skilled yet of superior weight and malicious cunning. A few more steps and Rand would be within reach of Graydon's sword. All McConnell had to do was lure him forward enough for his confederate, pausing for a single instant in his bout, to make a fatal thrust.

Her heart caught in her throat. She screamed a high-pitched warning.

It was unnecessary. Rand saw ploy.

He closed abruptly with McConnell, stepping into his guard. Catching him in a travesty of brotherly embrace, he swung him toward Graydon and gave him a hard shove.

Graydon's blade took McConnell in the back, driving upward. A single, guttural cry sounded in the throat of Rand's half brother before he sagged to the floor. His knees hit first and he fell forward. His sword clanked upon the carpet-softened stone of the floor, then spun across the bright-patterned wool, coming to a stop against the stiff skirt hem of the queen's gown. Elizabeth of York stooped to pick it up by its heavy hilt, holding it with the tip trailing to the floor.

The shock of what he had done stunned Graydon for a mortal instant. He jerked his blade up into guard position once more, but it was too late. David, leaning already into an attack, slid past his feeble defense and took him in the heart.

The stillness was so sudden, so complete, that the fluttering of lamp flames on their oiled wicks had the sound of a flight of birds. Then Henley's curse scalded the silence. Slewing around, he dived for the queen. Before Henry could bring up his sword again, Henley jerked the carmine-stained blade of his confederate from Elizabeth's hand. With a growl like the bear emblazoned on his tunic, he turned toward Isabel.

It was then that a shadow moved, circling from a darkened corner. Lithe, silent as death, it rose up behind Henley, casting over him a black pall that had within it a silvery gleam. A slender dark shape drew back an arm, struck deep with a slender blade. And when Henley sank down with a knife between his ribs, Leon, Master of Revels, was revealed in all his splendor of yellow doublet embroidered in black with musical notes. A knife of finest Spanish steel was in his hand and a smile of satisfaction on his beautiful mouth.

"For my sister," he said, sparing a brief, encompassing glance for those who stood watching in attitudes of stunned acceptance, "and for Lady Isabel. The man was an animal, and deserved to die."

Moving to the cradle then, he slid his arms under the girl child who lay mewling there and lifted her against his chest. He turned toward the door.

"Stay!" Henry commanded.

Leon turned back, simple inquiry in his face.

"You have our daughter there. You may not take her to become a pawn for France."

"I have my sister's child, my own niece — though I once claimed her as my daughter in hope of keeping her safe. She was dearly loved by Juliette, just as she is dearly loved now by her uncle. Think you some matter of state was why she was conceived?"

"Was it not?" Henry asked in grim doubt as he avoided the steady gaze of his wife.

"Not on my sister's part. She loved you, though she died with the sin of it upon her soul. If you would know who took payment from France, look to the good viscount. It was Henley who succumbed to the bribes of France while jaunting about the Continent from one tourney to another. He had need of it, being without lands or estates to go with his title."

The king's chin had a stubborn tilt to it, though he cleared his throat before he spoke. "Who took French coin matters little. The use this small body may be put to now concerns us. Can you guarantee she will never be harmed because of her birth, that she will not be held as a hostage for our goodwill? Yes, and even if she is well guarded, what can you give her compared to the riches of our court, or the marriage we may arrange for her one day?"

Leon glanced from the king to the baby in his arms and back again. Indecision crept like fog into the night darkness of his eyes.

Isabel stirred as if rousing from a bad dream. Taking a single step forward, she spoke in soft reason. "Dear Leon, how will you keep a child while you wander from one court to another? What safeguards can you place around her, indeed, if others would use her for their ends? The king has the power to keep her secure. Would it not be best to allow it?"

"As he kept her secure this night?" Leon asked with a twist to his smile, never taking his gaze from his niece.

"The fault in that was mine."

Rand made a sound of denial, striding forward as if to support her until halted by an abrupt gesture from the king.

"What if it happens again?" Leon demanded. "More than that, what if, in his fascination with his heir, Henry forgets little

Madeleine's existence?"

"It is unlikely, especially after tonight." Isabel's somber gaze skimmed the bodies of the fallen whose bright lifeblood was soaking into the solar's rugs.

"Who will love her, hold her, teach her to dance and to sing?" Leon went on as if she had not spoken. "Who will show her joy, make certain she knows how to laugh and to love? Who will see she is given to a husband who will treat her gently and well? These things matter, you see. They matter to me."

"I am certain —" she began.

"I am not. A king has other cares, other intentions that may loom as more important than the life of one small girl child. Such an uncertain fate cannot be allowed. I will not leave her unless . . ."

"Unless what?" Henry demanded, scowling, as well he might, considering the insults he had endured.

"Unless Lady Isabel is given charge of her," Leon said, turning a limpid yet unseeing gaze on the king. "She can be trusted to see to her, to give her the love a child requires. For protection, she has the sword arm of Sir Rand behind her, and his example of honor and chivalry before her. I could bear to leave her with the two of them, with your gracious permission."

"We rejoice to see you accord us some authority," Henry said in sardonic ire.

Isabel, ignoring that small sign of disagreeableness, turned toward him. "The responsibility is great, sire, but I would accept it should it be your will."

"As will I," Rand said, moving to her side in spite of the king's prohibition.

Henry stood in frowning thought for long moments. Then Elizabeth of York moved to his side with a soft whispering of silk skirts. "It is not my place to interfere in this matter, and yet, my dear husband, it seems agreement would be a kindness."

Henry looked down at his queen, his brow still furrowed. "I am seldom kind."

It was a sign of his perturbation that he had forgotten the royal plural, Isabel thought.

"So you would have it," Elizabeth said simply, "yet I know otherwise."

They stood for the space of several breaths while beyond the solar could be heard the tramp of marching feet. Then Henry reached to take Elizabeth's hand, lifting it to his lips before placing it on his arm. "How am I to refuse the mother of my son and heir?" he murmured. He released an audible sigh, squared his shoulders and resumed his royal persona like donning a cloak of great weight. "Enough. Have it as you will, our Master of the Revels. Only you must leave England and never return. We can endure no more of your tragic *danses macabre,* no more sad music and sadder tales."

Leon bowed his curly head.

"As for you, Sir Rand," the king went on as he turned to him, "we are in your debt yet again. When next we are at Westminster and you with us, we will invest you with the honors and privileges of the Order of the Garter given to you before. Then we shall discuss a barony to properly reward one whose strong arm, and stronger heart, is most prized by us."

Baron Braesford. It had an appropriate, noble sound to it, Isabel thought, even as she watched her husband flush to the roots of his hair, saw his bow of graceful acceptance and homage to his king.

Henry raised a hand in a gesture of farewell. He covered Elizabeth's hand with his own where it lay on his arm. The king and queen, heads held high, quitted the room. The nursemaid, summoned by a terse word, scurried after them with young Prince Arthur in her arms. They walked away down the dim passage beyond the door until finally even their shadows were gone.

The incident, beginning to end, had taken much less time than seemed possible. No sooner had Their Majesties left the room than the king's steward, drawn by the noise, appeared with a half-dozen men-at-arms at his back. In the confusion of explanations, Leon came to Isabel, kissed little Madeleine's soft cheek, handed her over and made his escape. Rand raised his voice to bring order to the chaos of questions and threats, recommending that the steward apply to the king for explanation for the dead, the blood and the ruined carpets. Offering his arm to Isabel then, he led her from the solar with David, pale and grim of face after his first kill, trailing behind them.

When they had retrieved Gwynne and passed from the great pile of stone that was the palace, emerging into the fresh night air, Isabel tugged on Rand's arm to bring him to a halt. "Where are we going?" she asked, keeping her voice low to avoid disturbing small Madeleine, who had quieted as she was held against her. "We have no place here."

"To find a wet nurse or a goat," he said. "Either will do. Then I thought we might set out for Braesford."

"Braesford?"

"You object, my lady?"

"It is night, and the journey is far. And you are no longer a nobody, nor yet a mere knight who may go where he wills without thought."

"No?" he asked, tipping his head.

"You are my Lord Baron Braesford of Braesford, or soon shall be, a man of rapidly increasing responsibilities that include a wife. Yes, and a growing family."

He watched her for long moments, there in the dimness lit only by flickering torchlight that fell upon them from some distance away. The strain eased from his features then, and a smile curved the firmly molded lines of his mouth. "You are increasing?" he asked in quiet inquiry.

"Just so."

"You are . . . ?"

"With child, or so it appears. Gwynne declares it so and she is never wrong." She waited with a hard knot of apprehension in her chest to see what he would say. He had been away from her for so long, so long.

A soft sound left him, as if he had been struck. Swooping down upon her, he caught her and Madeleine up together in his arms and whirled them in long steps down the corridor while laughter rumbled in his chest.

Abruptly, he stopped, carefully set Isabel

on her feet. Steadying her with a hand at her waist, he reached to touch her face. "You are all right? You aren't sick? I didn't . . ."

The fullness in her heart forced tears into her eyes. "No, no. I'm perfectly well."

"A father. I'm to be a father."

"And a baron."

He inclined his head. "With a new device, so my son need never carry the bend sinister on his shield, need never be a nobody."

The child might yet be a girl, but Isabel would not remind him and so spoil his vision. It would come true in time, God willing, for there would be more children. For now, she honored him that his thought was for their child's future rather than the riches and estates that would come with his new title.

"It has been some time," she said in soft sincerity, "since you were a nobody to me."

His chest swelled with the depth of the breath he drew and his hold upon her tightened. "I believe resting here for the night may be a wise move, my lady." He swung toward David, who had followed after them, though remaining some few paces away. "You heard? We require space in an inn as well as a goat."

"Or a wet nurse. I did hear," David answered. "Though with so many here for the queen's lying-in and the christening, we may be lucky to find a room anywhere." Stepping around them, the lad went to carry out his errand. Still, he turned to look back at them with a smile tugging at his lips.

"I'd rather have the goat," Rand muttered as they began to walk again, "if we are all forced to share a single chamber."

So would she, if it came to that, Isabel thought, though she could foresee other problems. "Have you ever milked a she-goat?"

"No more than have you," he answered. "Mayhap David . . ."

"Or Gwynne." She glanced back at the serving woman, who followed after them with a resigned look on her face. An instant later, a frown pleated her brow. "But it could be your good squire will bring back a wet nurse who likes swift travel. He is really . . . really most efficient."

"You are concerned for him." He gazed down at her, studying her features with care.

"Concerned, yes, but that is all. Is that what you wished to hear? I believe he requires to be told I don't hold him accountable in the death of my stepbrother, will never blame him for it."

"I'll see to it."

She looked deep into his eyes, her own steady as she braved the silvery darkness there. He not only understood her misgivings and unspoken apologies, she thought, but also her remorse that David must have Graydon's death upon his conscience, her regret that her stepbrother had not been a better man, that matters could not have been resolved with less hatred and greed for power. "I knew you would," she said quietly.

"You know a good deal too much about me, I think, including the fact that I loved you before I took you to wife."

"Did you?" she asked, the words not quite steady.

"Oh, aye. I wanted only you from the moment I saw you in Westminster's great hall, dancing with firelight in your hair and such passionate joy in your eyes that I longed to share it."

"So you never feared the curse of the Graces, as you had fulfilled its requirement? Or is it that you never believed there to be one?"

"I had no fear."

He would not mock her fabrication, for that might be to remove whatever protection remained in it for Cate and Marguerite. This further evidence of his care for the concerns of her heart brought the rise of tears behind her eyes. "My sisters . . ." she began.

"Will be sent for at once, to come to Braesford. Henry will not forbid it, I think, not while his gratitude lasts. They will be safe there. Well, as safe as they want to be."

She allowed her gaze to move over the strong angles and planes of his face while a smile trembled across her lips. "Thank you, Rand. You are kindness itself."

His gaze on the liquid that rimmed her eyes, he allowed a scowl to narrow his eyes, shielding their softness. "And is that all you have to say to a declaration from your husband for how he broke this curse of yours? Have you no interest in my affection, my lady, nothing you would say to it in return?"

"If you want my love, you have it," she said, her tone lilting as wild joy beat up inside her, engulfing her heart, her chest, her whole body.

He halted again, turned toward her. "Oh, I want it, Lady Isabel of Braesford, and would show you how much if you were not encumbered at the moment by a baby in swaddling. Yes, and with the likely addition soon of a wet nurse, a goat, an opinionated serving woman, two sisters still accursed and a knight in training who looks like an angel and worships the ground on which you tread. As do I, my lady. Aye, as do I."

She reached to catch the strip of ragged white silk tied still to his arm, wrapping its length slowly around her hand to draw him to her while gladness blazed in her eyes. "Show me, anyway, my brave and most favored lord of a husband," she murmured against his lips, "for I would see exactly how broken is this curse."

Thoroughly, merrily, it was shattered then, for the eldest Grace of Graydon.

Merrily, and forever.

AUTHOR'S NOTE

For those who may be curious about where history ends and fiction begins, the incident of the murdered newborn depicted in *By His Majesty's Grace* was never connected with Henry VII. This story from the sixteenth century, recorded as the "Littlecote Scandal," was taken from *Albion, A Guide to Legendary Britain* by Jennifer Westwood. Nevertheless, it is a fact that Henry VII brought a mistress with him from France when he arrived in England for the invasion of 1485. What became of the woman afterward is lost in time. Nothing more is heard of her after Henry's marriage to Elizabeth of York on January 18, 1486.

The disappearance of the two young sons of Edward IV from the Tower of London is a mystery that has never been satisfactorily explained. In the past few decades, it has become popular to second-guess the histories compiled in the late fifteenth and early sixteenth centuries, which indict Richard III, uncle to the boys, in their deaths. Many modern writers absolve him of ordering the deed, despite the fact that the princes were last seen in public shortly after he declared them illegitimate in order to seize the throne, and that rumors of their deaths were extant at that time. The confession to the crime by Sir James Tyrell fifteen years later, during the reign of Henry VII, has been dismissed as a political move to prevent false claims to the throne in the boys' names. My own conviction concerning this tragedy, developed after studying a multitude of both ancient and modern histories and numerous biographies of the principal players, is that Shakespeare got it right: Richard III was indeed the villain in the crime.

Arthur, the eldest son of Henry VII and Elizabeth of York, was born as described, at Winchester Priory on September 19, 1486. A studious and conscientious youth, he was betrothed to Catherine of Aragon as a child and married her at age fifteen on November 14, 1501. He was in Ludlow Castle on the Welsh border with his bride five months later when he apparently contracted a fever and died on April 2, 1502, at age sixteen. Had he lived to take the throne, Britain and the world would be far different today. Instead, it was Henry, third son of Henry VII, who put his own spin on history after becoming the infamous Henry VIII.

Jennifer Blake
November 24, 2010

ACKNOWLEDGMENTS

First, thanks beyond thanks to Bertrice Small, Roberta Gellis and the other authors and romance readers who greeted the beginning pages of this story with such enthusiasm when they were read for a workshop at the Romantic Times Convention in 2008. Without that grand reception, I might never have embarked upon this medieval tale.

My sincere appreciation to my editor, Susan Swinwood, for her attention to detail, unfailing support and lovely tact. To all the great people at MIRA Books, many thanks for wonderful covers and book expertise in the past, and especially for the inspired suggestion that I make the transition from my usual Victorian-era United States to medieval England.

Many thanks, as well, to my agent, Richard Curtis, for his faith in my ability, his support for this project and his constant effort to make my career the best it can be.

A thousand expressions of appreciation to all those online entities that were sources for special research books and historical details, including free Google eBooks, Project Gutenberg, Amazon.com, the Sony eBook Store, Melissa Snell at About.com: Medieval History, http://tudorhistory.org, Wikipedia, http://englishhistory.net/tudor .html and many others.

Finally, a special thank-you to my daughters Delinda Corbin and Katharine Faucheux, for acting as my first readers and making super suggestions that provided story enrichment, to my husband, Jerry, for unflagging interest and patience, and to all the rest of my grand family for simply being there.

DATE DUE

NOV 1 6 2011			
FEB 1 1 2012			